GENTEEL SPIRITS

SPIRITS, FEATURING
DAISY GUMM MAJESTY

GENTEEL SPIRITS

ALICE DUNCAN

FIVE STAR
A part of Gale, Cengage Learning

GALE
CENGAGE Learning·

Detroit • New York • San Francisco • New Haven, Conn • Waterville, Maine • London

GALE
CENGAGE Learning™

LIBRARY OF CONGRESS CATALOGING-IN-PUBLICATION DATA

Duncan, Alice, 1945–
    Genteel spirits : spirits, featuring Daisy Gumm Majesty / Alice Duncan. — 1st ed.
        p. cm.
    ISBN-13: 978-1-4328-2500-3 (hardcover)
    ISBN-10: 1-4328-2500-3 (hardcover)
    1. Majesty, Daisy Gumm (Fictitious character)—Fiction. 2. Spiritualists—Fiction. 3. Pasadena (Calif.)—Fiction. I. Title.
PS3554.U463394G46 2011
813'.54—dc22   2011013299

First Edition. First Printing: July 2011.
Published in 2011 in conjunction with Tekno Books.

For the real John Bohnert who, unlike Daisy, is an excellent cook and, what's more, is willing to share his excellent recipes!

Also for Lynne Welch and John Charles, who have been a constant source of support over the years, even when my so-called writing career seemed to be floating belly-up in the goldfish bowl of publishing.

I'd also like to give my appreciation to the folks connected with the real Pasanita Obedience Club, where I took my very first wiener dog, Hansel Schnitzel Fritzel Von Pancho Pooh Puddle Monsieur la Puppy Stink Duncan. Okay, so I was a kid then. My daughter Robin took her dog Apu, who isn't a dachshund but is still a good dog, there, too, and between Hansel and Apu, I can vouch for the Pasanita Obedience Club folks. I've never met two more well-behaved dogs.

CHAPTER ONE

The first few months of 1922 weren't what I'd call boring, exactly. Nevertheless, the fact was my best client, Mrs. Algernon Pinkerton, nee Madeline Kincaid—but no, I'm wrong about that. However, since I don't know her maiden name, it'll just have to do—was on another long, long trip with her new husband.

Mrs. Pinkerton's daughter Stacy Kincaid, formerly bane of my existence, had yet to fall from grace since she'd joined the Salvation Army, so she wasn't causing me any problems.

No ghosts requiring exorcism had taken possession of Mrs. Bissel's basement, as had happened once before.

Flossie Buckingham, a dear friend and the wife of Johnny Buckingham, captain in the Salvation Army and, therefore, firmly in charge of the aforementioned Stacy, was "with child," and elated about it. Actually, both Buckinghams were. And so was I. For them.

Pasadena, California, my hometown, remained serene and beautiful in all its bounteous spring glory, but . . . Well, the fact of the matter was that not much was going on in the Gumm-Majesty household. You'd think that was a good thing, wouldn't you? It might have been, except that all the nothing happening had me on pins and needles.

Mind you, the rest of the world continued to turn, and lots of stuff was going on in it. For one thing, a conference was taking place in Cannes, France, concerning retribution payments required of the Germans after the late Great War. As far as I was concerned, there was no way Germany could possibly repay the world for the damage it and its foul Kaiser had caused. Heck, I lived with one of the results of the Kaiser's insanity every day of my life.

My beloved husband, Billy Majesty, formerly tall, athletic and handsome, had joined up in 'seventeen when the USA entered the European Conflict, and had come back a little more than a year later a broken man. Literally. Not only had he been shot but, worse, his lungs had been permanently damaged by the most evil weapon ever perpetrated on the world: mustard gas. I expect someone, someday, will invent a weapon of war even worse than that blasted gas, but whoever does it will probably be a German. And damned for all eternity, if I have any say in the matter, which I don't, and which also means it's probably a good thing God is in charge of judgment and not Daisy Gumm Majesty.

I don't really mean that—the hating-all-Germans part. I'd learned late in 1921 that not all Germans are vicious and evil. But I still resented the blasted Kaiser and his partners in crime more than I can ever possibly say—and I've said a lot. My poor Billy was a wreck of his formerly wonderful self. What was worse was that, in the early months of 1922, he seemed to be weakening almost daily, which accounted for several of the aforementioned pins and needles. He used to try to walk, swearing he'd be able to leave his wheelchair behind one day. By early 1922, he almost never wanted even to try to walk. I feared he was giving up on life. That not only made me want to cry, but it made me want to personally tear a pound of flesh from the Kaiser's ugly body. And, unlike Shakespeare's Shylock, there'd be blood when I wielded *my* knife.

But I guess you don't need to know that much about my grievances against the Kaiser. I should probably get back to what had happened during the early months of 1922.

Billy had been interested when the American Professional Football Association renamed itself the National Football League in January, but I didn't much care. Fortunately for Billy, I'd bought him a radio-signal receiving set a year or so earlier, so he could listen to football and baseball games when they were broadcasted. Radio, which is a much more convenient way of referring to the things, seemed to be expanding its horizons like mad, too. Americans were buying radios by the thousands, and President Harding had even installed one in the White House.

"April Showers," by Al Jolson, was a top hit. I bought the sheet music to it because the Gumms and Majestys—Billy and I were the only Majestys in the house. Ma and Pa and Aunt Vi were the Gumms—liked to gather 'round the piano of an evening. I'd play and we'd all sing. I'd bought "Toot, Toot, Tootsie," which was also by Al Jolson, and which was a fun, toe-tapping melody; and "Way Down Yonder in New Orleans," by Margaret Young. I tell you, if we didn't have much else, we had music in the house.

Probably the most shocking thing that occurred in early 1922 was the as-yet-unsolved murder of William Desmond Taylor in Hollywood. There had been tons of scandals regarding moving-picture people in those days, but a real, honest-to-goodness murder was worse even than when Fatty Arbuckle was arrested, tried and found not guilty in another scandalous case involving picture people and what finally proved to be an accidental death. Even though he was found not to be guilty of murder, Mr. Arbuckle's career had been ruined. Scandals did that to a person.

That didn't mean the pictures themselves were bad, only that some of the people who worked in and around them were. In fact, my family and I really enjoyed *Blood and Sand*, which had starred Rudolph Valentino. I probably enjoyed that one more than I should have, given that I had no business ogling other men, for heaven's sake. Then again, how many Rudolph Valentinos are there in the world to ogle? Besides, every other red-blooded American female was doing the same thing. Valentino aside, we saw other pictures that were quite entertaining, including *Oliver Twist* and *The Prisoner of Zenda,* which made me cry. Nobility of character always does that to me.

The most exciting thing that had happened to my family in 1922 up to the time this story begins was that Billy and I had started taking Spike, our black-and-tan dachshund—which I'd taken in payment for ridding Mrs. Bissel's home of the ghost I mentioned earlier—to dog-obedience school. The Pasanita Dog Obedience Club held dog-training sessions on Saturday mornings in Brookside Park.

Billy, although confined to his wheelchair, nevertheless cheered Spike and me on from the sidelines, while Mrs. Pansy Hanratty, a rather mannish woman, but a darling, taught us humans how to teach our dogs to heel, sit, stay, lie down, fetch and so forth. All three of us had a great time at these training sessions, and Spike was doing swell, as long as I remembered how to make him obey, which I mostly did. Spike and I practiced every day, generally in the backyard with Billy and my father watching from the porch and laughing at us. Still and all, Spike was a more obedient specimen than were most of the human children I knew.

Obedience training aside, for the most part life was pretty much as it had always been in our household since Billy came home from the war. Ma worked at the Hotel Marengo as the chief bookkeeper, which was a darned impressive job for a woman in those days. Aunt Vi cooked for the Pinkertons, although they, as I've already mentioned, were on another long trip somewhere. They liked to travel. I didn't mind them being gone, even though my spiritualist business slumped a bit during their absences. For one thing, her being elsewhere in the world meant life was more peaceful in the Gumm-Majesty household, and I also had lots of time to practice obedience training with Spike.

You see, Mrs. Pinkerton's first husband, Eustace Kincaid, had been a horrid man, a thief and a general crumb, and it made me happy that Mrs. Kincaid had finally married a nice man. Mind you, I wasn't holding my breath waiting for Stacy to return to her formerly flapperish ways and depart from the Salvation Army, but her defection from said army wouldn't affect me too much one way or the other, except that when she behaved badly, Mrs. Pinkerton called on my services a lot. Then again, no matter what Stacy was doing at any given time, Mrs. Pinkerton always had tizzies that required me to bring my Ouija board or my tarot cards to her home for spiritualist sessions. That was lucky for me, as my family needed the dough.

Ma, Pa, Aunt Vi, Billy, Spike and I still lived in our tidy little bungalow on South Marengo Avenue in Pasadena, California. We still walked to the Methodist-Episcopal Church (North), where I sang alto in the choir, on the corner of Marengo and Colorado every Sunday. My best friend was still Harold Kincaid, a gentleman of whom Billy didn't approve because . . . well, because Harold was what Billy called a "faggot." I don't know why, although I do know what the slang term means, and I think it's cruel. Harold couldn't help being what he was. What's more, his . . . um . . . particular gentleman friend, Delray Farrington, was the person who had saved the Kincaid Bank when the evil Mr. Kincaid did a bunk and ran off with a bunch of bearer bonds. Why, if it hadn't been for Del, the bank would have crashed and all its investors would have lost their entire savings! So there, Billy Majesty.

Oh, and there was still Sam Rotondo. Sam, a detective with the Pasadena Police Department, was Billy's best friend.

Sometimes I considered Sam my worst enemy, because he'd entangled me in one or two of his cases. And it's not true, whatever Sam says, that said entanglement was all my fault. How could I have known the police would raid that speakeasy? Or that a crook had infiltrated the cooking class I taught at the Salvation Army? Of course, the fact that I, Daisy Gumm Majesty, who not only could but did burn water, was teaching the class in the first place might have been considered some sort of crime, but it wasn't the sort Sam Rotondo would ordinarily care about.

Sam and I didn't exactly get along together, if you haven't already figured that out for yourself. But Sam is neither here nor there—although I preferred him there. Unfortunately, he could generally be found in my very own living room, playing gin rummy with Billy and Pa. I was the only one in the family who didn't adore Sam Rotondo. Ma, Vi, Billy and Pa thought he was great. Even Spike, who had once perpetrated an indignity on one of his big, fat policemanly shoes as a puppy, liked Sam by that time. Oh, well.

Probably the most exciting thing that happened in my fair city of Pasadena in 1922 was that Mr. Montgomery "Monty" Mountjoy, an actor darned near as handsome as Rudolph Valentino, bought his elderly, genteel, Southern grandmother, Mrs. Beauregard "Lurlene" Winkworth, a fabulous home on San Pasqual Street. Both the *Pasadena Star News* and the *Evening Herald* had a field day with that tidbit of information. Supposedly, Mrs. Winkworth, while from an old and distinguished South Carolina family, had fallen on hard times, and her grandson had rescued her in fine heroic fashion, thus cementing his gallant image as an icon off as well as on the silver screen.

For the most part, Pasadena was a moral, not to say stuffy, community, where motion-picture people weren't exactly welcomed with open arms. This was especially true in light of the William Desmond Taylor affair and the constant news of drug and alcohol consumption among the members of the picture community. All this consumption was being carried out in the days of Prohibition, too. Huh.

Mind you, I doubted if anyone really knew anything against Mr. Mountjoy, although the press had tagged him as a gay blade and something of a lothario for some months. The gossip columnists had also claimed that his fame and fortune had gone to his head, that he was in danger of becoming positively decadent in the manner of, say, Nero or Caligula or another one of those old Roman guys who bathed in wine and killed people for fun, in spite of having rescued his elderly grandmother from the clutches of poverty.

I, however, Daisy Gumm Majesty, understood that the press often got things wrong. In actual fact, Harold Kincaid, my aforesaid best friend, was a costumier for a motion-picture studio in Los Angeles, and he had told me more than once that the studios actually hired people to make up fake backgrounds and personalities for their "stars." Harold had also informed me that Monty Mountjoy was in reality a kindhearted and relatively sober-sided gent who liked to read books and listen to classical music on his radio or gramophone most evenings. What's more, according to Harold, when Mr. Mountjoy did go out on the town and was seen with a young woman from the pictures, the outing was invariably arranged by his studio.

Gee, you'd think I'd become cynical, knowing all this stuff, wouldn't you? But I wasn't. I could still be swept away by a well-made picture, just like everyone else in America. Heck, probably the whole world was watching moving pictures by that time. Besides, I earned my living pretending to talk to dead people for people with more money than sense. If that hadn't made me cynical by 1922, after I'd been doing it for eleven years, I don't suppose anything could.

In any case, all of the above doesn't have anything to do with the story I'm about to relate. Well, some of it does, but I'll get to that later.

You see, Billy, Vi and I were sitting at the kitchen table one Friday morning, eating the delicious breakfast Vi had made—have I mentioned that Vi cooks for us as well as Mrs. Pinkerton? Well, she does. And a good thing, too, since neither Ma nor I could cook for anything—when the telephone rang. Vi looked at me. Billy lowered the newspaper he'd been reading and looked at me, too. I sighed, got up from the table, and went to the far kitchen wall to pick up the receiver.

"I thought Mrs. Pinkerton was out of town," Billy muttered under his breath. Billy didn't appreciate having his restful mornings interrupted by the shrill ringing of the telephone. I couldn't fault him for that. I also wondered who could be calling, since early-morning telephone calls generally came from Mrs. Pinkerton when she was in particular distress, and I was pretty sure she was riding a camel in Egypt at the moment.

"Gumm-Majesty residence," I said into the receiver, as I almost always did. "Mrs. Majesty speaking."

"I need to speak with Mrs. Desdemona Majesty, please."

Perhaps I should explain that *Desdemona* thing. You see, when I was ten years old and first pretended to communicate through the Ouija board Mrs. Pinkerton (then Mrs. Kincaid) gave Aunt Vi, people actually believed I was speaking with spirits. So I let 'em. I mean, if people wanted to believe that sort of rubbish and I could profit therefrom, why shouldn't I? At any rate, that's when my career as a spiritualist began. When I was ten years old. Honest. It's the truth. Shortly thereafter, I decided Daisy was too humdrum a name for a genuine spiritualist. Not that I was one of those, but people thought I was, and that's what mattered. So I selected Desdemona as my nom-de-whatever. Not until three or four years after that was I forced by a particularly mean-spirited English teacher to read *Othello,* or I'd probably have chosen another name. I mean, who wants to share a name with a famous fictional murderee, for heaven's sake?

Anyhow, I said, "This is she speaking." I did so in my low, smooth, soothing spiritualist voice, since I knew nobody'd be telephoning for "Desdemona Majesty" unless the call was work-related.

"Mrs. Majesty, my name is Gladys Pennywhistle—"

"*Gladys?*"

Silence on the other end of the wire. For good reason, as I didn't generally shriek into the telephone receiver and just had. But I was shocked. Gladys Pennywhistle and I had gone to school together ever since the first grade!

In an attempt to retrieve the moment, I said, "I beg your pardon, Gladys, but this is Daisy. You know, Daisy Gumm?"

"Daisy?" came uncertainly through the wire. Talk about sober-sided people, Gladys was probably the premier example of the species. Very smart, the Gladys I knew had absolutely no sense of humor and took everything seriously, even when it wasn't. We'd never been close friends, although we always got along well.

"Yes. It's Daisy. Only I'm Daisy Majesty now. Have been since 1917, in fact, when I married Billy Majesty, whom you may remember. He was a couple of years ahead of us in school. My professional name is Desdemona Majesty."

"Daisy?" she said again, as if she couldn't believe her ears.

"I'm sorry, Gladys. I didn't mean to startle you. But, yes, I am Desdemona Majesty, and I am the spiritualist for whom you're looking."

I decided not to startle her further by telling her I'd made up the Desdemona part of my name. For all she knew, I'd been named Desdemona at birth and Daisy was a nickname.

"I . . . I see." Gladys cleared her throat. "What . . . what an interesting line of work you're in, to be sure, Daisy. I mean Desdemona."

"Please call me Daisy, and it certainly is. How may I help you?" I couldn't quite imagine Gladys calling upon a spiritualist for herself. Although people do change over time, I couldn't reconcile the Gladys I'd known in school, and who'd actually understood and enjoyed algebra, with a person who possessed the need for a spiritualist. Personally, I'd liked geometry until we got out of the theorem stage and had to begin using algebra again. For my money, algebra is for the birds. Not that it matters.

"Um . . . yes. I see. Thank you, Daisy."

She didn't say for what. I gave her one of my low, comforting spiritualistic "hmmms." We spiritualists can make all sorts of gentling noises.

"Well, Daisy, you see . . ."

Poor Gladys seemed to be rather flustered. I probably shouldn't have screeched at her, even though my raised voice had been kindly meant. I tried to help her. "Do you or does someone you know need my services, perhaps?"

"Yes." There she was again: the no-nonsense, down-to-earth Gladys I'd known for most of my life. "You see, I work for Mrs. Lurlene Winkworth—"

"Oh, my! You *do?*" There I went again. Shoot, I was almost always more composed than this. I expect Mrs. Pinkerton having been away for so long had allowed my spiritualist mystique to rust a bit. "I beg your pardon, Gladys. I'm just surprised, is all. I mean, I just read about Mrs. Winkworth in the *Star News*. About her grandson buying her that mansion and all, I mean."

"I . . . see." Poor Gladys.

"I'm terribly sorry to have interrupted you again, Gladys. Please go on and tell me why you're calling."

She cleared her throat. Meticulous Gladys, whom I'd inter-rupted twice in one telephone call, and we hadn't even got to the meat of her call yet. I tried to suppress my feeling of guilt.

"Yes," she said eventually. "As I said, I work for Mrs. Lurlene Winkworth, as her private secretary."

I almost shrieked again. I'd always figured Gladys would become a college professor or something like that. I'd never once figured her for a private secretary. Not there's anything wrong with being a private secretary; it's just that I couldn't quite feature Gladys Pennywhistle in the role. I said, "Yes?" with becoming gentleness of tone.

"Mrs. Winkworth desired that I telephone you . . . as Desde-mona Majesty, I mean . . . Oh, dear."

I understood. "Please don't be dismayed, Gladys. I'm sure you're as surprised to find I've become a spiritualist as I am to discover you're a private secretary. By this time in my life, I expected to be married to Billy and rearing a family." I shot a glance at my beloved, who scowled back at me, and I wished I hadn't said that to Gladys. It wasn't Billy's fault we couldn't have children. It was the thrice-cursed-forever Kaiser's. Valiantly, I continued in spite of Billy's scowl, "And I rather expected you to go into teaching or nursing or something of that nature."

A heavy sigh made its way through the telephone wire. "You're right, Daisy. I attended two years of study at Pasadena College, but then I couldn't find a job, and I couldn't afford to continue my education at a university. Being a secretary to Mrs. Winkworth isn't exactly what I'd planned, but . . . well, the position is rewarding in its own way."

Have I mentioned that the country was in something of a depression in 1922? Well, it was. Gladys wasn't the only person out of work at that time. Thousands of soldiers had come back after risking their lives only to find they were apt to starve to death on the streets of America because they couldn't secure

17

employment, which didn't seem fair at all. I considered myself and my family fortunate.

"I should say so!" Realizing my voice had risen again, I lowered it. "I'm sure everyone asks you this when they learn you work for Mrs. Winkworth, but have you met Mr. Monty Mountjoy?" I tried not to pant, especially with Billy sitting there, watching me and still frowning.

"Oh, my, yes. And I suggest you don't believe anything the press has to say about him. He's always a perfect gentleman when he visits his grandmother."

Well, he'd better be, if his grandmother was anything like mine. Grandma Gumm, whom I'd only met twice because she lives in Massachusetts, never hesitated to give a girl a swat, whether the girl deserved it or not. Rather than reveal this, which spoke perhaps more about my childhood behavior than my grandmother's charms, I said, "I'm glad to hear it. I never believe what I read in the newspapers about celebrities. One of my best friends works in the pictures, and he says most of the stuff you read is all made up anyway."

"Yes, I believe that's so." Gladys didn't sound as if she considered the situation to be in any way commendable. A woman of high moral standards as well as a brain, our Gladys. "This friend of yours wouldn't be Mr. Harold Kincaid, would it?"

"Why, yes. Harold and I are great friends."

"I see. He and Mr. Mountjoy are acquainted, and he mentioned that he knew you and that you were highly recommended as a spiritualist."

I said, "How nice of him."

The conversation sagged for a moment. Then Gladys cleared her throat again. "At any rate, the reason I called for . . . well, Desdemona Majesty, is that Mrs. Winkworth desires to hold a séance sometime soon. And . . . and Desdemona Majesty is reputed to be the best spiritualist medium in Pasadena." I could tell Gladys still had trouble reconciling the Daisy Gumm she used to know, and who had been kind of a tomboy and definitely a prankster, with the Desdemona Majesty who conducted séances and communed with spirits. In truth, I couldn't fault her for any confusion in that regard.

"I see." All business now, I. "When does she want to hold this séance?"

"Two weeks from Saturday. That is the Saturday after tomorrow, if your schedule is free. In the evening. Around eight o'clock. Mr. Mountjoy, Mrs. Winkworth's daughter, and Miss Lola de la Monica will be among the attendees."

I darned near screamed *again*. But, my goodness gracious sakes alive! Miss Lola de la Monica was one of the leading lights of the motion-picture industry. What's more, she and Monty Mountjoy were reputed to be having a hot and sordid affair. I guess Miss de la Monica fitted Mr. Mountjoy in when she wasn't dallying with Mr. Rudolph Valentino, who was supposed to number among her many *amours*. Shoot, I don't know how the woman did it. I only had one man in my life, and he was too much for me most of the time. Of course, that was the Kaiser's fault, too.

But we've already discussed how imprecise published accounts of celebrities could be, haven't we?

"Let me check my calendar, Gladys. Hold the wire for a moment, please."

In truth, I knew darned well I was free to hold a séance the following Saturday evening. The only thing I had on schedule between now and then was a party at Mrs. Bissel's house, where I would read tarot cards and palms for the guests; and two dog-obedience lessons, but those were held in the morning. However, I paused long enough for Gladys to think I was very much in demand. Which I was. Most of the time. The present lull was actually rather like a vacation for me, although I hoped it wouldn't last too long, since my family needed my income.

When I again picked up the receiver, I made sure I sounded as though I were doing Mrs. Winkworth a favor. "I do have a commitment . . . but, no. I'm sure I can move that appointment to another time."

"Oh, dear. You have something else scheduled?" Gladys sounded worried, and I felt guilty again.

"Oh, no, not at all. I have no commitments that can't easily be changed. Yes, Gladys, I will be happy to hold a séance for Mrs. Winkworth on the Saturday after next."

"Ah! I'm so glad!"

For the first time, Gladys sounded other than confused. I guess Mrs. Winkworth was either a hard taskmistress or Gladys expected a lot of herself. I suspected the latter. She'd always been extremely precise and exacting, and if she didn't get the highest grade on any given test, she'd fall into a deep melancholy that would last until she again excelled at something academic. That sort of thing didn't happen often since, as noted before, Gladys had a largish brain in which she stored lots and lots of stuff that didn't matter a whit to me.

She went on, "Thank you so much, Daisy. Mrs. Winkworth will be so pleased."

"And I shall be very pleased to meet her." Not to mention her grandson and Miss de la Monica. "And I look forward to seeing her house. I understand it's quite lovely."

"Huge," said Gladys succinctly. "I actually get tired from all the running around I have to do, although the exercise is, I'm sure, good for me. But the gardens are quite beautiful and I do enjoy strolling in them of an evening."

I'd just bet they were. San Pasqual was one of the loveliest streets in our lovely city. "Well, it will be nice to see you again, Gladys," I said politely, wondering if the severe, bespectacled

Gladys I remembered would have changed as much as I had in the years since we'd graduated from high school.

"It will be a pleasure to see you again, too, Daisy," she said, sounding perfunctory rather than ecstatic.

I hung up the receiver and turned to face my husband and my aunt. I expected Billy to say something cutting—he'd gone so far as to say what I did for a living was evil a time or two—but Aunt Vi beat him to the punch.

"You're going to meet *Monty Mountjoy* and *Lola de la Monica?*" Her voice was breathy and very nearly reverent.

"I guess so. That was Gladys Pennywhistle, and she set up a séance at Mrs. Winkworth's house for next Saturday night."

"Oh, my dear goodness gracious sakes alive," said Aunt Vi, sinking into her chair—she'd been standing, clutching the back of it, I guess staring in awe at my back as I spoke with Gladys on the 'phone.

"I swear, Daisy," said Billy, "you do get around, don't you?"

He didn't sound too terribly snide, so I smiled and said, "I do. And in such exalted company, too." I wandered back to the kitchen table, wishing my helping of egg-and-potato casserole was still warm. But I ate it anyway. "Never turn down food" is my motto, which explains why I'll never achieve the lean and boyish shape that was so fashionable in those days. My bust flattener helped my image some, but I still had hips. Couldn't help having them without starving myself.

"Well, I guess that's all right," said Billy, surprising me. "It must be fun to meet all these celebrities."

"It is, in a way, but it also makes me nervous sometimes."

"You?" His left eyebrow lifted sardonically. I didn't appreciate that expression on my Billy's face. Before he'd gone off to war, he couldn't have looked sardonic if he'd tried.

"Yes. Me. Although I must admit I'm less nervous around big shots than I might have been if I hadn't met Harold Kincaid. He's told me so much about so many of the so-called stars, it's hard to keep from laughing when I meet some of them."

"Do you think Lola de la Monica is really from Spain?" breathed Aunt Vi, who was still impressed by what she read in the papers.

"I don't know, but I'll ask her," I said. "And I'll get autographs, too, if you want them."

Billy said, "Huh."

But Aunt Vi said, "Oh, thank you, Daisy! I'd just love to have autographs from Monty Mountjoy and Lola de la Monica!"

It was nice to know somebody in the family appreciated me.

CHAPTER TWO

Actually, Ma and Pa were pretty impressed, too, when I told them about my impending séance later in the day. Sam Rotondo, who came to dinner that night, was also impressed, although not in a good way. That came as no surprise to me, since nothing at all about me ever seemed to please Sam.

Perhaps I should say a little more about Sam. I didn't really dislike him. Not anymore, anyhow. I'd hated his guts when I'd first become entangled with one of his schemes. But he was a very good friend to Billy and Pa, who had a weak heart and could no longer work as a chauffeur for rich people as he'd once done. And, as I've already said, Ma and Aunt Vi liked him, too. Besides, late in 1921, when I'd discovered that my Billy had a whole boxful of morphine syrup stashed away in our closet, Sam had been surprisingly sympathetic when I'd spoken to him about it. His sincere conception of and insight into Billy's problem had taken me aback, to tell the truth. I hadn't expected compassion and understanding from someone like him. Well, from someone like I thought he was, I mean.

Mind you, Billy needed the drug. If it weren't for morphine syrup, I doubt he'd have been able to live at home, but would have had to spend his days in one of those hideous, gray-walled institutions where irreparably injured victims of the Kaiser's wrath had been locked away since he began his wretched war. But Billy had me. And he had Ma and Pa and Spike and the rest of my family, all of whom loved him. And Sam. He had Sam.

Still, the plain, unvarnished fact of the matter was that Billy's health had been deteriorating ever since the war ended, and his constant pain was debilitating and horrible. So were his lungs and his night terrors and his shell shock. *Damn* the Kaiser. But there I go again. Get me started on the Kaiser, and I never shut up. At any rate, Billy needed a good deal of morphine syrup by 1922, but when I found a box stuffed full of morphine bottles hidden away in the back of our bedroom closet, I'd become very frightened. *Suicide* is an ugly word, but it was never far from my mind in those days. Nor, I fear, was it far from Billy's.

Anyhow, after having heart-to-heart chats with Sam; Johnny Buckingham, our good friend as well as a captain at the Salvation Army; and Dr. Benjamin, I wouldn't have blamed Billy if he'd done himself in. I'd tried having a heart-to-heart talk with Billy, too, but he wouldn't allow me into his innermost hell. All I knew for certain was that he hated living as he did. Worse, he thought I hated it, too. He was right; I did, but not because I ever once regretted marrying Billy. I adored Billy; I only hated what had happened to him. Heck, if he were to live another forty or fifty years, I'd be right there at his side, cheering him on.

Billy thought I pitied him, and he didn't like it. I did pity him, and I didn't like it, either.

However, Dr. Benjamin, who saw Billy weekly, had told me more than once that influenza, pneumonia, bronchitis or some other chest ailment would probably take Billy away from me one day in the not-too-distant future. The notion depressed me greatly. I couldn't imagine life without Billy, even Billy as he had been returned to me after being gassed out of his foxhole in France and shot as he tried to crawl to safety. Naturally, when we married, we never anticipated the tragedy that had ended our life as we'd expected it to be. We'd believed our life together would be sunshine and flowers. Heck, we lived in the City of Roses, didn't we?

There I go again: digressing. To get back to Sam, he was good for Billy and for my father. Therefore, I tolerated him ever so much better than I had when we'd first met. I still wasn't sure what he thought about me, although I knew he disapproved of my line of work. When we'd first met and he'd accused me of fortune-telling, I'd become highly indignant. I didn't tell fortunes, darn it, and I told him so in no uncertain terms. I conducted séances, interpreted tarot cards, manipulated the Ouija board and read palms. If people with lots of money and no brains wanted to pay me for doing those things, more power to me, I say. None of my skills, even though people paid me to ply them, could be considered fortune-telling, unless one wanted to stretch a point until it snapped clean in half. It seemed to me that Sam did exactly that, and I'd detested him for it.

There was another thing I resented like fire: I could never get either Sam or Billy to acknowledge that my job truly helped people. But it did. Our country—indeed, the whole world—had been through two and a half hideous tragedies only a few years earlier: the Great War, the great influenza pandemic and the ensuing financial problems resulting therefrom. Both of Billy's parents had died in the epidemic, and many, many young men had died in the war, including Aunt Vi's only son, who'd been buried in France. After the war, the country had been plunged into a financial depression that was still devastating to common folk like the Gumms and the Majestys and, evidently, Gladys Pennywhistle. The only people who weren't affected by the depression were the ones who were so rich they weren't affected by anything. But that's not the point I'm trying to make here.

The point is that during the war and the concurrent pandemic, thousands—perhaps millions—of people had died. I considered it part of my job to give comfort to people who needed help coping with their losses. My work made my clients . . . not jovial, certainly, but contented. I made sure to let them know that their loved ones were happy on the Other Side, and that they wanted their survivors to live cheerful and fulfilled lives until called by God to join them. Does that sound evil to you? Well, it doesn't to me.

However, Sam and I now tolerated each other, which was a step in the right direction, at least for me, since he spent so much time at our house. I'd once kind of hoped he'd become interested in another friend of mine, a girl with whom I sang duets in church from time to time. But neither Sam nor Lucille Spinks, the girl in question, had seemed to be much taken with each other. Well, Lucille had been taken with Sam, but he hadn't returned her regard, so that was that. Anyhow, it was probably better that they hadn't become a couple, because then Sam would have spent more time with Lucy than he did with Billy, and that would have hurt Billy who had enough pain to contend with already.

Anyhow . . . where was I? Oh, yes, I remember. Sam came to dinner the night Gladys called, and I told him I was going to hold a séance for Mrs. Winkworth and meet Monty Mountjoy and Lola de la Monica. I was surprised and annoyed when he scowled at me.

I glared back at him. I wasn't about to take any guff from Sam Rotondo about my job. "Well? What's the matter with that?"

My voice held a challenge that Ma didn't like. She said, "Daisy," in *that* voice. You know the one I mean. All mothers use it to keep herd on their children.

"Nothing's the matter with that," said Sam, sounding as grumpy as all get-out.

"Then how come you're frowning at me?"

"I'm not frowning at you."

"Yes, you are! Darn you, Sam Rotondo, what's the matter with Lurlene Winkworth? For heaven's sake, from everything I've read about her, she's the most respectable female alive in this world today. I read an article in the *Herald* that traced her ancestors back to Plymouth Rock, for Pete's sake, although she belongs to the DOC rather than the DAR, which I consider silly, although that's probably because my folks are Yankees."

The Daughters of the Confederacy prided themselves on having come from Confederate stock. The Daughters of the American Revolution, on the other hand, prided themselves on having come from the stock of original Europeans to settle our grand land. Personally, I didn't care what my forebears did or didn't do. I had enough on my hands, what with dealing with Billy and helping to support my family. Besides that, I'd begun to consider wars of any kind at all complete failures of communication and diplomacy. I know. My views are probably radical, but don't forget that I lived every day with the result of one man's obsession, and I was far from the only one. My belief, in case anybody cares, is that the guys who want to start wars should jolly well go ahead and fight them. Themselves. And leave at home the young, healthy boys they'd normally send to fight and die for them.

Where was I? I'm sorry I keep getting distracted. Ah, yes.

"There's nothing wrong with Mrs. Winkworth," said Sam as though he didn't believe himself. "But that idiot grandson of hers is trouble."

"Oh?" I felt myself on firm ground here. "And why is that? Because the newspapers say so? Because reporters dog his footsteps and report salacious gossip that probably isn't true? The studios have entire publicity departments to make up stories about their stars, don't forget. Harold Kincaid has told me all about that, and if anyone should know, it's Harold." I felt like adding *so there*, but knew it would be childish, so I didn't.

"No. Not because the newspapers say so. I've heard things from other sources that I can't go into here. Police business."

Indignant, I cried, "If that isn't just like you, Sam Rotondo! First you bring up something to intrigue us and then tell us you can't talk about it! Nuts."

My mother said, "Daisy" again. Huh.

Sam sighed. By the way, that night Vi had prepared a delicious beef stew with lots of vegetables and the most tender biscuits you can even imagine with which to sop up the gravy. My aunt Vi was the best cook in Pasadena. Probably the entire United States of America. What's more, we were going to have floating island for dessert. I love floating island, which consists of a creamy custard sauce with little baked meringues floating on top of it. Hence, the name, in case you hadn't already guessed.

Billy, gallant as he was, tried to cut the hostility in the room. "If the woman's ancestors go back to infinity, why isn't she a member of the DAR? That would mean her family's older than some Confederate family that might have shipped over from Ireland during the potato famine in the earlier eighteen hundreds."

Boy, I loved my husband! He knew by that time that it would take a real distraction and not a mere "Daisy" from my mother to get Sam and me to quit fussing at each other. I looked over at him and grinned. "I think she's still fighting the Civil War in her mind, Billy. Some of those old Southern families just won't give it up."

Pa said, "Well, personally, I don't give a hoot. Maybe that's because my side won."

"Probably," said Sam, his voice still evincing a little strain, but evidently willing to turn the topic.

"I read in the *National Geographic* that some Southerners won't even call it the Civil War," Billy said. "To them it's the War Between the States or the Recent Unpleasantness."

"*Recent?*" I laughed. "The Civil War ended almost sixty years ago. Those guys have long memories."

Billy shrugged. "I reckon they do, and maybe for some cause. The South was well and truly destroyed during the war. Their whole economic way of life was ruined. I guess they carry grudges. Aside from the slave issue, Sherman cut a swath through some of those states so deep, they haven't recovered yet."

Billy's favorite magazine was the *National Geographic*, probably because it allowed him access to people and places he'd never be able to see for himself. Even if his health hadn't been ruined by the war, chances were slim that we middle-class Majestys would ever have been able to tour the world. Or even the South.

"Well, maybe so," said I. "But I don't understand how anybody can justify slavery, even if the institution of slavery did save the plantation owners money."

"I don't, either," said Sam.

"Everyone else has to hire workers," I pointed out. "Why not farmers and tobacco growers?"

"Right," said Billy. "Why not, indeed?"

Murmurs of agreement followed, and my sentiment seemed to be unanimous at the dinner table, which was nice since the conversation had begun with dissension.

Billy said, "Slaves were considered property. Sort of like horses and oxen. I read somewhere, probably in the *National Geographic*, that a slave had been hanged for running away from his master, and the State of Georgia gave the slave owner four hundred dollars in compensation for lost property."

I stared at him. "That's . . . horrible." My mind turned to

Jackson, Mrs. Pinkerton's gatekeeper, a fine colored gentleman who'd taught me some very interesting things about voodoo and other types of mystical stuff he'd gleaned from his boyhood in Louisiana. "It absolutely boggles my mind how evil people can be to each other, yet still call themselves Christians. Or whatever. I'm thinking Chinese emperors. Didn't those guys do some pretty horrid stuff to their people?"

"And," said Billy, smiling, "don't forget that good old Romanian guy, Vlad the Impaler. He nailed some Turkish officials' turbans to their heads at one point in his career."

Another gem culled from the pages of the *National Geographic*, I have no doubt. I said, "Ugh. Isn't that the legend that inspired Bram Stoker's book? I understand some German guy"—I tried not to shudder at the word *German*—"is turning *Dracula* into a movie. What's the title? I can't remember."

"*Nosferatu*," said Billy promptly. He had all sorts of facts at his disposal, since he spent most of his days reading everything from *National Geographic* to newspapers to just about anything else he could get his hands on.

"Interesting," said I, not voicing what I was thinking, which was, *It would be a German, wouldn't it?*

Sam then changed the subject with a bang that had us all goggling at him. "Some studio's making a picture in Pasadena, beginning next month, and it's going to be filmed at Mrs. Winkworth's mansion."

I think it was Ma who spoke first. "Really?"

Sam nodded. "Yes. It's some sort of epic, from what I hear. Along the lines of that Griffith picture. What was the name of that thing?" From this question, I got the impression that Sam, unlike Billy, didn't have the luxury—if you could call it that—of sitting around all day reading things.

"*Birth of a Nation*," I said. "Good picture."

"I liked it," confessed Billy. "Although they portrayed those night-rider guys in sheets in a good light. If you're against slavery, you probably should be against them, too."

"You're right," I said, meaning it. "But Sam, how come you know about this picture project? You don't generally keep up with stuff like that, do you?"

"No, I don't. I have a job to do," he said gruffly. "Unfortunately, I know about this one because I have to be on the blasted set. And the set is Mrs. Winkworth's estate."

I think the response to this was general, to judge by all the gaping mouths and staring eyes. I was the first to react. I'm always the one who talks the most; don't ask me why, because I don't know. "Oh, wow, Sam, that's the cat's meow!"

He gave me another frown. "You think so, do you?"

"Well . . . sure. I think it would be a lot of fun to see a picture being made. Harold's told me it can be a dead bore, but I'd still like to see for myself."

"Huh." Sam swiped a biscuit in his stew bowl and didn't say anything else.

"So why are you being made to do this arduous task, Sam?" Billy asked, as curious as I, if not more so.

Sam chewed and swallowed and then heaved a deep and melancholy sigh. "It's part of the case I can't talk about."

I'd have rolled my eyes, but I didn't want Ma to get mad at me. "Nerts. I wish you wouldn't talk about your cases unless you *could* talk about them," I said, nettled.

"I shouldn't have mentioned it," grumbled Sam. "But I'm not looking forward to having to hang around that dratted place for days at a time. That's not what my job is supposed to be about."

"Then why'd they assign it to you?" asked Billy.

"I'm the senior man. I'll have two other uniforms under me. We're supposed to keep an eye on things."

"Whatever's going on, it must be quite important for the

Pasadena Police Department to assign three men to a picture set," said Pa, surreptitiously handing Spike a bit of biscuit. None of us were supposed to feed the dog at the table, but we all did it, and we all pretended not to notice when the others did. It was kind of like a game, although Spike was beginning to show the results thereof.

"It must be," said Sam in a mildly savage voice. "Waste of manpower if you ask me."

"Well, maybe Pasadena doesn't have enough crime to go around these days," I suggested, knowing as I did so that the comment would annoy Sam. I couldn't seem to help myself.

He only glared at me some more.

"Daisy," said Aunt Vi, who had her own ways of keeping me under control, "why don't you pick up the plates while I go in and fetch dessert?"

Naturally, I did as my aunt asked, fuming as I did so. I continued to fume as Ma and I washed up the dinner dishes while Sam, Billy and Pa played gin rummy in the living room. Naturally, fuming did no good at all, and I was still mad at Sam for not divulging his precious mystery by the time I went to bed that night.

Fortunately for the state of my nerves and my mood, the following day was Saturday, and Saturdays were the days Billy and I took Spike to the Pasanita Dog Obedience Club at Brookside Park, where Pansy Hanratty tried to teach us dog owners to train our dogs. I loved those classes. Saturday mornings were the only times during the week when I knew for a certainty that Billy and I would be getting along.

That morning, I bundled Billy and Spike into our lovely new self-starting Chevrolet—bought with money given to me by a happy customer of my spiritualist business. Well, more or less. The money that bought the Chevrolet had been given to me by the mother of the ghost I'd exorcised from Mrs. Bissel's basement. But that sounds too absurd, and it's a whole 'nother story, so never mind.

Anyhow, after Billy and Spike were in the machine, I folded up the special bath chair I'd bought for Billy for just this purpose and stuffed it into the wooden rack Pa had built for it and installed on the back of our auto. Pa was clever about things like that. Billy used to be, too, but . . . well, never mind about that, too.

Anyhow, it was a perky threesome that drove down the twisty path to Brookside Park and pulled next to a field where several other people and their dogs already awaited that day's lesson, which began at ten o'clock sharp, Mrs. Hanratty being cut of a general's cloth. Although she was kind if she noticed one of us owners doing something wrong, she tolerated no tardiness or sloppiness, and she insisted that we *practice* what she taught us. We were there to train dogs, and she expected us to behave. I got the feeling Mrs. Hanratty liked her dogs considerably more than she liked most people. I understood her point of view, and even agreed with it to a degree.

I hauled Billy's bath chair out of its rack, unfolded it, helped a wobbly Billy into the chair, and the three of us joined the others at the training park. Billy wasn't the only observer of the action. Not only were there parents gathered to watch their children learn to train favorite pets, and husbands and wives of other participants, but there were also two other war-injured men who liked to come and watch the fun. One of them had lost both legs at the knee during the recent war, and the other poor fellow had lost an eye and an arm. In some ways, Billy was lucky.

No, he wasn't. Everyone who'd fought in that terrible conflict had suffered. So had their loved ones. There wasn't a single lucky thing about the whole damned war.

Sorry about my language. I don't usually swear.

Anyhow, I settled Billy near his chums—they were chums by that time, although they hadn't met each other until we'd begun taking Spike to the park for obedience training—and Spike and I set out to join the circle of eager dog lovers.

"Today, we are going to practice sitting, staying, and heeling," Mrs. Hanratty said in her characteristic voice, which was kind of loud and hollow, if that makes any sense. "Remember what we learned last week, and I trust"—she gave us all a stern look—"that you've been practicing with your animals *every day*, as I instructed you to do."

Most of us nodded meekly. It was the truth, at least in my case. Billy and I enjoyed taking Spike out to the backyard, where our spring-bearing orange tree was in full fruit, and there Billy would instruct me in Spike's training practice. Not that I needed his instruction, but I didn't mind. Telling me what to do made him feel good, and he had very little to feel good about in those days.

"So," Mrs. Hanratty continued. "Let us all get our dogs to heel. Then we'll walk for a few minutes. I'll tell you when to stop walking, and see how well you have done in getting your dogs to sit and stay."

By that time—I think we'd been coming to these classes for three weeks—Spike was an absolutely master at heeling, sitting and staying, so I was feeling pretty confident that we'd pass muster. Sure enough, as soon as Mrs. Hanratty gave the signal, we all began slowly speaking to our dogs.

"Spike, heel!" I said to Spike, and then I started walking in the prescribed circle. Spike heeled. What a good boy he was!

"All right now. Let's come to a halt," said Mrs. Hanratty after we'd been walking in a circle for a few minutes whilst she inspected our performance.

I halted. I looked down at Spike. Spike looked up at me. I

said, "Spike, sit." Spike appeared confused for a moment, so I bent and did as Mrs. Hanratty had instructed us to do: I squeezed the spot right in front of where his legs joined his hips. Spike sat. It's a foolproof way to get your dog to sit. Trust me on this.

Oh, and you're not supposed to repeat your commands, either. Mrs. Hanratty was very specific on this issue. You tell your dog what you want him to do, and then make sure he does it. I clearly remember what she'd told us the week before when we were taught the command "Sit." She said, "None of this 'sit, sit, sit' nonsense. *You're* the boss. You either train your dog, or your dog will train you."

She was right about that, too. Spike had already taught me to do many things for him. I figured it was past time to turn the table on him. So to speak. I didn't mean to bring my employment into this discussion.

At any rate, Spike sat.

Mrs. Hanratty said. "I trust you remember how to get your dog to stay." It wasn't a question. She meant what she said. "I will take note of those of you whose dogs follow you when you walk away from them." She meant that, too. She watched our progress like a hawk.

Therefore, I leaned over a little, put the flat of my palm in front of Spike's muzzle, shoved it toward him a bit, and said in a strong, authoritative voice, "Stay." Then, my heart in my throat, I dropped the leash, turned my back on my dog and walked away from him.

Darned if the little darling didn't stay! He was smart as a whip, Spike was.

He was so smart, in fact, that Mrs. Hanratty pointed out our excellent progress to several others in the class, whose pups had become confused and tried to follow them as they walked away.

"Let me congratulate Mrs. Majesty and Spike," said she. I

saw Billy grinning from the sidelines and was proud. "If you'll notice, she is very firm with her dog. You all need to be firm, yet kind. Never, ever, hit your dog. Don't forget, too, that some breeds are more amenable to correction than others, and believe me, dachshunds can be very stubborn. I trust you are using some sort of bait to help with his training at home, Mrs. Majesty?"

"Bait" in the doggy world meant "treat." I nodded and said, "Oh, yes. He loves his treats . . . er, bait. He'll do anything for food."

Mrs. Hanratty's smile beamed at Spike and me, and felt as if we'd been blessed by a holy angel or something. "It's not merely the bait, either," she said in her honking voice. "You *practice* with him, don't you?"

"Oh, my, yes. Mr. Majesty and I practice with Spike every day in our yard."

"Soon you'll be able to take him for walks in the neighborhood, I have no doubt, without a leash because he behaves so well. You're doing an excellent job with him, Mrs. Majesty."

I felt my cheeks heat, and I said, "Thank you." I meant my thanks sincerely, but I wasn't sure about the neighborhood walks. The only times we walked anymore were when Billy allowed me to push him in his wheelchair, and those times were becoming fewer and farther between.

But back to the class . . .

"All right," said Mrs. Hanratty. "Humans to the fore! Listen to me and practice. Do you hear me? *Practice!* Any time you meet an unruly dog, you'll know that its owner hasn't taken the time to train it. And in order to train your dog, *you* must be trained in the proper method of teaching him how to behave."

"Or her," said a woman I'd already tagged as silly, and who had a fuzzy little toy poodle on a pink leash.

I didn't mind poodles, although I considered Spike a much

more doggly dog, perhaps because he didn't have to have his hair cut in such a frilly way with puffs and poufs everywhere. Spike looked like a *dog*. What's more, he looked like a *boy* dog.

Mrs. Hanratty smiled at the woman, who had, after all, paid for the privilege of being there. I'd learned long ago that one should never show one's annoyance to a client, and I guess Mrs. Hanratty subscribed to the same principle. "Or her," she said. "But you must see, Mrs. Hinkledorn, that Mrs. Majesty has worked very hard with her pet." She gave the woman's poodle a small frown. "I suspect you need to practice more with Fluffy."

Can you imagine anyone naming a dog *Fluffy?* No wonder the poor poodle didn't obey as well as Spike did.

The class lasted for an hour, and when we got ready to leave, Mrs. Hanratty came over to speak to Billy and me. And Spike, of course. This was special attention, indeed.

"Mr. and Mrs. Majesty, I truly do mean to congratulate you on your progress with Spike. He's doing very well. How old is Spike, by the way?"

Billy and I looked at each other and I said, "About a year old, I suppose."

"Ah. That's good. Sometimes puppies are more difficult to train than more mature dogs."

Her words reminded me of one evening shortly after I'd brought Spike home. Billy had handed him a rag, and Spike had pulled Billy's wheelchair clear across the living room and back while Pa, Sam and the rest of the family laughed hysterically. I decided not to mention the incident to Mrs. Hanratty, whom I doubted would appreciate it.

"Anyway," Mrs. Hanratty continued. "I do want to congratulate you on your progress with Spike. Some people"—she shot a meaningful glance at the poodle lady—"refuse to become truly responsible for their pet's behavior. Obedience in a dog all depends on the *human*. Dogs are wonderful, but they don't learn on their own, any more than children do. I know that from experience, believe me." She gave us one of her hooting laughs, and I have to admit to being rather surprised. I hadn't pegged Mrs. Hanratty as a mother, although what did I know? But I'd always associated her with dogs, not children.

"Thank you very much," I said sincerely. "This class has been wonderful for all of us. I think Saturday is our favorite day of the week." I glanced at Billy for confirmation, and he nodded.

"It is. It makes me happy to see Spike and Daisy out there in the ring. You're an excellent teacher, Mrs. Hanratty."

"Why, thank you, young man."

Billy held out his hand, and Mrs. Hanratty shook it. Darned if she didn't blush!

The three of us, Billy, Spike and I, went home pleased as punch with ourselves that day.

CHAPTER THREE

It was Harold Kincaid who filled me in on what I thought were the details of Sam's case, but which turned out not to be the case, which was probably just as well. If Harold had been right, Sam would have been furious that Harold had talked.

As it was, Sam himself eventually let on why he'd been posted to the Winkworth place during the picture shoot. I don't know why he'd been so reticent about the matter at the dinner table, since the reason seemed trivial to me once he'd revealed it. I just chalked up his reticence to him being Sam. Anytime he could muddy an issue, he'd do it. Or so I thought in my crabby mood.

The Saturday of Mrs. Winkworth's séance had finally arrived. The morning, during which Spike had once again distinguished himself among the other dogs of Pasadena, had been lovely, but I had to go to work that night. In many ways, I was looking forward to the séance as an adventure. Heck, I was going to meet one of the most handsome and wealthy men on the planet, after all. That fact didn't stop me from wanting to spend a quiet evening home with my family. But needs must, so I did.

I drove our lovely Chevrolet down Lake Avenue to San Pasqual, where I dutifully turned left, drove to Mrs. Winkworth's magnificent estate, and pulled the machine up to the guardhouse in front of a massive wrought-iron gate. A guard posted at said gate asked who I was, I told him, and he pressed a button to allow me entry into the estate's grounds.

Let me tell you, the grounds were grand, too. I arrived, as requested by Gladys Pennywhistle in a follow-up telephone conversation, at seven o'clock. At the time of Gladys's call, I'd figured Mrs. Winkworth wanted to look me over and interview me before she allowed me to perpetrate my spiritualistic gifts on her guests. That was all right with me, since it gave me ample opportunity to study Mrs. Winkworth's beautiful home.

The drive up to the house was lined with jacaranda trees, all of which were blooming madly on this pleasant May evening. As I drove nearer to the house, one of the rose gardens—I learned later that there were several rose gardens on the estate grounds—came into view. Later in the summer, the roses would bloom like crazy, and there were blossoms even in May that took my breath away. Flowers flourished everywhere. I don't think I've ever seen so many anemones or ranunculus, and the hydrangea hedges made me blink.

I got the feeling Mrs. Winkworth liked her flowers. I wasn't surprised to see two magnificent magnolia trees standing guard at the portcullis. I figured she'd had them planted there as a reminder of her genteel Southern roots. It must have cost somebody—probably Mrs. Winkworth's grandson—a bundle to plant adult trees like that. Unless they were there when he'd bought the estate, although I doubted it, magnolias not being as plentiful in Pasadena as they were in South Carolina; at least I didn't think they were.

Gladys had told me to drive my Chevrolet under this spectacular piece of architecture—the portcullis, I mean—and park in a small paved area at the back of the house. I might be a spiritualist, but I was still hired help, and hired help entered through the back door. I didn't mind, being accustomed to such treatment by that time. Many of my regular clients like Mrs. Pinkerton and Mrs. Bissel were happy to have their staff greet me at their front doors, but when I worked at a house that was new to me, I tried to be polite and follow tradition. This seemed to me as though it might be especially important when it came to the elderly Southern belle who was Lurlene Winkworth.

As soon as I stepped out of the Chevrolet, however, who should rush up to greet me but Harold Kincaid! Boy, was I happy to see him.

"Harold! I didn't know you were going to be here!" I gave him a friendly hug, which he returned.

"Monty asked me to come."

"I didn't realize you knew him all that well," I said, surprised. Harold had told me lots of stuff about the picture business, and he'd also told me that Monty Mountjoy liked to read and listen to music, and Gladys had mentioned he and Mr. Mountjoy were acquainted, but I hadn't expected them to be such close friends that Harold would be invited to Mrs. Winkworth's séance.

Harold took the bag into which I'd placed my tarot cards—in case anyone wanted me to do a reading after the séance—in one hand, and hooked my arm through his on his other side. "I know him, all right, and he's in some pretty hot water. I'm hoping you can help us out with it."

Oh, dear. I didn't like the sound of that, especially when my mind instantly connected Monty Mountjoy's hot water with Sam Rotondo's next assignment. The one he refused to talk about. "Oh?" I tried not to sound as troubled as I felt.

Harold led me to a back door that didn't look like one, being every bit as beautiful, if not as elaborate, as the front one. But here, too, flowers abounded. A cunning Cecile Brunner rose arched over a trellis right before you got to the door, and geraniums lined the brick path leading to it. By the way, in Pasadena geraniums grow like weeds, and it had astonished me when I learned that people in colder climes cultivated them

41

with the same vigor and care they devoted to other plants. Somewhere nearby, I smelled the heavenly aroma of a couple of—or perhaps a couple of dozen—gardenia bushes.

"Boy, this place is really a doozy, isn't it? The gardens are almost more beautiful than your mother's."

"They're infinitely more spectacular than Mother's gardens," said Harold in a no-nonsense voice. "Monty's grandma loves her flowers almost as much as she cherishes her sacred Southern roots." I got the impression Harold wasn't particularly impressed with either of Mrs. Winkworth's partialities.

Then again, Harold had once told me that his special friend Del attended "Our Lady of Perpetual Malice" Church in Pasadena. He'd meant Saint Andrews. Harold wasn't impressed by much, probably because he grew up as a rich boy in the upper echelons of Pasadena society, whereas I'd climbed a perilous ladder to gain small glimpses into that same society, and I still felt as though I was merely peeking into heaven when I visited a place like Mrs. Winkworth's.

"I asked Gladys to have you come early," Harold continued, surprising me yet again, since I'd assumed Mrs. Winkworth had wanted to inspect me before allowing me at her guests. "You and I need to talk to Monty before this shindig begins." He opened the back door, I stepped inside, and Harold shut the door behind us. He studied me critically. "You look smashing as always, my dear. I presume you stitched that magnificent ensemble on your trusty Singer?"

I smiled, pleased that he'd noticed. Then again, Harold was a costumier, and he always took note of people's clothes. In fact, I had a superior wardrobe, thanks to the trusty White, not Singer, sewing machine Harold had mentioned. I bought material on sale at Maxime's Fabrics on Colorado Boulevard, and had a swell bevy of beautiful, tasteful evening gowns to wear when I conducted séances or attended spiritualistic parties. In those days, lots of rich folks enjoyed throwing spiritualistic parties. Spiritualism was the "in" thing, which made it handy for me.

That evening, I wore a fashionable but sober-hued velvet gown. Well, it was black, and I guess that's about as sober as you can get, isn't it? Anyhow, it was supposed to be a tubular shape, and it pretty much was, except where my hips marred the straight line. Naturally, I wore my bust flattener. The dress was augmented by a bias-cut, diaphanous, hip-length silk-chiffon cape that attached to it via narrow, beaded ribbons. I'd done the beading myself, by golly, with beads purchased cheaply at Nelson's Five and Dime. The beading was repeated on the V-shaped hip yoke and the edges of a short, straight train in back. I made sure never to let the sun damage my skin, which appeared milky white against the black of my gown. Believe me, I cultivated my spiritualist persona religiously, and it was nice to know that someone besides me appreciated my efforts. I felt elegant that night, and I was glad that Harold thought I looked it, too.

"Yes, indeedy. I did make it on my trusty sewing machine. Well, I did the beading with needle and thread," I confessed. "The White can't handle beads."

He shook his head. "I honestly don't know how you do it, Daisy. But you always look as if you just stepped out of *Vogue.*"

"That's the nicest thing anyone's ever said to me, Harold," I said, only half-teasing.

"Yes, it probably is. But come on, Daisy. We need to talk to Monty before the magnolia lady finds you're here."

At that moment, Gladys stepped into the little room occupied by Harold and me. She said, "Oh, good, you're here." Not a blink did she give my dazzling evening costume. Or me, for that matter, except to register my arrival. That was Gladys Penny-whistle all over.

I walked over to her and took her hand. "It's so good to see you again, Gladys." If she wasn't polite, I sure was going to be.

She blinked, her brown eyes huge behind the lenses of her strong spectacles. "Oh," said she. "Yes. It's good to see you, too, Daisy. I mean Desdemona."

"Just call me Daisy, please, Gladys." I glanced at Harold. "But Harold told me that Mr. Mountjoy wanted to see me before the séance begins."

Gladys wrung her hands. This gesture was one I hadn't seen on her before. The ever-confident Gladys Pennywhistle I'd known had never evinced any signs of distress unless her marks weren't up to her exacting standards in school. It surprised me to see her evincing them in spades that evening. "Yes. Yes, please. Come this way." She then blinked at Harold, whom I think she'd forgotten all about. "You, too, please, Mr. Kincaid." She lowered her voice. "Mrs. Winkworth is in the front parlor."

Ah, yes, the front parlor. The room we plebian Gumms and Majestys called the living room, I presume. I'd learned a lot in my business. Mrs. Pinkerton called her living room the drawing room. The only drawing that ever went on there, as far as I knew, was the withdrawing of my tarot cards from the darling little bag I'd sewn to hold them.

"Mr. Mountjoy would prefer to keep this meeting from her."

I shot a glance at Harold, who nodded vigorously. Oh, dear. This problem of Mr. Mountjoy's was beginning to sound worse and worse—and I didn't even know what it was yet.

Anyway, Harold and I followed Gladys. We'd been standing in a small room off the back door. That room led to the kitchen, and from there we walked through the butler's pantry. Then we turned left, walked through an enormous and elegant dining room into a broad hallway, and eventually got to a high, spiraling staircase. From what I could see of the décor of the home as Gladys sped us along, the entire place was fabulous. I wanted to stop and poke around, but didn't. I was the hired help. Perhaps

44

later, if I found favor with Mrs. Winkworth, I could have better access to the house and its furnishings.

Gladys kept up a speedy clip. Although I wore pointy-toed black evening slippers with Louis heels, I was able to keep up with her, but that's probably because I practiced training Spike a lot. A real lady would have been out of breath by the time we got to the top of that staircase. Harold and I then had to chase Gladys down another hallway, where I only caught glimpses of pictures on the wall and hoped I'd get to investigate them all more closely later.

At last, Gladys stopped at a closed door and tapped lightly upon it. A masculine but slightly reedy voice called, "Gladys?"

"Yes, Mr. Mountjoy, it is I." Proper. That's what Gladys was. "I've brought Mr. Kincaid and Mrs. Majesty."

The door opened and there, in all his manly perfection, stood the star of the silver screen, Mr. Monty Mountjoy. I very nearly fainted on the spot.

However, spiritualists are supposed to be above such unseemly behaviors, so I swallowed my excitement and smiled my beguiling spiritualist's smile at the absolutely *gorgeous* male who stood before me.

Harold didn't have the same problem I had. He said curtly, "Thanks, Gladys. I'll take it from here."

Gladys, holding her hands folded at her waist and gazing worshipfully at Mr. Mountjoy, said, "Very well."

"Thank you, Gladys. You're a gem."

Boy, oh boy, if Monty Mountjoy had smiled at me like that, spiritualist training or no, I do believe I'd have swooned. Even steady, practical Gladys gulped audibly.

With effortless efficiency, Mr. Mountjoy managed to get Harold and me inside the room and shut the door in Gladys's face. And he didn't even seem rude as he was doing it. Astonishing how suavity can assist people through ticklish situations, isn't it?

As soon as the door closed, Harold said, "I'm sure Daisy can find out who's doing it, Monty," leaving me as much in the dark as I was before.

Feeling a little sickish—I really, really hated to become embroiled in other people's problems, even though I seemed to do it all the time—I said, "Find out who's doing what?"

"That's what we need you for," said Harold. Big help.

"Please, Mrs. Majesty, take a seat. Harold, you're being a brute to my guest. Behave civilly, sir, or I shall have to call you out."

"Oh, please!" said Harold grumpily.

"No, really," said Mr. Mountjoy. "Please, Mrs. Majesty, have a chair."

For Monty Mountjoy I'd do pretty much anything. I didn't tell him that, of course. "Thank you." I made sure my voice didn't go shrill and I didn't simper or anything like that. I upheld my image, even in a room filled with Monty Mountjoy. Well, and Harold Kincaid, but he didn't count. Anyhow, I sat in the lovely chair to which Mr. Mountjoy gestured me.

Harold grabbed another elegant chair—I think those types of chairs were French and named after one of those Louises they had over there a long time ago. Louis XIV? If I'd been born rich, I'm sure I'd know—hauled it over to mine and sat with an irritated huff. "We don't have much time, Monty. I really think you need to get to the point. Don't worry about Daisy. She won't be shocked."

I turned my head and stared hard at Harold, not trusting this "she won't be shocked" thing one tiny little bit.

Monty Mountjoy turned his back on us and walked slowly to a window—which was covered, I might add, with perfectly beautiful lace curtains. There he drew one of the curtains aside and gazed out onto his grandmother's gardens. He sighed deeply. I'm sure the view from that window was gorgeous, but his sigh didn't sound like one of appreciation. My apprehension edged ever so slightly upward.

Silence grew thick in the room after that, until Harold finally burst out with, "Damn it, Monty, spill it!"

I smacked him on the knee, his knee being close by. "Don't swear, Harold."

Harold rolled his eyes. "Oh, for Christ's sake."

So much for that. Perhaps I should take Harold to Mrs. Hanratty's obedience class.

After what seemed like eons, Monty Mountjoy turned from the window and joined Harold and me, pulling up yet another elegant chair. I can't remember what those types of chairs are called either, although I'm almost sure they were French. You know the kind I mean. They had no arms, and they had medallion backs that were worked in a shiny brocade fabric as were the seats, and I'm pretty sure even one of them would cost as much as our Chevrolet.

"My problem is very embarrassing and troubling, Mrs. Majesty," Mr. Mountjoy said in a serious voice.

"Embarrassing, mainly," said Harold. "And if you don't nip it in the bud, it might well ruin your career, Monty. You know that as well as I do."

"Um . . . what problem is that?" I asked politely, trying to move things along. We had less than an hour before I had to go downstairs and conduct a séance, for heaven's sake.

Then Monty Mountjoy did something very unusual. He heaved a sobbing sigh, lifted his hands, and buried his face in them.

Harold huffed with annoyance yet again. Such a show of impatience wasn't like my good friend Harold, so I knew that, whatever the matter was, it was bad. "For God's sake, Monty,

I'll tell her then!"

"Yes. Please. You tell her," came his muffled voice, from behind Mr. Mountjoy's hands. "I don't think I can say it."

So Harold turned to me and said, "Monty's getting threatening letters."

I blinked. I probably gasped, too, but I don't remember. "Threatening letters? That's terrible!" I saw Mr. Mountjoy peeking between his fingers and said the first thing that popped into my mind. "Um . . . have you told the police about these letters?" I couldn't imagine Sam and two uniformed officers being assigned to a job featuring threatening letters, but what did I know?

"He *can't* tell the police, Daisy. If he tells the police, everything will come out, and then his career will be over."

"And my family," moaned Mr. Mountjoy pitifully. "It would ruin my family. I don't care about my career, but my family . . ." His words trickled out.

"You'll care about your career soon enough when the money stops flowing," Harold said in what could only be called a ruthless tone.

I shook my head, bewildered. "But what do you want me to do? If you can't go to the police, how on earth can I help?" After considering the matter for a second, I asked, "Why the heck can't you go to the police?"

Mr. Mountjoy's hands dropped to his lap. "Because then it will come *out!* And I'll be ruined."

Feeling quite frustrated by that time, I lifted my own hands and said rather more loudly than I probably should have, "Then *what* will come out? *Why* would you be ruined?"

Harold and Mr. Mountjoy exchanged a speaking glance, and I began to catch on. I was shocked. Mind you, I don't know why I should be shocked, but I was. I stammered, "Do . . . do you mean . . . ?"

"Yes," Harold said firmly. "That's exactly what we mean."

Good Lord in heaven. Whoever would have thunk it, as one of my school chums use to say. But . . . Monty Mountjoy? The epitome of swashbuckling masculinity? A man whose reputation with women was absolutely infamous? Who was reputed to have had affairs with most of the crowned female heads of Europe, not to mention all the Hollywoodland stars of the day? *That* Monty Mountjoy was . . . was . . .

"He's a faggot," said Harold brutally. "Just like Del and me."

I stared at both men in turn before I finally managed to whisper a feeble "Oh, my."

As you can well imagine, the séance that followed was not nearly as exciting as the revelations that preceded it. I still felt a trifle shaky when Harold and Mr. Mountjoy—who'd asked me to call him Monty, so I'll refer to him as Monty from here on—escorted me downstairs to meet the formidable Mrs. Winkworth. Have you ever heard of an iron fist in a velvet glove? Well, I got the impression that expression described Lurlene Winkworth to a T.

In fact, I was so impressed by her majesty that I actually curtsied when Monty introduced us. I'm not a curtsier by nature, but there was just something about that woman. She lifted a languid hand. Or perhaps she languidly lifted a hand. Whatever the proper terminology, the gesture seemed perfectly Southern, I couldn't seem to help myself, and so I curtsied.

"It's so good of you to come to my home this evening, Mrs. Majesty," she said in a voice as thick as honey. Magnolia honey, I'm sure.

"It's a pleasure to be here, Mrs. Winkworth," I said, maintaining my cultivated spiritualist's voice, in spite of the previous forty-five minutes, which had nearly knocked me flat.

"My guests will be arriving shortly. There won't be many of

them. I understand you like to work with small groups."

"Yes, I do. No more than eight, if at all possible."

"That's wonderful. We shall have exactly eight persons present at the séance."

"I'm so glad. Is there any person in particular with whom you would like to communicate this evening, Mrs. Winkworth?" Stupid question, but standard if you're in my business. "Someone who has recently crossed over, perhaps?"

"I should be very much interested in learning about some of my forebears and how they survived the War of Northern Aggression, although I don't particularly care which one you call up."

"I see." Yet another name for the Civil War. I wondered how many Southernisms there were for that brutal conflict. It was a darned good thing I'd done my homework and found out about Mrs. Winkworth's family connections and her grandparents' names and so forth. "I should think my spirit control will be able to satisfy some of your curiosity."

What I actually hoped was that the woman would be so intrigued by the few snippets of information Rolly, my spirit control, pulled out of thin air that she'd continue to hire me for séances. I know that sounds terrible, but I had to earn a living, darn it.

Oh, by the way, I'd made up Rolly, too, when I was ten and first started fiddling with Aunt Vi's Ouija board. As with the Desdemona part of my business, I often wished I'd named him something more elegant, but it was too late to change things now.

"I'm so very grateful to you for coming tonight. You can't begin to imagine how difficult my life has been since I had to leave my home and all my friends," said Mrs. Winkworth. I saw tears standing in her eyes!

Those tears startled me so much, I couldn't think of another single thing to say. Her life had been difficult because her grandson had moved her from a tumble-down wreck of a former plantation in South Carolina to paradise? Good Lord. Some people didn't realize their own luck.

Fortunately, my tongue-tied condition didn't matter, because a honking voice behind me bellowed, "Mrs. Majesty! It *is* you!"

I whirled, which isn't very spiritualistic behavior, but I knew that voice! "Mrs. Hanratty! How wonderful to see you here!" And it was. I was overwhelmingly grateful to see so normal a person as Pansy Hanratty in those elegant surroundings. I might even have kissed her feet if I were a person who did things like that.

She hurried over to me. "When Mother said somebody named Mrs. Majesty was going to conduct her séance, I couldn't think of another Mrs. Majesty, Majesty being such an uncommon name, but I just couldn't believe it was *the* Mrs. Majesty who belonged to Spike!"

"I am indeed that Mrs. Majesty, and . . ." Her words finally penetrated my reeling brain. "Your . . . your *mother?*" I glanced back to see Mrs. Winkworth leveling a quelling glance at Mrs. Hanratty.

"Really, Pansy," said Mrs. Winkworth. "One would think you were born in a stable."

Mrs. Hanratty laughed uproariously. "Not born in one, but I darned sure was raised in one!"

Mrs. Winkworth sighed. I could imagine what she was thinking: *First Pasadena and now this.* I couldn't for the life of me feel sorry for her.

"I'm really happy to see you here this evening, Mrs. Hanratty," I said with feeling.

Casting a glance of her own at her mother—it was more of a *can you believe I came from that?* glance than one of self-pity—Mrs. Hanratty went on, "Have you met my son?"

My mouth opened but I didn't have a chance to speak, which was probably just as well since Mrs. Hanratty then called out, "Monty! Come over here and meet Mrs. Majesty! She's doing the *best* job of training a dachshund I've ever seen!"

Monty Mountjoy was this woman's son? And Pansy Hanratty was Lurlene Winkworth's daughter? I swear, I think if I'd received any more surprises that evening, I might have gone 'round the bend.

Smiling his magnificent smile, Monty joined us in front of his grandmother's chair. "We've already met, Mother. Mrs. Majesty is a good friend of Harold's, you know."

"Oh, I didn't know that! My, my, it's a small world, isn't it?"

"It is indeed," said her son—Monty Mountjoy for heaven's sake!—and bowed over my hand.

"You should meet her dog, Monty. You'd love him. He's a black-and-tan dachshund, and he behaves better than the damned *poodle* in my class!"

I heard Mrs. Winkworth heave a small, tragic, genteel sigh behind us. I presume she didn't approve of her daughter's language.

"Harold's told me about Spike, Mother. But I thought you told me poodles were the smartest dogs in the canine world."

Talk about self-possession. Monty Mountjoy had tons of the stuff. Not only did he speak to his mother and me as if we were mere mortals, but he'd remembered my dog's name was Spike! And he'd only several minutes earlier been telling me about receiving poison-pen letters—and why he believed he was getting them. I was really impressed. No wonder he was such a smashing hit on the silver screen.

"Poodles are smart as whips. The poor poodle in Spike's class—Fluffy, if you can believe it—has an owner who's thick as a plank. You know my training methods, Monty. Train the owner, and the dog will behave itself."

"It worked on me," Monty said with a wink for me. My heart fluttered violently for a moment or two, even though I already knew he didn't care for women. You figure it out, because I sure can't.

Mrs. Hanratty smacked her son's arm playfully. "It certainly did work on you!"

I think that Pansy Hanratty had tried to spiff herself up for the evening. She wore a long green gown that looked rather like a horse blanket, although I'm sure it wasn't supposed to. If I weren't there to perform a job of work for which goggling was strictly prohibited, I might well have goggled, and not merely at Mrs. Hanratty's outfit. But, honestly. Never, in a million years, would I have connected Mrs. Pansy Hanratty, the dog lady, to Mrs. Lurlene Winkworth, proud and elegant daughter of the South, with a capital S; much less would I have pegged the dog-loving Mrs. Hanratty as the mother of Monty Mountjoy, the man over whom women swooned in packs and droves and he, who didn't give a fig for any of them.

Then a shriek came from the entryway—which was arched in the Spanish style—and we all whirled around to behold Lola de la Monica in all her glory. And she definitely radiated glory.

"Monty!" was the word she shrieked. She followed it up with, "My *darling!*" Then she all but flew across the front parlor's classy Persian rug and flung herself into the arms of Monty Mountjoy, who evidently had braced himself for this event, because he didn't even stagger.

My impressedness index got a huge boost that night. Not only did Lola de la Monica have an accent that gave no hint of her roots—which Harold Kincaid told me all about later on in the evening—but she actually sounded kind of Spanish. She also wore an ensemble that might have been painted by Goya in one of his more amorous moods. Flowing white covered her from creamy ivory shoulders to slender ankles. Naturally, the draperies were slender enough to show off her flawless figure. No bust flattener for Miss Lola de la Monica, thank you very much. Her shoes looked like those a Flamenco dancer might wear.

The séance went pretty well, all things considered. After I'd had Rolly chat with a couple of Mrs. Winkworth's more grandiose forebears, including a colonel of the Confederate Army who'd died shortly after the war ended, Lola de la Monica wanted me to get in touch with the spirit of William Desmond Taylor. Her request interested me, since she was one of the women whose names had been linked with Mr. Taylor's. The list of said women was long and illustrious and included such exalted names as Mary Miles Minter and Mabel Normand besides Miss de la Monica.

Naturally, although I hadn't expected to be chatting with Mr. Taylor that evening, Rolly and I pulled the matter off with élan. We also weaseled out of naming the murderer by having Mr. Taylor tell the assembled séance attendees that he hadn't seen the face of his killer. There are always ways out of these things if you stay on your toes.

Life is pretty darned interesting sometimes. It got even more interesting as the evening progressed, and not in a good way. In actual fact, when I drove home that night, I considered flinging myself off a high hill somewhere.

But Daisy Gumm Majesty is no coward, whatever else she might be. Anyhow, it was a long drive to a hill from which I could fling myself that would be high enough for me to land without merely breaking an arm or a leg, which would only have laid me up and hurt a lot, so I didn't.

Chapter Four

"Lola de la Monica wants you to do *what?*"

Once more Billy and I sat at the kitchen table, and once more we were eating a delicious breakfast prepared for us by Aunt Vi. Pa was there, too, but he didn't scowl at me as Billy was doing. In truth, Pa looked rather pleased to learn about his daughter's next assignment, which didn't really have a thing to do with spiritualism, except in the most pedestrian way. He'd already taken Spike for his walk—Pa and Spike went for a walk (with a leash) around the neighborhood every morning—but I'd slept in because I'd come home so late the night before.

Billy had waited breakfast for me, which might have been endearing if it hadn't signified to me yet one more indication of a decline in his overall condition. The Billy I'd married would have wolfed down his breakfast, walked with Pa and Spike, then come home and had another breakfast with me. I mean, he'd have done all that on a weekend, since he'd have been at work during the week. Before he'd gone off to war, he'd been prepared to work as an automobile mechanic at the Hull Motor Works. Mr. Hull had said the job was Billy's as soon as the war ended. But we already know how that had turned out. At any rate, the morning after Mrs. Winkworth's séance, I got the impression Billy was only eating because if he didn't, I'd nag him. I also got the impression he'd been drinking rather deeply of his morphine syrup.

Poor Billy. I honestly and truly despaired for him.

As for me, I toyed with my food that morning. I've read that expression in lots of books, but my appetite wasn't often dulled by care; hence, as I've already mentioned, my failure to achieve the slim and boyish figure so admired in those days. It was dulled that morning, though, with a vengeance. What's more, my heart ached, and I positively dreaded what I'd be facing during the next few weeks.

I repeated for my husband's sake, "She wants me to be her spiritual guide during the filming of *The Fire at Sunset*. That's the picture they're going to shoot at Mrs. Winkworth's place."

"Good God," said Billy.

Pa shot him a swift glance. I'm sure he was as worried about Billy as I, although he never said a single thing about his own cares or Billy's health, bless his heart. He said, "What's her place like, by the way? I understand it's grand and glorious."

"It is both of those things, all right, and it's beautiful, too." I told both of the men in my life—and Spike, too, since he always sat next to the table, hoping for handouts—all about the magnificent gardens and gorgeous home belonging to Lurlene Winkworth. "I understand there are more houses on the property, too, although I don't know how many."

"I swear to God," said Billy, sounding savage, "those picture people make too much money for what they do."

With a sigh, I nibbled a piece of toast. "It does seem rather unfair, doesn't it? There are people doing truly useful things in the world, and who makes the money? People who star in the pictures. Not the ones who write the scripts or the ones who make the costumes or create the cameras and stuff, but the actors, and all they have to do is look good on the screen. Heck, they don't even have to learn lines, since the pictures are silent. For all we know, they're reciting their grocery lists while the camera's cranking away."

"I'm sure," said Pa with judicious good will, "that there's

more to acting than merely looking good on screen." Pa always gave everyone the benefit of the doubt.

Recalling the prior evening, I said, "I'm not so sure about that, Pa. For instance, Lola de la Monica might look like a seductive lady of Spain, but I swear to heaven, once she forgets her audience is listening, her accent is just like Sam's."

That turned out to be a good thing to say, because Billy laughed. "You're kidding!"

I shook my head. "Am not. When she first made her entrance—and believe me, she *did* make an entrance—she put on a phony Spanish accent. But once she forgot to keep up her act, she actually sounded worse than Sam." Sam Rotondo was a native of New York City, by the by. "In fact, she sounded more like Mrs. Barrow." Mrs. Barrow, a native of The Bronx, New York, was the nosiest of our telephone's party-line members. She also had an accent you could cut with a knife, although I could think of other things I'd rather cut with said knife. Like her throat, for instance. But I'm being mean. Please forgive me.

"Good heavens," said Billy, marveling. "She sounds like a washer woman from The Bronx, and she's making hundreds of thousands of dollars by pretending to be a Spanish *femme fatale* on the silver screen." He shook his head in awe and wonder and no little disgust.

"She's a looker, all right," said Pa. "Whoever would have thought her to be from back East. None of my kin look like she does." But his expression was troubled.

I said, "What's the matter, Pa?" I didn't want my father to be troubled. We all worried about his health, ever since he'd had a heart attack several years earlier, and I wanted to keep him around for as long as possible.

"Nothing's the matter with me," he said. "But I sense something's the matter with you. What is it, Daisy?"

Perceptive, too, my father. That day I wished he wasn't. I

heaved a largish sigh. "Oh, it's nothing, really. But honestly, Pa, that woman is definitely what they call temperamental."

"Yeah?" Billy quirked an eyebrow at me. He was still grinning, so I decided to milk my first encounter with Miss de la Monica for all I was worth.

"She actually shrieked when we were introduced. It was all I could do not to wince, and you know how little emotion we spiritualists are supposed to display."

Billy said, "Huh."

Pa said, "She shrieked, eh?"

"Yes. She positively shrieked. And then she said, 'Oh, my God, I *need* you! You simply *must* be my spirit guide as I endure this next wretched picture.' "

"This wretched picture?" said Pa. "How much money are they paying her?"

"I don't know, but I'm sure it's not a wretched amount," I answered drily.

"She wants you to be her spirit guide? I thought that Rolly guy of yours was the spirit guide." Billy. Not as snidely as usual.

"He's supposed to be, but Lola de la Monica doesn't see it that way."

"Well," said Pa with a shrug, "it's money, and that's the point, I guess."

What I wanted to do was unburden my soul to both of them. To tell them that Monty Mountjoy had hired me, against my will and better judgment, to find out who'd been writing him threatening letters, and, if the reason was the one he feared it was, to do something about it. God alone knew what I was supposed to do to dry the ink in a poison pen. I wanted to tell them that Lurlene Winkworth was a spoiled, rotten daughter of the South who disapproved of her own daughter, and who deplored her grandson's line of work—kind of like Billy deplored mine, actually—even though his line of work had garnered her a home that was as close to heaven as a person could get without dying first. I wanted to tell them that Monty Mountjoy was terrified of being discovered to be one of "those" creatures whom Billy despised. Then I wanted to tell them that I didn't want to be on the set of a moving picture, especially since Sam Rotondo was expected to be there, too. I wanted to say that Sam and I had only recently begun being civil to each other and that I had no idea what daily proximity might do to our relationship, but I doubted it was anything good. I wanted to tell them that Harold and Monty Mountjoy and Del Farrington couldn't help being what they were, and that I thought people who considered them sinners or crazy were bigots of the very worst sort.

What I said was, "Personally, I don't think Miss de la Monica's problem is temperament. I think it's hysteria. With an extra dollop of extreme self-absorption thrown in for good measure."

"Sounds like a great gal," said Billy.

"Right," said I.

Pa laughed.

Billy asked, "So what's Mrs. Winkworth like? Does she appreciate her good fortune? I mean, if somebody bought me a fabulous mansion on San Pasqual, I'd appreciate it."

After heaving a sigh, I figured it wouldn't hurt to tell a little bit of the truth. "She deplores her good fortune, actually."

"She *what?*" Billy lowered his paper, and his expression changed from one of disapproval—of me—to one of wonder.

I nodded. "She deplores everything about her life. Including her grandson." Then I remembered something else. "Oh, Billy!" cried I, brightening momentarily. "She also deplores her daughter, and you'll never in a million years guess who her daughter is!"

After blinking at me once, Billy said, "You're right. I won't.

Who is she?"

"Mrs. Hanratty!"

Since Billy's profession didn't deny him the comfort of goggling, he goggled at me. "You're pulling my leg!"

"Am not. It's God's honest truth. Pansy Hanratty is Lurlene Winkworth's daughter. What's more," I continued, "Monty Mountjoy is Pansy Hanratty's son!"

"Good Lord," said Billy. "Lola de la Monica is from The Bronx, Mrs. Hanratty is from Mrs. Winkworth, and Monty Mountjoy is from Mrs. Hanratty. Sounds like one of those dog lines Mrs. Bissel and Mrs. Hanratty are so fond of telling us about."

"It does, kind of. Mrs. Hanratty lives on one of the other houses on the Winkworth property with her pack of dogs."

"What kinds of dogs does she have?" asked Pa.

It was a good question, but I didn't have an answer. "I don't know. I'll ask her when I start working there." The notion of my upcoming job made me grumpy again.

"Anybody know who the sires of all these people are?" Billy asked.

"What people?" asked Pa.

"Mrs. Hanratty and Monty Mountjoy," Billy enlightened him.

I shook my head. " 'Fraid not. I mean, I'm sure Mrs. Winkworth and Mrs. Hanratty know, but I don't."

"And are they properly registered with the American Kennel Club?"

"Billy!" I said, only marginally shocked.

Billy grunted and lifted his paper again.

Pa laughed.

Fortunately for the state of my appetite that morning, Spike loved eggs and toast.

★　★　★　★　★

As luck would have it, filming for *The Fire at Sunset* was set to begin two Mondays following the séance, which meant that Billy, Spike and I got to attend another dog-training class before the fateful day. Pa decided to accompany us the next Saturday, which I appreciated, because Billy always behaved when other members of my family were with us. Spike pretty much behaved all the time by then, bless his heart.

Mrs. Hanratty rushed up to greet us as soon as she saw me pushing Billy's chair up to the group gathered at the field designated for Pasanita's use.

"Daisy!" she cried. "I'm so glad to know you're going to be at Mother's house during the filming of Monty's picture. Monty is such a sweetheart and he never says anything at all unpleasant to his grandmother, but Mother is a *very* trying person to live with."

Since I didn't have a single clue what to say to that—one can't very well agree that one of one's clients is a selfish old biddy, now can one?—I only smiled and said, "I enjoyed meeting your mother very much. I had no idea you were related."

"Yes, well, one can't choose one's relatives, can one?"

I couldn't think of an answer to that question, either, so I introduced her to my father.

"So happy to meet you, Mr. Gumm," said Mrs. Hanratty, shaking his hand with hearty vigor. From what I'd seen of her so far, just about everything Pansy Hanratty did was either hearty or vigorous or both. She was as unlike her mother as a daughter could be. "Your daughter and Mr. Majesty are doing an absolutely wonderful job training Spike."

"They practice all the time with him," Pa said, preening under this glowing commendation from his daughter's teacher. "But you could have knocked me down with a feather when Daisy told us you were Monty Mountjoy's mother."

"Astonishing, isn't it?" Mrs. Hanratty gave one of her hooting laughs. "You'd never know to look at the two of us that we were related. He takes after his father's side of the family, fortunately for him."

"I enjoyed meeting him last Saturday evening," I said, not wanting to get into the looks issue. In truth, Mrs. Hanratty was a handsome woman—but she was right when she said nobody would ever connect her and Monty Mountjoy as belonging to the same family.

"Isn't he a darling boy?" Mrs. Hanratty all but crooned.

For some reason, my mind's eye pictured her holding out a treat to the infant Monty Mountjoy as an enticement to get him to sit up and beg. I shook my head to rid it of the silly image. "He's a lovely young man. Um . . . did he choose the last name Mountjoy himself?" Was that a snoopy question? Well, too bad. I'd already asked it.

"Good Lord, no. The studio tacked that one on him. I don't mind, though. Hanratty isn't exactly a name you'd expect to see on a theater marquee, would you? Mountjoy is much more . . . romantic."

"I suppose so," I muttered, recalling where Monty Mountjoy's romantic interests lay.

"And isn't that Lola de la Monica a stitch?" Mrs. Hanratty went on. "Now you *know* somebody at the studio tacked that moniker on her. Lola de la Monica, my hind leg."

Pa, Billy and I all laughed. "I told them about her phony Spanish accent and what she sounds like when she's not putting it on."

Mrs. Hanratty shook her head in good-natured wonder, Pa and Billy joined Billy's war-injured friends, Spike and I walked with Mrs. Hanratty to join the circle of dog-obedience trainees, and then commenced the only truly good hour of my weekend.

Oh, very well, so life wasn't all bad. At church the next day, we choir members produced a rousing rendition of "Come, Christians, Join to Sing," and following that, we all partook of the covered-dish social in Fellowship Hall. Generally we only had cookies and coffee after church, but one Sunday each month was designated covered-dish Sunday. Aunt Vi had brought one of her more delicious chicken-in-cream-sauce dishes *and* a caramel cake. What with Vi's contribution and the rest of the wonderful food the other women of the church brought, about all that went on in the Gumm-Majesty household that particular Sunday afternoon was a whole lot of napping.

And then it was Monday. Or Doomsday, if you were me.

Mind you, I've been in worse places and predicaments in my life. I was arrested in a speakeasy one time, for pity's sake, and all I'd been doing there was conducting a séance, being too intelligent to drink my hard-earned money away or to break the law . . . well, not on purpose, anyway. And I'd darned near been killed by a couple of thieving anarchists a few months earlier, and I hadn't done anything wrong that time except teach a cooking class for which I was totally unqualified. But except when Harold had been driving me to that wretched speakeasy, I can't recall a single time when I'd experienced such dread heading to a job.

I didn't mind so much being spiritual advisor to Lola de la Monica, although I can't really say I liked the woman very much. But attempting to discover who was sending poison-pen letters to Monty Mountjoy—under Sam Rotondo's nose, and without allowing Sam to find out what I was doing and why—was a prospect that thrilled me not at all. In fact, it made me want to run away and hide.

Also, why was Sam going to be there? He wouldn't tell me. Did he know about the threatening letters? Why would the Pasadena Police Department deploy a detective and two uniformed outriders to seek out the author of threatening letters? I feared there was a deeper and far more sinister purpose for Sam's attendance at the picture shoot, and he'd already let slip that it concerned Monty Mountjoy.

Was Monty Mountjoy a secret drug addict?

Was he a secret drug *pusher*?

Was he hand in glove with bootleggers?

Was he, God forbid, some kind of perverted person who enjoyed dallying with children? The mere thought made me sick.

In any case, if he was any of those things, I didn't want to know. My initial impression of Monty was that he was a kind and gentle and genuinely nice man. I didn't want him to be a crook.

And I really and truly didn't want to have to hang out anywhere near Sam Rotondo for a job that might well last for weeks and weeks.

CHAPTER FIVE

As soon as I entered the drive and stopped the Chevrolet before the grand iron gateway separating Mrs. Winkworth's estate from the vulgar world, I understood why at least one of the Pasadena coppers had been sent to this so-called set. In all his uniformed glory, he stood guard at the gate. I guess the regular gatekeeper wasn't tough enough for the job. Or perhaps the picture makers expected violence to erupt on the set and needed men with guns to quell it. Ghastly thought.

The policeman, whose badge said his name was Thomas J. Doan, approached the driver's side of the machine. "Name please?" he snapped. It didn't sound to me as if he much wanted to be there. I understood completely, as I shared his sentiment.

"Mrs. Majesty," said I, similarly snappish.

He lifted a clipboard I hadn't noticed before and scanned what seemed to be a list of typewritten names. Then he squinted at me again. "Mrs. Desdemona Majesty?"

Swallowing a sigh—my advice to anyone who might be reading this journal is never to make a life-altering decision when you're ten years old—I said, "Yes."

"Identification?"

"Identification? What do you mean?"

"Do you have some form of identification on you? I'll need to see confirmation that you are who you say you are."

My jaw dropped. "You need to see identification to allow me onto a picture set?"

"Yes, ma'am."

"Good heavens, why?"

Officer Doan's complexion had begun to deepen to a slightly mauve hue, and I decided to ask somebody else why armed guards were needed at Mrs. Winkworth's gates. This man clearly didn't care to be questioned about his duties by little old me.

"Just a minute." I fumbled in my handbag and eventually found my California State driving license, which said I was Mrs. William "Daisy" Majesty. No mention of anyone named Desdemona, but how many Majestys were there in this particular policeman's world? I shoved the license at him and said, "Here."

He squinted at my license for what seemed like eons. Mind you, the sun that day was glorious, but I think he only squinted because he thought it made him look rugged. Maybe he wanted to get a part in the next Western picture the studio made. Stupid man. Then he looked at me again. "Daisy is a nickname? Short for Desdemona?"

"Yes."

"Well . . ."

All right, here's the thing. I didn't want to be there. I was already in a bad mood. If this wretched policeman kept me waiting much longer, I'd jolly well snatch my license from his brutish grip and drive back home. I could always telephone Monty and tell him I'd been turned away at the gate.

No such luck.

Officer Doan handed back my license and said, "Go on in." Not a smile did the man crack. He might have been made of stone, except that he could move his limbs.

I guess the regular gate guard pressed the button from inside the gatehouse at a signal from Doan, because the big gates swung open, and there was no escape. I drove through them.

The day only got better when the first person I saw after I'd driven onto the Winkworth grounds was Sam Rotondo. I'm being sarcastic, in case you didn't notice. Anyhow, Sam was just walking down the wide marble steps of the front entrance, which led to the drive over which the portico arched. Therefore, he saw me coming.

Naturally, Sam—being who he was—scowled at me. I pulled the Chevrolet to a stop beside him. "This isn't my idea, Sam Rotondo, so don't you start in on me. I practically had to be fingerprinted by one of your policeman pals in order to gain access to this stupid picture set."

"I wasn't going to start in on you. Officer Doan was only doing his job."

We frowned at each other for another second or two.

Then Sam said, "You're in a good mood today, aren't you?"

"I'm not the one who frowned first," I told him.

He rolled his eyes and muttered something I didn't catch. It was probably just as well.

So, Officer Doan having proved such a dud, I asked Sam, "What's the reason for the tight security, Sam? Do you expect a mob of respectable Pasadenans to storm the palace in revolt against the moving-picture industry or something?"

"Of course not," Sam said, as if my question had been utterly ridiculous.

"Well, then, why'd I have to show my identification? I felt as though I were being allowed into the presence of a royal personage."

"Where are you going now?" Sam asked, completely ignoring my question.

I held on to my temper with some effort. "Mr. Mountjoy told me to drive through the portico and head out to what he called the north forty. I guess there's a big field somewhere on these massive grounds that they're using to build the set."

"There is. There are signs tacked up to point people in the

right direction. Will you drive me out there so I don't have to walk? It's getting hot."

I considered Sam's question. Which was a heck of a lot more than he'd done to mine.

He must have realized that, because he said, I presume as an inducement, "I'll tell you why security's so tight."

I thought I already knew why security was tight but didn't let on. Anyway, I kind of hoped I was wrong. Not that I thought the Pasadena Police Department would blab about Monty Mountjoy's sexual preferences, but news had a tendency to leak out. However, I was kind of surprised that Sam was breaking his silence on the issue, and I definitely wanted to know what he knew.

"All right, then. Get in." I lifted my handbag off the passenger's seat, threw it in the back, and Sam opened the door and entered the Chevrolet. I thought I was being pretty darned nice, all things considered.

As soon as Sam had settled into the machine and shut the door, I put my foot on the gas pedal, let up on the choke, and we putted off to the north forty, which Monty had told me was somewhere beyond the rose gardens. He'd said all I needed to do was follow the first right-hand road I got to, and continue to be guided by the arrows tacked up on trees along the way. Except for the prior year when I'd visited the gigantic Castleton estate in San Marino, I'd never seen such extensive grounds. They looked as if they were manicured by a herd of professional gardeners every single day, too.

In spite of myself, before Sam could satisfy my curiosity about the security question, I said, "Boy, this place is the cat's pajamas, isn't it? It's positively gorgeous. It must take a staff of hundreds to keep it in trim."

"It does," grumbled Sam.

I got the feeling he shared Billy's opinion of picture stars who made monstrous amounts of money while the rest of us common folk plodded along, scraping by from week to week whilst working every bit as hard, if not harder, than the rich picture stars. I'd learned in my tenth year that worth and wealth have nothing to do with each other, so I was used to it.

Lawns rolled on forever, and flowers grew positively everywhere. Sure enough, we soon came to a road that bisected the one we were on. A big white arrow pointed to the right-hand path. This place was as big as a village all by itself. In actual fact, it had some outbuildings that looked like they might house permanent staff. And all for the sake of one little, old woman who didn't appreciate her good luck. I tried not to be bitter.

"So tell me about the security," I said as soon as I'd turned onto the appropriate road.

"New invention," said Sam, as if that explained everything there was to know about the security question.

I'd have stared at him balefully if I weren't driving. "What do you mean, *new invention,* Sam Rotondo? People are inventing new things all the time, and they don't all require armed guards and detectives to keep people away from them. Darn you! What's going on?"

"All right, all right," Sam said with a deep sigh. "Some guy named Homer Fellowes—he's one of those scientific geniuses at Cal Tech—has invented a new motion-picture device. From what I've been told, you put the camera on it, strap it down—the camera, I mean—and this special devise is supposed to hold the camera steady, so the picture doesn't wobble. The thing rolls, which, naturally, allows the camera to be moved around from place to place. It's supposed to make the pictures look more realistic."

I chewed on that notion for a while. "Heck, the only reason I go to the pictures is to escape from reality. I don't particularly want them to look more realistic."

Sam grunted, which was no more than I'd come to expect of him.

"So why was this supposed to be such a big secret that you couldn't tell my family about it?" I asked. I thought the question a reasonable one.

Sam glanced at me, his lips compressed into a tight line for a minute. Then he let out a chuff of breath. "I just mainly didn't want to talk about it. It's such a stupid assignment. A detective and two uniforms on a picture set. God!"

I could tell he considered his assignment a particularly asinine one—and I agreed with him. Granted, Pasadena wasn't a crime-ridden city; still, I could understand why he considered his talents were being wasted on this particular job.

But by that time I could see a big huddle of people gathered ahead of us, so I didn't tell him that, but pulled the Chevrolet over to the side of the road and parked behind a snazzy red, low-slung Stutz Bearcat that looked like Harold Kincaid's. My heart rose slightly. If Harold had come to the set, perhaps the day might not be as awful as I feared.

Sam and I both got out of the car and stood glancing around at the other automobiles for a moment. Sam grunted again. "These people make too much money. Look over there. It's a Pierce Arrow Special. And that's a Bugatti racing car, or I'll eat my hat."

"A what?" I glanced from the machine he'd pointed out to Sam's hat. It didn't look awfully tasty.

"A Bugatti. Bugatti's an Italian company that makes race cars. Huh. Damned picture people."

Clearly Sam's mood was as bad as, if not worse than, my own. I stared at the machine he'd called a Bugatti racing machine. "It looks like a couple of Franco-American Spaghetti cans welded together and painted blue," I said. "It's ugly."

"It might be ugly, but it's fast. And expensive. And look at that Daimler touring car. I swear, your Chevrolet is the cheapest automobile on this piece of land."

"It might be cheap," I said, feeling a good deal of loyalty to my precious automobile—which had been run into a ditch not long ago and tenderly repaired by the Hull Motor Works people—"but it's a good car."

"I'm not saying it isn't. All I'm saying is that these people make too much money."

"Are you a Communist, Sam Rotondo?"

"No, I'm not a damned Communist! But I still think people ought to be paid what they're worth. Not less, and definitely not more, and I'd say these picture people make way more than they should be making."

"Maybe so," I said somewhat wistfully. "Still, I'm glad some people make lots of money. Otherwise I'd be out of a job."

"Huh."

"But why is this fellow's invention so important, anyhow? Do they honestly need three policemen, one of them a detective, to guard it? Do you really have to be here on the set every day because of a stupid invention?"

"The picture people think it's that important." Sam didn't sound as if he agreed. "They say the German picture makers are out to steal American ideas."

After a judicious pause, during which I reviewed my many grudges against Germans in general and the Kaiser in particular, I grunted, too. "They're probably right. I wouldn't put anything past the Germans."

Sam gave me an ironic grin. "Is that why you begged the police department to let those two Germans into the country a couple of months ago?"

He would have to remind me of that, wouldn't he? "They were different. They weren't the Kaiser, and they were only trying to get by in the world, like the rest of us. And they weren't

71

thieves. Or picture people."

Sam said, "Huh" again.

"But why does the Pasadena Police Department care what the motion-picture thieves do? Aren't you guys generally called in after the crime is committed? Why all the support from the PPD? I still don't understand."

"It all comes down to money," Sam told me, still grumpy. "The picture folks pay the City of Pasadena boocoo bucks to film within Pasadena city limits."

"Really? I had no idea."

"Yeah. Well, now you know."

"I'm surprised Mrs. Winkworth allowed them to film on her property. She's so prissy about how her grandson makes his money."

"I don't suppose she had much of a choice in the matter unless she wanted him to send her back to Arkansas."

"South Carolina," I said.

"Some damned Southern state."

And Sam Rotondo stomped off toward the huddled masses.

I followed him more slowly, scanning the crowd for someone I knew, preferably Harold Kincaid. But I didn't see him. People in overalls were hammering away at something or other, men in knickerbockers and sporty tam-o'-shanters conversed in groups, and several women had clumped together and stood under a spreading oak tree, one of them fanning herself with her hand.

Then I heard, from the direction I wasn't looking, "Daisy! Daisy! Over here!"

Harold Kincaid. Thank God. I turned and squinted, and sure enough, there was Harold, standing with another man and a woman. The trio stood beneath yet another spreading oak tree. I don't know when this place had been built, but either somebody had built the houses around the trees, or the trees had been transplanted fully grown onto the grounds after the houses were built. Not that it matters, but I was glad the trees were there because they were beautiful.

With a grateful heart, I made my way to Harold. That day, although I was technically there to work, I'd dressed for the weather, which had been warm for several days. It was almost June, after all. Mind you, sometimes June and July in my fair city could be kind of cool and foggy, but the weather was prime that day. Anyhow, I wore a white-and-cream-spotted voile dress with a wide boat-shaped neck trimmed with some embroidered ribbon I'd got cheap at Maxime's. The dress was comfortable, with a hip-length, unfitted bodice, which means I didn't have to wear any particular corseting. Heck, for all I knew, I was going to spend the entire day out of doors, and I didn't aim on being any more uncomfortable than I had to be. In addition to low-heeled shoes, I also had on a wide-brimmed straw hat that I'd decorated with more of the cheap embroidered ribbon. Believe me, nothing I wore that day looked cheap. I'd gone to great lengths to make sure of it. I looked as fashionable as any darned picture star, if I do say so myself.

Actually, Harold said so too, as soon as I got close enough for us to chat without hollering. Good old Harold. He always made me feel good about myself, which is a marvelous quality in a friend.

"You are absolutely ravishing today, Daisy. Love the ensemble. It goes perfectly with your hair."

I'd thought the same thing when I'd bought the fabric, but I didn't say so. My hair is kind of a darkish red-brown color. Maybe auburn describes it. Anyhow, the tan embroidery accentuated the color of my hair. My eyes are blue, and my outfit didn't do a darned thing for them, but you can't have everything.

"Thanks, Harold. You're looking pretty spiffy yourself."

He, too, wore knickerbockers and appeared as if he were about to step out onto the golf course. I presume the men were dressed sportily in deference to the weather, just as I was.

"Standard set wear," he said. "Let me introduce you to my assistant, Lillian Marshall. Lillian, this is my dear friend and my mother's particular spiritualist, Desdemona Majesty. If you're a friend, she might let you call her Daisy."

I held out my hand and laughed lightly. "How do you do, Miss Marshall? Please do call me Daisy. Desdemona is my professional name."

"Oh. Kind of like Lola de la Monica?" Lillian shook my hand and grinned. "Pleased to meet you, Daisy. Harold's told me ever so much about you. Please call me Lillian."

After shooting Harold a suspicious glance, I said, "I hope he hasn't told you too much."

Harold laughed. "Don't worry, sweetie. Some secrets I keep locked tight in my heart."

"Didn't know you had one, old man," said the fellow who stood with Harold and Lillian.

"Oh, yes," Harold said, turning a lifted-eyebrow gaze upon his male companion. "I guess I forgot you, John. Daisy, please allow me to introduce you to John Bohnert. John's the head director for this picture. Don't believe a word the man says to you."

"Harold!" But Mr. Bohnert chuckled. "He's being terribly unkind to me, Miss Majesty."

"She's *Missus* Majesty, John, and she means it, so none of your shenanigans," Harold said sternly.

Lillian giggled again. John heaved what I'm sure was meant to be a heart-wrenching sigh. "Be still my heart. Such a sad tragedy."

He was trying to be funny. If he only knew.

And then a high-pitched shriek came to us from what looked like a marble building standing some yards off.

The four of us said as one, in a rather melodious chorus,

"Lola de la Monica."

"God, the woman drives me insane," said Harold.

"Oh, goody. And I'm supposed to be her mainstay and support whilst this picture is being made." I grimaced at Harold.

"You're the one?" John said, sounding surprised. "Why, I expected some old Gypsy crone in a black dress and flowing scarves."

"No," said I. "The only flowing scarves you'll see around here, if the one time I met her is any indication, will be those on Miss de la Monica."

"What's she yelling about now?" wondered Lillian.

"God knows," said Harold.

John heaved a sigh that sounded genuine this time. "I'd better go find out. Lord, I love my job."

And he strode off in the direction from which Miss de la Monica's scream had come.

"Brave fellow," I said.

"You betcha," said Lillian. "Wait until you have to sit through a fitting."

I gazed with horror at her. "Will I have to do that?"

Harold answered that question. "Probably. When Lola hires someone, she expects that person to be at her beck and call."

Sagging slightly, I said, "Wonderful."

"Buck up, kiddo," Harold said, patting me on the back. "This shoot won't last forever. Today they're finishing building the stable."

"The stable? Oh, yeah. I guess I forgot to ask what the picture's about."

"Can't you guess?" Harold made a sweeping gesture. "It's the Old South, risen again, with ladies in hoop skirts and gents in buckskin riding trousers. And horses. Lots of horses." Harold wrinkled his nose.

"Your stepfather has horses," I reminded him.

"And he can keep 'em," said Harold firmly. "What's more, he can keep them away from me."

"Gee, I think they're pretty," said Lillian in a wistful tone.

"Do you ride, Lillian?" I asked her.

"Good heavens, no. But I do think horses are pretty. And I think the ladies in their full skirts and the gentlemen in their riding habits look ever so elegant and graceful."

I surreptitiously gave Lillian the once-over, and could understand her romantic notions. There she stood, lost in admiration of her mental images, her hands clutched to her meager bosom—and I don't believe the meagerness of her bosom had anything to do with a bust flattener. Her hair was what they call a mouse-brown color, and it had been carved into a severe, practical bob. Lillian Marshall was definitely no beauty. Mind you, she wasn't ugly, but she was about as plain as a woman could be and she evidently took no pains with her wardrobe or hair, which seemed kind of odd to me as she was Harold's assistant. She wore a plain brown skirt and a plain white shirt, thick cotton stockings and extremely sensible shoes.

Harold must have seen me eyeing Lillian because he leaned over and whispered, "You shouldn't believe what you see any more than you should believe anything John Bohnert says. Lillian is the best assistant any costumier ever had."

"I'm sure she is," I whispered back.

Then we saw, coming toward us at a dead run, Gladys Pennywhistle, her spectacles bouncing. "Daisy!" she cried. "Daisy, we need you at once. *Now!* Oh, please, come at once!"

Harold, Lillian and I exchanged a glance. I gulped. Lillian adopted a pitying expression and reached out to pat my arm. Harold said, "Good luck, kiddo."

So, bracing myself for what was to come and pasting on a smile that felt as phony as a three-dollar bill, I called out to

Gladys, "Coming, Gladys! I'm right here," and I walked toward my doom.

CHAPTER SIX

Very well, so it wasn't my doom toward which I walked. What I walked toward was the huddle of people surrounding Lola de la Monica, who was, according to Gladys's panting explanation, experiencing a major temperament.

"Having a temper tantrum, is she? How come?"

Gladys drew a handkerchief from a pocket of her sensible blue suit pocket, wiped her brow, and said, "Who knows? The woman is impossible."

Oh, boy. Was I ever happy to hear that.

"I thought you were Mrs. Winkworth's secretary, Gladys."

She huffed. "I am, but she's *lending* me to the picture folks for the duration of this shoot."

"You don't sound awfully happy about that."

"I'm not," she said succinctly, and speeded up her pace. I got the impression she didn't want to talk about how she managed to get "borrowed" by the picture folks.

I heard the sobs as we approached the group, and a man turned toward us. John Bohnert. As soon as he saw me, he heaved a breath of relief and smiled. I smiled back, but I didn't mean it.

"Thank God." He turned back to a heap on the ground I presumed to be Lola de la Monica. "Everything's all right, Lola. She's right here."

Up from the ground she arose. I think that's a slightly revised line from an old hymn, but I don't mean it in any sort of reverential context here. What she did was leap to her feet, and I saw that her dark hair streamed wildly down her back, her face was beet red, her eyes swollen, and her garments, which had started out that morning white, were streaked with grass stains. Harold was going to love that, if she was wearing a costume he'd designed for the picture. In short, she put me in mind of the mad Mrs. Rochester before she threw herself from the burning roof of Thornfield Hall—or did she burn up in the hall? Pooh, I can't remember. At any rate, she was every inch a wild woman.

"Mrs. Majesty!" Lola cried, using every ounce of dramatic training she'd ever had and then some. "I *need* you! Come to my dressing room at once!"

One glance at my companions told me I was stuck. Nobody else evinced the slightest tendency to come to my aid or that of Miss de la Monica. In fact, all the persons gathered there stepped back a pace or six and left me to the demented female.

I reminded myself that I was being paid for this—and a good deal, too—held out one of my well-manicured, very white (because I always wore heavy gloves and a wide-brimmed hat when working in the garden or pruning our orange trees) hands, and said in my most soothingly ethereal spiritualist's voice, "My dear Miss de la Monica, this will never do. You must take control of the demons haunting you. Yes, I will come to your dressing room, and we will deal with this problem."

Although I noticed a good deal of eye rolling and significant-glance-passing going on among the assembled watchers, I paid no heed. My focus was on Lola de la Monica, and Gladys had been absolutely correct: she was in the very midst of a major temperament. Lucky me. I'd been elected the animal trainer in this particular circus.

Taking one of Lola's arms, I guided her to—And then I stopped in my tracks and remembered something vital. I had no earthly idea where her dressing room was. I turned toward where I'd last seen John Bohnert. Where he'd been standing not seconds earlier, now stood, rather like a largish, immovable boulder, Sam Rotondo, his fists on his hips, his legs apart and planted solidly on the well-tended lawn, frowning at me.

Giving him back a good, hot scowl of my own, I let my glance slide sideways and whispered to the stranger standing beside Sam and whom I hadn't yet met, "Can you direct me to Miss de la Monica's dressing room, please? I fear she's rather too upset to provide coherent directions."

The man I'd addressed gulped, exposing a fairly protuberant Adam's apple as he did so, and said, "Yes, ma'am. I'll take you right there."

Bless the fellow, he stepped right up, took Lola's other arm, and we headed toward the marble-like building I'd noticed a few minutes earlier, Lola staggering every now and then as if the weight of her problems was tilting her slightly off-kilter. It passed through my mind to wonder if the woman had been drinking, but it was only about nine in the morning. Then again, she *did* belong to the maniacal world of moving pictures, and those folks were an odd lot, even if you didn't believe everything you read in the papers.

The building we arrived at in a few moments turned out to be yet another grand house on the grounds of the Winkworth estate. I learned later that there were a total of three houses situated on those massive grounds: Mrs. Winkworth's, Mrs. Hanratty's and this one, which had been unoccupied until the motion-picture folks took it over for *The Fire at Sunset*.

The fellow helping with Lola dropped her arm, which precipitated another stagger, this one guiding us right for several steps. By the time I'd managed to get us on course again, the man had opened the door and was hurrying back to us, looking as if he feared his departure might have permanently damaged Our Star.

"I'm so very sorry, Miss de la Monica!" cried he. "I only wanted to open the door for you."

For this man, evidently I didn't exist. Huh.

"It's all right, Homer, darling," whispered Lola in a failing voice. "I know you meant well."

Homer, eh? Was this the genius Cal Tech professor who'd invented the wobble-free camera-moving device? As I helped him heave Lola into the house, I gave him a good once-over and decided he fitted the absent-minded-professor stereotype fairly well, except that he wasn't bald. His eyeglasses were every bit as thick as those Gladys wore, and the expression on his face matched Gladys's when she'd gazed with adoration at Monty Mountjoy. I felt sorry for both of them in that moment: Gladys because Monty would never be hers for reasons already pointed out; and Mr. Fellowes because Lola de la Monica didn't have a care for anyone in the universe except herself.

"Just take me to the sofa, please, will you?" Lola murmured as if she were Carmen dying in the last act.

"Tell me where it is, and I'll be delighted to do so," I said with a trifle more acid in my voice than I'd meant to allow.

It didn't matter. Lola was performing for the male present at the moment, which was a good thing since he seemed to know where the desired sofa was. He steered us left into a big living room, and together we managed to get Lola over to the massive red crushed-velvet sofa against the far wall. I don't know why she couldn't have used the smaller, plainer one near the door, but I guess she knew her business. As she sank onto the sofa, I saw with some amusement that the deep red of the velvet, her grass-smeared white gown, her black hair, and her makeup formed another nearly perfect rendition of an artwork, this one perhaps by one of those pre-Raphaelite guys. Rosetti maybe. Or

81

perhaps Burne-Jones. Lola would have done either one of them proud.

After she did her sinking routine, Mr. Fellowes, if it was he, knelt beside her and took her hand. "Is there anything I can get for you, Miss de la Monica? A glass of water perhaps?"

I felt like telling him that nothing so prosaic as a glass of water would do for this particular fainting maiden, but didn't. Rather, I glanced toward the doorway through which we'd just entered the room and was relieved to espy Gladys Pennywhistle bustling toward us, John Bohnert at her heels and looking peeved.

"Thank you so much, Homer darling, but I need Mrs. Majesty right now," Lola said in a voice that might have heralded her eminent demise if she weren't acting, which she was, so it didn't.

Homer Fellowes got to his feet, his expression radiating his defeat and unhappiness that he couldn't continue to be the hero of the hour.

"I'm right here, Miss de la Monica," I said, my tone reverting to its soothing spiritualist quality. I reminded myself to keep it there, no matter what this ridiculous female did in the future.

"Is everything all right in here?" John Bohnert gazed down with displeasure at his star. I guess some directors get used to all types of histrionics, but John appeared to be reaching the end of his tether with this particular actress.

"I believe Miss de la Monica only needs a little spiritual guidance. We won't be long," I assured him, praying I was right. Glancing at the solid, ever-practical Gladys Pennywhistle and then at the awe-stricken Homer Fellowes, I had a brilliant idea. "Why don't you and Mr. Fellowes make up some tea, Gladys? After Miss de la Monica and I chat for a while, I think a bracing cup of tea will be just the thing."

"It's *Doctor* Fellowes," Gladys said in her practical voice. She wasn't reproving me, only setting me straight. "And that might be a good idea."

"Please, Dr. Fellowes," I said, latching on to the man's arm, "go with Miss Pennywhistle, if you will. I'll deal with this situation."

"Eh?" Dr. Fellowes glanced from the sprawling star on the sofa and blinked at me. "Beg pardon?"

"If you will please accompany Miss Pennywhistle to the kitchen and prepare some tea, we should be ready for you again in about ten minutes."

"Uh . . . I mean . . . I don't know how to prepare tea," said the hapless Dr. Fellowes.

"I'm sure Gladys does. You can carry the tray," I told him, thinking that he and Gladys would make a perfect pair. They were both brainy, and Gladys had that helpful, practical streak that would assist the ineffectual professor, who only, apparently, knew how to invent things.

"Yes, indeed. Thank you, Dr. Fellowes. I can use your help." And Gladys led him away, much as Mrs. Hanratty might lead one of her well-trained pups.

"It won't take any longer than ten minutes?" John asked in my ear. "We've got to finish dealing with the costumes today, and this damned temperament has already set us behind schedule." He glanced at his watch, one of those nifty new wristband varieties, and frowned down at the sofa some more.

"I'll deal with her," I promised him. "I've had lots of practice with hysterical women."

And *that* was the truth. My spiritualist persona had been weaned, so to speak, during the former Mrs. Kincaid's many hysterical moments.

He huffed with irritation. "I hope to hell you're right." And he stomped off, I guess to do something director-like.

After sending one exasperated glance ceilingwards, I sat next to Lola on the sofa and took one of her limp hands. "Now, you must let me help you, Miss de la Monica. What has happened that has you so upset? I'm sure that, with the help of the spirits, my constant guides and companions, I can assist you through whatever has transpired." I wanted to add, *to put you in this nonsensical state,* but didn't.

With a dramatic moan and a theatrical sigh, Lola de la Monica reached into one of her grass-stained white pockets and withdrew a crumpled sheet of paper. She whispered, "Read this."

So I did. By golly, it was a threatening letter! The poison seemed to be spreading. The thing said, in big, black letters that looked to have been cut from a newspaper:

CHANGE YOUR WICKED WAYS OR TRAGEDY WILL STRIKE!

Whoever had cut the words out of the newspaper couldn't find a decent exclamation point, I guess, because he or she had added one at the end of the message in bold, black ink that was darker than the newsprint.

"My goodness," I said, considerably taken aback. I'd figured she'd been throwing her fit to garner attention. That motivation probably had a good deal to do with it, but this particular fit had been precipitated by considerably more than mere dramatic instinct. This might well be serious. I wondered if Monty had received another letter. "When did this arrive?"

With a preliminary moan of weary tragedy, Miss de la Monica said, "It was waiting for me in my dressing room."

That seemed odd. An inside job, in fact! "Where is your dressing room?"

She looked upward, as if she were a petitioner beseeching God for some type of miracle. "Upstairs," she whispered. "At the end of the hall to the right."

"I think I'd better go up there and look around. Do you—"

My words ceased abruptly. I'd been going to ask her if she wanted me to telephone for the police, but then I remembered that the police were on the premises already in the person of Sam Rotondo, and that if I called this letter to his attention, the discovery of Monty Mountjoy's letters probably wouldn't be far behind. And behind the discovery of them, might well come the reasons for the letters having been written in the first place, if Harold and Monty were right about that. Sam might be annoying, but he definitely wasn't stupid. However, any such discovery would put an end to a very nice man's career as a picture idol. Then where would his stupid, ungrateful grandmother be?

Drat Sam Rotondo and the entire motion-picture industry! Except Harold Kincaid. None of this was his fault.

"No!" cried Lola, seizing my hand and holding onto it in an iron grip. "Don't leave me!"

Oh, brother.

But I only said, "Very well. I believe now would be the proper time for some spiritual intervention. Shall I pray with you?"

By the way, I'd only begun praying with my clients after Johnny Buckingham had prayed with—and for—Billy and me when I'd found Billy's secret stash of morphine syrup. Anyhow, Johnny's prayer had comforted me, and my prayers seemed to comfort my clients. I felt a little cheesy about praying with them, since I had my own personal doubts about God . . . well, not about God, *per se*. But I had a hard time believing that everyone who didn't believe exactly as we Methodist-Episcopals did were going straight to hell. Judging others didn't sound much like Jesus-thought to me. But who was I? Merely a young, married spiritualist who was trying to make a living. So I asked the woman if she wanted me to pray with her.

Lola whispered, "Oh, yes. Please."

Since she still wore her fake Spanish accent, I considered her request all part of her act. Nevertheless, I acquitted her of being entirely at fault in this case, given the nasty letter and all. So I prayed with her, calling upon God to protect His precious daughter Lola de la Monica. I hoped to heck God would know who I was talking about, since I was certain that wasn't her real name.

After a fervently whispered "Amen" that immediately followed my own, Lola said, "I must be a mess. Can you go with me to my dressing room now? I should freshen up, but I don't want to go up there alone."

At that moment, Gladys returned with Dr. Fellowes, who carried a heavy tea tray laden with tea things. Bother. Now I wished I hadn't asked the two of them to prepare tea.

"Here's the tea," Gladys said unnecessarily.

Dr. Fellowes carefully laid the tea tray down on the coffee table before the crushed-velvet sofa and stepped back, the better to gaze worshipfully at Lola de la Monica. He didn't speak.

"Thank you very much, Gladys and Dr. Fellowes. As soon as Miss de la Monica freshens up a bit, I'll see that she gets a good, strong cup of tea to carry her through the next few hours."

Gladys glanced at the watch pinned to her shirtwaist. "Better hurry. You've only five minutes left. I don't think Mr. Bohnert will be pleased if Miss de la Monica delays production further."

Lucky me. Now I was responsible for getting John's schedule back in line. *Why me, God?* But I already knew the answer to that stupid question. This was my life. And I had to deal with it.

"We'll hurry," I assured Gladys. Then I grabbed one of Lola de la Monica's hands and all but yanked her off the sofa.

She grunted softly, but didn't object. Rather, she meekly followed me up the stairs. When we reached the top, I stepped aside and followed her, since she knew where her dressing room was. As she'd said, it was the last room on the right. As we approached the door, she seemed to shrink back. I braced myself for another fit, but she only said, "Please. You open the door.

I'm so afraid."

Since she couldn't see me, I puffed out my cheeks and rolled my eyes. Then I passed her and turned the knob on her door. Voila! The dressing room, presumably as she'd left it.

"Do you see anything amiss?" I asked as soon as we'd entered the room.

Lola stood at the door, her hands clasped at her bosom, glancing with profound fear around the room.

I waited.

And waited.

Until I got fed up with waiting. "Well? Do you see anything amiss?"

Gradually, Lola drifted into the room, still glancing around as if she were a gazelle who expected a lion to pop out and devour her at any moment. At last she spoke. Goody gumdrops. "I . . . don't know. My maid picked up after me."

Must be nice. I said, "Well, can you poke around and tell me if anything is different than it should be? Where did you find the letter, by the way?" I probably should have asked her that in the first place.

She pointed a willowy finger at the huge, ornate mirror in front of which sat a huge vanity covered all over with pots and boxes and bottles. Face cream, powder and perfume, I presumed. "There. It was propped against the mirror."

Hmm. I walked over to the mirror and inspected it, looking for fingerprints. Not that fingerprints would have helped me one teensy bit, since I'd already determined not to tell Sam Rotondo about the lousy letters. What a stupid job I'd taken on! It didn't matter, though. I guess the maid had cleaned the mirror, too, because it sparkled, fingerprint-free against the wall. It was probably all for the best.

It took some prodding, but at last, after only ten or fifteen minutes, I got Lola de la Monica downstairs and out of the house. We forwent—is that a word?—the tea, since I didn't want to irritate Mr. Bohnert any more than was absolutely necessary.

I hadn't anticipated receiving any praise for my valiant efforts on behalf of *The Fire at Sunset,* but I sure as anything didn't expect John Bohnert to yell, "For God's sake, what *took* you so damned long?"

CHAPTER SEVEN

I must have looked as annoyed as I felt, because John instantly came to my side. "I'm sorry, Daisy. I know this isn't your fault." He turned like a tiger on Lola de la Monica. "Get into the costume tent instantly, Lola. You've delayed us long enough for one day."

Lola sniffed and said, "I received a great shock, John, and I think you're a brute to treat me so."

"Sorry for your shock. Sorry I'm a brute. Now get the hell over to the costume tent."

With drooping shoulders and a heartbreaking sigh, Lola took off in the direction of a huge, white tent: the costume tent, I presumed. At least she'd changed clothes and was no longer clad in grass-stained white. Now she wore a simple white day dress. I guess the woman had a thing for white. Perhaps she'd read Wilkie Collins's *Woman in White* recently or something. For what it's worth, I always thought Collins missed the boat on that one. Why any man would prefer the simpering heroine to her go-get-'em sister just because the heroine was beautiful is beyond my understanding. Not that it matters what I think.

"Maybe I'd better go with her," I said, feeling tentative. I wasn't sure exactly what my job was here, after all. Sure, I was supposed to be Lola's spiritual advisor, but I'd already performed that duty admirably—in spite of having taken a trifle too much time about it, which wasn't my fault but that of Lola, who hurried for no man, not even John Bohnert—and didn't know what to do next.

"You might as well. She's apt to throw another fit unless you're close by." John eyed me keenly. "I don't suppose you have any idea what prompted the first one, do you?"

I sure did. Rather than lie outright, I said, "I'm sorry. I'm not well acquainted with Miss de la Monica yet. Perhaps I'll come to understand her better in the days to come."

"God help you," snapped John, and he turned on his heel and stamped off toward a group of people who shuffled about some yards away. I guess Lola's antics had made them late with their duties, too.

This job was going to be a miserable one if it required keeping Lola de la Monica on schedule. From what I'd seen of her so far, the woman thrived on drama. It actually occurred to me that she might have manufactured the letter trick in order to have an excuse to throw her recent temperament.

But, no. She couldn't know about the letters Monty Mountjoy had received, so she couldn't have taken the idea of her threatening letter from his. As far as I understood at the time, the only person who knew about Monty's letters except Monty was Harold. And me. Nuts.

Anyhow, I headed to the costume tent without any enthusiasm at all for what I might find within it.

The first thing I found within it was Sam Rotondo. So far, my day was perfect (I'm being sarcastic). Naturally, he scowled when he saw me. Figuring *what the heck* I walked over to him. "H'lo again, Sam."

"What the devil took that confounded woman so long to get to the tent? She was supposed to be here forty minutes ago."

I frowned up at him. "What do you care?"

"I care because the City of Pasadena is paying a good chunk of money to have a detective and two uniformed officers at this idiotic picture shoot. If Miss de la Monica is late every damned day, it'll delay production and cost the city far more money than they budgeted for."

As much as I hate to admit it, that made sense to me. I'd already discovered that Sam didn't want to be here any more than I did, so I could hardly fault him for his sour mood, although he didn't have to take it out on me.

"You can thank me that it didn't take longer than forty minutes," I told him with asperity. "The woman threw a fit, and I had to calm her down."

"Good God."

"Yeah, I know. I don't like having to be here, either, after this morning's scene. I thought it might be fun to observe a picture being made, but so far it's just boring. Well, except for calming down Miss de la Monica, but that's just business as usual. Well," I amended for the sake of honesty, "she's more annoying than most of my other clients."

A corner of Sam's mouth slanted up. "You've had plenty of practice dealing with frantic women, I reckon."

"I reckon." Then I glanced around the interior of the tent, which was hot and stuffy and would probably only get hotter and stuffier as the day progressed. There were tons of people there, some of them worker bees and some of them picture folks. Well, the picture folks were worker bees, too. Drones. I guess Lola de la Monica was their queen, to continue with the beehive motif. Shoot, with a queen like her, this particular hive was going to be in big trouble. I'll bet regular queen bees don't have dramatic tantrums and throw the rest of the hive off-kilter. "It sure takes a lot of people to make a movie, doesn't it?"

"Sure does. And this is just for the costumes."

"I saw more people outside, waiting for Mr. Bohnert. Miss de la Monica held up their daily duties, too, from what I could gather from the frowns directed at her."

Sam eyed me with what appeared to be real sympathy. "I

don't like my job here, Daisy, but I'd rather have mine than yours."

"Thanks, Sam. I think I would, too."

Just then I spotted Lillian Marshall, who appeared harried, talking earnestly with Miss de la Monica, who wore a mulish expression on her beautiful face. Oh, dear. I had a feeling my services were going to be called upon again soon.

I was right. Harold Kincaid popped out of the cluster of people surrounding Lola, glared wildly around the tent, spied me and hollered, "*Daisy!* Over here!"

Giving Sam one last, forlorn peek, I headed for Harold.

Sam said, "Good luck" as I walked off. I appreciated him in that instant, which didn't surprise me until later, when I related the incident at the supper table.

Harold dashed over to hurry me along. "The damned woman is giving Lillian the fidgets. She doesn't like her costumes."

"What's not to like? I think long skirts and petticoats and hoop skirts are really pretty."

"They are. Lola de la Monica isn't."

"She actually is, Harold," I said reprovingly. "She's beautiful, in fact."

"On the outside, maybe. On the inside, she's filth and dirt."

"Powerful words, Harold Kincaid. Methinks you're annoyed with the lady."

"Lady, my foot. If she didn't have those dark looks, she'd be a nobody." Meditatively, he added, "I wonder how many directors she had to sleep with in order to climb the ladder."

"Harold!" It was probably silly of me, but I was shocked. I'd heard all the stories and read all the articles. I understood that some women were willing to do pretty much anything to get parts in the pictures, but . . . Well, I didn't like to think about it.

"Don't kid yourself, Daisy. Happens all the time. God knows her talent is mediocre. The only thing she's got going for her is her looks, and they aren't going to carry her much farther if she keeps slowing down production on picture sets."

"Has she done this sort of thing before?"

Harold made a horrible grimace. "All the time. Her fame has gone to her head, and she's become practically impossible to work with."

Suddenly, he grabbed my arm and pulled me to a stop. Leaning so that he could whisper in my ear, he said, "Monty got another letter this morning. He's really worried, Daisy. I hope you can find out who's sending the damned things."

"I'm so sorry. Miss de la Monica got one, too. That's what precipitated this latest bout of nerves."

Harold snapped to attention and stared at me, astounded. "Good Lord, really?"

"Yes. She showed it to me. Hmm. It might be interesting to compare her letter to the one Monty received."

"Yes, it would be." He began walking again and I gamely tagged along. "They have to be from the same person, don't you think?"

I shook my head. "I guess. I don't have any prior experience with poison-pen letters, but I doubt there could be more than one writer of them on a picture set. Lola's letter was propped against her mirror when she got to her dressing room this morning."

"So was Monty's."

I didn't like to see my friend appear so worried. "Can you get me Monty's letter? Maybe, after today's work is done, we can compare the one to the other. I saved Lola's letter in my pocket." I patted said pocket.

"Yes. We'll do that. But right now you're going to have to get the damned woman into her costume."

"Lucky me."

"Yeah," said Harold. "Lucky you."

So, sucking in a deep breath and praying my temper wouldn't snap, I knelt beside Lola. Smiling at Lillian, I said in my silkiest spiritualist voice, "What seems to be the problem here?"

Lillian spoke. I saw her jaw bulge and had a feeling she'd been grinding her teeth. "Miss de la Monica doesn't like her costume." Lillian waved at an absolutely gorgeous dress that looked as if it had been sewn for a debutante attending a ball held in an old Georgian plantation ballroom. Dark blue with pretty flounces and a full skirt that must have taken yards and yards of fabric, I thought it was swell. I glanced at Lillian, who shrugged as if she couldn't comprehend Lola's obstinacy any more than I could.

Swallowing my sigh, I turned to Lola. "Why don't you like the gown, Lola? It's beautiful, and it fits the period perfectly."

She frowned at me. "It's blue."

Lillian and I exchanged a glance. I asked, genuinely puzzled, "What's wrong with blue?"

Pressing a manicured hand to her heart, if she had one, Lola said, her Spanish accent considerably thicker than it had been a minute before, "Lola de la Monica wears white."

I thought for a second or two, trying to make sense of her words. "You *only* wear white?"

"Yes." If she lifted her chin any higher, she'd be able to see down the back of her dress.

"Um . . ." I cast my mind back to the last flicker I'd seen with Lola de la Monica in the cast. "Is this wearing-white thing something new? I distinctly recall you wearing a dark gown in *By the Light of the Moon,* with Douglas Fairbanks."

She nodded regally. "I had a vision. The Virgin Mary came to me in my vision and told me to wear nothing but white."

Good Lord. Stalling for time, I said, "What an amazing vision."

I could feel Lillian steaming like a teakettle about to start whistling any second. I also heard her teeth grinding. For the sake of her dentition, I hit upon what seemed to me to be a brilliant idea. "Perhaps the Virgin Mary meant for you to wear white as a rule. While you're working, I'm sure she wouldn't mind if you wore colors."

Lola's head snapped around, and she gave me a good, hot glare. "Nonsense. *Es mi vida.*"

I knew that much Spanish from school. She'd just told me this was her life; meaning, I'm sure, that she'd darned well wear anything she wanted to, and to heck with anyone who told her otherwise. Therefore, feeling desperate, I decided to take another tack. First I opened my eyes wide. Then, although I still knelt, I reeled slightly, grabbing for Lillian's arm. Turning my face away from Lola, who seemed startled by these antics, I tipped Lillian a wink, hoping she'd catch on that I was performing.

She must have had lots of experience dealing with actors, because she understood instantly. "Oh, my goodness, Mrs. Majesty! Whatever is the matter?" She overdid it a trifle, but that was all right.

"I . . . I feel . . . I feel the spirits gathering. They . . ."

Then I flopped down to the tent floor, which, fortunately for me, was covered with some kind of canvas carpeting. Or maybe all tents had canvas flooring. I wasn't a camper, so I didn't know beans about tents.

"What the hell's going on here?"

Sam. Heck and darnation! He was on his knees beside me in a flash and reaching for me, I presumed, to pick me up. Opening my eyes a slit, I mouthed at him, *"No!"* I guess he understood, because he withdrew his hands, stood, glowered at Lola and Lillian and repeated his question. "What the hell is going on here?"

When Lillian next spoke, her voice quivered. Either she was trying not to laugh, or Sam had scared her. Knowing what Sam looked like when angered, I suspected the latter. "M-Mrs. Majesty was speaking with Miss de la Monica when . . . when she muttered something about spirits and fell over."

Lola said, her voice awed, "The spirits, they came to her. For me."

Jeez Louise. I could imagine the conceited woman with her hands still pressed to her bosom, looking down upon me, certain she believed she'd just spoken the truth.

Sam knew better, of course. He also knew why I was there. Fortunately for me, Sam had a brain, even if he did use it against me more often than not. This time, he actually helped matters along. "Well, you'd better listen to her. I didn't believe that spiritualist bullsh—nonsense when I first met her and her husband, but she's made a believer out of me."

Liar, thought I to myself. Still, I also thought, *Thank you, Sam,* and began to moan softly.

"Oh, my goodness!" Lillian cried. "Whatever can be the matter with her?"

Don't overact, Lillian, I told her silently.

But Lola, who always overacted, didn't seem to notice. Rather, she reached out a hand to me as my eyes fluttered open. I was an expert at that eye-fluttering maneuver. Used it all the time during séances.

"Mrs. Majesty?" she said softly. "Daisy?"

I sat up and said unoriginally, "Wh-where am I?" Very well, it was a hackneyed line; so what? It was probably invented for scenes like this. I pressed a hand to my forehead, as if I felt woozy.

Sam said, "In the costume tent." His voice was as dry as old bones. I wasn't surprised.

"Wh-what happened?"

Sam said, "You fainted. The spirits attacked you."

Darn him anyhow! Not daring to show anyone watching how

peeved I was, I said a breathy, "Oh. Oh, yes. I remember now. It's coming back to me."

All right. I know the dialogue wasn't prime. It didn't matter. I was an expert at my craft, and I knew what I was doing, as you'll soon see.

"Need any help getting up?" Sam asked sardonically.

I didn't dare give him the scowl he deserved. Instead, I said in a shaky voice, "Yes. Please."

He reached down and yanked me to my feet. That time I did frown at him, because Lola couldn't see my face. He grimaced back at me. He would.

"Here, Daisy. Please take this chair."

Lillian thrust a folding chair under me, as if she feared I was going to fall over again, bless her. I gave her a wan, grateful smile and whispered, "Thank you."

"What did the spirits say?" Lola asked, eager to get to her part of the story, which was the only one that counted in her estimation.

"May I please have a drink of water first?" I asked plaintively. "These spells take *so* much out of me."

Rolling his eyes, Sam said, "I'll get you some water. Tell the lady what she wants to know, and let's get this show on the road. It's already behind schedule."

What a chivalrous gent.

Lola snarled, *"Men."* Then she said, "While he's getting your water, please tell me what the spirits said."

Boy, there was sure nothing subtle about Lola de la Monica, or whatever her name was. Because Sam was right and the picture was already behind schedule, I decided to give in. At a séance, of course, there would have been no time pressure, but this was a picture set. I heaved a sigh, which felt good and seemed appropriate.

"The spirits told me that you may wear colors during

pictures, Lola. They said your job is to grace the silver screen, and the contrast between your beautiful skin and the deep blue of the gown will look much better on black-and-white film than white on white will."

There. If that didn't move things along, I didn't know what would. A glance at Lillian showed me she was grinning like a fiend and liked my act better than Lola's.

"That's very true, Lola," she said.

"Yes, it is." It was Harold. Where had he come from? Well, it didn't matter.

"It is?" That was me, and I'd asked because I was honestly curious.

"White on you would completely wash you out of the picture, Lola," said Harold brutally. "It would look like hell, and *you* would look like hell. Your vast number of fans wouldn't like that, and neither would you. All you have is your looks, after all."

He could have left off that last part, but evidently the first part of his speech had struck Lola. Hard.

She lifted a hand to her generous mouth and said, "Oh, my. I hadn't thought of that."

"Nor did the Virgin Mary," muttered Lillian.

I hoped Lola hadn't heard her.

After that little glitch about colors, the fitting of Lola's costumes went well. She didn't throw another tantrum until the cast, crew, Sam and I went to take lunch, which was a catered affair taken *al fresco* on a cement slab that had been poured under yet more spreading oak trees in back of the house Pansy Hanratty used as hers. Folding tables and chairs had been set up, and the lunch was served buffet-style. I thought it was a very accommodating and nifty way to serve a whole bunch of people in a short period of time.

Genteel Spirits

Not Lola.

I'd walked to the lunch area with her, Sam clomping at our heels, and Homer Fellowes fawning along at Lola's side. I wanted to let him have her, but Lola clung to me as if I were hers and hers alone. Which, all things considered, I kind of was.

As soon as we entered the dining area, Lola stopped dead. Naturally, since she was attached to my arm, I stopped, too. By this time, I had a headache, was quite hungry and was finding it difficult to keep my temper.

In a very sweet spiritualist voice, I asked, "What's the matter, Lola?"

She lifted her chin, making me want to pop it with my fist. Of course I didn't do anything so unrefined. "I cannot dine among this mob."

Homer Fellowes, chump that he was, said, "I'll get something for you and take it to your dressing room, Miss de la Monica."

She eyed him as if he were a worm she wanted someone to squish for her. Naturally, she wouldn't squish anything herself. "My good man, I never want to see that dressing room again."

John Bohnert, who had come to the dining area shortly after we did, overheard her. "What do you mean you never want to see that dressing room again?"

Lola whirled, taking me with her. I darned near stumbled and fell. Fortunately for me—boy, I never thought I'd ever say *that*—Sam was right there and caught me before I could skin my knees on the cement.

"Evil has penetrated that room. I cannot use it again."

Oh, boy, she was back on her high horse with a vengeance. I gazed pleadingly at Sam, God knows why.

But, by gum, he came through again!

"The police will make sure that your room is safe, Miss de la Monica."

She turned to give Sam a scowl. I guess she didn't like her

99

temperamental turns met with such practicality.

"What a brilliant idea!" I said brightly. "And I can make sure there are no evil spirits remaining in the room, too. I've done an exorcism before." That was technically true, even though the being I exorcised wasn't a spirit.

Suffice it to say, I never did get lunch that day. Poor Homer Fellowes carried a tray of food back and forth from the mobile canteen—that's what the picture folks called it—to various spots on the grounds where Lola thought she might be able to take sustenance. She finally settled on a bench about a mile and a half away from the canteen. I'm only exaggerating a little bit. However, she got her lunch. When she finally allowed me to return to the canteen, everything was on its way to being cleaned up.

Sam, who had wisely stayed behind whilst Lola was searching for exactly the right spot to partake of her luncheon, took pity on me and gave me the last couple of bites of his cherry pie and a biscuit he'd been saving for later. Neither one was as good as anything Aunt Vi might have fixed, but by that time, I didn't care.

I sank down onto a bench opposite Sam and gratefully swallowed his leavings. "Thanks, Sam. I don't think I'm going to survive this job."

"She's a piece of work, all right."

I couldn't have said it better myself.

By the time I got home after the shoot that day I had a raging headache, and I never wanted to see Lola de la Monica again in my lifetime. Since, however, I'd signed on for the duration, I staggered into the house, said a brief howdy to Billy and Aunt Vi, and retired to our room, where I downed some salicylic powders and lay down for twenty minutes or so. That's all the time I was allowed before I had to get up and set the table for dinner.

CHAPTER EIGHT

"And that Homer Fellowes person, the one who's supposed to be so smart and who's got three entire policemen there to guard his invention, thinks she's the cat's meow."

My family and I were gathered round the table on the evening of my first day on the job, and I regaled them all with the events of the day. Fortunately for me, the powders had worked, and my headache was down to a dull throb by dinnertime. I hate to admit it, but I hadn't been able to wait until Vi got the chicken on the table, but snabbed a wing and got my hand slapped for my efforts. I told Vi I'd been deprived of food since breakfast and hadn't eaten anything except an old dry biscuit all day long, but she said that wasn't any excuse for bad manners. I told her she ought to spend a day with Lola de la Monica and see how mannerly *she* was. Vi only clucked her tongue at me and said, "Go on with you, Daisy." She said that a lot. I'm not sure what it means.

"Good Lord," said Billy, staring at me. "I can't believe anyone can be that . . ."

He apparently couldn't think of a good word for what Lola de la Monica was, so I tried to help him out. "Self-absorbed? Conceited? An obnoxious care-for-nobody? Self-centered? A selfish pig? A ridiculous human being?"

My mother said, "Daisy," in the tone she used when she disapproved of something I've said, generally to Sam. But Sam was in my good book that day. He'd saved my skin several times,

101

in fact. Tonight, all my grievances were directed at Lola de la Monica. I hadn't yet told Billy that I had to return to the Winkworth mansion that evening, since Harold, Monty and I still had to compare threatening letters. Billy wouldn't like that one little bit. Neither did I, but I'd promised.

"She sounds like all of those things," said my darling Billy, who occasionally still showed remnants of the wonderful person he used to be.

"She is," I said, reaching for another piece of chicken. "And then some."

"It's such a shame," said Aunt Vi, tutting. "She's such a beauty to look at. It's too bad she's not lovely on the inside, too."

"Sure is," said Pa. "I'll never be able to watch one of her pictures again without remembering how hard she is to work with."

"You can say that again," I told him. I took another helping of mashed potatoes and gravy to go along with my second piece of chicken.

"Didn't they feed you on the set?" asked Billy, eyeing my plate. "I know you like your food, but . . ."

Again he ran out of words. Again I helped him out. "No! No, they didn't feed me on the set. That's why I came home with a roaring headache. They *would* have fed me on the set, if Lola de la Monica hadn't latched herself onto my arm and not let me go. By the time I finally got back to the canteen, they'd cleaned up everything."

"That stinks," said Pa, who didn't like to hear about people going hungry.

"My goodness," said Ma. "No wonder you're eating like a pig."

I frowned at her. "I'm not eating like a pig. I'm taking second helpings because I'm starving to death. But I'm using good table manners as I do it."

Ma primmed her lips, but didn't comment. Therefore, I took a second helping of green beans, feeling defiant, although not nearly so hungry as I'd been when we sat down to dinner.

"So that's why Sam's there? To guard this fellow's invention? And the fellow's name is Fellowes? That's kind of funny." Billy actually grinned.

"It would be, if he weren't so pathetic. I was hoping to fix him up with Gladys Pennywhistle, since they seem so admirably suited to each other, but he's got eyes only for Lola de la Monica, and Gladys has eyes only for Monty Mountjoy."

"Yeah?" said Billy. "And what about your eyes?"

This wasn't the first time Billy had shown signs of jealousy. For pity's sake, a year or so ago, he accused me of running around with Johnny Buckingham! Johnny Buckingham, the most upright, moral person on the entire face of the earth! And besides that, I'd never cheat on my Billy, no matter that our circumstances were far from ideal. I didn't do things like that. I loved him, and I was loyal to him.

Therefore, I gave him a good, hot frown. "My eyes, Billy Majesty, are firmly fixed in my head. I'm doing a job at that wretched mansion, and that's it." I didn't think it was up to me to tell him that Monty wouldn't have gone for me even if I were the most beautiful woman in the world, since he didn't go for girls, period.

I noticed the gazes of everyone else were fixed firmly on their plates. The rest of the family hated to hear us spat. I hated it, too, but golly! You'd think my husband would have known me well enough by that time not to be jealous.

"Anyhow," I said, lying through my teeth, "I think he's having some torrid affair with Theda Bara." I'd just slandered two people and felt kind of guilty about it, but neither Monty Mountjoy nor Theda Bara would ever know about it, and Monty would probably appreciate the publicity if he ever learned of it, so I figured it didn't count.

After Ma and I cleaned up the dinner dishes and Aunt Vi had gone upstairs to her rooms—the upstairs of our bungalow consisted of two rooms, which would have been a swell place for a young couple to live, except that Billy couldn't negotiate stairs by the time the Kaiser got through with him—I decided to face the announcement of my evening's assignment head-on. No use shilly-shallying. Billy was going to hate it; I knew that, and I also knew he wouldn't like it even if I told him the truth, since he didn't like "faggots." Idiotic bias if you ask me.

Therefore, feeling tired, abused and unwilling, I went into the living room where Pa was engaged in reading *The Devil's Paw,* by E. Phillips Oppenheim. I'd got it for him from the library on my last jaunt there. The librarian knew me and managed to hold all the good detective novels for me if she thought I'd like them. I loved the library. Still do, actually.

Billy sat in his chair, thumbing through the latest issue of *The Saturday Evening Post.* I noticed he had the latest *National Geographic* on his lap along with *Helen Vardon's Confession,* by R. Austin Freeman. This was a brand-new book, and Miss Petrie said I was the first patron of the Pasadena Public Library to check it out. Since I was pretty sure she'd sneaked it to me as sort of a preview, I'd promised her I'd have it back within the week. Which meant Billy had to read it fast, because I wanted to read it, too. However, if he didn't read fast, I suppose my being unable to read it before it had to be returned was just punishment for the disappointment I was about to inflict upon him.

Ma was knitting, God knows why. Ma didn't know how to knit very well, but she kept trying. She'd attempted to knit a sweater for my niece last Christmas, and it had turned out to have arms of different lengths. We'd tried it on Spike, but his legs are so short, he couldn't move them when he had the sweater on. I'm not sure what Ma did with the thing after that.

Anyhow, my family was snug and secure in our nice little home, and I was about to desert them all. Again. I heaved a deep and heartfelt sigh and headed for Billy, who'd rolled his chair into the inglenook, which was lined on both sides with padded bench seats. Billy liked to sit there during the wintertime when we had fires in the fireplace, but this was May. I guess he still liked it even without the fire. I sat on one of the benches.

He glanced up at me from his *Saturday Evening Post.* I must have looked guilty because he said, "Let me guess: you have a job this evening." His sneer was a work of art.

I closed my eyes and swallowed another sigh. He clearly wasn't going to make this easy. Therefore, to keep matters simple, I said, "Yes. I have to return to Mrs. Winkworth's estate. Harold needs to talk to me about something."

"Harold?" Billy's nose wrinkled. "What could he have to discuss with you?"

"I'll tell you when I get home," I said. It had been a hard day, and I didn't like Billy's tone of voice. "All I know is that it involves me making more money, and, therefore, I'm going to visit with him at Mrs. Winkworth's home. I'm sorry if you don't approve."

"Doesn't much matter if I approve or not, does it? I don't have any say in these matters, since you're the one who brings home the bacon. Right?"

I laid a hand over his. "Please, Billy. I don't know what Harold needs, but he's my friend and he evidently requires my help with something."

He looked at me for a long time, and I nearly started crying. Then he gave my hand a short squeeze and said softly, "I'm sorry, Daisy. You work too hard. What you need is a whole man."

That nearly undid me completely. With vehemence—but

keeping my voice low so my folks wouldn't hear me—I said, "What I need is *you*, darn it, Billy Majesty. I love you. I married you because I loved you, and I still love you, and I don't want anybody else. I wish you'd get that through your thick skull!"

His expression softened and he squeezed my hand again. "I believe you, Daisy." Shaking his head, he said, "But you deserve so much more."

"I want *you*, Billy," I said, my voice thick. I hated my tendency to get emotional all the time, but I couldn't help it. "I don't *want* anybody else."

He'd have heaved a sigh of his own if he could have. "Well, you've got me, for whatever I'm worth."

"You're worth the world to me," I said stoutly. Then, figuring more words would only start me crying again, I rose, kissed him, and said, "I hope to heaven this isn't going to take too long. I'm about to fall over in my tracks. I didn't realize being Lola de la Monica's so-called spiritual advisor would be such hard work."

"Good luck," he said, smiling. And he went back to his *Saturday Evening Post*.

Feeling like the Wreck of the Hesperus, I rose from the window seat, told my parents I'd be back in a little bit and why, and went out to the Chevrolet. When I got behind the wheel, I took a minute to stare into the dark night sky—it was about eight o'clock by that time—and wish things were different.

But they weren't, so I pushed the self-starter, let out the clutch, and chugged down the hill to Del Mar, where I hooked a left, drove to Allen Avenue, turned right, and then took a left on San Pasqual. The guard at the gate knew me by that time, so he opened the gates as soon as I gave my name. I drove to the same parking area I'd used on the night of the séance, walked to the back door, and knocked.

For the longest time I stood there, wondering what was taking the door-answerer so long to get to the stupid door. Then the door was flung open in my face, and there stood Harold Kincaid, frowning at me. "Why the devil did you come to the back door? You're not a servant, for God's sake!"

Oh, brother. I didn't bother to explain, but just walked into the little room off the kitchen and said, "I'm really tired, Harold. I hope this won't take long."

"I hope so, too. I still have work to do on costumes. That damned de la Monster creature has put us behind schedule already, and we haven't even begun to shoot the picture yet."

"Good name for her," I told him, meaning it sincerely.

He took my hand. "I'm sorry, Daisy. I didn't mean to take my bad mood out on you. I'm just so frustrated with that female. You'd think I'd have become accustomed to stupid women by this time."

"I hope you're talking about your sister and Lola de la Monster and not me, Harold Kincaid." I meant it as a joke. I think.

"My sister and my mother," said Harold, shocking me, although I don't know why. I thought his mother was stupid, too, though I'd never tell him that.

"I brought Lola's letter," I said in order to change the subject.

"Good. Come upstairs to Monty's room, and we'll show you the latest one he got."

As we passed through the dining room into the front hallway, Gladys Pennywhistle entered the hallway from another room. She jumped when she saw me. "Daisy! What are you doing here at this hour?"

Because I couldn't think of anything else to say, I told her, "Harold needed me to go over something with him."

She squinted at me as if she didn't believe me. "Were you going upstairs?"

I glanced at Harold, hoping he'd take it from here. He did, bless him.

"I need Daisy's advice on a couple of things. We're going to be visiting in Monty's rooms because we need his input."

"I see."

I could feel Gladys's eyes on us as we climbed the stairs, and the incredible thought that she might be jealous crossed my mind. I felt like screaming at her that Monty didn't care any more about me as an object of desire than he did her. That snotty thought had only been prompted by my state of exhaustion, I'm sure. But I could feel my headache creeping back on stealthy feet, stopping right behind my eyeballs and taking up residence there. Stupid day.

Anyhow, we got to Monty's door, and Harold knocked. Monty smiled his award-winning smile when he saw me and stepped back. "Please come in, Daisy. I'm very happy you could join us tonight. I know it's a terrible imposition."

He was so nice, and I was feeling so nasty, it took some effort for me to say, "It's nothing. Really."

"I hope it's nothing, but I'm afraid it's not. I mean I'm afraid it's something." Monty led the way to the sitting room, which housed a sofa, the chairs I mentioned earlier and a coffee table. Well, and a fireplace, but there was no fire. Did I mention that his "bedroom" consisted of a suite of rooms? Well, it did. I didn't inspect it at any length, since I was there merely to do a job, but I deduced there to be a sitting room, a bedroom, a dressing room and a bathroom, mainly because that's the way the suites in Mrs. Pinkerton's house were set up. "Now that Lola's getting letters, too, I don't know what to do or where to turn."

"Daisy will help us get to the bottom of the matter," Harold said bracingly.

I'd have snorted, but knew better. I did, however, eye the two men with some interest. As far as I knew, Harold and his special gentleman friend, Delray Farrington were happy as a couple of clams. They shared quarters together in San Marino, which was just down the street from San Pasqual. Well, perhaps "quarters" is insufficient to describe Harold and Del's home. It was, in short, another mansion.

But that's beside the point. At that moment, I tried to determine if I could spot anything warmer than friendship between Harold and Monty. I decided there wasn't and felt better, although I did ask Monty if he had a headache powder.

He looked at me with some concern. "Yes, I do. Do you have a headache? I'm so sorry. It's probably Lola, isn't it?"

I closed my eyes and breathed deeply, grateful for his understanding. "Yes. She's driving me crazy."

He shook his head with what seemed like sincere sympathy. "She drives everyone crazy. If she doesn't shape up, she's going to be blacklisted pretty soon."

"Blacklisted?"

"Unless the pictures a person makes earn so much money that it's worthwhile to put up with their quirks and idiosyncrasies," Harold answered for Monty, "the person soon becomes useless as a property. Lola is quickly becoming more trouble than she's worth."

My goodness. That sounded terrible. Although I guess it wasn't. Heck, if any employee caused his employer too much grief, the employee would be fired, wouldn't he? Or, in this instance, she? I guess it wasn't any different in the pictures than it was in real life. For some reason, that made me feel better, don't ask me why. Maybe it was because these people made *so much money,* as Billy had pointed out. It was kind of nice to know the folks behind the scenes didn't tolerate too much nonsense from idiots like Lola de la Monica.

Then Monty handed me a paper filled with salicylic powders,

a glass of water and a spoon, so I stirred the powders into the water and downed them, hoping that, if nothing else, the vile taste would drive my headache away. When the ghastly mixture was all the way down, I shuddered, handed the glass back to Monty and said, "Thanks."

"You're welcome. I'm sorry this mess is so hard on you."

He sounded so genuinely concerned that I studied his face for any sign of fraudulent emotion. I didn't see any. The man's aspect exuded honest anxiety about my welfare. I appreciated him for that. "It's not your fault. My life isn't exactly rosy at the best of times."

As he turned and carried the glass and spoon back to the bathroom, where, I suspected, a maid would clean it up the next day, he said, "Yes. I'm awfully sorry about your husband, too. Harold has told me the horrors he went through in the war and how you're both doing your best to cope now."

I shot a glance at Harold, who frowned. Harold did a lot of covering-up of honest emotions with humor, but I gathered he'd had a serious chat with Monty about Billy and me. Then he gave me a little shrug, and I smiled at him to show him I appreciated his friendship.

And then I thought *Enough of this maudlin stuff*, and said, "May I see the letter you found this morning, Monty? I want to compare it to the one Lola got."

"I have it right here," said Harold, reaching into his pocket and withdrawing a slightly crumpled, folded piece of paper.

So I dug in my handbag and found the note Lola had received.

"The paper looks the same," I said before we'd unfolded either document.

"Well," said Harold, "lots of paper looks alike. Paper's paper, after all."

"Don't let Sherlock Holmes hear you say that," I warned

him. "He'd point out the different grades of fiber and the watermarks and all sorts of other stuff."

"Good God. You're not going to compare watermarks and grades of paper, are you?"

"Are you kidding? I wouldn't know a watermark from a milk stain."

Monty rejoined us. "What are you two laughing about?"

He sounded a trifle peeved, so I tried to soothe him. This was no joke to him. The letters might not be a life-or-death matter, but they were possibly career-ending, and that was important.

"We were just comparing watermarks," said Harold.

"Watermarks?" Monty split a glance between us and pulled up another of those medallion-backed chairs that were so pretty. "I didn't notice a watermark on my letter."

"No," said I, deciding to get down to business. The powders I'd drunk hadn't affected the pain in my head yet, and I truly didn't feel like joking around. "I didn't see one on Lola's either. Let's spread them out on the coffee table and compare them."

Following this sensible suggestion, we did just that. I leaned over and squinted, trying to discern any differences between the two missives. Both letters said exactly the same thing, exactly the same way, even down to the penned-in exclamation points at the end of each:

CHANGE YOUR WICKED WAYS OR TRAGEDY WILL STRIKE!

I pointed to the bottoms of the pieces of paper. "Do you suppose this started out as one sheet of paper and somebody folded it and then tore it across the fold? That's what it looks like to me."

Reaching out, I turned Lola's letter upside down so that its torn bottom matched up with the torn bottom of Monty's letter. "Well . . ."

"I can't tell," said Harold. "One piece of paper being very

like another." He shot me a tiny grin. "But you might be right."

"You might well be right," said Monty, "although I don't know where that gets us."

With a sigh, I said, "I don't, either. However, it's pretty clear to me that the same person is responsible for both letters." I turned Lola's letter around again and pointed between the two. "See? It looks as if the words were cut from the same newspaper."

Harold scratched his head. "We really could use Sherlock Holmes for this. He would undoubtedly be able tell us which newspaper the words were cut from."

"Wasn't he always going on about short-bladed, curved scissors or something like that?" I asked, picking up Monty's letter and doing some more squinting. Then I shook my head. "Heck, I can't tell. The words are so small, I can't tell what kind of instrument cut them out. I suspect scissors, but I suppose someone might have used a razor blade and a straight edge to do the deed. And I have no earthly idea what kind of glue was used."

"Flour-and-water paste would be my guess," said Harold. "I think it's an inside job."

"Inside?" Monty gaped at Harold. "What do you mean, Harold?"

Harold waved a hand in the air in an isn't-it-obvious gesture. "Hell, Monty, how else could someone get into both of your dressing rooms?"

Monty appeared genuinely distressed. "Do you mean to tell me that someone I *know* is doing this?"

With a shrug, Harold said, "I don't know. There are a whole lot of people on a picture set. You began to get these things before you settled here for the duration of the picture, didn't you?"

After a brief hesitation, Monty said, "Yes. The first two were sent to my home in Los Angeles."

"They weren't propped against your mirror?" I asked, thinking maybe Harold was getting somewhere.

Monty shook his head. "No. They came through the mail and were addressed to me."

"How?"

He stared at me. "What do you mean, how?"

Fighting fatigue, a headache and tetchiness, I tried to keep my voice calm. "Were the envelopes typewritten? Handwritten? Was your name cut out of a newspaper? That's what I mean."

"Oh. Well . . ." He rose and began pacing. I guess the poor guy was awfully nervous about this, for which I couldn't fault him. These stupid letters might bring about an inglorious end to what had been a stellar career. "I don't know." He threw his hands out in a helpless gesture. "I have a secretary to open my mail. He brought me the letters as soon as they began to arrive, but I never thought to ask him to keep the envelopes."

Figures. Anything to make my life more difficult. Rather than saying that aloud, I said, "That's too bad. If you should, by chance, get another letter mailed to you, be sure to keep the envelope, all right?"

He shrugged, still looking helpless, which irked me. Darn it, it was *his* life being ruined. Helplessness didn't seem appropriate to yours truly. Then again, he was a man and accustomed to having everything done for him, unlike most of us women, who had to wait on everybody else.

Can you tell I was in a really bad mood?

Monty finally said, "Sure."

For several seconds, we all stared at each other, Harold and I from our chairs, and Monty from the middle of the room. Then I decided I'd had enough. Scooping up both letters, I folded them and put them into my handbag.

As I rose, I said, "I think the best thing we can do is study the people around us for the rest of the week. Maybe one of them will give some kind of clue."

"What kind of clue?" asked Monty.

The question was sensible, but I didn't like it. It annoyed me. Then again, everything seemed to be annoying me that evening. "*I* don't know! If anyone acts or looks suspicious, keep an eye on him. Or her." It occurred to me that Gladys Pennywhistle might have a reason for sending threatening letters to Lola de la Monica, if she really thought Lola and Monty were carrying on a steamy affair. She might have sent similar letters to Monty for the same reason, although that seemed a far stretch of the imagination, given what appeared to be her fondness for him. Still, you never knew about these things.

And then I bethought myself of Homer Fellowes.

My eyes must have registered something, because Harold said, "What is it, Daisy?"

I shook my head, making the pains behind my eyes clank together and hurt. "Nothing, probably. I was just thinking of Homer Fellowes. He's got a definite *thing* for Lola. He's one of those absent-minded professor types, and from everything I've ever read, they tend to be a little crazy. Maybe he thinks he can win her if he drives you off or scares her away from you."

It sounded feeble to my own ears, but Harold and Monty exchanged a speaking glance.

"By God," said Harold. "You might have something there, Daisy." Turning to Monty, he said, "Let's keep an eye on him, Monty. It can't hurt, and it just might help."

The demon of logic overtook me at that moment, and I asked, sounding pathetic to my own ears, "Are you *sure* you don't want to tell Sam Rotondo about these letters? He's a detective, after all, and he's stationed here through the end of the shoot. It would give him something to do besides bother me, too."

A resounding duet of "No!" struck my ears, so I sighed and

took my leave.

I fell into bed about nine-thirty that night, thinking longingly of the morphine syrup in Billy's dresser drawer. But I figured sleep would cure my headache eventually.

CHAPTER NINE

Shakespeare was right about sleep being good medicine. While it didn't exactly knit up the raveled sleeve of all my cares, it did cure my headache. Even sans headache, I was still loath to face another day with Lola de la Monica.

"It's your own fault," said Billy unsympathetically as I hunched over my coffee cup the morning after my first day on the set. "You get yourself into the darnedest messes sometimes, Daisy."

"I know it," I said. Actually, it was more of a whimper.

To my surprise, Billy reached across the table and took one of my hands, which had been gripping my coffee cup. "I'm sorry, sweetheart. I know you're doing your best to make a good living for us. And you're doing a swell job. I just hate that you have to be the one to do it."

Good Lord. Was this my Billy Majesty speaking? I blinked at him and said, "Thanks, Billy. That means a lot to me, especially now that I have to deal with that stupid actress. I do try, you know."

"I know you do."

Spike stuck his cold, wet nose on my bare calf at that moment—I being clad in my nightie and bathrobe—and I squeaked, breaking the mood. "Darn it, Spike, don't *do* that!" I dropped a piece of bacon for him, which was his point in nosing me in the first place. He didn't have to go to obedience school to get his humans to obey him. And they say dogs aren't as smart as people. Huh.

"Do you think we're spoiling Spike?" I asked Billy.

He chuckled. "Of course, we're spoiling Spike. He's our child."

Good Lord. I stared at my husband again. It was probably just as well that he'd lifted the morning paper and couldn't see me, because his words had touched something deep within me.

When we got married all those years ago—well, five years ago, but it seemed longer—Billy and I had planned our life together. We'd aimed to have three children, and it didn't matter to either of us if they were boys or girls. We were going to live with his folks for a couple of years before Billy, working at the Hull Motor Works, had saved enough money to purchase a little home of our own. He'd already begun saving, in fact, since he'd always had a job or two even during his high-school days. We married right after I graduated from high school, and we were on top of the world.

Now look at us. Thanks to the Kaiser, Billy couldn't father children, thereby assuring that I'd never have any; Billy's parents had perished in the influenza pandemic, weakened, no doubt, by grief over their mutilated son; and we lived with my mother and father and my aunt, whose only son had been killed in the war and whose husband had also succumbed to the Spanish flu. Oh, boy. You just never knew what life was going to throw at you, did you?

Feeling like crying but restraining myself, I said, "I guess you're right. I just never expected a child of mine to have such short legs."

Fortunately for my state of mind, Billy chuckled again. "Heck, you're short. I guess he took after you."

Ah, yes. Billy had been tall. And strong. And so very handsome, especially in his army uniform. I suppressed my sigh. "I guess so."

Then, because I had to, I rose from the table and began gathering dishes. Pa had gone out already. He aimed to walk to the little corner grocery store on the corner a couple of blocks south of us and buy some navy beans. His Massachusetts boyhood had given him a fondness for baked beans and brown bread. His family had eaten baked beans and brown bread every Saturday evening during his entire childhood. I guess every section of the country has its own traditions. Personally, I liked baked beans, but I was kind of glad Pa didn't insist we eat them every Saturday.

"Good luck at the set today," Billy said, his nose still buried in the newspaper.

"Thanks. I'll need it. Yesterday, Miss de la Monster was so fussy, I never even got lunch. Well, I guess you knew that. I made up for it at dinner, but I never did get rid of my headache until I slept it off. Shoot. I hope she behaves better today."

"I don't suppose you can turn her over your knee and spank her, could you? Spanking did wonders for my behavior when I was a kid."

I stared dreamily out the kitchen window as I rinsed the breakfast dishes, thinking about how much Billy's suggestion appealed to me. From the kitchen window I had a lovely view of our next-door neighbors' driveway, which didn't look nearly as ugly as it sounds because it was lined with pretty flowers. "Boy, I wish I could. The thought holds a whole bunch of charm."

"But," Billy said, understanding lacing his voice, which surprised me, "if you did that, you'd lose your job."

"I sure would. And word would probably get around, and then my business would suffer."

"Not if they knew anything about Miss de la—what did you call her?"

"De la Monster. That's Harold's affectionate name for her."

118

"Huh. Harold comes up with some good ones. I have to give him that."

"He's a nice man, Billy," I said, always a little defensive about Harold around Billy.

"I know. You're forever telling me so. You're probably right."

I turned from the kitchen sink to stare at my husband's head. It wasn't like Billy to be so kindhearted when it came to Harold and men like him. Wondering about his change of attitude and not a little worried about it, I said, "Are you feeling all right, Billy? Do you need me to call Dr. Benjamin or anything?"

The paper lowered and Billy turned his head to stare back at me. "What? Why? Do I sound sick? Well, sicker? I'm not. I'm still the same. Crippled, unable to breathe, in pain. The usual. You don't need to call the doctor."

"It's just that you usually aren't so easygoing when it comes to Harold."

Billy only shrugged, so I was left to make what I could of his mood, which seemed quite mellow this morning when compared to his moods most mornings.

Because I couldn't help myself, I decided the change in mood on Billy's part meant something. The only problem was I couldn't figure out what.

And then I decided there was no use worrying about Billy's moods. I had to get ready to go to work.

After I dried and put away the last dish, I slumped off to our bedroom, which was directly off the kitchen. There I took a careful squint at my collection of clothes, which was, as I may have already mentioned, extensive, due to my sewing skills and my enjoyment of sewing. I justified what might have seemed an extravagant wardrobe by telling myself I had to look good for my job. People didn't expect their spiritualists to show up to work in pretty little gingham house dresses or plain old skirts and shirtwaists. No. I had to *look* like a spiritualist.

However, the merry month of May was still upon us, and the day would indubitably be warm. Therefore, I removed from the closet a becoming cotton day dress that came to about my mid-calf—not an especially flattering length for anyone, but all the mode—with blue-and-white checked cap sleeves and bodice and a blue flared skirt. The dress was extremely comfortable and wouldn't look out of place with my short-heeled, black, pointy-toed shoes. I could wear my straw hat and plop a ribbon of the same blue-and-white checked fabric around the brim to take the place of the tan ribbon the same hat had sported the day before. See how easy it is to look modish when you sew your own clothes? Well, it is.

After I'd selected my costume for the day and laid it out on the bed, I went to the bathroom, performed my ablutions, fixed my hair, which, in a daring mood I'd had bobbed and shingled the year before, dabbed a mere trace of light face powder over my freckles—freckles are *not* fashionable on spiritualists—and returned to our room to dress, fetch my handbag and put on my hat.

And there was Billy, swigging morphine syrup from the bottle he kept in the top drawer of our birdseye-maple bureau. Before he spotted me, I stepped aside, hoping he hadn't seen me. As soon as I heard the drawer close, I made a noise in the hall and entered the room. Billy smiled at me, and I was pretty sure he hadn't seen me see him.

Lord, Lord, Lord, sometimes I wondered why our lives had to be like this. Then I remembered I was a Methodist, and Methodists believe all humans have been provided with a set of rules and free will, and that it was up to us what we made of our lives. I guess that doctrine included evil Kaisers and young soldiers with romantic notions of going off to war to fight against evil to save the world. And their brides. It's that free-will thing that gets so many of us into trouble, although I wasn't sure what free will had to do with my current life situation, except that I had selected to marry Billy and he had chosen to go off to war. I hadn't done anything to stop him, either, because I'd been imbued with the same romantic notions he'd had. Boy, were we stupid. But we weren't alone in our stupidity.

Knowing there wasn't a single, solitary thing I could do in aid of Billy's problems, I smiled as I tossed the dress over my head. "I'm really glad I can sew," I said as I tugged it down over my hips. "This entire ensemble cost twenty-five cents. Well, plus two cents for the thread. I got the material from two bolt ends at Maxime's, and the hat at Nelson's Five and Dime."

"You're very thrifty, Daisy," said Billy.

I thought I detected a note of admiration in his voice, and glanced up quickly. By golly, I was right. His face expressed admiration, too. I grinned. "Thanks. I do try, you know."

"You try very hard," said he. "I'm sorry you have to try so damned hard."

I went over to him. Since I hadn't yet put on my shoes and he hadn't yet regained his wheelchair, I had to reach up and stand on tiptoes, but I put my arms around him and kissed him soundly. "I love you, Billy. I don't have to try so very hard, you know. I love to sew, and I love making my own clothes. And being a spiritualist is really fun *most* of the time."

"I know."

He returned my embrace and even my kiss, which surprised me, Billy not being given to shows of open affection very often. I guess he felt so diminished as a man, he didn't want to start anything he wouldn't be able to finish. Not that I cared about that. Our first few fumblings after we wed and before he went off to war had been perfectly satisfactory for him, but they hadn't done much for me. I imagine we were just too young at the time to know what we were doing. And now it was too late. But I've said more than enough about that.

121

"Well, I'd better put my shoes on and get going. Lola awaits. Darn it."

"I hope she treats you better today than she did yesterday."

"You and me both."

Shortly thereafter, I sailed out to the Chevrolet with a heaviness in my heart for which I couldn't account. I guess I felt guilty because Billy had been so nice to me that morning. Now I ask you: how much sense does that make? None. That's how much.

Nevertheless, by the time I got to the Winkworth estate, told the guard who I was, and drove the Chevrolet to the area provided for parking, I hadn't been able to put Billy's strange morning mood completely out of my mind. It was shoved out, hard, as soon as I stepped out of the automobile.

"Daisy!"

Harold. It looked as if he'd been waiting for me. Impatiently. Rushing up to me, he grabbed my arm and started tugging. "Harold!" I cried. "Wait a minute! I have to get my handbag."

"To hell with your handbag. You forgot to exorcise the demons from the monster's dressing room yesterday, and she refuses to set foot in it today until you do so. You can come back for your handbag after you get her moving."

Already annoyed at being hauled along behind Harold like a sack of potatoes, I snapped, "I'm not late. Why are you in such a tizzy? I'm supposed to arrive at the set at nine o'clock, and it's got to be earlier than nine."

"You're not late, and it's not you," Harold said grimly. "It's *her*. We were supposed to be rehearsing by the time you got here." He snorted. I've heard that bulls will do the same thing before they charge at one. Being a city girl and not acquainted with the habits of bulls, I don't know that for a fact. "She didn't even need to go to her dressing room this morning, but she refuses to begin rehearsal until she can get in there and powder her damned nose, or whatever it is she wants to do with it. Personally, I'd like to flatten it for her."

Golly, Lola must really have got Harold's goat this morning. I'd never heard him express violent wishes before. "I'm sorry she's such a pill, but slow down, will you? My hat's falling off."

Harold stopped walking as abruptly as he'd started, let go of my arm and ran both hands through his hair. I don't know if I've described Harold, but he was of about average height, slightly overweight, had a face that might be described as cherubic and thinning brown hair, which probably didn't take kindly to having hands run through it. His gentleman friend, Del Farrington, was tall and handsome. Yet the two of them seemed to go together like ham and eggs. Or something more romantic. Actually, the first time I ever saw Del, he was in his army uniform, had his back to me, and he looked so much like my Billy that I nearly fainted dead away on the spot.

Gazing at my friend with honest concern as I straightened my hat and caught my breath, I said, "Good heavens, Harold, she must be having a truly terrible fit if she's got you in this state."

"She's driving everyone *nuts*," he said bluntly. "I have a feeling this is her last picture. I'm only sorry her last picture wasn't *her* last picture." He squinted at me. "If you know what I mean."

I nodded. "I understand. Um . . . where are we going? To that big marble building with the dressing rooms?"

"Yes." Harold sucked in a lungful of air. The morning was fine, with none of the smog that sometimes settles in the beautiful San Gabriel Valley where Pasadena is located. "Can you put a spell on her room or something, so she won't do this to us again?"

We started walking once more, albeit more slowly, thank God, and I thought about Harold's question. "As to that, I can do it, but it's going to take more than a spell to make sure no

123

more notes appear there. I mean, I'm a fake, remember?"

"I remember. Too bad."

When I glanced at him, I saw that his eyebrows were lowered, and he looked to be in deep contemplation. Probably of breaking Lola de la Monica's neck. He said, "I guess I can get the carpenters to put a special lock on her door."

"That might help, as long as it's not one of the carpenters sending the letters."

"Oh, God, don't say that!"

"Sorry, Harold. I suspect it's someone closer to the action than a carpenter who's the poison penner. Still, we don't really know who the letter writer is."

"Don't remind me."

"I don't suppose you've taken any particular note of Professor Fellowes this morning, have you?"

Harold let out a breath. "Yeah. He's hovering over Lola as if he's afraid she's going to expire from her fear of dressing-room ghosts."

"Really? Gee, I don't understand how anyone can find behavior like hers attractive."

"I don't, either, but he seems to."

"What's going on with Gladys Pennywhistle?" I asked then, thinking that, while I could imagine her detesting Lola, I couldn't quite feature her sending nasty notes to Monty Mountjoy. Now if she'd sent a threatening letter to *me* in the misguided assumption that Monty favored me, Gladys would seem a more probable letter writer.

"Gladys?" Harold shrugged. "She's doing her best. She's the old lady's secretary and, as such, doesn't have a lot to do with the set as a rule, but even she tried to talk to Lola this morning. So far nothing's worked."

"Oh, dear." Sounded as if it was going to be another spectacular day for yours truly.

As long as we were walking on these glorious grounds, I decided to look around and appreciate the beauty of my surroundings. What lay ahead for Harold and me—that is to say Lola de la Monica and her hysterics—was most assuredly going to be ugly, so I figured I'd take in as much beauty as I could along the way.

The Winkworth place was honestly exquisite. It was, as I've mentioned earlier, immense, fully capable of supporting three large, mansion-like houses, and each of those houses had its own grounds. I don't know how many square acres of prime Pasadena real estate the Winkworth estate took up, but it was probably as much as was used by the California Institute of Technology nearby.

Paths led here and there on the grounds, each leading to different places—you know, special gardens and so forth. In the distance to the right, I noticed a pretty pergola, which would be a delightful place to sit and read a book with one's dog at one's feet, or on one's lap if one's dog was Spike. The path Harold and I trod upon led past one of the rose gardens, too. I don't think I've ever seen so many rosebushes in my life as had been planted on the Winkworth estate.

Curious, I asked, "Did this place come with all three houses on it already, or did Monty have to buy three separate properties and tack them together?"

"Oh, no. He bought up the old Hollis place. In the old days, it was sort of a compound, where old man Hollis kept his family corralled. Or as much of the family as he could tolerate, anyhow."

"Ah. Wasn't Charles Hollis in partnership with Henry Castleton?"

"Yes. They owned the railroad together and made millions."

"On the backs of all those poor Chinamen," I muttered, remembering a conversation I'd had with Mr. Castleton's daughter a few months earlier.

Harold shot me a grin. "Don't forget the backs of the Irish and a bunch of other poor immigrants who laid out those tracks and died for the privilege of doing so."

"Yeah, but nobody ever says someone has an Irishman's chance. It's always a Chinaman's chance," I reminded Harold. Which, in turn, reminded me of how unfair Fate is, with total impartiality, to everyone. Fate hadn't dug its vicious claws only into Billy and me. I heaved a huge sigh.

"What's the matter, sweetie?"

Good old Harold; back to being his own lovable self again. I was glad for it. "Nothing, really. I was just thinking about how unfair life is sometimes."

"Oh, Lord, don't start in on that, or I might begin to feel guilty." Harold had come from a very wealthy family.

"You have nothing to feel guilty about," I said staunchly. "Your father might have been a crook and your sister might be a witch, but you're neither of those things."

My sentiments might have been pure, but I could have phrased my opinion better. However, it didn't matter. Harold threw his head back and roared with laughter, so I guess he didn't mind. Well, I knew he didn't mind. We'd been over this ground before. Not physically. I mean we'd talked about our families together. The Winkworth place was new, to me at least.

"I'm glad you're my friend, Daisy," he said when he stopped laughing and wiped his eyes with the back of his hand.

"I'm glad you're my friend, too, Harold." For some stupid reason, I felt like crying again. Shoot. To cover it up and change the subject, I said, "I don't suppose Monty's received any more ugly letters, has he?"

"Not yet, but the day's young."

His good mood had fled, and I felt a little bad about that until I realized the path upon which we walked had bent, and the dressing-room house loomed ahead, looking like an enormous marble tomb in the sunlight. Gaggles of people stood about outside of it, I presume waiting for Lola to get over her temperament so they could all start working. It irked me, watching all those folks waiting for one silly woman to stop being stupid and start to work. "Are all of those people waiting for Lola?"

"Yes," said Harold grimly. "They're all awaiting her majesty's pleasure. Damn her."

"Good heavens. Is she really worth everyone's time?"

"Of course, she isn't!" He practically snarled it. "But she's in this picture, under contract, she's the damned star, and nobody can do anything until you can calm her down."

Oh, goody. Lucky me. I said weakly, "Lead on, Harold."

CHAPTER TEN

Harold hadn't been exaggerating the state of Lola's hysteria. I could hear her wailing long before we got near the first bunch of people, from which broke away Gladys Pennywhistle, Sam Rotondo and John Bohnert as soon as they spotted us. They hurried over. To me, naturally.

"She's really in a state this morning, according to Harold," I said before Gladys or John could both regale me with separate accounts of Lola's antics.

John wiped a handkerchief across his brow. "This is going to kill the picture! We *have* to get that woman to do her job, or we're all sunk."

"Can't you fire her and call in another actress?" I asked, honestly curious. "I mean, filming hasn't started yet, has it? How much trouble would it be to replace her?" Of course, if they replaced her, I'd be out of a job, but it wasn't a job I liked a whole lot.

"Sounds like a smart plan to me," grumbled Sam, who didn't care for women throwing tantrums on his watch. Not that I'd ever thrown a tantrum in front of him, mind you, because I didn't do stuff like that. But I'd listened to enough of his stories around the dinner table to know how little he cared for hysterical females.

"It sounds like a brilliant plan," snarled John. "But the producers want Lola. Besides, she's under contract and she'd sue us if we fired her."

"But she's not fulfilling her contract," said Gladys. She *would* point that out. Practical. That was Gladys. "How could she sue you? Isn't there some kind of clause in her contract that requires her to do her job in a timely manner?"

"Anyone can sue anyone," said Sam. His voice carried a trace of cynicism, and I remember him, too, delivering a dinner-table diatribe or two about lawyers. "She might not win a suit, but it could cost the studio a bundle."

"Precisely," said John. "It would cost the studio more money and publicity than it would be worth, providing we can get the bitch to do her job at all."

I was a little surprised he'd used the B-word with ladies present, but I guess he'd come to the end of his rope.

He turned to me. "Can you *please* do something with her, Daisy? Everybody else has tried and failed."

Feeling poorly equipped for the task before me, I nevertheless said, "I'll do my best."

"She's going to put a spell on her dressing room," said Harold drily. "In the meantime, will you get the carpenters to get a stout lock installed on the damned door? And put someone there overnight to watch the place, too, will you?"

"Why do you need anyone to watch the room?" Sam's keen gaze flipped from Harold to me and back again.

Oh, dear. Nobody was supposed to know about those stupid letters. I'd have to remind Harold in private that Sam was a lot smarter than he looked, and that he'd better watch what he said in front of him if he didn't want Sam finding out about them.

Fortunately for us, Harold was a quick thinker. "Lola thinks some spirit or ghost has been rummaging around in her dressing room. So Daisy offered to put a spell on it to keep out evildoers from beyond this pale. But I figure a new lock and a guard would help, too. Something she can see, don't you know."

"Huh," said Sam, sounding far from convinced. Darn him. I

guess this is what comes from being in a profession like his for so long. Without proof, he never believed anything anyone ever said to him.

With a deep and heartfelt sigh, I decided not to stick in my two cents, since that would only deepen Sam's mistrust. Rather, I said to Gladys, "Will you please lead me to the lady?" My voice, I fear, conveyed my reluctance.

Gladys gave an indignant sniff. "I don't know how much of a lady she is. She certainly doesn't act like any lady I've ever known."

"I'm sure that's true," said I. I remembered my handbag, but decided it couldn't come to any harm in the Chevrolet. There was no money in it, after all, and I didn't expect I'd need my tarot cards for this. Lola was in no state to sit still and be foretold to.

As ever, Gladys was garbed sensibly. She wore a plain brown-and-white striped skirt along with a plain white shirtwaist. Eyeing her from behind, I decided the skirt was probably part of a suit, the jacket of which Gladys had opted not to wear due to the heat. Smart girl, Gladys. Naturally, she wore sensible, lace-up shoes with cotton stockings. I still thought that, providing neither she nor Homer Fellowes was the nutty letter writer, they'd be perfect together.

That thought, as well as any others that might have been floating around in my brain, flew out of it as soon as we approached the front parlor of the marble house. I cast a beseeching glance at the ceiling, hoping God would see me and take pity upon me, although I didn't expect much from that quarter. I'm sure God had his attention on bigger, more important things.

"No, no, no, no, *no!*" screeched the voice of Lola de la Monica. Even though she was supposed to be hysterical, I noticed she was keeping her pseudo-Spanish accent in place. "I can't do it! There's *evil* there!"

"But you don't need to go there at all this morning, Miss de la Monica." Homer Fellowes. Trying to reason with her, which, under these circumstances, might be likened to someone trying to reason with a tornado. Lola was wound up and spinning out of control, and it was going to take more than mere reasoned persuasion to get her calmed down.

Gladys gave a peremptory rap on the open door, and we entered the room. Homer glanced up, saw me, and his relief was almost palpable. "Oh, good." Turning back to a weeping Lola, who'd flung her white-clad self on the crushed-velvet sofa again, he said, "Mrs. Majesty is here, Miss de la Monica. I'm sure she'll be able to . . . um, do something for you."

Completely disregarding Homer's tentative hands, which were hovering over her—I guess he didn't have the nerve to put them on her writhing form—Lola nearly upended him as she leaped up from the sofa. "Daisy! Oh, my God! Daisy! I *need* you!"

Because I anticipated her next move, I braced myself so that we both didn't fall over backwards when she flung herself at me; she only managed to spin me around so that I was facing the other direction. "There, there," I said, patting her on the back. I felt like paddling a different part of her anatomy. Hard. As she sobbed onto my shoulder—thank God I'd worn a lightweight, washable cotton frock that day—I glanced over her heaving back and saw a line of men glaring at the spectacle, all with their hands fisted and planted firmly at their waists. I rolled my eyes at them.

Sam looked the most disgusted of the lineup.

Harold shook his head. He appeared pretty disgusted, too.

John Bohnert said, "Can you do something about her?" as if Lola were a troublesome pest in need of an exterminator. He was probably right.

Lola lifted her head and shrieked, her voice right, smack next to my ear and nearly deafening me, "*Do* something about *me?* I'm in psychical *torment,* you horrid beast!" And she recommenced sobbing onto my shoulder.

After heaving a heavy sigh, I said, "Why don't you gentlemen wait outside for a moment or two? I'll take care of this."

Sam said, "Huh."

Harold said, "Good."

John Bohnert snapped, "Be quick about it." He looked at his wristwatch as he turned and marched out of the room, his knickerbockers flapping in the wind he made. The man was definitely tense.

"Get hold of yourself, Lola," I said in a firm but soothing spiritualist voice. I'd had tons of practice soothing Mrs. Pinkerton when she was hysterical, although I have to admit that Mrs. Pinkerton wasn't nearly as physical in her frantic fits as Lola. "This will never do. If you need my help, you must calm down at once."

I led her to the sofa across from the crushed-red-velvet one. The beige one. I figured it would be difficult for darned near anyone to carry on effectively against a beige background. Firmly but gently, I pressed her down. Then I sat next to her quickly, just in case she decided to try flinging herself flat in spite of the dull background. Taking her hands, I said, "Tell me why you're in this state this morning. Surely you haven't received another letter. Have you?" I hoped she hadn't. She was difficult to deal with even without real threats complicating matters.

She shook her head. "No. But I know where yesterday's letter came from."

"You do?" Boy, maybe this would solve all of our problems. I was ecstatic for about a second and a half, until Lola spoke again.

"Yes. From the *Beyond.*"

Nuts. Stupid woman. I said, "Nonsense. The spirits don't need to write poison-pen letters. In fact, they couldn't if they wanted to. They're insubstantial beings. They may visit from time to time, if given sufficient cause, but they never write letters."

Her lower lip stuck out so far, she looked like my niece in a pout, and she crossed her arms over her chest in a posture of defiance.

Figuring I'd best hurry this along, I ignored both her posture and her pout and went on, "There's no need for this carrying-on, Lola. By delaying production this way, you're only annoying the people you need to further your career. I'll be more than happy to conduct an individual séance with you this evening, after the rehearsal is over." Oh, boy, Billy was going to love another late night out on my part. Still, this, as I kept reminding us both, was my job.

She brightened minimally and looked at me. Her eyes, for all the supposed crying she'd been doing, were remarkably dry and un-puffy. Hmm. Playacting all along, by golly. After the day's work was done, I might just remind her that she was in danger of ruining her reputation and that people who mattered in the industry were getting sick of her antics. Naturally, I'd couch my lecture in esoteric, spiritualistic terms. And I'd probably call Rolly in to impart it. Even though Lola de la Monica seemed to possess a thickish head, I believed I could get Rolly to do his part in straightening her out.

Which brings up a salient point, but it's one I'd run across before. People were ever so much more apt to take home truths from Rolly, a fictional gentleman I'd made up when I was ten years old, than they were from a real, honest-to-goodness human being. You figure it out. It's beyond me.

Lola sat in mulish silence for a moment or two, then sniffled once to show me she was still in distress. With some difficulty, I refrained from smacking her. "You neglected to put a charm on my dressing room yesterday," she said sulkily.

"I'll do that first thing. As soon as you go on out to the set and begin rehearsing."

"No! I must be there with you when you do it."

I was very firm in my reply. "You may *not* be there when I do it. When I cast charms, I have to work alone." Figuring it wouldn't hurt and might just help, I went into one of my patented spiritualist routines. "You see, Lola, I have a special ability to communicate with those from the Other Side." *Whatever that was.* I didn't add that part. "It is very important that I attain a special spiritual state of mind, and in order to do that, I need to meditate and concentrate on the realm beyond our understanding. My spiritual conductor to that other realm will assist me. Any other human being present will only disrupt the psychical connection. It's exhausting work, and it takes a lot out of me. I definitely need to work alone with my control."

Was I good at this nonsense, or was I not?

"Well . . ."

Lola clearly wanted to pout some more, but I put the kibosh on her stubbornness. I wasn't above doing some playacting of my own, by gum. "If you won't take my advice on spiritual matters," I said, icing up my spiritualist's voice a notch, "there's no reason for me to be here. Perhaps you can find another—"

"*No!*" she squealed, again nearly rendering me deaf. "You can't desert me!"

"I can and will, if you refuse to follow my instructions. I believe I've been referred to you as a competent spiritualist, Miss de la Monica. Is that correct?"

She sniffled again, sounding less pouty and more desperate. "You're the best. Everyone says so."

"Then," said I, gentling my voice, "you need to allow me to

do my job whilst you do yours. Your job in this instance is to go out to the set and begin rehearsing. My job is to place a special spell on your dressing room so that no otherworldly entities can harm you. The letter," I reminded her, "was *not* placed against your mirror by a supernatural force. It was put there by a human being, so you don't need to fear the Other Side when it comes to letter writing."

Bowing her head and folding her hands in her lap, she whispered soulfully, "Very well. But you must come out with me. When I am with the others, you may then come back to this house and place your spell." She thought for a micro-second. "Perhaps you should place a charm on the entire house."

Oh, brother. Was this woman a selfish cat, or was she not a selfish cat? I ask you! I said, "Placing charms and spells is an exhausting business, Lola. One room a day is my limit. If I drain my psychical abilities, I won't be able to conduct a proper individual séance with you this evening."

Billy was absolutely right about my line of work. That is to say, he was right in that it was pure hogwash. I still maintain it wasn't evil.

Lola heaved herself up from the sofa and expelled a long, weary sigh. "Very well. I understand. I, too, must suffer for my art."

With effort, I refrained from rolling my eyes and giving her the raspberry. Rather, gathering my self-control around me like a mantle—or perhaps a mantilla would be more appropriate, given Lola's Spanish mien—I rose from the sofa and took her arm. "Good. I'll see you out to the others, and then I'll go to your dressing room." Maybe I'd just take a little nap there, in fact. In Lola de la Monica's stupid dressing room, there wasn't anything else I could do that would benefit anyone.

It's a good thing I didn't anticipate applause when I led Lola out to do her job, because we sure didn't get any. Lola got black looks from most everyone. Harold mouthed, "Thank you, Daisy," but had the good sense not to say it aloud. John Bohnert, who'd been pacing and had his back to us, received a tap on the shoulder from Lillian Marshall, whirled around, saw us walking toward the set, and looked as if he wanted to bellow at Lola. In order to prevent any more theatrical displays from her, I grimaced at him, and he controlled his urge. He seemed mighty peeved when he stomped over to us, but at least he didn't yell.

"So." He glared at Lola. "Let's get busy. We're at least an hour behind schedule already. Add this delay to yesterday's, and we may never get this picture in the can."

With no reluctance whatsoever, I handed Lola over to the not-so-gentle hands of John Bohnert. It might have done her good if he *had* hollered at her, but it would also have probably precipitated some more delays, so I only breathed a sigh of relief.

Shoot, the day had barely begun, and I was a wreck.

"Do you think the woman's nuts, or is she just an idiot?"

Sam.

My shoulders sagged. "I don't know, Sam. One of those things, I expect. Maybe both."

"She's definitely a pain in the neck. And other parts of the body."

Harold.

I said, "You've got that right."

"Thanks for getting her out here," Harold said. "I've got to check with Lillian about the costumes. Then I need to talk to you. Will you be in the dressing room?"

"I guess so," I told him. "I don't have anything else to do."

"I can offer you a job as a seamstress. You sew better than anyone I have on staff."

I think Harold was only joking, but I said, "How much do you pay?"

"Not as much as you make casting spells." Harold trotted off toward the gathered mob at the rehearsal set.

"Are you really going to cast a spell on her dressing room?" Sam again.

"I suppose so. Might as well." I heaved yet another sigh. "Casting spells is a darned sight easier than dealing with Lola."

"I'll go with you," said Sam. "I want to see how you do this."

"You would."

He chuckled. I didn't really mind him coming along. It wasn't as if he didn't already know I was as phony as the tooth fairy.

"No. Really," he said. "It will be interesting to watch you work."

I frowned at him. "You're as much of a fraud as I am, Sam Rotondo, you know that?"

He splayed a big hand across his chest. "Me? *Me?* A fraud? Perish the thought."

For a minute or two, we silently stumped along back to the big marble house where the dressing rooms were located. Then I said, "You know very well I'm not going to be casting any sort of charm on that idiot's stupid dressing room."

"I know it." He chuckled again. "But I've only been here for an hour or so, and already I'm bored to death. I honestly don't think anyone is going to try to steal Professor Fellowes's invention. It galls me that I have to spend all my time here for however many days or weeks this picture is being filmed. Talk about a waste of manpower and the city's money."

"I know. I'm sorry, Sam."

"Me, too." He stuffed his hands into his pockets. "So, what are you going to do? Just stand in the dressing room and say 'boo'?"

After glancing around to make sure nobody who counted

could overhear our conversation, I said, "Actually, I was thinking of taking a nap."

For the first time I could ever remember, Sam Rotondo burst out laughing. Gee, he was usually so grim. His good humor took me somewhat aback.

He got over it quickly. I wasn't surprised about that. What had surprised me was his laughing in the first place.

"So how's Billy doing?" he asked, back to being serious again.

"Not very well." I glanced up at him. "You already know that, Sam. You're with him darned near as much as I am." Before he could say anything nasty, I hastened to assure him my comment wasn't intended as a barb. "And he needs your friendship, especially now. He . . . he seems to be getting weaker. Worse, he seems to have lost hope. He won't even try to walk anymore." I swallowed the lump of tears that had formed in my throat, as it always did when I considered the state of my husband's health. "The only thing he seems to enjoy doing anymore is attending Spike's dog-obedience lessons on Saturday mornings, and they aren't going to last forever. I don't know what to do to help him."

Sam had already shocked me once that morning. He did so again when he laid his hand on my shoulder. "I don't think there's anything you can do about it, Daisy. You're doing the best you can."

Boy, a year and a half ago, if anyone had told me that Sam Rotondo would one day say something kind to me in regard to my husband, I'd have scoffed—after I stopped laughing. I darned near cried again. But I didn't and was proud of myself. "Thanks, Sam. It's . . . it's really rough. I love him so much, you know. I've loved him all my life."

"I know."

"And it's so difficult to watch someone you love decline the way Billy's doing."

"I know."

"That's right. You do know, don't you?"

It was Sam's turn to sigh. "When Margaret was dying of tuberculosis, I kept thinking there *must* have been something I could do for her. For a long time I thought that if I'd only found a job out here on the west coast sooner, it might have made a difference to her health. It's taken me years to believe the doctors were right when they told me I couldn't have done anything to help her, no matter how much I tried. She had tuberculosis, and that was that."

"Yeah," I said, feeling miserable. "It's so hard."

We were interrupted at that maudlin point by the sound of someone hurrying up behind us. Turning, we found Harold approaching.

"Daisy, I need to talk to you for a minute."

"Sure, Harold."

Sam, who shared Billy's opinion about men of Harold's stamp, frowned, but he didn't say anything cutting. "Want to watch Daisy cast a spell on Miss de la Monica's dressing room? That's what I'm going to do."

With a brief laugh, Harold said, "Sure. Why not?"

So the three of us tramped into the big, cold marble building and walked up the carpeted stairs. Since we couldn't fit three across on the staircase, I gestured for Sam to go first, sensing Harold had a reason for having hailed me. As Sam tromped up the steps ahead of us, sure enough, Harold gave me a significant look. I lifted my right eyebrow. Or maybe it was my left. It doesn't matter. Harold understood my unspoken question, and he nodded.

Oh, dear. Monty had received another letter.

Chapter Eleven

Sam came to dinner at our house that night. That wasn't anything unusual. What was unusual was that I was the one who invited him.

"It's because I told Lola I'd perform a personal séance for her this evening," I explained after I'd proffered the invitation. "Billy's going to hate my going out two nights in a row, and I was hoping you could play gin rummy with him and Pa while I'm at the Winkworth place."

Naturally, Sam frowned. "I don't know, Daisy. I hate to spring myself on your aunt unannounced."

"I'm *inviting* you, Sam. Billy needs you, because I won't be there, and he's going to pitch a fit. *I* need you." Boy, I hated saying that. "If you're there—"

"He won't throw a fit in front of me. Is that it?"

Feeling defeated, deflated, abused and battered by the Fates, I snapped. "Yes! Yes, that's it. Darn it, Sam, this is my job! Maybe I shouldn't have taken it but I did take it, and now I have to do it to the best of my ability. If I can get Lola to stop delaying the action every day, maybe the picture will finally get finished and we can all go home again. Do you think I *like* dealing with that ghastly woman?"

Sam held up his hands in a placating gesture. "No. I know you don't like dealing with her. And I know you're just doing your job. Sort of like I'm just doing mine." He scowled hideously for a second. "But will you at least telephone your

140

aunt and let her know to expect an extra person for dinner? Heck, I wouldn't be surprised if the woman wanted to rest from her duties, too, and had planned to serve Campbell's soup and toasted-cheese sandwiches. Which would be all right with me," he hastened to assure me.

I eyed him speculatively. "Would Campbell's soup and cheese sandwiches be much different from what you generally fix for yourself?"

The sound he made was something between a snort and a laugh. "Hell, no. It would be considerably better than what I generally fix for myself."

"Very well. I'll 'phone Aunt Vi. She'll probably be thrilled." I turned to Harold. "Is there a telephone in this house?"

"Sure. I'll show you."

Turning to Sam, I said, "Will you excuse us for a minute? I'll be right back to cast my spell."

Sam said, "Huh."

It figured.

Anyhow, I did call Vi, propounded my scheme for Sam coming to dinner and why, and she seemed quite pleased, at least about the Sam part. "Really, Daisy, I know you earn a good income doing what you do, but deserting your husband day *and* night is going pretty far."

I was stunned. While Vi occasionally chastised me for saying something she didn't approve of, she'd never before chided me about my wife-hood.

"Deserting him?" I repeated, hardly able to believe my ears.

"Well . . . I don't mean *deserting* him, exactly," Vi said, backtracking slightly. "But I know he hates it when you leave him after you've been away all day."

She was right. I told her so. "You're right, Aunt Vi. I'm so sorry about all this. It's Lola de la Monica. She's an absolute horror to work with, and in order to get her onto the set I had

141

to promise to hold a personal séance for her this evening. I *promise* you and Billy that it won't happen again."

"Oh, Daisy." Vi hesitated for so long, I thought we'd been disconnected by the operator. "I know I shouldn't say anything, but I worry about Billy. He seems so different lately."

So she'd noticed, too, had she? "I know, Vi. Sam and I were just talking about the same thing. That's why I wanted him to come over tonight, so he could keep Billy and Pa company. I *really* don't want to have to come back to this place tonight. I just feel so responsible now that I've been hired. Nobody else can get the woman to behave herself. I plan to sic Rolly on her tonight."

"I understand," said Vi. "I know you're doing your very best, Daisy."

She sounded so sincere, my emotions nearly got the best of me. Again. I really had to get a grip on my nerves. "Thanks, Vi. See you after work."

"Take care of yourself, Daisy."

"I will."

Turning from the telephone, I met the handkerchief Harold was holding out for me. "You looked like you might need it," he said kindly and without a hint of sarcasm.

"Thanks, Harold, but I'm not crying."

"You sure?" He eyed me keenly.

"Well . . . not yet anyway."

"Before we go back up to the monster's dressing room, I want you to see this."

The telephone kiosk was directly beneath the staircase, and I didn't trust Sam to keep to his own business. Therefore, after casting a glance upstairs—I didn't see a lurking Sam—I snagged Harold's sleeve and hauled him into another room. This one looked as if it might serve as a kitchen if this house were ever to house anything akin to a family rather than a bunch of actors' dressing rooms.

Lowering my voice, I said, "All right. What is it?"

Harold handed me a sheet of paper. On it, in the same cut-from-the-newspaper format as the other letters I'd seen, I read:

CHANGE YOUR WICKED WAYS OR TRAGEDY WILL STRIKE!

Again, the exclamation point had been penned in. I frowned at the missive for a moment. "Not a particularly original thinker, our letter writer, is he?"

"Or she."

"Or she," I admitted. I didn't want to, being a woman myself. However, since I knew it to be only fair, I said, "Women have so little power in the ordinary course of nature, they might just feel letter writing is the only way they have to express themselves."

"You aren't like that," Harold reminded me.

"True, but I'm not an ordinary woman. And I catch heck for it all the time, too, even though I make more money doing what I do than if I held a regular woman's job."

"Well," said Harold, probably thinking he was speaking judiciously, "don't forget that men traditionally have families to support."

I lifted my head so fast, I almost sprained my neck. "Darn it, Harold Kincaid, *I* have a family to support! Why I should earn less than a man for doing it is beyond me!"

Harold winced. He should, the rat. I'd never heard such rubbish come from his mouth before, and it had shocked me. "You're right. I'm wrong. Sorry about that, Daisy. I really do know better."

"I should hope so."

Still feeling a little miffy, I shoved the letter back at Harold. "Here. You'd better keep this. We can discuss it with Monty this evening. I've got to come back here to do a personal séance for Lola."

"Lola," said Harold. "Fah."

I couldn't have phrased it better myself.

Anyhow, Harold and I reclimbed the stairs, entered the room, and found Sam waiting for us, his arms crossed over his broad chest, a frown on his face. I frowned back. "I was only using the telephone," I told him. "Just like I said I'd do."

"How's your aunt?" he said, unfolding his arms—and a good thing, too. Rotten, suspicious man!

"She's fine, and she says she'll be pleased as punch for you to come to dinner. Then she scolded me for leaving Billy again." I don't know why I added that last part. I really do know better.

"Good for her," said Sam.

I wasn't surprised, but I'd had enough of being bullied for one day and let Sam know it. "Curse you, Sam Rotondo! I have to earn a living for my husband and myself! And my father, too, for Pete's sake, since he can't work any longer. If you think I enjoy leaving Billy to deal with idiots like Lola de la Monica, you're an even bigger fool than I thought you were!"

He held up his hands in a defensive gesture, and I noticed that both he and Harold stepped away from me. I guess they could tell I was nearing my breaking point. What I wanted to do was continue ranting for another fifteen or twenty minutes at the both of them.

Instead, I sucked in at least a gallon and a half of Lola-scented air—we were in her dressing room, and it smelled just like she did. Whatever the scent, it was probably "white" something-or-other—and said, "Enough of this." I turned to Harold, who dared step forward a pace. Brave man. "Are you getting a new lock for the door?"

"Yes. The crew's going to install it today."

"Good. Then let me wave my magic wand for a second or two, and we can get the heck out of here. I hate this room. It smells like her."

"Tell me again why you need a special lock for this particular door," said Sam, blast him.

I, being accustomed to Sam's suspicions being directed my way, answered for Harold. "Lola thinks somebody's out to get her."

Sam scratched his chin. "How does she figure that? Anyhow, you said she thought spirits were haunting her."

"That, too," I said, not wanting to get into the letter situation.

"I don't see how a new lock will keep out a ghost." I just hated when Sam got logical on me.

"A new lock won't keep out a ghost. Or it wouldn't if ghosts existed." I shrugged. "You figure it out. I think she wants the spell and a new lock because she's an egomaniacal crazy woman."

"That would be my guess, too," said Harold, bless him. "But since she *does* believe someone's out to get her—either spirit or human—and she's already caused so many delays, I figured a lock and a guard would be cheaper than more delays."

"I see," said Sam, as if he were reserving judgment until he discovered exactly which one of us was lying to him.

"So I'd better put a spell on this room and get it over with," said I.

"Are you serious?" Sam again.

"Why not." So I walked to the middle of Lola's dressing room, turned a full circle, and said, "Boo!" Dusting my hands together, I said, "There. That should do it. Let's get to the set in case Lola decides to pitch another fit."

Both Sam and Harold laughed, and I felt minimally better.

Ma and I were setting the table when I heard Sam and Billy whispering together in the hall. Mind you, they talked together all the time when Sam came to dinner or to play cards, but I hadn't noticed them whispering before. Therefore, when Ma went back to the kitchen to retrieve an extra bowl—Aunt Vi had prepared her special French onion soup as a first course that evening, bless her heart—I tiptoed to the door to the hall and listened. I know one isn't supposed to eavesdrop, but I'd been doing more than my share of it lately. Anyhow, this was my husband and his best friend whispering. I was mortally worried about my Billy and was curious as to why he deemed it necessary to speak to Sam in secret. The following is what I heard:

"Don't talk that way," Sam whispered vehemently.

Oh, dear. I didn't like the sound of that.

"Listen, Sam. You know as well as I do that I'm not going to last much longer. I'm getting weaker all the time. I'm just asking you to watch out for Daisy after I'm gone. Is that such a bad thing for a fellow to ask of his best friend?"

My hand flew to my mouth of its own volition. I wasn't going to cry out or burst into tears or anything, but Billy's words both shocked me and chilled me to the bone. I just *hated* that I couldn't do anything for him. Worse, I hated that Billy seemed to have become resigned to his fate. More than resigned. It sounded to me as if he positively looked forward to dying to get away from his misery.

I could feel Sam's frown from where I stood. I could heard it, too, when he finally answered Billy. "I don't like to hear you talking like this, Billy. You need to keep trying to get stronger. You may never be what you were before the war, but you can get stronger. You can't give up."

"To hell with that, Sam. I am what I am, and that's a ruined man. Will you please just answer my question? Daisy's been forced to take care of too many people since I got back from the damned war. Will you please just promise to look after her for me? If anything should happen to me." The final sentence sounded as though he'd tacked it on as an afterthought.

My heart hammered so hard it hurt, and my hand remained firmly attached to my mouth as I waited for Sam's response to Billy's request.

A huge sigh came from the hall. I presumed it had come from Sam, because it was followed with, "I doubt that she'll let me, Billy. We haven't exactly been best friends since we met, you know."

"I know it, but I think you and she would get along really well if you'd forget about her job. I love her, Sam. She's the only woman I've ever loved. If you don't watch out for her when I'm gone, all she'll have is her father, who's liable to die even before I do, and that faggot Harold Kincaid."

As bitterly as I wanted to interrupt this conversation and chastise the two bigoted men for their opinion of Harold, still less did I want Billy and Sam to know I'd been listening to them in secret.

Ma returned to the dining room just then, and I only had time to hear Sam's muttered, "Oh, all right. But there's no need for this, you know. You've got many years left in you," before I had to give up my listening post.

All through dinner, Billy and Sam's conversation haunted me. Did Billy anticipate his demise? Was he *planning* his demise? My thoughts kept snagging on that box filled with bottles of morphine syrup I'd discovered in our closet. *Oh, Lord. Oh, Lord. Please protect my Billy*, I prayed over and over even as I sipped my soup.

Which was a stupid prayer. The Lord had already failed to protect my Billy. He was a shell of his former self: ruined in mind and body and, apparently, merely waiting for the moment he could shuffle off this mortal coil into a better beyond.

Boy, I wished I believed in a better beyond.

As a firm Methodist, I should. I know that. But the only thing I knew about for a sure certainty was this life I was living, and I didn't want to live it without Billy, no matter how much I knew he suffered. Was that selfish? I guess it was.

But . . . oh, Billy.

Billy took my defection from the family that evening better than I'd expected him to. It was good that I'd asked Sam to come to dinner, I guess.

"Try not to be too late," was all Billy said to me as I headed toward the front door.

"I'll try." Because I wanted him to know it, I returned to his wheelchair, bent over and kissed him on the lips. "I don't want to do this, you know. It's my stupid job. If somebody doesn't get that Lola creature on the right track, the picture will never be finished. John Bohnert—he's the director—is always carping because it's behind schedule. I'm hoping good old Rolly will be able to drum some sense into Lola's thick skull."

He smiled at me. Definitely not a good sign. The old Billy would have been surly and probably even lectured me on how evil my line of work was. Instead, he said only, "I know it, Daisy. Don't let the woman aggravate you."

With a deep sigh, I said, "It's too late for that. She already has."

Billy chuckled as I returned to the front door. Fortunately for all of us, Spike sat on Billy's lap, so I didn't have to fight with the dog to get outside. My heart ached all the way back to the Winkworth mansion.

By the by, I'd changed my clothing for this evening's séance. Deciding it was incumbent upon me to impress Lola with the importance of behaving herself, I dressed in truly spiritualistic splendor: a black wool crepe dress with a U-shaped neckline and an ankle-length straight skirt. The bodice bloused across the front, and was gathered with two ebony disks on the sides, purchased at Nelson's Five and Dime for a penny each. I'd copied the pattern from one of Worth's I'd seen in *Vogue* magazine. Mind you, I didn't subscribe to *Vogue,* but I kept up to date on the current Worth and Chanel designs at the library. I know I've mentioned it before, but it does need stressing: I was very, very good at my job.

That night I wore very light powder and dark mascara, so that I carried off a pale-and-interesting, vaguely ethereal bearing to perfection. My light complexion, the dark eye makeup and the black dress, which I wore with black pointy-toed shoes with Louis heels, made me appear every inch the spiritualist I pretended to be. If Lola didn't shape up after tonight's performance (mine, I mean), it wouldn't be my fault.

This time I parked the Chevrolet in the front of the house and boldly walked up the marble steps to the massive front porch, which was flanked on either side by marble beasts. I'm not sure what kinds of beasts they were. Lions, probably.

Gladys Pennywhistle answered my ring of the bell.

I smiled at her. "Good evening, Gladys. I have to perform a séance for Miss de la Monster . . . I mean Miss de la Monica."

She didn't even crack a smile. Not an ounce of humor in her bones, Gladys. "Yes. Mr. Kincaid told me as much. He also said you and he have some business to transact with Mr. Mountjoy." She sounded a trifle snippy when she spoke the latter sentence.

"Right." She wasn't truly jealous, was she? It was difficult to tell, since her countenance exhibited no emotion at all. Crisp efficiency. That was Gladys.

"Is Miss de la Monica here? Or is she at the dressing-room house?" I didn't know what else to call it.

"Miss de la Monica has taken up quarters here for the duration of the picture shoot. Come with me."

So I did. I, who'd rather be home with my sick husband, followed a stuffed-shirt secretary through a magnificent mansion bought with money from a business built on fantasy. And people had the nerve to disapprove of spiritualists!

Gladys led me through the front parlor, where I was surprised to see a card table set up. By gum, maybe it wasn't only my family that played cards of an evening! I was even more surprised to see Mrs. Winkworth, Mrs. Pansy Hanratty and Dr. Homer Fellowes seated around the table, along with an empty chair, which I assumed had once been filled by Gladys. Although I had little to feel optimistic about that evening, this seemed a good sign to me. Perhaps Gladys and Homer would get together after all.

Mrs. Hanratty, who was friendlier than anyone else in the room, called out, "Mrs. Majesty! Have you come to play bridge with us?"

Bridge, eh? I guess bridge was somewhat classier than gin rummy, which is what Billy, Sam and Pa played.

Glad that someone in the world was happy, I went to the card table, shook Mrs. Hanratty's hand, smiled at the other bridge players, and said, "No. Unfortunately, I have to conduct a private séance for Miss de la Monica."

Homer Fellowes frowned. "A private séance? Good God, don't tell me the woman truly believes in that rubbish, does she?"

"Rubbish?" This, from Mrs. Winkworth. I presumed Dr. Fellowes didn't know about Mrs. Winkworth's fascination with spiritualism. "There's nothing rubbishing about it, Dr. Fellowes. Mrs. Majesty is the premier spiritualist in our community. Why, you know very well she's conducted séances for me."

The look she gave Homer Fellowes might have frozen him into an icicle if he were a normal person. Instead, Homer being akin to Gladys in the stiffness department, he only said, "I beg your pardon, Mrs. Winkworth. I meant no disrespect."

Mrs. Winkworth sniffed imperiously.

"Anyhow," I said, in an attempt to get out of an awkward situation, "this isn't going to take long. Billy and I are really looking forward to your Saturday class, Mrs. Hanratty. I think Saturday is the happiest day of our entire week." Actually, I knew it was.

Mrs. Hanratty's broad and genuine smile made me feel better for about a minute and a half. But then I had to continue following Gladys through the parlor, up the stairs to Lola's suite of rooms, and all feelings of happiness fled. As soon as Gladys tapped on the door, it was flung open, and Gladys and I were met by Lola de la Monica in a State, with a capital S. She reached out, yanked me into the room, and slammed the door in Gladys's face.

Oh, boy, was I ever looking forward to this.

CHAPTER TWELVE

Extricating myself from Lola's grip, which felt like a steel trap, I opened the door and peered out to see if Lola had managed to squash Gladys's nose, break her eyeglasses, or mangle any other body part by her precipitate action.

She hadn't. Gladys didn't look any too happy, but she appeared intact. I said, "Sorry, Gladys. Just try to remember whom you're dealing with."

"How," she asked tartly, "could I ever forget?" And she turned on her heel and went back downstairs to resume playing bridge. I envied her, even though I didn't know how to play bridge.

"It's happened again!" Lola shrieked at my back. "Why do you delay matters to deal with that peasant?"

I turned and stared at her for a moment. I'm sure I appeared as incredulous as I felt. "Peasant?" I asked at last. "Gladys Pennywhistle is no peasant, Miss de la Monica. I believe your status as a moving-picture star has skewed your view of the world. To the spirits in the Great Beyond and to God Almighty, Gladys is every bit as important as you and I are. Besides," I added after thinking about it for a moment, "where would the world be without the peasants? They're the ones who do the work to put food on all our tables, don't forget."

"Fah!" she cried, waving my philosophy about peasants and Gladys away with a delicate hand. "It's happened *again!*"

"What's happened again?"

Never blow up at a client. That was my motto, and I stuck to it through thick and thin—and this was getting pretty darned thick. But I had my own personal powers, by gum, and Lola needed them. She didn't know I was a fake. In actual fact, she believed in my powers to communicate with spirits. In plain English, in other words, the woman was as stupid as a baked brick.

Reaching behind her, she snatched something off her dressing table and presented it to me with the same delicate hand with which she'd waved away the majority of the earth's inhabitants. "Read this."

Oh, dear. Another letter. I knew it even before I took the thing from her hand and scanned it. By that time, I could have recited it without going to the bother of reading it, since the letter writer evidently had only one thing to say to his or her recipients:

CHANGE YOUR WICKED WAYS OR TRAGEDY WILL STRIKE!

Same newsprint. Same inked-in exclamation point.

"Well, whoever's sending these is definitely not a spirit," I said. "Do you mind if I keep this? I'd like to compare it to the other ones."

Lola opened her beautiful eyes wide. "The other *ones?* Do you mean to say I'm not the only victim of this vicious person's malice?"

To tell the truth, I was impressed with her phrasing. She was so dim-witted, I hadn't expected such a coherent sentence from her. I was also as stupid as she, blast it. Monty and Harold would skin me alive if I let on to Lola that Monty was receiving letters, too.

"I mean the other one," I said in a world-weary tone that I hoped conveyed conviction. "I have the other letter you received." Recalling that her dressing room door was supposed to have had a special lock installed upon it and that a guard was supposed to have been posted at the door to said room, and that this wasn't her dressing room, I asked, "How'd you get this one? Was it propped against the mirror in this room?"

If it was, Harold, Monty and I were in trouble, because it meant that someone extremely close to the family had means we knew nothing about with which to perpetrate his or her evil deeds. I couldn't imagine who it could be. Mrs. Hanratty would no more write poison-pen letters than she would fly to the moon. Gladys didn't have enough imagination—although, as I've mentioned, this particular letter writer didn't exhibit much imagination. Homer Fellowes was an unknown quantity, but I suspected him of being too Gladys-like to perpetrate nasty letters. And I couldn't in a million years imagine the dignified, misplaced Mrs. Winkworth of doing anything so unrefined as writing threatening letters.

Lola shook her sleek, dark head. "No. I discovered it had been slipped into my pocket sometime after dinner this evening."

"Oh? Where'd you dine?" Gee, maybe somebody was following her around Pasadena, which would give us an entire city's population to work from. The notion didn't appeal.

"Here."

"With the Winkworths? I mean, with Mrs. Winkworth, Mrs. Hanratty and Mr. Mountjoy?" That cut down on the possibilities, although it didn't make me feel appreciably better.

"Yes. And that other creature."

"What other creature?"

"That costume person. Harold."

My temper spiked. "Harold is not a creature, any more than Gladys is a peasant!" Then I recalled my spiritualist's motto and said more mildly, "Mr. Harold Kincaid is one of the most talented costumiers in Los Angeles. Perhaps the world. He is also a dear friend of mine." I'd have liked to have set her straight about Gladys being smart as two whips and infinitely more intelligent than Lola de la Monica, too, but decided any comment about Gladys's understanding and appreciation of algebra would only muddy waters that were already murky.

She sniffed. "Well, I prefer men who like women."

"I see." I suppressed the urge to ask her why she hung out with Monty Mountjoy if she preferred men who liked women. Every now and then I can show a modicum of good sense. Wish I could do it more often. However, common sense attacked me that night. "So," I continued, "may I keep this letter? I'd like to compare it to the other one you received."

The letter having been slipped into her pocket at dinner was every bit as appalling as it having been propped against her mirror. Clearly someone in the Winkworth household, either a family member or a member of the staff in very close contact with the family, was writing—or cutting and pasting—the stupid letters. I didn't know a single thing about the staff, except for Gladys, and I'd pretty much ruled her out. Perhaps I'd been too quick to do so. Fiddlesticks.

"I don't care what you do with it," Lola said in a high-pitched, slightly panicky voice. "I just want them to stop! Are you sure they aren't written by the spirits?"

"Positive," said I truthfully. "The spirits can't write letters."

I don't think she believed me. She turned in a swirl of white fabric and made her way to stand in front of the sofa in her sitting room. This particular sofa wasn't red, but a tweedy brown. And I defy anyone, even Lola de la Monica, to perform a grandiose tragedy on a tweedy brown sofa. "Then let's get on with the séance," she said in a pouty voice. "Although I don't know why we should be doing one if the spirits aren't responsible for the letters."

Suppressing yet another unseemly urge, this one to throttle the aggravating woman, I said sweetly, "Your inner mind is troubled. Perhaps the spirit world can guide you toward a path that will ease your way."

Giving yet another abrupt, dramatic swirl, she said, "Yes! Yes, that's true. Yes, I need inner calm. The Virgin Mary came to me, you know."

"I know," I said quickly, not caring to hear again the nonsense about Mary having given Lola fashion instructions. "But the spirits with which I deal are very good at giving advice, too." And they wouldn't say a thing about clothing preferences; I could guarantee it.

Lola bowed her head. "Very well. Let us begin."

I glanced around the room, endeavoring to find a good place to conduct my so-called "personal séance" for Lola. "One moment, please," I said, lowering my voice to a becoming spiritualistic level. "First I must prepare the room."

With big eyes—she truly had magnificent eyes—Lola watched as I surveyed the room. The furnishings in her sitting room were as lovely as those in Monty's suite; I assume they came with the house, although I don't know that for a fact.

Fortunately, I espied two medallion-backed chairs with a cunning little piecrust table set between them. Therefore, I positioned the two chairs facing each other and left the piecrust table where it was. I'd come prepared with my cranberry-red lamp loaded with a candle. I placed the lamp on the small table, lit the candle, walked to the electrical light fixture and pressed the button. The room went dark, except for that small, glowing red light between the two chairs.

Lola, as might have been expected, gasped dramatically.

Then I stood back, clasped my hands together, stared at the positioning of the chairs, and bowed my head. Lola had nothing on me when it came to drama. I pretended to fall into a transcendent state for a moment or two, then lifted my head and murmured, "The spirits are ready."

My performance seemed to have struck Lola with some kind

of awe, because she whispered when she asked, "What do we do now?"

I gestured at one of the chairs. "We each take a seat."

"Which one should I take?" Her voice was still tiny.

"It matters not," I told her in sepulchral accents.

"Are you sure?"

I only gazed at her, expressionless, and she quickly sat in one of the chairs. Much more gracefully, if I do say so myself, I took the chair opposite hers, folded my hands in my lap, and bowed my head yet once more. "One moment. I need to make contact with my spiritual control."

"Aren't we supposed to hold hands?"

Again I lifted my head and stared at her, and she shut up. It occurred to me, irrelevantly to be sure, that I might have taken up teaching as a profession. Would my special looks make children shut up and be still as they did adults? Well, it didn't matter. Besides, I'd bet anything that I made more as a spiritualist than teachers made. Didn't seem fair, but there you go. After Lola's mouth snapped shut, I once more bowed my head, continued to hold my hands in my lap and was silent.

You have to time these matters carefully. If you remain mute for too long, your client gets fidgety. I'd been studying what passed for Lola's character for a couple of days by that time, so I timed my silence to perfection. After what probably seemed like hours to Lola, but was actually only thirty seconds or so, I lifted my head and gazed directly into her eyes across the cranberry lamp. Her face was quite beautiful in that soft pink light and, I presumed, my own face was similarly illuminated. Only I wanted to appear not beautiful, but mysterious. I think I carried the act off well, because Lola said not a word, but only gaped at me with what looked a good deal like trepidation. Perfect.

"We must hold hands now," I told her, using my best mystical tone. "I shall consult with Rolly, my spirit control. Say not a word while in his presence," I warned her. "Should you interrupt communication, I will be in great peril."

"How?"

"My soul could well be lost in the otherworld if anything interrupts the séance." I was in the middle of a séance at a speakeasy once when the coppers raided that place. Talk about peril! But Lola didn't need to know that.

"Oh." She sounded good and scared now.

I'd often wished I'd named my spirit control something more dignified than Rolly, but it couldn't be helped at this point. Anyway, what can one expect from a ten-year-old? Fortunately for me, Mrs. Pinkerton believed his name was spelled Raleigh, so if anyone asked, that's the way I spelled it for them.

Lola held out her shaking hands, and I took them in mine. My grip was gentle but firm, and Lola seemed to relax. I didn't want her too relaxed. I wanted her to be impressed by this show. Therefore, I shut my eyes, breathed deeply several times, and then let my head flop forward—not too hard, since I didn't want to damage myself.

After another several seconds—which probably seemed like eons to Lola—I spoke in my Rolly voice, a deep, richly accented Scottish voice. Not only did my family possess a phonograph record of John Barrymore playing Macbeth, but I'd also gone to first and second grades with a girl from Scotland, so I had the accent down pat.

"I'm here, my love," said Rolly.

Lola gasped. Not an unexpected reaction, I'd learned. I squeezed her hands slightly to keep her from blurting out anything else.

Since I'd invented him, I'd felt it was my privilege to make him into what I wanted, and what I'd wanted when I was ten was to have a man who loved me and me alone with a love that endured for centuries. What's more, I'd decided we'd been married in the eleventh century in Scotland, had five sons together, we were soul mates, and he'd been with me in spirit ever since. You can't get much more loyal than that. Even better, Rolly was a magnificent specimen of a man, rather like my Billy had once been. Only Rolly hadn't been damaged by war as had Billy.

But enough of that. On with the séance.

"Rolly," said I in my own voice, only slightly modified to sound enigmatic—this was a show, after all—"Miss de la Monica needs peace in her life. She's been receiving very ugly letters that have upset her so much that they're affecting her performance on this picture."

Lola made a noise, I think because she didn't appreciate my words, but I rolled right along. The nonsensical woman was going to understand my point before I left her room. If she still insisted on delaying the shooting of the picture, it wouldn't be my fault.

"She's in danger of being labeled a troublemaker by the motion-picture people, and such a reputation might well end her career. We need to get her set upon the right path for the sake of her career and her many fans."

I heard Lola swallow hard. Good. Maybe she was paying attention.

"Aye, my love, I understand," said Rolly, bless his phony little heart. "Let me consult for a moment with my minions."

Don't ask me how Rolly managed to end up with minions, because I'm honestly not sure. I mean, supposedly he was a mere soldier under one of those old Scottish kings. Maybe he was a general or something. Anyhow, I don't suppose it matters.

Silence reigned once more. When Lola's hand began to vibrate in mine and I suspected she was about to burst with frustration, I allowed Rolly to speak again.

"Och," he said. I don't know where I'd learned that Scottish people said "och." Probably from novels, but it sounded good in Rolly's deep voice. "She needs to behave herself, the silly wench."

Lola gulped. I guess she didn't like being called a silly wench. Too blasted bad.

Rolly went on, "The powers are gathering, and if she continues to misbehave, her career will end in disgrace and indignity. Such a fine talent must not be wasted."

I added the last part because I figured it wouldn't hurt to boost her ego a little, although her ego was probably what was getting her into trouble in the first place.

Lola said, "But . . ."

I squeezed her hand again, a little harder.

"This is important," said Rolly. "The lassie must pay more attention to time. The folks whose money creates her pictures are becoming impatient with her. She has fine dramatic skills. It would be a shame to waste them on ruining her career rather than upon building it."

"And you really believe she's hurting herself by delaying production?" I wanted to say *by her stupid antics,* but didn't. My job held me back.

"Definitely, my love. This is her last chance. She won't get another."

Lola gasped more loudly than she had before.

"Is there anything specific she needs to do, Rolly?" I asked him.

"Aye. She needs to show up on time and behave herself."

Lola made a noise, but Rolly pushed on in spite of her.

"She mayn't delay production one more time. She has to do her job so that others can do theirs. When she delays production, she antagonizes the entire cast and crew. This picture is her very last chance."

I heard Lola gurgle, and decided to say something to mitigate

160

Rolly's harsh words. "You know, Rolly, Miss de la Monica is truly upset about some awful letters she's been receiving."

Lola's gurgling subsided.

"Aye. The letters," said Rolly, as if he were pondering the deep mysteries of the world. "The writer of the letters will be discovered soon. The lass needs pay no attention to them. The writer will not harm her."

Lola said, "Huh."

I made Rolly chuckle. "Och, the lass doubts me, but she needn't. People who write letters do so because they are powerless to do aught else. Tell the lass that, my love. She needs to fear nothing from the writer of those nasty letters."

"I will tell her, Rolly. Thank you for your wise counsel."

"Och, 'tis nothing, my love. You know how much I delight in communicating with you. But I must return to the Other Side now."

"Thank you for visiting us this evening, Rolly."

"Och, my love, you know I desire nothing more than to be of service to you."

Very well, in spite of his ungenteel name, Rolly was a good guy. Personally, I'd like to know a man who desired nothing more than to be of service to me. Ah, well . . .

At that point in the proceedings, I had to sort of collapse into myself and sag in my chair. My hands went limp, and it took Lola a moment or two to realize the séance was over. I lolled my head and moaned a little to give her a larger clue.

Naturally, she didn't know what to do. Nobody ever does. It's kind of fun to leave them in suspense like that for several seconds. Or in suspenders, as my father would say. He's a real card, my pa. Gradually, however, understanding the volatile nature of Lola's personality, I stirred and lifted my head, doing my best to appear confused.

Lola had taken to staring at me in fascinated horror. "Are

you all right?" she asked softly, without even bothering with her Spanish accent. I guess my performance had gone so well, she feared I'd managed to get myself lost in the otherworld, whatever that is.

I said, "Ah," in a weak little voice, as if the séance had taken a good deal out of me. Well, it had, darn it. I wanted to be home with my family, not here with this vain, stupid woman.

"Mrs. Majesty?"

Good. She was worried.

I lifted a white hand to my supposedly fevered brow. "Wh-where am I?" There it was again: the old, tired where-am-I line. Nevertheless, I figured correctly that Lola would respond well to it.

"You're in my sitting room. You just consulted with your spirit control." She sounded slightly stronger, curse her. It would have served her right if I *had* become lost in the otherworld.

With my hand still pressed to my forehead, I said faintly, "Did Rolly come?"

"Don't you remember?" She sounded astonished, which was a reasonable reaction, even if it did come from her.

I gave a very slight shake of my head, trying to appear as if my head were only hanging on to my neck in some kind of fragile manner, if you can picture it. I know. It sounds strange. "I never remember what has transpired after the spirits have come to me." I figured people wouldn't want me to know their innermost secrets, so I generally told them that to assuage their mangled feelings, especially if the message was a harsh one, as it had been tonight.

"Oh." She was definitely impressed. And relieved; I could tell.

"Did Rolly visit us?"

"Yes." Lola swallowed. "He came."

"Do you think his message will assist you?"

She looked mutinous for a moment, and I held my breath. I *really* wanted her to take Rolly's message to heart—if she had a heart. At that point in time, I doubted it. Then she sniffed and said, "I believe so. He told me the letters are nothing to fear."

"Ah," said I. "I believe he's correct about that. From everything I've read about people who write poison-pen letters, they aren't generally violent."

"*Violent!*" Lola gaped at me, and I cursed my stupidity. Again.

"Well, yes," I said. "They derive satisfaction from frightening people. If they had the power to hurt anyone, they wouldn't resort to letters. That's what I've read, anyway."

"Oh. Well. I see."

I wanted to get out of that darned room. I was fed up to the brim with Lola de la Monica and her silly ways, and I still had to have a heart-to-heart chat with Harold and Monty. However, I couldn't rush this aspect of the evening's performance. Every moment of a séance, from my entry into the séance room to my departure from it, needed to be carefully choreographed. In other words, I couldn't just jump to my feet, blow out the candle, grab the lamp and scram out of there. I had to "recover" first.

"Do you have a glass of water, Miss de la Monica? I feel rather faint. These things take so much out of me, don't you know."

"Water?" she asked if she'd never heard the word.

"*Agua*," I said. I might not have been the world's best student, but I remembered a little of my Spanish. Probably knew more than Lola did, in fact.

"Oh. Oh, of course. One moment, please." Her Spanish accent had returned.

And darned if Lola de la Monica, star of the moving pictures, didn't go to her bathroom and fetch lowly little me, Daisy Gumm Majesty, a glass of water. I made sure my hand trembled when I took the glass, and that my voice sounded weak when I said, "Thank you."

From then on, it was easy going. I recovered from my enervated state, smiled sweetly at Lola, blew out the candle. After waiting for the lamp to cool, I gathered it up, stuck it in my handbag, and stood. I held out my hand for Lola to shake.

"I do hope this evening's séance has been of benefit to you, Miss de la Monica."

"Yes," she said doubtfully. "I hope so, too."

Because I didn't want her to miss Rolly's message, I said, "The spirits are very wise, you know. They've lived and they've died, and they occasionally visit us mortals with sound counsel. I do trust you won't waste this opportunity to learn from them."

She said, "Yes," again.

Well, I'd done what I could. If she failed to heed Rolly's advice, the end of her career would be her own darned fault. Rolly and I had given our best to the cause, however silly that cause seemed to me.

"I must be going now," I told her, eager to visit Harold and Monty and go home.

"Thank you, Mrs. Majesty."

Was it my imagination, or was Lola's voice a shade on the humble side?

It was probably my imagination.

CHAPTER THIRTEEN

Thanking my lucky stars *that* was over, I made my way down the hall to Monty Mountjoy's room and rapped lightly.

Harold opened the door, a mighty frown on his face. I sighed. "Don't tell me. Monty got another letter. That makes two in one day."

"How'd you guess?" Harold, eyebrows now steeply arched, stepped aside and I entered the room.

"I'm psychic, remember?"

"Right."

With a sigh, I said, "I know because Lola got one, too." I retrieved Lola's missive from my handbag and waved it in front of Harold.

Monty joined us, holding a glass filled with some amber-colored liquid that I assumed wasn't apple juice. Prohibition might as well have been a joke to some people. I stuck Lola's letter back into my handbag for the moment.

"Did your letter get put in your pocket at dinner? That's how Lola claims she got hers," I asked him.

"More or less," said Monty. "I found it in my dinner jacket when I retired to my room after dinner. But, please, Mrs. Majesty, have a seat. Would you like a drink?"

"Thank you." I sat wearily in yet another of the medallion-backed chairs with which the mansion seemed so liberally littered. "I don't care for anything to drink. I just had a glass of water in Lola's room."

"Water?" Monty shuddered and downed some more of his drink. "These letters require more than water, if you ask me."

"Yeah. Lola was mildly hysterical about hers."

"Only mildly? Lola's always at least mildly hysterical about something," Harold said drily. "I should think a nasty letter would have her in full rant."

"True, true. Only this evening she mainly seemed spooked and scared. Anyhow, I guess we have to acquit her of making things up this time. I mean, these letters are real."

"Too bloody true," muttered Monty.

"But I really don't think either you or Lola should be too worried about the letter writer doing anything substantive." I proceeded to tell Harold and Monty the same thing I'd told Lola, and which I'd honestly and truly gathered from reading books that featured poison-pen letters. Mind you, the reading had been primarily in the form of detective fiction, but I had no reason to doubt my favorite authors. "You know, Harold and Monty, poison-pen writers are generally forced to write letters because they have no other power to do harm. I don't think you have much to fear from that source, especially since Lola's getting the letters, too, and she . . . er, doesn't share your . . . um . . ."

"I understand," Monty said. Then he sat with a thump on another chair. So did Harold.

It was Harold who spoke next, and it was to Monty. "You know, Monty, Daisy might have a point there. Why would the person who's writing to you because of your life preferences write to Lola? It can't be for the reason we feared on your account, since Lola definitely likes men. Well, so do you, but that's not what I mean."

"I know what you mean." Monty made a face at Harold. I held my tongue. "But why would anyone want to write nasty letters to me for any other reason?" he said in a voice that fully conveyed his fear and frustration. "There's no other reason I can think of for someone to want to blackmail me. The only secret in my life is . . . that one."

"That brings up another important point," I told him. "You mentioned blackmail, and that's what we first assumed the letters were leading up to, but have you received any specific threat or demand for money from the letter writer to keep your secret?"

"No. Nothing like that so far. The letters I've received have all said exactly the same thing about changing my wicked ways or tragedy striking."

"Which means our letter writer either has no imagination—well, we already knew that, or he'd vary his message—or he hasn't figured out how much money he or she wants to screw out of you," grumbled Harold.

I wrinkled my nose, disliking the next point of interest I aimed to impart. "From everything I've read, poison-pen letters are always sent by women. That eliminates a whole lot of people."

"That makes us feel ever so much better," said Harold, rolling his eyes.

"Well, it eliminates all the men, I reckon. And whoever it is has to be involved in this picture, or how could he or she slip the letters into people's pockets?" I said reasonably.

"Somehow that doesn't make me feel a whole lot better," muttered Monty.

"I do understand your frustration, Monty," I told him. "But you know, this whole letter thing is beginning to make absolutely no sense to me. Look at this." I took Lola's letter from my handbag once more and spread it out on the same sort of piecrust table I'd used in Lola's room. "See? It's exactly the same as the other ones. Is yours like this, too?"

"Exactly," Monty said. "Harold, where's that damned letter?"

"I've got it." Harold reached into a pocket in his trousers and hauled out a crinkled piece of paper. "It looks precisely the

167

same to me."

To prove his point, he spread Monty's letter out on top of Lola's. They might have been twins of each other. Or maybe they were quintuplets by that time. I passed a hand over my eyes, feeling very weary indeed. "This whole letter thing makes no sense at all to me."

"I sure don't understand it," said Harold.

"Me, neither," said Monty. "But I don't like it."

"Nor do I." I peered from the letter to Monty's face, searching it closely. "Are you sure you can't think of another reason for anyone to be sending these types of letters to you? You haven't annoyed anyone in particular or made an enemy you don't know about?"

"If he doesn't know about an enemy, how could he tell you who it is?" asked Harold.

I confess he had reason on his side. Nevertheless, the question irked me. I was tired, confound it, and I wanted to go home. I maintained my composure, since the letters weren't Harold or Monty's fault any more than they were mine. "Good point, Harold. But . . . well, could someone be envious of your success?"

It was Harold who answered. I got the feeling he was quicker on his feet—with his tongue—than Monty. "I'm sure lots of people are jealous of Monty's success. But why would a person who's jealous of Monty also be jealous of Lola?"

He had me stumped with that one. After thinking over the question for a moment, I ventured, "Perhaps someone's jealous of anyone who makes it big in the pictures because he or she hasn't been able to do so?"

Monty and Harold exchanged a glance. Then both men shrugged. "It makes as much sense as anything else, I guess," said Monty.

I think he was humoring me. I said, "But there have to be

hundreds of people who envy your success, Monty. Are any of them working on the set of *The Fire at Sunset?*"

"Now how the devil could he know that?" Harold asked.

It was another valid question, and one to which I had no answer. "Beats me."

The three of us sat in Monty Mountjoy's room, thinking. I don't know what the guys were thinking about, but I was considering the nature of fame, envy, and what I considered to be the very odd compulsion to write threatening letters to both Monty Mountjoy and Lola de la Monica. Monty's letters made sense, knowing what I now knew about his personal life and sexual orientation, but Lola's? I could imagine someone becoming so annoyed with her personally that he or she would like to do her an injury, but would that person write exactly the same type of poison-pen letters to her as s/he wrote to Monty?

And then I bethought myself of recent current events, and I perked up a bit.

Harold, who knew me well, said, "What? You have an idea, Daisy. What is it?"

"Well . . . I don't know. But I suppose it's possible that some Bolshevist might resent Monty and Lola both for making a lot of money in motion pictures when other people, with valid skills and so forth, can't seem to get jobs these days."

Monty and Harold glanced at each other and then at me.

"Um . . ." Monty evidently couldn't think of anything else to say, because the word just sat there in the room all by itself, naked and unadorned.

Harold, like me, never had that problem. We didn't need scripts in order to talk; in fact, it took a good deal to make either of us shut up, as a rule. "That's nuts, Daisy. Although it's no more nuts than anything else about those lousy letters. What about that Fellowes guy? Don't college professors tend to be political radicals? Maybe he's a Communist and hates all rich people just because they're rich. That would include both Monty and Lola."

"Good God," said Monty, clearly taken aback by Harold's suggestion.

"That would be a fine idea," I said, "except that everything I've read about the situation points out that only women write poison-pen letters."

"I thought you were a blazing feminist," said Harold, managing a grin. "Why should any form of employment be restricted to a single sex?"

He had me there, and I told him so. "I guess it doesn't have to be." That still didn't negate the fact that everything I'd ever read pointed the finger at women when it came to writing nasty letters. But I didn't feel up to arguing with Harold. Besides, I'd just as soon discover a man was responsible for sending the horrid things. It would sure help if we could figure out a reason for the person to be writing to both Monty and Lola, though. And it would also help, although it would be sort of icky, if the stupid writer would make a demand for money or something tangible like that. This "change your wicked ways or tragedy will strike" nonsense was too darned vague to be of any use in solving the mystery. I mean, what did it really mean? How were they supposed to change their wicked ways? Which wicked ways? Phooey.

"I'm not sure that's funny, Harold," said Monty.

"It wasn't meant to be," said Harold.

"I can't figure any of it out," said I. And we all subsided into silence, which was broken only once, when Monty got up to refill his glass with whatever it was that wasn't apple juice.

After a few minutes of stillness, I heaved a deep sigh, rose from the pretty chair and said, "I'm beat. I'd better get going. This whole letter thing is only confusing the heck out of me and giving me a headache. I want to go home." I fear the last sentence came out a trifle whiny.

The two men rose. Being gentlemen, they didn't pounce upon my weakness. In fact, Monty thanked me for coming and shook my hand as if he meant it.

Harold saw me out to my automobile. "This whole thing is driving poor Monty crazy," he said, his hands shoved into his pockets and looking worried. "I'm sorry I got you involved in the mess, Daisy."

"It's all right, Harold. I understand. Anyhow, I was going to be here anyway. Might as well try to solve the mystery of the letters. That'll probably ultimately turn out to be easier than dealing with Lola. But the letter thing is driving me crazy, too. In fact, it's confusing me so much, I can't even think any longer. I need to go home, sleep for a long, long time, and come back here tomorrow morning." Because I couldn't help myself, I added, "I *really* don't want to come back here tomorrow. I hate this job."

"I understand the feeling, Daisy. Working with Lola would drive any sane person around the bend. Besides, you have more important things to think about than that stupid woman."

Suddenly, every bad thing in my life tackled me at once, and I turned to Harold. "Oh, Harold! I can't stand it any longer!" And I subsided, weeping, into his arms.

Poor Harold. He was such a good friend. He understood, even though I didn't articulate to him what the *it* was that I couldn't stand any longer. Putting his arms around me, he allowed me to cry on his shoulder for several minutes, crooning softly all the while.

"I know, Daisy. You have too much to bear. But you're a trump, you know. Anyone who can put up with my mother for as many years as you have is definitely a trump. Add to that your personal situation, and I think you deserve a halo. Failing that, you deserve a whole lot of money and some peace of mind."

His words made me chuckle. It was a weak and watery

chuckle, but still . . .

I withdrew my pitiful self from his arms, yanked a hankie out of my pocketbook, and wiped my eyes. "Thank you, Harold. Sorry I fell apart."

"If anyone deserves to fall apart, Daisy Majesty, it's you. Think nothing of it. I'm always available if you need someone to talk to. Or a shoulder to cry on," he added with a grin.

"I know. You're my best friend, Harold."

"And you're mine," he said.

I didn't believe him. Harold had tons of friends. But I did know he considered me one of his special favorites, and that made me feel good.

The rest of that week passed miserably, but not quite as miserably as it might have. For one thing, Lola actually seemed to take Rolly's words to heart and was only late four or five times for the entire duration of the week, most of which was devoted to filming the picture. She threw minor fits and tantrums every now and then, but they were easily subdued, primarily because I reminded her what Rolly'd told her she had to lose if she kept misbehaving.

Both Harold and I kept a weather eye on Dr. Homer Fellowes. He not only didn't seem to notice that he was under observation, but he did nothing of a suspicious nature. I wasn't sure whether to be disappointed about that or not.

"Do you think he might be a Communist?" I whispered as we watched the shooting one day. The scene being filmed was one in which Lola, wearing a beautiful black gown with big hoop skirts and a wide-brimmed black hat, tearfully bade Monty Mountjoy, clad in a pristine Confederate Army uniform, farewell as he went off to war. I was, of course, talking about Dr. Homer Fellowes, whose grand invention was being used at that very moment. I was only whispering, by the way, because I didn't want Sam to overhear our conversation. There was no other reason to be quiet, since the picture being shot was a silent. Well, they all were in those days. As the camera cranked away, it made so much noise any dialogue would have been drowned out.

"I don't know," said Harold. "I've been watching him, and so far the only odd thing I've been able to detect about him is his fondness for Lola."

"Oddly enough, I think that's fading a trifle. He was actually looking at her askance during this morning's tantrum."

Harold rolled his eyes. "Askance? If he had the gigantic brain he's supposed to have, he'd have strangled her and then walked out of the room and slammed the door."

It had been a fairly awful scene. Lola had been peeved about the fit of her costume. Rather than discussing the matter with Harold and Lillian Marshall in a sane and civilized manner, she'd ripped out a side seam and pitched a fit. Poor Gladys Pennywhistle had been caught in the middle of her antics and received an arm across the face that knocked her glasses askew and sent her sprawling onto her bottom in the costume tent. I was more pleased than not when Dr. Fellowes assisted her to her feet and frowned at Lola. Maybe there was hope for those two yet.

Unless, of course, he turned out to be a rampant Bolshevist who was writing nasty letters to screen stars because they were rich. The more I thought about that scenario, the less I liked it. Dr. Fellowes must have made a ton of money with his invention. Besides, if he was so creative about motion-picture equipment, wouldn't he have been able to think of something different to write in those letters than the identical silly message time and time again? The repetition of the same tired line seemed to point to a lesser intelligence than the one lodged in Dr. Fellowes's head.

Of course, there was always Gladys. She was not only female, but, while she had great intelligence, she was possessed of no imagination at all. I'd been keeping my eye on her, too, but she hadn't done anything out of the ordinary except gaze moony-eyed at Monty once or twice. After that morning's scene, when Monty hadn't rushed to her rescue and Dr. Fellowes had, I got the impression her infatuation with Monty might just be slipping a trifle, as was Dr. Fellowes's with Lola. As far as I was concerned, it was past time for the both of them to come to their senses.

Then again, Harold had once told me that smart people are no more sensible than stupid ones when it came to matters of the heart, and I suppose he was right. I'd noticed before that common sense has very little to do with romantic love.

"What about Gladys?" asked Harold, as if he'd read my mind. "She seems gooey about Monty. Do you suppose she might be writing the letters? She's female, at least, and you claim all these letter writers are female."

"I've thought about her," I admitted.

"Personally, I think she fits the frame better than Dr. Fellowes does."

"But you just said she's gooey about Monty. Why would she write to him as well as Lola?"

Harold huffed. "You know what the press has made of Monty's so-called Casanova image. According to the press, he uses women like hankies and tosses them aside when he's through with them. Maybe she's trying to get him to lay off the other girls and stick to her." He eyed Gladys, who stood under an elm tree across the set from where we were. "If she believes his press, she's not as smart as Mrs. Winkworth claims she is."

"Oh, she's smart, all right," I confirmed. "I went to school with her. She actually understood and enjoyed algebra."

Harold turned to gaze at me with horror-filled eyes. "You're not serious!"

"I am serious."

"Good God."

I couldn't have agreed more, although I was unable to say so because suddenly Sam Rotondo appeared at my side. How typical.

I said, "Hey, Sam."

"What are you two talking about?"

I eyed him with some disfavor and felt like asking "What's it to you?" but didn't. "We're not conspiring to rob a bank, if that's what you're insinuating." My tone was rather chilly.

"I didn't mean that," said Sam, sounding disgruntled. As well he should. "I'm only bored to death and thought maybe you were discussing something interesting."

Hmmm. Did he mean that? I searched his face. By gum, he appeared honestly dejected. "You really hate your job here, don't you, Sam?" The chill in my voice warmed up some.

"I detest it. It's a rotten job. I should be out solving crimes, not here guarding a damned motion-picture invention that nobody cares about."

"I thought you said the Germans wanted to steal it," I reminded him.

"Huh. That's what the chief told me. I think the German scenario was just a bunch of hooey invented by the studio. They only wanted people to think that infernal machine is important so people will come to see this picture when it comes out. It's what they call 'good press,' I think."

Harold, who didn't talk to Sam much because he knew what Sam thought about men like him, actually grinned at Sam. "You've finally got a grasp on the motion-picture biz, Detective Rotondo. It's all razzle-dazzle and has no substance to it at all. You hit the nail right, smack on the head."

Sam grunted again. "I think it stinks. This is a waste of

manpower and money. The only person on this set who might do anything criminal is that idiot actress. Lola what's-her-name."

"De la Monster," I said softly.

"Beg pardon?" Sam eyed me oddly.

I sighed. "De la Monica."

"Yeah. Stupid name for a stupid woman."

It later seemed odd to me that Sam Rotondo, of all people, should have given me the only laugh I had all week.

CHAPTER FOURTEEN

But Saturday rolled around at last, and Billy and I got to take Spike to the Pasanita Dog Obedience Club in Brookside Park.

Ma and Pa were taking a walk in our lovely neighborhood, which positively dripped with pepper trees during the springtime, and Aunt Vi had gone upstairs to her room where, she said, she aimed to write a letter to her sister in Kentucky. Kentucky sounded like a pretty exotic place to a Westerner like me. I'd read about the Kentucky Derby and seen photographs of beautiful women in huge hats and mustachioed gentlemen in white suits. I'd also seen pictures of Kentucky in the *National Geographic* and had noted how green and lush everything was there. Aunt Vi had told me drily that people paid for all that green with suffocating heat and humidity, not to mention mosquitoes and other buggy beasts, so I'd decided I liked California just fine, thank you.

I was just about ready to fold up Billy's collapsible bath chair and stick it in the carrier on the back of the Chevrolet when a knock came at the door. Spike, who was already excited—he loved these Saturday outings, too—set up a barking fit that might have awakened the dead.

"That must be Sam," Billy said, stopping me in mid-stride as I aimed for the front door.

I turned. "Sam?"

"I asked him to come with us today," said Billy. "Thought he might enjoy watching you teach Spike how to behave." He grinned.

Oh, boy. It wasn't bad enough that I had to endure Sam Rotondo five days a week; I now had to endure him on Saturdays, too? Life truly didn't seem fair to me. I said, "Oh. How nice." Then, with more vehemence than usual, I hollered, "Spike! Sit!"

Darned if he didn't sit. I tell you, those Pasanita Dog Obedience people really knew their stuff.

"Good boy," said I to my obedient dog, who was straining every nerve in his body to get to the door. His black tail whipped back and forth across the floor like mad. It occurred to me that if we attached a dust cloth to Spike's tail, he could clean the wooden areas of the living room that weren't covered with rugs. What's more, now that I knew how to teach him stuff, I'd bet I could train him to do it!

I'd already forgiven Billy and Sam for planning this morning's jaunt by the time I opened the door. "Hey, Sam. Come on in."

"Thanks." He eyed Spike, who was still, against his nature but obedient to his training, sitting. "Wow, did he learn how to do that at school?"

"Practice makes perfect," I said, so proud of my dog, I could bust.

What a good boy! Beaming at Spike, I said, "Okay!" thereby giving him the signal that it was all right for him to relax and greet his friend. Have I mentioned that Spike once piddled on Sam's shoe when he was a very young puppy? Well, he did, and that action forever cemented Spike's place in my heart.

He didn't piddle on Sam that day. In fact, you'd have thought Sam was his long-lost best friend whom he hadn't seen in eons instead of the man who came over to play cards several evenings out of every week. Sam bent over and gave Spike a good petting. I watched, my head tilted to one side, trying to decide if I still disliked Sam as much as I thought I did.

But thinking proved as useless as it ever did, I not being cut of Homer Fellowes's cloth, so I gave it up. Besides, Mrs. Hanratty didn't tolerate lateness in her students. Therefore, I folded the bath chair and headed out to the Chevrolet, which was parked in our driveway.

Sam forestalled me. "Hey, let me do that."

"Thanks, Sam, but it's not heavy," I told him. "I can carry it."

"For crumb's sake, Daisy, let the man act like a gentleman, will you?" said Billy.

I got the feeling he was annoyed about something—probably the fact that he couldn't do gentlemanly things any longer—so I didn't fight for the privilege of carrying out the bath chair. I said, "Thanks, Sam," and left it at that.

"There. That wasn't so hard, was it?"

I turned to look at Billy, who had uttered the comment. "Beg pardon? What do you mean?"

"It's all right to let people do things for you from time to time, Daisy. I can absolutely assure you that Sam has no ulterior motive. He only wanted to help."

His words confounded me, and I told him so. "I still don't understand, Billy. It's okay with me if Sam wants to carry the bath chair to the motor."

"You don't like Sam doing anything for you. Admit it, Daisy. I don't know why the devil you dislike him so much."

"I don't dislike him!" I declared, feeling my face flush, mainly because I'd just been wondering if I still hated Sam or didn't hate him. "He irks me sometimes because he's got me involved in some scary situations, don't forget."

"Hey, don't you forget that it was your blasted job that got you involved in those situations. If you worked as an elevator operator, you never would have become embroiled with bank robbers or bootleggers or anarchists."

Feeling miffed and unsettled—Billy had only told the truth—I fell back on my good old standby excuse. "My job as a spiritualist—"

"Pays better than a job as an elevator operator. I know. I know." There was a note of defeat in Billy's voice that unsettled me.

"Well, it does."

"I know."

"Anyhow, most of the time my work is perfectly innocuous. Those examples you mentioned were . . . anomalies."

Billy rolled his eyes. I hated it when he did that. But then he grinned and said, "Right. Well, roll me out onto the porch, and you can help me to the motor."

So I gave up our stale old argument and did as he asked. Our nice bungalow had two double doors leading onto a side porch, which was basically a concrete slab and not particularly beautiful, although Ma had some pots of geraniums out there, mainly for the benefit of our neighbors to the south, the Longneckers. The night before, I'd parked the Chevrolet right next to the side porch so that Billy would have easy—well, easier, anyhow—access to the motor. I opened the two doors and the screens and pushed Billy's chair out onto the porch.

Sam had already put the bath chair onto the rack on the back of the Chevrolet, so he trotted up the porch stairs, and together we steered Billy to the passenger's side of the motorcar. Billy groaned a little as he managed to settle himself onto the seat. Even morphine syrup had its limits, I reckoned. I realized I was chewing my lower lip. Because I didn't want Billy to worry about my anxiety over him, I stopped chewing as soon as I realized I was doing it.

Then I rolled his wheelchair back into the house, shut the side doors and the screens, took up Spike's leash and led him to the car, where he jumped onto Billy's lap. I held my breath—it always worried me that Spike would hurt Billy when he did that—but all seemed well. So I strode to the driver's side of the motor and was astonished to see Sam there, holding the door open for me. What was going on here? First he carried Billy's bath chair, and now he was opening the door for me. I didn't care what Billy thought; to me this was unusual behavior on Sam's part and, thus, highly suspicious.

Had Sam somehow found out about the poison-pen letters? If so, did he aim to do anything about them? If he did, would police involvement in the case expose Monty Mountjoy as a homosexual to his adoring public? If that happened, I had no doubt whatsoever that Monty's career would be as dead as Fatty Arbuckle's. Probably deader, actually, since Arbuckle had been found not guilty, and Monty was definitely a man who preferred men. Not that his doing so made him guilty of anything, although the general public didn't share my opinion. Most of the people I knew could almost comprehend murder, but they were positively horrified by any hint of aberrant sexual behavior. To my mind, that spoke of extremely limited thinking, but I've already established myself as an oddity so you probably shouldn't pay any attention to my opinion.

Anyhow, I squinted up at Sam and said, "Thanks," and feared he was only buttering me up and intended to pounce later. If he'd somehow discovered—or if he only suspected—Lola and Monty were receiving threatening letters, he'd get no confirmation from me, curse the man.

My voice must have conveyed my uncertainty and confusion, because Sam said, "You're welcome," in as wry a voice as I'd ever heard issued from his lips.

He got into the backseat and shut the door. I pressed the self-starter, and we began backing up. Silence reigned in the auto as we made our way to Brookside Park. I felt uncomfort-

181

able with it, so I said, "How come you wanted to see this spectacle, Sam? Are you interested in getting a dog?"

"No. I don't think they allow dogs in my apartment building. Even if they did, I'm gone all the time, so it wouldn't be fair to the pooch."

"That makes sense."

"Besides, you've got Spike," said Billy. "At least when you're at our house. So you aren't completely dogless."

"I meet dogs on the job sometimes, too," said Sam, sounding wry again. "We broke up a gambling ring not long ago and met a couple of Doberman pinschers that darned near killed one of my deputies before somebody shot it."

I cringed. "They had to shoot the dog? Poor dog."

"Poor dog, my a—foot," said Sam. "He darned near chewed the arm off Paul Winslip's shoulder before we could get a good aim."

"Oh." I still didn't like it.

"The gambling gents had trained the dog to attack," Sam explained. "And he'd learned his lessons as well as Spike's learning his, I guess."

Ah. It all made sense to me now. "I see. So it was the fault of the humans who owned the dog that he had to be shot. People have a lot to answer for."

"I guess so." Sam didn't sound as if he cared a whole lot.

Naturally, that riled me, since it seems to me that it's people who cause most of the trouble in the world. The poor dog wasn't at fault if a gang of criminals had trained it to do a certain job and the dog had done it. Darn people, anyway. I sensed my audience wouldn't care to listen to my outlook on the matter, or share it if they did listen, so I didn't pursue it. "What happened to the other dog?" I asked, truly curious.

"What other dog?"

"You said you met a couple of Dobermans. What happened

to the other one?"

"One of our guys got him around the neck, and we stuffed him in a closet. The Humane Society folks picked him up—very carefully."

"Well, I'm glad one of the dogs survived. It wasn't their fault, you know. The dogs, I mean. Stupid people."

"They were pretty smart people, actually," said Sam.

"But they caused the death of an innocent dog." Very well, I couldn't help myself.

Billy patted my knee. "It's all right, Daisy. Spike will never chew anyone's arm off. He couldn't reach, for one thing."

When I glanced over at him, I saw Spike wagging his tail as if he agreed wholeheartedly with whatever his master chose to say about any matter at all.

Sam chuckled. "Oddly enough, Spike looks a lot like those Dobermans. They had that same black fur with the tan dots over their eyes and the same tan around the feet and mouth and on the chest. The dobies were just taller, is all. A whole lot taller. And not nearly so friendly."

"Hmm," I said.

Fortunately, since a lecture on the evils of people versus the goodness of dogs was dancing on my tongue begging to be let out, we arrived at the parking area at Brookside Park at that moment. Spike began woofing happily. He loved these lessons. Not only did he get an hour of my undivided attention (almost undivided—I had to pay some attention to Mrs. Hanratty), but he got to say hi to a bunch of other dogs and people at the same time.

Sam hurried out of his seat first and opened the door for me. What was going on here? Was Sam beginning to "take care of me" even before Billy's demise? God help me. Still, I doubted it. No. It seemed far more likely that, if he didn't already know about the letter plot, he thought I was up to something at the

Winkworth place, wanted to know what it was and was doing his best to soften my attitude toward him so I'd spill the beans. Darn it. I swear, Sam Rotondo was the bane of my existence!

He then opened the door for Billy, but I forestalled any further gentlemanly behavior on his part by saying, "Why don't you get the bath chair, Sam? I'll take Spike and help Billy get out."

"Sure," he said, and trotted off to do my bidding. *Most* unusual behavior. I mistrusted it intensely.

I decided to ask Billy about it. "Why's Sam being so nice to me all of a sudden?"

Billy glanced up at me as if he thought I'd lost my mind. "Huh? Sam's only Sam. He's always nice."

Not to me, he wasn't. But I didn't want to argue. Besides, getting Billy out of the Chevrolet whilst clinging to Spike's leash—Spike was trying doggedly, as was only proper, to go visit his friends—was hard work. My arms and shoulders were probably stronger than those of most baseball pitchers after having to deal with Billy and his wheelchair for so long. It finally occurred to me to say, "Spike, sit," and Spike sat. Boy, I loved these obedience lessons, once I remembered to use them! Too bad they didn't offer one aimed at wives for the training of their husbands.

And then Sam showed up with the bath chair, unfolded it, and Billy sank into it. Those few seconds of standing had him trembling, with sweat bedewing his forehead from the effort thereof, and my heart ached anew at the realization of how much his condition had deteriorated in the past months. I shoved Billy-thoughts out of my head with grim determination and said, "Sam, can you roll Billy up to those two men in the wheelchairs?" I pointed to Billy's fellow wounded warriors. "The class is about to start, and I have to get Spike over there or risk being scolded by Mrs. Hanratty."

"Absolutely," said Sam.

I waited for an added barb, but none came. Mysterious. Very mysterious.

But I could no more think about Sam's odd behavior than I could about Billy's problems because obedience training awaited. When we first began taking Spike to these classes, I'd determined to make this one blessed hour of the week free from any thoughts at all except those imparted to us by Mrs. Hanratty.

"Spike, heel," said I in my firm master's—or mistress's, although that sounds so unrefined somehow—voice.

And Spike, wagging his entire hind end out of pure joy, heeled, and we joined the other Pasanita attendees in the circle Mrs. Hanratty required of us. She, naturally, stood in the middle as she taught us stuff. Today we were going to practice having our dogs lie down and stay. I'd been practicing with Spike, but to tell the truth, at first I sometimes found it difficult to tell if he was lying down or not, because his legs were so short to begin with. However, Spike, genius dog that he was, had learned anyway, and I was eager to show off his brilliance to the class.

The class went swell. I was ever so proud of Spike, who lay and stayed better than any other dog there, and I don't think it was because he was basically lazy, either, which is the theory Mrs. Hinkledorn, the poodle lady, propounded. I was really glad when Mrs. Hanratty agreed with me.

"Nonsense," Mrs. Hanratty honked. It's difficult to describe her voice in any other way. "Spike is no lazier than most dogs. Mrs. Majesty *works* with him. Isn't that so, Mrs. Majesty?"

"Every day," I said, frowning at Mrs. Hinkledorn. Lazy, my foot. She, by the way, looked kind of like a marshmallow, all soft and fluffy. Like her stupid poodle. But, no. I'm almost sure I'm wrong about that, and I shouldn't malign her poor poodle. It wasn't the dog's fault it had a silly haircut and had been named Fluffy.

"There. You see? *Practice* is the key word," Mrs. Hanratty said, smiling at me as if she'd taught me to sit up and beg and I'd just done so. "It's *we* who are responsible for our dogs' behavior. You need to work harder with Fluffy, Mrs. Hinkledorn, or Fluffy will end up teaching *you* what she wants you to do."

She was right about that. I knew it for a fact. Spike had taught me all sorts of things, although I didn't want to tell Mrs. Hanratty that. She'd have disapproved.

"Now," she went on, "let's form a line and see how we do with our dogs. If you've worked with your pet, you should be able to walk away from him without him stirring."

"Or her," said Mrs. Hinkledorn. She would.

"Or her," said Mrs. Hanratty upon an irritated sigh. "Your dog's attention should be on you and you alone. That's the whole point of this class: to teach your dog you're the boss. Everything your dog does reflects on how much authority you have over him. Or her." She added that part to prevent further interruptions, I'm sure. "You are the leader of your pack. Your dog needs to understand that and take his—or her—clues from you and you alone. Unless, of course, other members of your family are also going to be handling the dog. Then those other members need to be trained by you."

This was interesting stuff. I'd already learned from experience that Billy could get Spike to sit and stay and come and fetch, because he'd come to all the classes, watched and learned. He'd also sat on the porch with Pa every day and watched me work with Spike. Probably Pa could achieve the same results, because we all spoke the same language: Spike's.

I glanced over to see if Billy was appreciating the full impact of Mrs. Hanratty's words about the glories of his dog, only to discover he wasn't paying any attention at all. In fact, none of the four men, Billy, his two war-injured pals and Sam, were paying attention to the class. Sam had squatted in front of them, and they all seemed engrossed in a very serious conversation. Then Billy said something I couldn't hear from where I stood, and the man who'd lost an arm and an eye shook his head. Billy said something else, and Sam put his hand on one of his arms. Billy appeared frustrated, and the fellow who'd lost both legs said something. Billy frowned.

Darn it! What was going on over there?

"Mrs. Majesty? Are you still with us?"

Startled, I jerked to attention. Mrs. Hanratty was watching me as if she were disappointed that her favorite student had allowed her mind to stray from the important stuff. I could feel myself blush, which was embarrassing. "I'm sorry, Mrs. Hanratty. Yes, indeedy. I'm here and ready to go." I straightened and decided *to heck with the men.*

I was somewhat distracted for the duration of the class that day, though, and I can't deny it. The one hour of the week during which I generally relaxed and had a good time had been spoiled, and all because of that darned secret male conclave. It had looked to me as though Sam and Billy, and maybe the other two war relics, were cooking up something. If they were, I knew I wasn't going to like it, and that worried me more than Sam finding out about the poison-pen letters.

Spike, however, remained blissfully unaware of any undercurrents of tension on my part. Or maybe he was aware of my anxiety and didn't allow it to distract him. I do recall that he looked up and frowned at me a couple of times, which he generally didn't do. I know, I know. Dogs can't frown. Try telling that to Spike. *He* could frown, and he did it that day. It was as if he were telling me to pay attention to the matter at hand and let things I couldn't affect one way or another go chase themselves for the nonce. Do you think I was, perhaps, projecting? Or do you believe, as I do, that dogs are superior forms of animal life? I don't suppose it matters one way or the other.

Whether Spike caught my mood or not, he performed beautifully. When I told him, "Spike, lie down," he flattened himself out on the grass like nobody's business. When I dropped the leash and said, "Stay," then walked away from him, he stayed right where he was and didn't move a muscle. I could feel his beady little doggie eyes on me until Mrs. Hanratty gestured for me to stop walking and turn around. Spike was still there, splat on his tummy, in spite of Fluffy and a cocker spaniel named Buddy frolicking around gaily nearby. Not only that, but Hamlet, a Great Dane, now stood over Spike and sniffed his butt while his owner tried and tried to drag him away. I'm pretty sure Hamlet weighed more than his owner, who was maybe ten years old. Talk about concentration! I could have taken lessons from Spike.

I have to admit to being a trifle alarmed when I realized how much commotion was going on in the field of action, yet Spike lay there and stared at me, willing to sacrifice not merely play, but even his life—if Hamlet had been an ill-natured Great Dane instead of a big baby—rather than move before I gave him the order to move.

Mrs. Hanratty evidently noticed my startled expression, because she said, "It's perfectly all right, Mrs. Majesty. Hamlet is only a puppy and won't harm Spike, and the other dogs are no threat. Spike is doing beautifully. You may call him to you now."

You can bet I did! And quick. I shouted, "Spike, come!" and Spike shot out from under Hamlet's nose as if he couldn't do so fast enough. Unfortunately for Hamlet's owner, Hamlet took it into his head to lope off after Spike, thinking, I presume, that this was some sort of game. Naturally, his owner came with him, because he wasn't big enough not to. Hamlet dragged the poor boy on his stomach all the way across the grass, haring after Spike as if Spike was game and he was a mighty hunter. As soon as Spike got within scooping distance, I scooped him up. Not that I believed Hamlet would do anything nasty to my dog, since he mainly seemed big, clumsy and friendly, but I didn't want to take any chances. He was *huge*. Puppy, my foot.

Mrs. Hanratty walked over to Spike, Hamlet, Hamlet's owner and me. "You know, Tommy, it might be better if your father were to stay with you during these classes. Old Hamlet here needs a slightly firmer hand."

"I'm really sorry," said Tommy. He sounded as if he might cry. "I'm practicing with him all the time. Honest, I am."

"I'm sure that's so, dear," said Mrs. Hanratty, oozing sympathy. "But classes are different. At home, you're alone with your dog. In class, the dogs can become distracted with so many other canines around. Is your father here?"

"I'm here," came a grumbly voice from behind Tommy. Mr. Tommy appeared as embarrassed by Hamlet's unruly behavior as was Tommy.

Mrs. Hanratty discussed with him the advisability of him helping Tommy in future classes, and Mr. Tommy said he thought that was a good idea.

"I'm real sorry, Mrs. Majesty," said Tommy. "I just couldn't hold him."

"I understand, Tommy," I said. "I was only a little worried about Spike." I glanced from the dog in my arms to the Great Dane now being held by the leash by Mr. Tommy, and shook my head. Hamlet's gigantic head was about level with Spike's— and I was holding Spike! "Boy, you'd never know the two of them belonged to the same species, would you?"

"I don't think they do," said Mr. Tommy, sounding crabby. "Your dog comes from the species of good dogs, and Hamlet comes from the species of idiots."

I laughed and said, "I think you're being too hard on him. Dogs are smart. Hamlet knows he outweighs Tommy. Once you take him firmly in hand, he'll obey both of you, I'm sure."

"Precisely," hooted Mrs. Hanratty. "I was just going to say the same thing."

Mr. Tommy sighed. "All right. I have to be here anyway. Might as well join in the fun."

"Thanks, Pa," said Tommy, and I got the feeling his father's capitulation to Mrs. Hanratty's suggestion was a relief to him.

At any rate, Spike won top honors at Pasanita that day. You've got to admire a dachshund who isn't intimidated by a looming Great Dane.

The Hamlet incident successfully diverted my attention from whatever my husband and his friends had been plotting, and that was probably a good thing. When the class was over, all four men applauded as Spike swaggered over to them. I guess they'd watched the day's final exam, because Billy was grinning from ear to ear, the other wounded soldiers were smiling, and even Sam had an expression of approval on his face. Boy, I didn't see that expression aimed at me very often!

But wait. It wasn't aimed at me. It was fixed firmly on Spike. It figured.

CHAPTER FIFTEEN

Sam stayed for dinner that night. No surprise there. What surprised me was that he remained civil to me for the entire rest of the day. My nerves began to skip like Mexican jumping beans by the time we all sat down to Vi's superb Boston baked beans, which she served with Polish sausages and coleslaw. Pa said the sausages and coleslaw weren't authentic Massachusetts chow, but I don't think anyone minded that. I know I'd rather have a Polish sausage than a hunk of brown bread. Not that brown bread is icky or anything, but there's just something about a good sausage, you know?

Naturally, we talked about Spike's spectacular behavior during class that day.

"A Great Dane, eh?" Pa looked down with wonder upon my precious pooch. Well, technically, Spike was Billy's precious pooch, but I figured he was what the lawyers called community property. "You're really something, Spike."

"He is, isn't he?" I said, happy to hear praise heaped upon Spike's head.

"It's a good thing that other dog didn't have murder on its mind," said Sam. "Spike wouldn't have stood a chance."

I bridled. I would. "I'm not so sure about that. I'm sure Spike would be good in a fight."

Sam shrugged. "Wouldn't matter if he was a dachshund Hercules if he was pitted against a Great Dane. The Dane might have lost a kneecap, but I doubt that Spike could triumph in the end."

"That's a dismal thing to say," I told him.

"Sorry." Sam didn't sound the least bit sorry.

"Say," said Billy.

I was glad he'd interrupted, or Sam and I might have exchanged heated words, and Ma and Aunt Vi would have scolded me. Oh, boy. I, a married woman, still being scolded by my mother and my aunt. I regretted the cozy cottage Billy and I had once intended to live in even more than usual that evening.

"Do dogs have kneecaps?" Billy finished his thought.

There was a lot of looking at each other going on for a minute or so before anyone spoke. "Do dogs have knees?" I asked, curiosity having pushed my annoyance with Sam out of my mind for the moment, even though I still resented him having killed off Spike during the fictitious battle with the fictitious Great Dane.

"I don't know," said Ma. She appeared quite baffled.

"Perhaps you can ask a veterinarian," said Aunt Vi.

"Is there a veterinarian in Pasadena?" I asked. It would probably be a good idea to find out if there was one, since Spike might get sick one day, God forbid.

"I think so," said Billy. "Maybe someone at the Humane Society would know about knees on dogs."

He and I both looked at Sam, who had mentioned the Humane Society once already that day.

"Don't ask me," he said. "The only dealings I ever have with the folks from the Humane Society is when a dog or a cat is owned by someone affected by a crime. Then they send someone out to pick up the animal. I never thought to ask about dogs having knees or kneecaps."

"Then why'd you say Spike might deprive a Great Dane of a kneecap if they got into a fight?" I challenged him, feeling feisty on Spike's behalf, although I'm not sure why except that Sam always seemed to get my goat.

He rolled his eyes which, naturally, peeved me. "It was only an example. A stupid one. Spike might be able to bite a Great Dane's foot before the Dane chomped him in half. Is that better?"

"No, it's not better!" I cried indignantly. "I don't want anything to happen to Spike. Ever."

Sam mumbled something I didn't catch into his baked beans.

Ma said, "Daisy, really." See what I mean?

Pa laughed. "You'll never get her to admit any dog is better in any way than Spike, Sam, so you might as well give it up. Maybe Spike would turn out to be a David, and the supposed Great Dane would be Goliath." He turned to me. "You like that scenario better, sweetie?"

Now I felt foolish. But I said, "Yes, I do," because I figured I should.

"I don't know why we talk about half the things we end up talking about at dinner," Ma complained. "I should think dogfighting too disgusting a topic to discuss at the table."

"You're right, Mrs. Gumm," said Sam. "Sorry I brought it up."

"You didn't bring it up," said Ma, peering at me. "Daisy did."

There was no way out. "I'm sorry."

"There's a great article about Egypt in this month's *National Geographic*," Billy said hopefully.

You can see why I loved the man. Even though he'd gone through hell and come back singed, he still did his best to protect me. What's more, his ploy worked, and we all enjoyed a spirited discussion about Egyptian exploration. Most of us said we'd love to go to Egypt one day and see the pyramids and the sphinx and so forth. As if that would ever happen.

Nevertheless, and in spite of me, the rest of the evening passed pleasantly.

We Gumms and Majestys spent the following day peacefully, too. First came church, then a wonderful dinner prepared by Aunt Vi—roast beef and Yorkshire pudding, if you're interested— and then general napping, dog walking, reading, a little piano playing, and then bed. I have absolutely no idea how Sam spent his Sunday, since he didn't intrude into our family that day.

And then came Monday.

May was almost over, and June was looming on the horizon that particular Monday morning, and I decided that I'd chance fate and select a summery costume for my spiritualistic duties that day. There's a fine art to this dressing-as-a-spiritualist thing, as I'm sure you've gathered by this time. The day was going to be warm, if the past few days were anything by which to judge, yet I couldn't be seen in any old house dress.

Therefore, I selected a plain black cotton dress with a dropped waist and short sleeves. Black isn't a very summery color, but the fabric was thin, and besides, black fit my image. Not to mention my mood. The notion of tangling with Lola de la Monica for another week or so made my innards curl up and squeeze. However, according to Howard, now that I'd more or less frightened Lola into fearing for the future of her career, he didn't expect filming to take much longer than another week. Providing Lola didn't backslide into her old temperamental ways. I tried to brace up by telling myself I could always haul out Rolly again. The notion didn't make me feel appreciably better.

Black was a good color for me, I decided as I patted some light powder on my cheeks. It didn't so much wash me out as stand in contrast to my pale skin, which was a good thing for a spiritualist. We spiritualists can't go around looking too healthy and robust, after all. I even had a black straw hat to go with my ensemble, so that I would look appropriately spiritualistic whilst maintaining my own personal comfort.

"Jeez, Daisy, are you going to a funeral or something?" Billy asked as I left our bedroom, ready to depart and face my day. "Not that you don't look good," he added, probably because he noticed my glower.

"I feel as though I'm going to a funeral," I admitted. "I hate this job."

"Maybe you should quit?" he said, with a little lift to the end of the sentence as if it were more of a question than a statement.

"Maybe I should." I sank down into a kitchen chair, since Billy was still at the table and still plowing through the *Pasadena Star News*. He read every word of that newspaper every single day. Well, he didn't have anything else to do. Oh, my poor Billy.

"I know you don't like to give up on a job that pays well," he said.

I heaved a huge sigh. "It's not so much that," I said after thinking about what he'd said for a moment or two. "It's that I have to protect my reputation. If people started talking about me as quitting before a job was done, my business might suffer."

Billy gazed at me for a few seconds and then shook his head. "Your business." That's all he said, but there was a world of meaning in the two words.

I sagged. "I know. Stupid business. But—"

"It pays well," he finished for me.

"Yes." We sat at the table for a couple of minutes, me staring at the tablecloth, Billy doing I don't know what—because I was staring at the tablecloth.

"Do you think the family would suffer a whole lot if you, say, became a telephone exchange operator?" he asked suddenly.

I looked up. "A telephone exchange operator?" I repeated

blankly. "Wouldn't that put Mildred out of a job?" Mildred Rafferty was an old pal of mine from high school. She was the one who always placed calls for me when I needed to call an operator.

"The phone company has more people than Mildred on its payroll."

I began drawing little circles on the tablecloth. "Gee, Billy, I'd never see you if I got a regular job."

He shrugged. "You're gone most of the time anyway."

"That's not true," I said, defending myself a bit too hotly since this present job of mine seemed to be taking me away from my family day and night. "Not most of the time, at any rate. I get to spend lots of days with you."

"That's true," he admitted. "But you might get to meet more . . . normal people if you worked at a regular job."

"Normal people?" I wasn't sure what he meant. Sure, he'd beefed at me about hanging out with rich people, and at one time he even accused me of being a social climber, but he didn't mean it. Any more than he'd meant it when he'd accused me of running around on him with Johnny Buckingham. Johnny Buckingham, a minister of God, for Pete's sake.

He gave me another shrug. "Yeah. I mean people like us. Not rich people. You know, people like your family. Wouldn't you feel more comfortable being around folks like us than all those rich picture people? They sure aren't normal."

"I hope to heck they aren't." I actually shuddered as I contemplated Lola de la Monica. If that was normal, I didn't want anything to do with normality. Or "normalcy," as our president had called it once. Then again, he'd offered somebody a "generalcy," too. He might not have been too smart, President Harding, but he sure looked presidential. Actually, thinking about politicians made my mood lighten slightly. "Picture people may be a strange lot, but they're better than politicians, who are all crooks," I told Billy.

He laughed. I always felt good when Billy laughed.

"You're probably right about that," he said. Then he gave a little sigh. "Well, don't take any guff from Lola today, all right?"

"I'll sure try not to," I said. Then I got up, feeling as if I were hefting a ninety-pound sack of sand rather than my own regulation-sized body. "I'd better go. I need to get there before Lola begins kicking up a fuss."

Billy lifted the newspaper and snapped it open. "Say hello to Sam for me."

That's right. Not only did I have to deal with Lola the Lunatic, but I also had to endure another day of Sam Rotondo's company. I don't suppose dealing with Sam would bother me so much if I weren't attempting with all my wits and strength to keep him from learning about the letters Lola and Monty had been getting.

It then occurred to me that ever since I'd met him, my entire life seemed to have been involved in keeping things from Sam Rotondo. It got darned tiring, too, curse it.

And then something much better occurred to me: it was way past time I dropped by to see how Flossie Buckingham was getting along; you know, now that she was going to have a baby and all. Flossie, having come from very dire circumstances, was easy to talk to about stuff. So was Johnny, who, as a captain in the Salvation Army, had seen and heard darned near everything and knew all there was to know about Billy's situation. And mine. Maybe I'd just pop by the Salvation Army after I got off work today. Heck, I might even leave the wretched set early.

Life didn't seem so bleak after I'd made that decision. Mind you, I wasn't exactly cheerful, but thinking about friends made me feel not so alone with my problems, if you know what I mean.

My mood lifted even more when I set out to drive to the

Winkworth mansion. The Chevrolet tootled down the pepper-tree-lined Marengo Avenue where our modest bungalow sat, and it seemed to me as though the entire neighborhood shone in the morning sunlight. Mrs. Killebrew, our neighbor across the street, waved to me as I drove past, and I waved back. Mrs. Killebrew had been most grateful for a service I'd rendered the citizens of Pasadena a few months earlier, and recalling that made me feel not nearly so glum. I *did* do some good in the world, even when, as then, I didn't much want to.

Everyone's gardens were looking lovely. Even our garden looked good. Pa had planted rosebushes near the porch, along with a hydrangea plant that was budding already. Pa was careful to prune the bush so that the blue clusters, which would burst into bloom any day now, would be huge. It was a good thing that Pa liked tending to the garden, since Billy wasn't able to do it and all the women in the family had to go out to work. Gee, that seemed so backward. But it worked for us. Anyhow, we didn't seem to have much choice in the matter.

But there I went again, thinking negatively. I sucked in a big breath of fresh May air and turned my mind to other people's yards, which were very pretty. What was more, the house—or estate, I suppose is a better word—to which I was at that moment driving, had spectacular gardens and magnificent green, rolling lawns. The fact that it also contained a crazy actress was an aberration. A single blot on an otherwise perfect setting.

Well, except for those thrice-cursed letters. Oh, bother. I wished I hadn't thought about those blasted letters.

Anyhow, my nominally sunny mood didn't last much past the great gate of the Winkworth estate. Even before I parked the Chevrolet, my heart sank. An entire delegation seemed to await my arrival, and I darned near turned around and motored the other way. But there was no escape. By the time I got the Chevrolet headed in the right direction, the gate would be shut against me. I was trapped.

Harold was the first to greet me. He rushed to my door and flung it open, in fact. Not bothering with pleasantries, I asked, "What's wrong now?"

"Lola got a letter, and your detective friend got hold of it. Now Lola's hysterical and Detective Rotondo is furious."

Oh, goody. Just what I wanted to hear. "Why's Sam mad? Does he know about Monty's letters?"

"No, but he suspects you knew about Lola's letters and didn't tell him."

"Is that what Lola told him?"

"No. He guessed."

"Darn him anyhow! How come he always thinks I'm at fault when bad things happen?"

Harold grinned. "Because you are?"

"That isn't funny, Harold Kincaid."

He sobered at once. "I know it's not. We've got to keep him from finding out about Monty's letters. Even if the writer doesn't aim to expose his secret, we have to keep it from the police."

"Mrs. Majesty, I hate to bother you so early on a Monday morning, but could you please come? Quickly? Lola's in a state, and that detective fellow isn't helping matters."

I glanced over Harold's shoulder to see the man who'd spoken: a grim-faced John Bohnert, who looked as if he wanted to murder someone. My guess would be Lola.

Lillian Marshall stood beside him, wringing her hands, and Gladys Pennywhistle's eyeglasses glared in the sunlight much as I suspected Gladys herself was glaring behind them. I didn't see Homer Fellowes anywhere. If the man was still enamored of Lola de la Monica, I'd have to reassess my notion of pairing him with Gladys. If he still had what my friends called a "crush" on Lola after all her shenanigans, he was definitely not the right person for Gladys, who wouldn't have a crush on an idiot like Lola for worlds. Well . . . all right, so I guess she had a crush on Monty Mountjoy, but at least he wasn't always throwing fits and tantrums. I suppressed a sigh.

"Sure, John. I'll be there as soon as I can be."

And, with a sinking feeling in my middle, I walked with Harold, John and the others to the marble dressing-room building, where Harold told me Lola was in the process of pitching her fit.

I'd barely rounded the corner of the building and had only just taken in the mob scene, when one man broke away from it and stomped toward Harold, John, Lillian, Gladys and me. Sam. Naturally. I gave him a little finger wave.

He didn't wave back. In truth, he looked kind of like a thunderhead that was about to burst and rain all over us. Not that we in sunny southern California had much to do with thunderheads as a rule, but Billy had shown me a picture in the *National Geographic,* so I knew what one looked like. The thunderhead in that *National Geographic* photograph had looked a lot like Sam Rotondo did at that very moment. Dark and dangerous and unpredictable.

As he approached, more or less like a speeding freight train, Harold, John and their outriders seemed to melt away from me. Cowards. I frowned at all of them to let them know my opinion of people who deserted other people in times of crisis. On the other hand, it probably wouldn't have made much difference. Sam was a force of nature when he was riled.

Before he reached me, he started waving a sheet of paper at me. I recognized the paper. It looked precisely like the other poison-pen letters had looked, even though I couldn't yet read the words pasted thereon. I knew what they said before Sam stamped to a stop in front of me and shoved the letter in my face: CHANGE YOUR WICKED WAYS OR TRAGEDY WILL

STRIKE! Yup. There was that inked-in exclamation point.

"You knew Miss de la Monica was getting these letters, didn't you?" Sam roared as he stood before me. I fancied I could see steam coming out of his ears.

For the merest moment, I considered lying, but then I gave it up. Sam wouldn't believe me anyway. He never believed me. I took a largish breath, told myself I hadn't done anything wrong, and said, "Yes."

"Why the devil didn't you tell me about them?"

"Please don't shout, Sam. I can hear you quite well without you yelling at me."

That was definitely the wrong thing to say. I knew it at once when Sam seemed to grow right there until he loomed over me like a mountain. Gee, he was looking like all sorts of natural and man-made phenomena that morning, wasn't he? Before he could burst out of his detectival suit—a detectival suit being one of modest cost, as opposed to suits worn by the Harold Kincaids of this world, who were rich—I said, "I didn't tell you because the letters seemed . . . well, stupid."

Still looming—and probably fulminating, too—Sam stood there, glaring at me for what seemed like about a year and a half before he said, in measured accents which boded ill for me, "*You* thought the letters seemed stupid. That's why you didn't tell the police that the star of this picture was being threatened. *You* decided that, did you?"

I shrugged. Couldn't do much else under the circumstances, what with a wrathful police detective towering over me and all my friends having deserted me. "That's just it, Sam. They didn't threaten anything. Let me guess what that letter says." I shut my eyes and recited, " 'Change your wicked ways or tragedy will strike.' Right?" I attempted to smile at him, but my effort didn't produce much more than a tight little grimace.

"You know this how?" asked Sam furiously. "Psychic powers?"

"Of course not. I've seen the other letters she's received. They never vary by so much as a word. Or an exclamation point, which is always inked in, presumably because newspapers don't go in for exclamation points very often. And they don't threaten anything specific."

Sam sucked in some air, just as I'd done. "They don't threaten anything specific," he repeated, his voice tight. "How many of these things do you know about?"

"Um . . . I guess that one's the third." I pointed at the paper flapping in the gentle breeze.

"Three of them. I see." He took another deep breath.

I held on to my own breath, scared and waiting for the explosion. A police detective couldn't arrest anyone for not saying anything about anonymous letters, could he? I sure hoped not.

He didn't explode—yet. "And you say the letters don't threaten anything specific."

"Well . . . no. They all say exactly the same thing, and they never relate precise consequences. I mean, they don't ask for money or anything. For that matter, they don't even tell the recipient what types of behaviors the writer deems wicked or what kind of tragedy will befall her. They're silly, is all. At least from my perspective."

"From your perspective. Exactly what do you consider 'tragedy,' Daisy? Does that word bring pictures of happiness to your mind?"

"Well, of course not. But don't you see, Sam? Nothing's happened. Nothing at all, except more letters. Lola thought the letters were being sent to her by ghosts, for Pete's sake!"

"Ghosts."

"Yes. Ghosts. So naturally, I disabused her of that insane notion."

"I see. Ghosts aren't responsible for writing threatening letters. Did it occur to you that a human being *might* be responsible for them?"

"Of course, it did! Jeez, Sam I'm not stupid." Any more than I was psychic, but he already knew that.

"Sometimes I wonder about that," said Sam, rather cruelly, I thought.

"Darn it, Sam. You're dealing with a hysterical woman! For all I know Lola's writing the letters to herself so that she can get people to pay attention to her!"

Actually, the notion hadn't once occurred to me until that very minute when it came to me in a burst of desperation. What's more, I knew the suggestion to be wide of the mark. This was mainly because Monty was also getting the same letters and I knew for a fact that they worried him a whole lot, and for a very good reason. If it weren't for Monty, I might actually have believed Lola was writing the things to herself. But she wasn't, and I knew it. What's more, I was being unconscionably callous toward Lola for having uttered such a thing and was ashamed of myself. Lola might be a nitwit and a pain in the neck, but the letters were truly upsetting to her. Well, they would be to anyone. Nevertheless, my words seemed to give Sam pause, so I didn't take them back. I didn't dare let down my guard, but I could tell he was thinking hard about what I'd just said.

Still glowering—Sam never wanted to give up a good bout of anger easily, especially when it was directed at me—he said, "Hmm. You might have a point there."

I gave yet another shrug, feeling helpless to do anything more useful, not to mention guiltier by the second. "I don't know that for a fact, mind you. Still, I wouldn't put much past her if she thought she could get a good temperament or two out of it." Was I mean, or was I not mean? I hated myself, not for the first time by any means.

As if by magic, Sam seemed to shrink until he stood before me in his normal size. Which was still pretty darned big, but not mountainous, thunderous or trainly. "Do you know if anyone else has been getting these things?" Again he flapped the letter at me.

Oh, boy. I really hated to lie outright, especially since I'd just slandered Lola de la Monica. Still and all . . . I said, "No. Not to my knowledge, anyway."

I was pretty sure in that moment that I was headed straight for hell.

Chapter Sixteen

Evidently, Harold and John Bohnert also judged the worst to be over at that point because they appeared, one on each side of me, as if by magic. I still considered them abject cowards.

"Is it all right if I take Daisy to Lola, Detective Rotondo?" Harold asked, considerably more courageous than his colleague, by gum.

Sam huffed for a second or two, but then acquiesced. "I suppose so. Somebody's got to calm that idiot woman down. And I guess she relies on Daisy for that." He sneered. I wasn't surprised.

After having braved Sam Rotondo all by myself, I wasn't eager to confront a hysterical Lola. I regret to say I began to whine. "Do I have to?"

This time it was John who stepped in and said, "Yes, you damned well have to! You're the only one she'll listen to. Besides," he added rather meanly, "she's paying you a small fortune to deal with her."

"You're right," I said, drooping in body and spirit. "You're absolutely right. She's paying me for this. Although it's not a small fortune." I felt honor-bound to add the last sentence, since it was the truth. I lowered my head. "Oh, God, please help me." It was kind of a prayer, even though I knew I was unworthy to utter one, having just told Sam Rotondo a bold-faced lie and all but accusing Lola of writing those letters to herself. Not to mention tricking people for a living. You can tell how low I felt. I don't often agree with Billy about the way I make my living.

Fortunately for me, I had Harold Kincaid as a friend. "Buck up, Daisy," he said. "I'll reward you as soon as this thing is over by taking you out to lunch at Mijares."

I turned a wan smile upon him. "Thanks, Harold. That'll make this misery almost worth it."

Sam grunted. He grunted a lot. "You ought to take the whole damned family out to dinner," he told Harold. "While Daisy's here, her husband's at home alone."

Well, I liked that! "Darn you, Sam Rotondo! Billy is not alone! Pa is always there with him, and so is Aunt Vi, at least now, while Mrs. Pinkerton is on her trip. Besides, Billy has Spike for comfort. That's more than I have!"

Sam, as might have been expected, rolled his eyes. "What he needs is his wife," he told me.

And this was the man whom Billy had asked to look out for me if anything should happen to him. Bah! If this was the way Sam Rotondo took care of people, I disapproved. A lot.

But I didn't have any more time to fret and fume about Sam, because we were approaching the mob. There were at least two dozen people there, all gazing in rapt amazement at something going on in the center of the circle they made. I knew that something must be Lola. The only thing I didn't know was what she was doing. I didn't *want* to know what she was doing, either.

But as Aunt Vi might have said, I'd made my bed and now I had to lie in it.

Putting on my mantle of spiritualism rather like Dracula's cape, I tapped on a shoulder. "Pardon me, please," I said, using my best, lowest-pitched, most soothing voice. "I need to assist Miss de la Monica."

The crowd parted much like the Red Sea must have parted

for Moses lo, those many years ago. As soon as Lola, who was on her hands and knees and seemed to be trying to pound the grass into submission, lifted her head and saw me, she uttered a piercing shriek. Her dark hair was wild and straggled over her face. Her white gown, a flowing number that must have been pretty once, was wrinkled and smeared with grass stains. She got grass stains on her white clothing a lot. I'll bet she never got them out, either.

"*Daisy!* Thank *God* you're here!"

Ah. There was Dr. Homer Fellowes. He'd been hovering over Lola, clearly without a clue what to do. At Lola's shriek, he leaped backwards, and his gaze searched furiously beyond me to—ta-da!—Gladys Pennywhistle! I knew that, because I turned to see Gladys receive his glance and return it with a speaking one of her own. Well, well.

But I didn't have time to congratulate myself on what looked to be a budding, and infinitely suitable, romance on the parts of Gladys and Homer. I had to steel myself for the onslaught of Lola, who lifted herself up from the pounded grass and flung herself at me. I was almost used to this behavior on her part by that time. I remained standing, thanks to strong muscles built up by years of assisting my husband to do various things, and hardly staggered backward at all when she hit. I gently patted her on the back.

"There, there," I said softly. "There's no need for this."

"But I got another letter!" she cried—in full Spanish-accent mode. "And that beastly detective fellow is being *horrid* to me."

"There, there," I said again. "Think nothing of that. Sam is beastly to everyone."

"Hey," said Sam, nettled.

But I'd spoken only what I perceived as the truth and my hot glare over Lola's heaving shoulders told him so. He rolled his eyes again. Darn him, anyhow!

"I'm sure you're upset about getting another letter," I began.

"Yes! Oh, yes!" she wailed in my ear.

I swear, I was going to be completely deaf before this job was finished. "However, there's no need to carry on so. I believe these letters to be written by someone who has no real power. I don't believe the threat is to be taken seriously."

Her shudders subsided slightly. "You don't?" She lifted her head from my shoulder and peered at me through wet eyes. At least this time she'd been crying genuine tears. Unless she'd just got grass in her eyes from the thumping she'd given the lawn. "Why not?"

"Because if any real threat were intended, something bad would have happened by this time, don't you think?"

"Well . . . how can you tell? How do you know?"

"For one thing, the letters all say the same thing. There's not one mention of what might happen if you don't change your ways. And the writer certainly hasn't explained what he or she considers 'wicked,' which he or she should if he expects your behavior to change."

"But . . ."

I went on doggedly, reminding myself of Spike. "From everything I've read about poison-pen letter writers," I told her, imparting the same information I'd given to Harold and Monty recently, "they're written by people who feel they have no power. The only way they can express their disapproval or vent their spleens is to write nasty letters."

Lola blinked at me. "What's a spleen?"

Oh, boy. "I mean, writing letters is the only way they believe they have to . . . to get back at someone they don't like. If you know what I mean."

"But why would anyone want to get back at me? Why would anyone not like *me?*" asked Lola.

I heard a murmur spread through the crowd gathered and

felt like doing a little eye rolling of my own.

"I have no idea." Figuring the time to comfort was over—I saw John Bohnert frowning at his wristwatch—I spoke more bracingly when I continued, "But you have a job to do. You shouldn't allow these letters to upset you so much. That's precisely what the letter writer wants. Whoever is doing this is hoping that you—or perhaps the entire picture—will be so badly affected by the letters that the studio will suffer."

Boy, I'd just that second thought about someone maybe having it in for the studio, but it seemed like a really solid idea! I glanced at Sam and saw that he was frowning, only not at me this time, but in thought. I was proud of myself for about a second and a half before Lola captured my attention once more, this time by wailing again. I winced before I could stop myself.

"No! No! *No!* This evil person is out to get *me!* I know it! I can feel evil coming toward me! Oh, Daisy, you *have* to help me!"

How, I wanted to ask her. Did she want me to go out stalking the letter writer? But Lola, never one for common sense, clearly had no more idea than I about how I could help her to get the letter writer to cease and desist. "I'm doing my best to help you," I said, trying to keep the sharpness out of my voice. "And the best way to do that is to ignore the letters and do your job. Remember what Rolly told you."

"But he didn't know about the letters!" she cried.

My poor ears couldn't take any more of being screeched into, so I pulled slightly away from Lola. "Yes, he did," I reminded her. "We talked to him about them, remember? Anyhow, the spirits know everything, so even if we hadn't told Rolly about the letters, he'd know." I spoke firmly.

"We told him?" she asked uncertainly.

Brother. Why bother to give the woman her own personal, private séance if she wasn't going to remember anything about it? For the first time, I began to wonder if Lola tippled on the side. I'd never smelled alcohol on her breath, but the Hollywoodland people were notorious for taking all sorts of drugs, as well as drinking to excess. Maybe she took drugs and they had made her stupid.

"Yes, indeed. If you'll recall, he told you not to worry about the letters, but to do your job."

"But I thought you didn't remember what went on during séances."

Nuts. She would have to remember that, wouldn't she? "I don't recall immediately after the séance is over, but I remember as days pass."

"Oh." Lola appeared confused for a second or two, which only made sense.

Therefore, I hurried on, hoping she'd decide thought was something meant for other people to do. "Right now your job is to get dressed for today's filming." I shot a glance at John Bohnert, hoping I'd said the right thing. He nodded vigorously, so I guessed I had.

"Well . . ." Lola seemed to be wavering. I already knew she loved being the center of attention. Too bad for everyone working with her that she seemed to take delight in garnering negative, instead of positive, attention.

"Come with me, Lola. I'll help you get cleaned up. You're all over grass stains."

She glanced down at her formerly white gown.

"I'll go fetch her costume," Lillian Marshall said brightly. "And bring it to her dressing room."

"Make it snappy," said John, not at all amused by his female star's antics.

"I'll help you, Daisy," said Harold. He stepped up to Lola's side and took an arm.

Bless Harold for a saint, the woman finally released me. Not, mind you, before she'd dampened the shoulder of my black cotton frock. However, I'd dressed appropriately both for the day and for Lola, so it didn't matter. I'd dry out quickly once we were all outdoors in the warm May sunshine with the camera rolling. "Thanks, Harold."

"I'm not through investigating this matter," Sam said with a tone of authority that fit him.

"Well, can you investigate it while we get Lola ready for work?" I asked him, glancing at John and beginning to feel a little desperate, although I'm not altogether sure why. I suppose it was because I felt responsible every time Lola acted up, which was silly of me, but there you go.

"I guess so." Sam spoke grudgingly. Too bad for him.

"Thank you, Daisy. Please don't leave me," pleaded Lola as if she expected Sam to haul out the manacles and leg irons— which might not be a bad idea, actually. If we chained her up, at least we could haul her where she needed to be and keep to the schedule.

But there I go again, being absurd. Life was never as simple as that.

"I won't leave you," I assured Lola.

"Oh, thank you!" Lola said upon a sob.

With Harold on one side and me on the other, we managed to get Lola upstairs and into her dressing room. Sam followed us. I could practically feel him seething behind us.

"Here we are." I spoke with considerably more brightness than I felt. I could already tell that I wasn't going to be able to leave work early in order to visit Flossie and Johnny. Not with Lola in this fragile state. Darn and blast.

Harold let go of Lola long enough to open the dressing-room door, and Lola and I more or less staggered in, Lola feigning great weakness. Or maybe she wasn't feigning.

Naw. She was feigning. That's what she did for a living, was act, after all.

Sam stomped into the room behind us, and I saw Lillian, looking nervous and holding a pretty green dress in one hand and a bunch of petticoats and a hoop skirt in the other. Costume time. I wanted to talk to Harold alone to find out if Monty, too, had received another letter, but so far we'd been surrounded by people and I hadn't dared ask. Now that Sam was there, I didn't think it prudent to ask Harold any silent questions, either. Sam invariably noticed stuff like that and quizzed me ruthlessly about it.

"I think you need to wash up before you change your clothes," I said gently. "Would you like me to help you?"

"Help her wash up?" Sam. Grumpily. What a surprise (I'm joking).

Lola eyed him with loathing. "My spirits have been crushed, Detective Rotondo." She rolled the R in Rotondo beautifully. "I need Mrs. Majesty's assistance."

"All right," said Sam as if he didn't understand Lola now, never had and, what's more, didn't want to.

After sending him a peeved glance—he wasn't helping in the least to get Lola calmed down and ready for work—I went into the small bathroom leading from the dressing room with Lola, who decided only a full, hot bubble bath would do for her. In a way I didn't blame her, since she'd been grubbing around on the lawn for God alone knew how long before I came onto the scene. On the other hand, that grubbing had been her idea, and she was already late for the day's filming.

"Please," she said, "draw my bath for me."

Golly, now maid duties had been added to my list of responsibilities! However, I didn't feel it prudent to cavil at that point, so I turned the water on in the bath. "Are these the salts you prefer?" I asked, holding up a bottle of purple crystal-like stuff.

"Yes. That's my own fragrance, you know. It's even called Lola."

I could hear the pride in her voice. Personally, I'd rather have a rose or something named after me, scent not appealing to me much—besides, who'd want to hire a spiritualist who reeked of some god-awful perfume? Unless maybe it was sandalwood. I think sandalwood is approved of in spiritualistic circles. Not that this has anything to do with Lola.

Suffice it to say I dumped a quantity of the bath crystals into the tub, and they foamed and emitted an enticing scent. "This smells nice," I said, hoping to sooth Lola's ruffled spirits. Besides, it was the truth. The salts smelled like Lola always smelled. I guess maybe some perfume maker somewhere really had created a scent just for her.

"Of course. Guerlain created it for me."

Now she sounded smug, and any trace of sympathy I'd been harboring for her vanished like the steam from the tub. "That's very nice. Now, why don't you get out of that stained dress and clean yourself up."

And then I got a most unpleasant shock. Lola, no shrinking violet, had already shed her stained dress. She wafted past me, stark naked, and sank into the tub. Thank God for bubbles. She might have been beautiful, and she might have had a great figure, but I sure as the dickens didn't want to see it. I whirled around, and she laughed softly.

"Ah, Daisy, don't be such a prude."

"Thank you. I prefer being a prude to being an—" Fortunately, I stopped myself before uttering the word *exhibitionist*. As little as I liked Lola, still less did I want to be fired from this detestable job. "Um . . . I'll just wait with the others in the sitting room. Please don't take long, Lola. Mr. Bohnert is quite distressed about the continued delays in the filming of this picture."

"Bah. Mr. Bohnert is a Philistine!"

"He's also the boss," I reminded her with something of a snap to my voice. "Try, please, to remember what Rolly told you. He meant it, Lola. The spirits don't lie."

A short space of silence preceded Lola's whispered, "Very well."

So I left her to her bubbles, prayed she'd hurry, and went back to the sitting room, where everyone was, as seemed appropriate, sitting. I heaved a huge sigh as I shut the bathroom door behind me.

"What's she doing in there?" Harold asked.

"Bathing. I told her to hurry it up."

"Bathing?"

I jumped, turned, and saw that John Bohnert had joined us. It was he who'd bellowed the word. "I told her to hurry. During our private séance, my spirit control—"

"Rolly," Harold interrupted, grinning.

"Yes. Rolly told her to behave herself or this would be her last picture because she was getting a reputation as a troublemaker, and nobody would be willing to work with her again if she didn't shape up."

"That was darned severe of him," said Harold. "I'm proud of you, Daisy."

"Thank you."

"Thank *you*," said John. "I only hope she starts taking his advice." He frowned. "Although I almost understand why she was upset this morning. Why didn't anyone tell me she was getting these letters, anyhow?"

"We didn't see the point," said Harold before I could.

"You didn't see the *point?* Damn it, Harold, Lola's a bitch to work with even without threatening letters showing up."

Harold shrugged. "Sorry, John."

"So tell me what you know about the letters Miss de la Monica has been receiving, Daisy." Sam. Always business, Sam.

"There's not much to tell. She told me she'd found a letter propped up against her dressing-room mirror last Monday—"

"Which accounts for the lock and the guard," Sam said drily.

"Well, yes," I admitted. "And then she got another one stuffed into her pocket at dinner on another occasion."

"At dinner? Dammit Daisy—"

This time it was I who interrupted him. Turnabout being fair play and all that. Before he could continue to scold me, I asked, "Where was this one?"

Sam gave a horrible frown. "I have no idea. She was hysterical when I got here, and I wasn't able to get a word out of her. She was too busy tearing up the lawn."

"Yeah," I said. "That was an interesting reaction."

"Most entertaining," said John acidly.

"That white dress will probably never come clean of all those grass stains," Lillian murmured, and she heaved a little sigh. I got the impression Lillian took clothes seriously and didn't care to see them ruined on the whim of a demented actress.

"So," said Sam loudly, obviously attempting to get the topic back to the appropriate subject, "she's received three of these letters, and neither you nor she felt it appropriate to tell the police about them. Why is that, I wonder."

I shook my head. "Honestly, Sam, I really didn't think there was any validity to the so-called threat in the letters."

"You know all about anonymous letters, do you?"

"Well . . . I do read a lot, you know." I lifted my chin, feeling guilty as heck but hoping Sam would take my mien as defiant.

"You read a lot. I see. And you say you don't know if anyone else is getting these letters?"

I *really* wanted to look at Harold, but I didn't dare, Sam being the snoopy and, I must admit, insightful person that he was. If he caught a glance pass between the two of us, he'd pounce on it like Spike on his ball.

"I haven't heard about anyone else getting letters," said John. He lifted an eyebrow at Harold, who shook his head.

"I think she's writing them herself," said Harold, giving credence to my own slanderous utterance to Sam only minutes earlier. "She'd do anything to get herself in the spotlight."

"Hmm." Sam didn't appear to want to give any validity to this idea, which, while quite likely, given Lola's personality, was dead wrong. But he didn't have to know that, curse the man.

"You know," said John in a thoughtful voice, "I hadn't thought about that, but you might be right, Kincaid. It's exactly the sort of thing Lola *would* do to get attention."

"I think so, too," said Lillian, who'd clearly been through the wringer as she'd dealt with the woman.

Sam shook his head, not in denial, but in disgust. "Well, you might all be right, but I'm still going to have to investigate the matter."

"If it turns out she's been writing them herself, can she get into trouble for it?" Lillian's voice held a note of optimism.

"Oh, boy, wouldn't the studio love that?" said John. His voice, unlike Lillian's, held nothing but dread. "And wouldn't the papers like to get their hands on a story like that?"

I ventured cautiously, "Well, people would probably flock to see the picture."

"Not bloody likely," said John bitterly. "You surely remember what happened to Fatty Arbuckle."

"Oh," I said. "You're right. People aren't eager to forgive fallen idols, are they?"

"To hell with the picture and the studio," Sam burst out suddenly. "What *I* need to know about are these damned letters. Can't *anyone* tell me *anything* about them? Anything at all?"

Raised eyebrows and puzzled expressions passed among those of us gathered there. I know my own expression of bafflement was totally fake, and so was Harold's. Lillian and John can be acquitted of any sort of flummery.

Lifting my hands in what I hoped was a helpless gesture, I said, "Sorry, Sam. I don't know anything except that Lola's been getting the letters. I don't know who's sending them. Or placing them, I guess is a better word for it."

"Whoever it is has access to the estate," said Sam. "You say she got one at dinner?"

"That's what she told me," I said. "She said someone put it in her pocket, and she found it there after she went up to her room."

"What do you mean, 'up to her room'? Is the woman living on the estate?"

"Well . . ." This time I did glance at Harold.

It was he who answered, "Lola is so much trouble, the studio thought it would be better to house her here for the duration of the picture shoot."

John took up the explanation. "God, yes. We that is, the studio—figured she'd be less apt to disrupt the shooting if she were confined to the grounds of the Winkworth estate, and since Monty's grandmother owns the place, it made sense. Besides," he said sourly, "Lola likes fancy surroundings, and these are about as fancy as you can get without going to a five-star hotel somewhere."

"Hmm." Sam thought about what Harold and John had said. "That does make some sense."

"It sure does. The last time I worked with Lola, we put her up at a hotel in the desert, and she caused no end of trouble. The place was *not* up to her exacting standards." John's nose wrinkled. "I swear to God, if they ever assign me to another of her pictures, I'm going to shoot myself."

Harold chuckled. "Don't do that. She's not worth it."

At that moment, the bathroom door was flung open, and

Lola stood there, steam wafting around her, clad in a white satin robe. "My costume," she said imperiously. "Bring me my costume."

After exchanging a speaking glance with Harold, Lillian rose from the chair she'd been sitting in, gathered the green dress, petticoats, hoop skirt, etc., and walked to the bathroom. With a dramatic sigh, Lola backed up. I didn't envy Lillian trying to dress a damp Lola in a room full of hot air, especially since the gown was supposed to be a Civil War–era one that probably weighed a ton and a half.

Glancing at his wristwatch, John said, "Do you suppose it's safe for me to go down and get the technical people set up?"

"I think so," said Harold, a note of caution in his voice. "Daisy's here. If Lola cuts up, Daisy can deal with her."

"Thanks, Harold." I grimaced at my best friend.

He winked back. "Hey, it's your job, Daisy, remember?"

"How could I ever forget?"

As soon as Harold and John left the room, Sam turned to me. "All right, Daisy, tell me the truth about those damned letters."

Aw, crumb.

Chapter Seventeen

"Darn you, Sam Rotondo, I've *told* you everything I know about those letters!" My protest was hot, although my heart thumped like a demented drummer in a speakeasy.

"I don't believe you."

The statement was so bold and bare of ornamentation that I actually gasped. Then I got indignant. I know, I know. I was lying through my teeth. What right did I have to be indignant? Nevertheless, I managed it quite nicely. "You never believe me about anything! Curse you, Sam, I don't know what Billy sees in you!"

"I might say the same thing about you," he said, getting indignant himself.

I gasped again. Sam's comment had been, possibly, the cruelest one he could have made to me at that particular moment in time when I was so terribly worried about Billy. I began to shake, I was so mad. "How dare you?" I whispered intensely. "I love my husband more than you'll ever know, Sam Rotondo, and I've been especially worried about him recently. He's . . . he's . . ." And then, like a complete fool, I began to cry.

"Aw, cripes," Sam grumbled. "I know it, Daisy. I'm sorry. I didn't mean what I said."

"Yes, you did," I said, getting myself under control in record time. "You think I'm a terrible wife. You think I'm a terrible *person!* Don't deny it, Sam. You do. If you didn't think those things, you wouldn't always be rebuking me. For your information, I do everything I can for my Billy. I *love* him! I've loved him my whole life. I'd never do anything to hurt Billy." Scenes from the past several months smote my mind's eye, and I muttered, "Not on purpose, anyway."

"Ah, sh—shoot, Daisy. Don't you think I know that? But you have to admit, you haven't been honest with me about a whole lot of things in the past."

"I have, too. I've never kept anything from you, darn it! I've actually helped you." A recent grievance against Sam and the Pasadena Police Department leapt into my mind, and I straightened on the sofa. "In fact, it was *you* who kept things from me when I was teaching that wretched cooking class! If you'd told me what you suspected, I wouldn't have been put in danger, and you know it! What's more," I added with a sniff, "our lovely new motorcar wouldn't have been wrecked."

"It wasn't wrecked," Sam grumbled. "You only drove it into a ditch."

"I was *forced* into that ditch, blast you!"

"Right. Anyway, I couldn't tell you what I suspected. I was under orders."

"Huh."

It was probably a good thing that Lola and a wilted-looking Lillian came out from the bathroom at that moment. Sam and I had to quit quarrelling and get Lola downstairs and onto the set before John Bohnert suffered an apoplexy.

I smiled as brightly as I could and said, "Ready to go? I'll walk with you to the set."

"Me, too," said Harold, and we assumed our former positions, one on either side of Lola so she couldn't escape. Lillian, bedraggled and panting, followed us, and Sam took up the rear. I thought I heard him grumbling under his breath. Served him right, the brute.

The tension in the air around the set practically crackled.

One of the assistant directors—I think his name was Paul something-or-other—ran toward us as soon as he saw us heading camera-wards. As soon as he got near enough for us to hear him, I realized he was repeating, "Thank God. Thank God. Thank God," over and over.

Lola, as serene as a Spanish Madonna, and with her chin lifted, gently detached herself from Harold and me and walked toward the worried man.

"Brother," I said, watching her performance with something akin to awe. "If I didn't know she'd been throwing a screaming tantrum not a half hour ago, I'd never know she'd thrown a screaming tantrum not a half hour ago. If you know what I mean."

"I know exactly what you mean," said Harold.

"It galls me that she makes so damned much money," said Sam, surprising me. "She sure isn't worth it."

"Don't tell her fans that," said Harold. "The studio might not like it."

Sam chuffed out an angry noise. "The studio." He made the word *studio* sound as if it tasted bad. Which it probably did, given his enforced state of entrapment on this wretched picture set.

"I'm just glad I can sit down for a bit," Lillian Marshall said upon a heavy sigh. "I'm completely worn out, and it's only . . . What time is it, anyhow?"

Harold glanced at his wristwatch. "It's only a quarter past nine."

"Lord. It feels like months since she got that stupid letter."

"Where was this one, by the way?" I asked.

"Under her plate at the breakfast table," said Harold.

"Good God," said Sam, thundering again. "That means it's someone in the house who's responsible for them."

"Must be," said Harold.

I almost reiterated the idea that Lola herself might be responsible for the letters, but I already felt guilty enough about propounding that theory the first time. I didn't want to pile sin upon sin, as it were.

"Hmm." Sam rubbed his chin thoughtfully. "I think you might be right about those letters, Daisy. Miss de la Monica is such a dramatic piece of work, I wouldn't put it past her to write the damned things to herself, just for the spectacle of it all."

There you go. I didn't even have to suggest the idea again. Sam had already picked it up and was chewing on it. Naughty Daisy. If Ma or Aunt Vi ever found out about this bit of meddling on my part, they'd never let me live it down. In that moment, I almost felt it a shame that Methodists didn't go in for confession as Roman Catholics did. I could use some cleansing-of-the-soul right about then.

"Do you need me on the set, Harold?" Lillian asked, bless her for jerking my mind away from my own unconscionable behavior and to her. "I'm exhausted, and want to go get a cup of tea and sit for a few minutes."

"Sounds like a good idea to me," said Harold. "What about you, Daisy? You probably need some kind of refreshment after your dealings with de la Monster this morning."

Along with his suggestion, Harold gave me what I considered a significant look. I took that look to mean that Lola wasn't the only person to have received an anonymous letter under her breakfast plate that morning. Golly, I was getting really tired of dealing with these people and their problems, especially since I couldn't tell Sam about them, and he was always *there*. In my way. Watching. Thinking. The darned man thought entirely too much, and his years as a policeman had given him a very suspicious mind. He believed—correctly—that I knew more about the letters than I was letting on, and he'd be scrutinizing my every movement in order to catch me out. Staying clear of Sam could be extremely tiring. I already knew that from bitter experience.

"Yes," I said, meaning it sincerely. "I'd love to take a cup of tea and maybe a little sustenance, if you've got a doughnut or something handy." Although I didn't want to, I said, "How about you, Sam? You want some coffee or anything?" This was my way of trying to make him think I had nothing to hide. Not that any of my similar stratagems had ever worked in the past, but I figured it was worth a shot.

"No, thanks," he said, relieving my mind a whole lot. "I think I'll watch this picture being filmed. I'm still trying to figure out why that invention of Dr. Fellowes is so blessed important that it requires a detective and two uniformed policemen."

"It's probably all for the sake of publicity," I said.

However, since Sam had brought up the subject of Homer Fellowes, I glanced around to see where he might be in the overall scheme of things. It pleased me to see him standing with Gladys Pennywhistle. The two seemed to be chatting amiably—*amiably* being a relative term, given the natural tendency of both parties to be serious and sober at all times.

So Lillian, Harold and I walked away from the set and toward Mrs. Winkworth's grand mansion. Naturally, Harold and I didn't instantly begin talking about the letter problem, since Lillian didn't know that Monty, too, was receiving letters. Instead, we talked about Lola, which helped all three of us get our frustrations out. *We* knew all about the venting of spleens, unlike some other uneducated and ill-informed people I might mention.

We vented in glorious surroundings. Even though I was worried about Sam and Monty Mountjoy, severely annoyed at Lola de la Monica, and wished I were home, I couldn't help but admire the swell gardens as we strolled past them.

"Oh, my," I said at one point. "Smell that fragrance! What is it, do you know?"

Harold lifted his nose in the air, reminding me of Spike, and sniffed. "Jasmine, I think."

"It's heavenly. I think I'll ask Pa to plant some jasmine. Maybe he could plant it along the driveway so the Longneckers can enjoy the smell, too."

"It does smell sweet," said Lillian. "I like the gardenias by the back door, too."

"Oh, my, yes," I said upon a pensive breath. "We have a gardenia bush. It's not blooming yet, but it probably will start soon. It's near the deck in the back of our house, so when Billy and I sit out there, we can smell it."

"I like flowers as much as the next guy," said Harold, making me smile, "but what I want to know is how to keep Lola from kicking up a fuss for the rest of the week. If we can get this week over with, the shoot should be over. Then they'll have to do publicity stills, and then she'll go away. After that, it's all editing, and they do that in the studio."

"Really?" I was interested, not having a clue how moving pictures were made.

"Sure," said Harold. "They don't just send the cans to the movie houses as is. They have to cut the film, take out parts, stick in parts and do all sorts of stuff like that."

"My goodness. I had no idea."

We were quiet for a few moments as we wandered the gravel path toward the Winkworth place. I wished I could just sit on one of the convenient benches placed here and there and read a book for an hour or so. But I hadn't brought a book with me, and anyway, I had a job to do.

"I swear, Harold, I think I'm going to have to go into another line of work. I don't believe I can take too many more Lolas," Lillian grumbled, breaking the silence. The poor thing looked as if she'd been through a minor battle.

"Buck up, Lillian," said Harold. "There's only one Lola in the world, and I wouldn't be surprised if rumors of her shenanigans on the set here put an end to her career."

"That's kind of a shame," I said, although I don't honestly know why. I neither liked nor approved of Lola de la Monica, who seemed more like a spoiled brat than a talented actress to me.

Harold shrugged. "Her choice. She's been warned." Turning, he gave me a broad grin, "Heck, Daisy, even Rolly's warned her."

"Who's Rolly?" Lillian wanted to know.

"Daisy's spirit control. Weren't you and Rolly married some thousand years or so ago, Daisy?"

I gave Harold a small frown. He made what I did for a living sound like a joke, and I didn't like it, even if he was partly right. "Yes, Harold. He is, and we were."

"Golly," breathed Lillian. "How fascinating."

"Daisy can tell you all about Rolly later, Lillian. Right now, I have to talk to Daisy about something else."

We'd reached the Winkworth mansion by that time, and we entered via the back door into the little room leading into the kitchen.

"Would you mind making a pot of tea, Lillian? I need to show Daisy something upstairs. This might take a half hour or so. You can relax and drink all the tea you want."

"Don't mind at all," said Lillian affably. "It'll be a pleasure to be alone for a while. Even a little bit of Lola is too many people for me."

Harold and I both laughed as we left Lillian in the kitchen. Our laughter died instantly when the door to the butler's pantry closed and we walked through to the dining room and toward the staircase. I whispered, "Did Monty get a letter, too?"

"Yes, and he's worried to death. So what you and I are going to do, my dear, is snoop."

"Snoop?" I blinked at Harold, puzzled.

"Snoop," he confirmed. "Your buddy Sam—"

"He's *not* my buddy!"

"Very well. Your *acquaintance* Detective Sam Rotondo was right when he said whoever is writing those thrice-damned letters is in this house, and you and I, my dear, are going to find out who the culprit is."

"We are?"

"Yes. Old lady Winkworth is out shopping with one of her maids, she's given leave for the rest of the domestic staff to watch the filming, and there's not another person in the house at the moment."

"Jeepers, how many people does it take to run this place, anyhow?"

"I don't know for sure. I think there are a couple of maids, a cook and a butler. And Miss Pennywhistle, of course."

"All those people for one cranky old lady," I said, disapproving, even though it wasn't any of my business how rich people lived.

"It's about like my mother's house," said Harold.

"I guess so. I just never thought much about it. Yet the woman has the nerve to deprecate her grandson's line of work." I made an unseemly huffing sound. "She reminds me of Billy." Naturally, I felt instantly guilty. Luckily, I was with Harold, who only chuckled softly.

"I know. People are never satisfied. At any rate, this is about the only chance we'll have to go through all the rooms and see if we can discover who's behind those letters."

"Excellent idea, Harold," I told him.

"I think so, too. Naturally, snooping is beneath the dignity of Mrs. Lurlene Winkworth, but she doesn't have to know anything about it. We have Monty's blessing. This letter thing has been really hard on him."

"I know. I'm sorry for him. I hope we can unearth the culprit."

"Me, too. Where should we start?"

I thought about it for a minute. "Don't people usually begin with the servants' quarters? That's what happens in all the detective novels I read."

"Well . . . I guess so. They're on the third floor."

So Harold led the way to an unobtrusive door on the second floor not far from Monty's bedroom suite, and opened it. There before us was a staircase.

"Oh, my," said I. "I didn't even realize that door opened onto a staircase. I thought it was a closet or something."

"One does tend to hide the servants, don't you know," Harold said drily.

"I guess so," I said doubtfully. "We don't have any. Servants, I mean. So I don't know how to go about hiding them."

"Mother stashes hers in a little suite of rooms off the breakfast room, and Algie uses the area belowstairs for his."

"Oh, yeah. I remember now. Edie and Quincy Applewood live in the kitchen suite, don't they?"

"I have no idea," said Harold. "Who are Edie and Quincy Applewood?"

"Good Lord, Harold! Edie and Quincy have worked for your mother for years."

I was kind of appalled until Harold said, "I haven't lived in my mother's house for ten years, Daisy. I don't know anything about her domestic arrangements, except for Featherstone, and he lives in an upstairs suite probably much like the one we're going to see now."

"Oh. I didn't know that." I'd always loved Featherstone, Mrs. Pinkerton's butler. He was so . . . I don't know. To my mind, he was the epitome of all things butlerish. Or butlerine. I don't

227

know if there's a word for it, actually.

Anyhow, as we chatted, we climbed the narrow staircase. Indeed, it was too narrow for us to walk side by side, so Harold went up first, gentleman that he was, in order that any dragons lurking up there would attack him first, I guess. I've often wondered how the rules of polite behavior came about.

The upstairs room was neat as a pin. It contained two narrow beds, two dressers, two wardrobes, and it led out onto the roof of the house, which was flat. Someone, probably one of the maids, who I assumed shared these quarters, had set out a couple of folding chairs and a card table on the roof. Curious, I walked onto the roof, and thought that whoever had set the table and chairs out there had acted on a brilliant idea. What a view! Why, you could see almost forever from up there.

"Wow, these are pretty nice slaves' quarters," I said to Harold. "Something like this would be great for Billy and me. If he could climb stairs." I sighed, as I nearly always did when I thought about my poor husband.

Harold snorted. "Slaves' quarters, indeed."

"Well, you know what I mean."

We didn't find anything even resembling the makings of anonymous letters in the maids' room, even though we looked into the wardrobes and through drawers. I felt like the worst kind of meddler, but I kept reminding myself that we were on an important mission, and stuffed my offended feelings inside myself and just did it.

Nothing.

"Very well," said Harold. "On to the second floor. That's where Monty and Mrs. Winkworth's apartments are."

"Do we need to search Monty's room?" I asked, surprised. "After all, he's the one getting the letters."

Harold shook his head. "We'd better. As little as I believe it, he might be writing the letters himself. God knows why. And I don't think he's doing it. The damned letters are upsetting him too much. Still, needs must."

"I guess," I said doubtfully. Then Gladys Pennywhistle occurred to me. "Where does Gladys sleep in this giant house?"

"She has a suite downstairs. Off that little room that leads into the kitchen. I doubt she's writing the letters, although you never know."

"True," I said. "You never know." I'd already considered Gladys before as the possible letter writer, but didn't say so to Harold. Gladys had so little imagination, it was difficult to imagine her as doing anything so outré as writing poison-pen letters. "Is Dr. Fellowes staying here for the duration? Will we have to search his rooms?"

"No. He has his own home near Cal Tech. He arrives after breakfast and generally leaves before dinner, unless Mrs. Winkworth needs a fourth for bridge. Thank God I never learned the game, or she might try to hook me." Harold shuddered. "Anyhow, I don't think he's the culprit, mainly because he hasn't had the opportunity to stick the letters where they've been found."

"That makes sense." I wasn't disappointed. Now that a romance seemed to be blossoming between Dr. Fellowes and Gladys, I didn't want either of them to be the guilty party.

The search of Monty's quarters didn't take long, and we didn't find anything. However, as we went through his drawers—actually, I let Howard handle the drawers as I searched the closet, I was impressed by the elegance of his belongings. To my practiced eye, it looked as if everything had been hand-tailored. No surprise there. The man was rich as Croesus, whoever he was.

"Nothing." Harold sounded relieved.

I was relieved, too. "I'm glad. I could almost picture Lola writing those letters, but I'd be awfully disappointed to learn that Monty was the culprit."

"You and me both."

"So who else is left?" I asked, my mind having wandered during my appraisal of Monty's fabulous duds. Then I thought about Monty's mother. I couldn't imagine Mrs. Hanratty as the letter writer, but figured I'd better ask. "Say, what about Mrs. Hanratty? Do we need to search her house, too?" It would kill me to discover that she'd been writing nasty letters to her own son."

"Next Saturday morning. That's when I plan to search her place."

"Good heavens, how do you expect to manage that?" I was impressed at the coolness of his plan, if a little appalled.

"Saturday morning is when she teaches her dog-obedience classes. You know that. For God's sake, you take Spike there."

"Well, I know that, but how will you get in?"

"Easy. I've already visited her home, and Mrs. Hanratty, just like everyone else in the known universe, keeps a spare key under the doormat. I'll just unlock the door and walk right in."

"What about any servants? Won't they think it odd that you're there while Mrs. Hanratty isn't?"

"Mrs. Hanratty, unlike her mother Mrs. Winkworth, doesn't need a staff of thousands to cater to her needs. She has a daily maid during the week and nobody at all on weekends, when she takes her meals with her mother and Monty, when he's in town."

"Oh." I was already fond of Mrs. Hanratty. Learning of her simple—well, simpler, anyway—living habits, only boosted her in my esteem. "Okay. So that takes care of her. Who's next on our list in this house?"

"Mrs. Winkworth."

"You honestly think we need to search Mrs. Winkworth's quarters?" I asked him. "Surely she can't be the one sending nasty notes to her own grandson. A grandson, moreover, who provided her these magnificent digs." I threw my arms wide in an all-encompassing gesture meant to include the entire estate and its three mansions and extensive grounds.

"She violently disapproves of the way Monty makes his moola," said Harold with a shrug. "She keeps wanting him to quit the pictures."

"But then she wouldn't have this great house, would she?"

"Probably not. I'm sure Monty still owes a good deal on this property. If he no longer worked in the pictures, he'd undoubtedly have to sell the place."

"Does she know that?"

"I'm sure she must."

"Good Lord. The woman's an idiot."

"Perhaps. But she's old and set in her ways. She keeps waiting for her beloved South to rise again."

I chuffed out an undignified breath. "She ought to be grateful she lives in southern California, at least. Heck, Monty might have bought her a mansion in San Francisco, and then wouldn't she have a lot to complain about?"

A laugh was all the response I got to that silly question.

"Well," said I as we traversed the mammoth hallway to the other end of the house where Mrs. Winkworth's suite of rooms lay, "I sure hope Mrs. Hanratty will turn out not to be the culprit. I like her a whole lot."

"I know what you mean. Monty thinks she's a dear, even if she is a little loud for him. He's quite the sensitive plant, you know."

"Oh."

Harold laughed again, and opened the door to Mrs. Winkworth's suite of rooms.

CHAPTER EIGHTEEN

Elegant is the word that springs to mind when I recall stepping into Mrs. Winkworth's sitting room. The furniture was all the same variety as furnished the rest of the house. Louis the Whateverth.

I stood, staring around me for a moment or two, then said, "Wow."

"Yeah," agreed Harold. "And every stick of furniture was paid for by Monty Mountjoy."

Shaking my head, I said, "Why in the world would anybody complain about living in this kind of luxury, especially if she'd been saved from abject poverty?"

"Beats me," said Harold. "I guess it was *genteel* abject poverty, and she misses the genteel part."

"Hey, I think we in Pasadena are pretty darned genteel."

"So do I, but she's from the great State of South Carolina, and I guess they're more genteel than we are. According to Monty, she thinks all people from the North are heathens and bullies."

"I see. Therefore she considers genteel poverty superior to crass wealth?"

"Your guess is as good as mine." Harold heaved a sigh. "Well, let's get to it. Her maid does a pretty good job of keeping everything spiffy, doesn't she?"

"Yes," I said, admiring a built-in bookcase crafted of some no-doubt wildly expensive imported wood. Curious, I walked to the bookcase and scanned the book titles. No murder mysteries for Mrs. Winkworth, thank you very much. Poetry seemed to be her particular pleasure in life. Old poetry. The sonnets of Shakespeare, James Leigh Hunt, William Wordsworth. I was kind of surprised to see an Edith Wharton novel on the shelves, and wondered if Mrs. Winkworth had disapproved of *The Age of Innocence*. Probably.

But I most assuredly wouldn't find a glue pot and cut-up newspapers in the bookcase, so I wandered off to another room, which turned out to be the bed chamber. Hoity-toity, indeed. But no signs of crumpled newspapers or chicanery.

Then I walked into a room that looked as if Mrs. Winkworth used it as sort of an office. There stood one of those dainty little French desks, with curly edges and gilt, adorned with scented paper and an array of pen holders and so forth. Believing that this particular search was doomed to failure, I pulled open the top drawer.

And I gasped.

"Harold!" I cried. "Come here!"

Harold did, at a run, and we both stared into the open drawer. Here's what lay there: shreds of clipped-up newspapers, a pair of scissors, a glue pot, and a jar of black ink. I inspected the pens in the pen holders and, sure enough, there resided a fountain pen with the exactly width of nib that had been used to create all those blasted exclamation points. I lifted out a sheet of newspaper. "This is the *Los Angeles Times*," I told Harold, feeling more than slightly stunned.

"And here's a *Pasadena Herald*." He lifted up another newspaper. "And a *Star News*."

"I'm surprised the word *tragedy* appears so often in the papers," I said musingly.

Harold, who knew his stuff, said, "I'm not. Look here."

I looked. There before me, bold as brass, on the theatrical offerings page of the *Los Angeles Times,* I read the words: "*King Lear,* a tragedy by William Shakespeare." Only the word *tragedy* had been neatly snipped out. "Well, I'll be darned," I whispered, faintly benumbed. "Why, the wicked old crone."

"Speaking of *wicked,*" said Harold, "I wonder . . ." He flipped through more of the *Times.* "No. I don't see it here."

A thought occurred to me at that moment, and I picked up the *Pasadena Herald.* Yup. There it was: *The Wizard of Oz,* by L. Frank Baum, being presented as a play for children at the Shakespearean Society. "Look here, Harold. See the cast of characters? She's cut out the 'wicked' before the witch."

"Funny that the Shakespearean Society is putting on the Baum play instead of *King Lear,* huh?"

"I suppose so, but that's immaterial. Whatever are we supposed to do now?"

"Lord, I don't know. I guess I'll have to tell Monty."

"But we can't tell Lola," I said, my mind conjuring images of Lola murdering Mrs. Winkworth in a fit of passion. "And somehow or other we have to get the old bat to stop sending the letters."

"You're right, of course," said Harold. "Lord, what a pickle."

"I can't *believe* that woman sent her own grandson those awful letters!" I said, becoming indignant all over again. "Why, he's done everything for her! What ingratitude! Shakespeare had it backwards. What's sharper than a serpent's tooth is a nasty old granny who doesn't appreciate what her grandson's done for her."

"Well . . . Don't forget Stacy, Daisy."

Stacy Kincaid, Harold's ghastly sister, was indeed a problem child, and not even I could deny that. Stacy had been a thorn in my side for as long as I'd known her. "I guess that's true. Maybe it works both ways."

"The next important question is whether or not to tell your

detective buddy."

"Sam?" I stared at Harold, aghast. "No! We should definitely *not* tell Sam!"

"I don't know. If we don't tell him, he might keep snooping and discover that Monty's been getting letters as well as Lola, and then Monty's secret will come out, and his career will be over. Let's talk about it some more later. Can you come over tonight? Maybe the three of us—you, Monty, and I—can work out some sort of strategy that will keep the secret from Lola and at the same time get the old woman to stop writing the letters. We don't want the police to know Monty's been getting the letters, that's for sure."

"True."

"Can you get away tonight?"

I heaved yet another heavy sigh. "I suppose so. Billy's going to hate it." It occurred to me that I might ask Sam over for dinner again that night. And maybe Flossie and Johnny Buckingham, too, if Aunt Vi didn't mind. That would give Billy lots of company while I was at the Winkworth mansion, plotting. *Plotting.* Gee, that sounds like such an ominous word. But we'd be plotting for good and not for evil, so that took some of the bite out of the word.

"But we'd better get downstairs now. Poor Lillian's probably wondering what's happened to us." Harold grinned at me. "Maybe she'll start a rumor that the two of us are having an affair."

My eyes must have opened wide in horror, because Harold said, "Not really, Daisy. Lillian knows exactly what I am. And your own moral rectitude is well known in the City of Pasadena and its outer reaches."

"I should hope so. That wasn't even funny, Harold."

"I guess not."

We put things back into Mrs. Winkworth's desk drawer as

closely as possible to the way we'd found them. I was still figuratively shaking my head in wonder and disgust as we descended the grand staircase and moseyed to the kitchen. Mrs. Winkworth. Of all people. Writing snotty letters to the grandson who'd provided her with the means to live a life of ease and luxury. It sure didn't seem fair to me.

As soon as we entered the kitchen, Lillian said, "Gee, you guys, I was about to send out a search party."

"Sorry. We had some stuff to discuss. My mother's coming home soon, you know, and I want Daisy to perform a special séance for her."

Could Harold lie like a rug, or could he not? I was impressed.

"Oh, boy," said Lillian. "I'd love to come to one of your séances, Daisy. I've never been to one."

Because I had an image to protect and project, I said, "Perhaps we can arrange that one of these days. Séances take a lot out of me, but the attendees seem to get benefit from them."

I noticed Harold rolling his eyes but didn't kick him, because I didn't want Lillian to see. "Daisy's the best spiritualist in Pasadena," he said, so I forgave him the eye roll.

"That's what everyone says," agreed Lillian, perking me up some. It was nice to have a good reputation.

She poured Harold and me each a cup of tea and set a plate with two doughnuts on it on the kitchen table. I reached for a doughnut and took a sip of tea.

And then an absolutely brilliant idea occurred to me, and I knew exactly what we might do to make Mrs. Winkworth cease and desist from writing those God-awful letters. A séance! If Rolly could (almost) make Lola de la Monica behave herself, I'd be willing to bet he could threaten the silly Mrs. Winkworth into submission. But I couldn't tell Harold about my bright idea then; the revelation would have to wait until the evening. In the meantime . . .

I finished my doughnut and tea and said, "Say, Harold, where's the telephone in this place? I need to make a couple of 'phone calls."

"Under the stairwell, I think, just like in my mother's house."

"Be right back," said I.

Harold was right about the positioning of the telephone. So I first dialed Aunt Vi to ask if she'd mind if we had three guests for dinner that night, providing two of the guests could come. Sam was a given. He always came over when we invited him to dinner.

"Why, I guess so, Daisy. Who do you plan to invite?"

"Sam, for one. And then I've been wanting to see Flossie and Johnny Buckingham for the longest time, but this stupid job is keeping me away from home and visiting all day. I thought maybe we could invite them for dinner, too."

"Oh, my!" said Aunt Vi, and I could hear the eagerness in her voice. "That's a lovely idea, Daisy. I'd be happy to see Johnny again. And isn't his wife expecting?"

"She sure is, and I bet she'd be pleased as punch not to have to cook for one night."

"I'm sure that's so. Have you already asked them, or will you ring me back and tell me if they're able to make it. If they can, I do believe I'm going to fix a pork roast."

Oh, yum! I loved Aunt Vi's pork roast. Of course, I loved everything Aunt Vi cooked. "I'll telephone the Salvation Army right now and get back to you, Vi. Thank you!"

Fortunately for me, it was Flossie herself who answered the telephone. She worked in the office a lot, doing secretarial stuff for Johnny. I don't think the Salvation Army could afford to hire a professional secretary, but Flossie just loved doing good works now that she'd changed her wicked ways, as Mrs. Winkworth might have said. Genteelly of course.

"How nice!" she cried, true joy in her voice. "I've been want-

ing to see you for the longest time, Daisy. We've been so busy
here lately."

"Likewise. Aunt Vi is going to fix a roast pork, which is one
of her most delicious things to eat." Then I remembered that
Flossie was pregnant—or *with child,* as the prudes put it—and
asked cautiously, "That won't make you sick or anything, will
it?"

She laughed, a happy sound that was so unlike the Flossie I'd
met a little over a year ago that my heart gave a little leap. I'd
done my part in that relationship and was proud of it. Flossie
and Johnny had practically been made for each other.

"Oh, no. I'm past the morning-sickness time. In fact, I've
been eating like a pig for weeks now."

"Good, then tonight you can eat a real one. See you at six?
Will that be all right? I've got to go back to work again at eight-
thirty or so, but we should have a good chat before then."

"Oh, my, Daisy, you work too hard."

"Nuts," I said, even though I agreed with her. "I don't mind
at all." And there was yet another lie to add to my growing list.
Ah, well. According to the Methodist principles that had been
drummed into my ears since I could walk, God would forgive
me if I asked him to. Good thing, too, because it looked as
though I was going to be requiring a whole lot of forgiveness.

I called Vi back, told her to expect Johnny, Flossie and Sam
for dinner, and then joined Harold and Lillian as they walked
back to the set.

Naturally, Sam was suspicious when I asked him to come to
our house for dinner that night. He squinted at me. "Why?
What are you going to be doing that you require someone to
divert Billy's attention from it?"

"Nuts to you, Sam. I have to come back here after dinner,
and I don't like leaving Billy alone. Flossie and Johnny Buckingham are going to come to dinner, too, so you'll have lots of

company, and so will Billy." I hesitated, and then admitted, "I've been really worried about Billy lately, Sam. His attitude has changed somehow. I can't quite put my finger on it, but it worries me."

Sam honored me with a frown. How typical. "I haven't noticed any difference. I think it's your guilty conscience playing tricks on you."

Drat the man! "It is not! You're so unfair, Sam Rotondo. I don't know why Billy and the rest of my family like you so much."

He chuckled. "I'm a nice guy, Daisy."

"You are not," I said bitterly. "You're always suspecting me of things."

"That's because you're usually up to something."

"I am not! Anyhow, I've helped your stupid police department more than once, if you'll recall."

"It's not my police department. It's the police department belonging to the fair city of Pasadena, and you only helped us because you had to."

"Oh, you drive me crazy!" I said, and stamped away from him toward more congenial company. Unfortunately, there wasn't any to be had. Harold and Lillian were in a huddle over costumes, and the camera people and the rest of the crew were busily cranking away, filming a love scene between Monty and Lola. Poor Monty. The things he had to do for his art. On the other hand, he got paid plenty to do it.

Which reminded me that it was his very grandmother who'd had him in a tizzy for however long she'd been sending him those awful letters. I could almost understand why she sent them to Lola, because she undoubtedly had read all the newspaper accounts of Lola and Monty being thick with each other. I wonder if it would shock her more to learn Monty's true predilection and suspected it would. I still didn't think she'd be

willing to give up her grand home on San Pasqual for the sake
of moral indignation. Stupid woman. And completely illogical,
too. Talk about biting the hand that fed her! Monty ought to
take her to his mother's obedience training classes and teach
her some manners.

My attempt to rid myself of Sam's company came to naught.
As I stood watching John Bohnert direct Monty and Lola in
their love scene and contemplating the nature of manners, I
nearly jumped out of my skin when Sam's voice came from
right smack next to me. I whipped my head around so fast, I
nearly got whiplash.

"So have you given any more thought to the letters Lola's
been getting?" he asked as if I hadn't just walked away from
him in a huff. Imperturbable. That was Sam all over. What's
more, he'd taken to looming over me again.

I took a step away from him and snapped, "Yes."

"Oh? Come to any conclusions?"

Hmm. This presented a problem. There were so darned many
things to consider. Bother. I decided I'd just have to hash it all
out with Monty and Harold that evening after dinner.

Therefore, I said, "No."

Sam said, "Huh."

I thinned my eyes and peered up at him. "You don't believe
me, do you?"

"Not for a second."

"For crumb's sake, Sam, do you think *I've* been writing the
stupid letters?"

"Of course not. But I know damned well you know more
about them than you've told me."

"Nuts. I don't know any more about them than you do."
Another lie. Shoot. I was really piling them up, wasn't I? The
words *divine retribution* flitted through my mind, but I drove
them out. None of this was my fault, curse it!

"Right," said Sam.

What nominally passed for our conversation was interrupted by a sharp cry from Lola. I looked at the set again and saw that she was in a flaming temper and stamping her foot. Poor Monty, clearly unhappy about it, stepped away from her. I felt sorry for him. If what Harold had told me about him was correct, all he wanted in this life was peace and quiet. And what was he getting? Poison-pen letters and Lola de la Monica, not a combination geared toward either peace or quiet.

"I *won't* do it again!" Lola shrieked. "You can't make me!"

"Dammit, Lola, I'm the director, I say we need another take, and *I'll* make you, if you don't cooperate on your own. I want to get the angle right."

"I," declared Lola, "am beautiful from all angles."

"Good God, the woman is a real shrew, isn't she?" said Sam.

"She is that," I agreed. It was kind of nice to agree with Sam about something every now and then.

"I thought you'd got her to behave herself. Wasn't that the point of your so-called private séance?"

"Yes," I said upon a heartfelt sigh. "That was precisely the point of the private séance. Lola, however, is a tough nut to crack." Knowing where my duty lay, I murmured, "Well, I guess I'd better intervene. It's my job, after all."

"Huh," said Sam. "Crappy job you have."

I agreed with him about that, too.

CHAPTER NINETEEN

"She objected to having to kiss Monty Mountjoy?" Flossie said, clearly astounded, her fork halfway to her mouth.

"She objected to having to kiss him *again*," I corrected her. Then I looked toward Johnny, who seemed perfectly serene in the face of his wife's obvious appreciation of Monty's manly beauties. Well, he should be. Flossie was as devoted to him as a woman could be to a man. Just like I was devoted to Billy, as a matter of fact.

"She's a general pain in the a—neck," said Sam, who was devouring Aunt Vi's delicious pork roast and mashed potatoes as if he hadn't eaten for a week and a half. "If she hadn't objected to that, she'd have objected to something else."

"Sounds like a very unpleasant female," Johnny commented, and forked another carrot into his mouth. "Not that I should say so, being a man of the cloth and all." He grinned as he chewed. Johnny had a great sense of humor, man of the cloth or not.

"She's about the most unpleasant female I've ever met," I told the assembled diners. "I'm sorry I ever took this job. Not only is Lola a pain to work with, but she's always causing me to leave home at night." I figured it was time to tell my family my plans for the evening. "In fact, I've got to go back there again tonight, and I don't want to."

"Shoot, Daisy, not again?" Billy eyed me with something less than disfavor and more like disappointment.

My heart lurched, and I reached across the table and took his hand. "I'm so sorry, Billy. I swear, I'll never take another job like this again in my life. I promise."

He'd have sighed if he could, I'm sure. "That's all right. I understand. The job sounded pretty good at first."

I stared at him, still holding his hand. Why was Billy all of a sudden being understanding about my job? His behavior had undergone an enormous change in recent weeks, and I didn't trust it. Was he finally coming to grips with his disabilities and my work? I didn't think so. But what the heck was going on here?

I said, "Thanks, Billy. I'd much rather stay home, believe me." I let go of his hand so we could both get back to Vi's delicious meal.

"Why do you have to go back tonight?" asked Sam.

I should have expected the question from him. Everyone else at the table just took it for granted that someone at the Winkworth estate needed my services. Not Sam. He suspected I was up to something. The fact that he was right didn't endear him to me one little bit.

"When I was trying to calm Lola down today, she asked me to come over and comfort her with the Ouija board and the tarot cards after dinner tonight."

"She's staying at the Winkworth place?" asked Ma.

"Yes. She and Monty Mountjoy both are staying there for the duration of the shoot. Of course, it's natural for Mr. Mountjoy to stay there, since both his mother and his grandmother live on the property."

"You're sure it's Lola you're going to see?" asked Billy.

I gaped at him. "Who else would I be going to see? I work for her." Oh, Lord, he wasn't going to have a fit of jealousy again, was he? Last year he'd practically accused me of having an affair with Johnny Buckingham, of all people.

Billy shrugged. "Mountjoy's a good-looking man. You're a good-looking woman."

"Thank you. I'm also a *married* woman, Billy Majesty." My feelings were honestly hurt by his words. I would never, ever, cheat on my husband, and if he didn't know that by this time he'd never learn.

"Daisy's a good girl," said my staunch father. "We brought her up right."

Billy smiled at him. "I know. I guess I just can't help worrying sometimes. Heck, look at me." He gestured at the wheelchair, which Sam had pushed up to the table. "I'd hardly blame her for being interested in a whole man."

"Billy," I said, shaking my head. "You honestly don't understand by this time that I love you? I've loved you all my life. Well, since I was five, anyhow."

He gave a comical grimace. "I guess I can't forget that. Heck, you chased me all over creation when we were kids."

"Darned right I did," I said, striving for a light tone that didn't feel right at all. Inside, I felt as heavy as if my heart were made of lead. "And I finally wore you down, too."

"You did," agreed Billy. "I tried to escape, but you caught me in the end." He grinned, looking genuinely happy. I didn't know what to think.

"I think that's so romantic," breathed Flossie, who had a romantic disposition in spite of her early life of hardship on the mean streets of New York City. She'd been working on trying to rid herself of her Eastern accent, and was doing a darned good job of it. I really liked Flossie. She'd been through a lot and had lifted herself up by her bootstraps, as it were. Sort of like Johnny, actually. The two were good for each other.

After we'd eaten entirely too much of Vi's delicious pork roast, mashed potatoes and gravy, carrots, and a lovely gelled salad into which she'd inserted celery, pineapple and a bunch of other goodies, Ma and I cleared the plates from the table and brought out the dessert dishes.

"Apple crumble for dessert," said Vi, fetching it. "With cream."

Be still, my heart. "I love your apple crumble, Vi," I said in a rapturous voice.

"You love everything," she said, but she appreciated my words; I could tell.

Dessert, as ever, was a wonderful end to a wonderful meal. I felt very sorry for Vi, who had lost her only child in the war and then her husband to the Spanish flu, but the Gumm-Majesty household was much the richer for her tragic losses.

Flossie, Ma and I washed the dishes while the men settled in the living room, chatting. I was sure they'd break out the card table pretty soon and begin playing gin rummy, since that's what always happened when Sam came to dinner. I hoped Flossie wouldn't mind if Johnny joined them, and told her so.

She laughed. "Oh, my, no. My poor Johnny works too hard. He needs some time to have fun with friends every once in a while. Anyhow, I brought my knitting."

"You knit?" I asked her, impressed. "I've always wanted to learn to knit."

"I can teach you."

Ma heaved a sigh. "I try to knit every now and then, but I'm terrible at it. I'm much better at crocheting."

"I can teach you, too."

"I'd love that. Thank you, Flossie. What are you knitting at the moment? Baby things, I expect."

"I'm knitting a little matinee sweater. Actually, this is the third one. People have told me that you can never have too many of them."

"That's the truth," said Ma, nodding wisely.

I'd never even thought about matinee sweaters for babies,

since I'd never have any, but the notion brought up an interesting question. At least I thought it was. "What colors are you using? I mean, you won't know if the baby's a boy or a girl until it's born, so I guess you're steering clear of blue and pink."

"Yellow, green and white so far," she said.

"You look so happy, Flossie," I blurted out. "I'm so glad."

"I am happy, Daisy. And it's all because of you."

"Nuts. You and Johnny were destined to find each other."

She shook her head. "I don't know about that. If you hadn't shown up when you did, I'd probably be dead by now."

"Now that's a dismal thought," said Ma, interested in our conversation in spite of herself.

"But it's the truth. Surely you know the story, Mrs. Gumm," said Flossie.

Ma colored slightly. She knew the story, all right, every sordid inch of it. "Um . . . yes. You were most unfortunate, dear. But that's in the past now."

"It is. And it's all because of Daisy," Flossie repeated.

I said, "Nuts," again, and dropped the subject, because it embarrassed me. Flossie and I had met in a speakeasy. She had at the time been what's commonly known as a "gangster's moll," and I was there to do a séance. Honest to God. What's more, I didn't want to be there at all. I'd been all but forced into doing the séance for the sake of Mrs. Pinkerton, then Mrs. Kincaid. Anyhow, life had been pretty darned perilous for a while, but it all turned out all right in the end, which I guess is the important part.

At any rate, I was glad Flossie didn't anticipate being bored when I took my leave, which I did shortly thereafter. I didn't want to go to the Winkworth estate again that night almost as much as I hadn't wanted to go to that accursed speakeasy. But duty called.

After the last dish had been put away, I decided to do

something I'd been dreading. Heading into the living room, I smiled at the company and said, bold as brass, "Say, Sam, if you figure out who's been writing Lola those letters, will you arrest the writer?"

I guess I'd interrupted some kind of interesting conversation, because Billy, Sam, Johnny and Pa all swiveled to gape at me. Billy said, "What letters?"

Bother. Sometimes I wish I weren't so precipitate. Often, in fact. I blame my straight-arrow nature on my being born under the sign of Sagittarius, although I'm sure that's unchristian thinking on my part. "Lola de la Monica has been getting threatening letters," I told my husband. And the rest of the guys, but he'd asked the question.

"Why are you asking about arresting the letter writer?" Sam asked in full suspicious-of-Daisy mode.

"Just wondering," I said with a smile that felt as counterfeit as it probably looked.

Sam rose from the sofa, where he'd been sitting next to Pa. "Daisy, if you know who's—"

"Darn it, Sam, all I want to know is if you can arrest someone for writing the stupid letters. Or does somebody have to . . . what do you call it?" I couldn't think of the right word, not being particularly acute about police matters, even though I read detective novels all the time.

"Press charges?" Billy asked, trying to be helpful.

I shot him a grateful smile. "That's the word! Does someone have to press charges, or can you arrest a person for writing anonymous letters without anyone, um, pressing charges?"

The way Sam was glowering at me, you'd think he suspected *me* of writing the idiotic letters. "Why do you want to know that?" he asked again.

I huffed. "Oh, never mind," I said. "I was just curious, was all." Not to mention the fact that I really needed to know. It

247

would make all the difference in the world if Monty would have to press charges against his grandmother, because he wouldn't. However, if Sam could arrest the old lady without having charges pressed against her—gee, that sounds odd—then it wouldn't matter, and I'd be more than happy to tell Sam all about her misguided attempts to get her grandson to quit the picture business.

Much to my disappointment, Sam didn't blurt out an answer. Rather, he scowled at me every minute as I kissed my husband and my father, gave Johnny a sunny smile, and even allowed Sam a pleasant look as I headed toward the front door.

By the time I'd said my good-byes, persuaded Spike that he couldn't go with me and got into the Chevrolet, night had fallen, so I didn't even have the consolation of pretty scenery as I drove south on Marengo. What's more, I was bone-tired. Lola de la Monica could really take the stuffing out of the people who had to work with her.

Harold and Monty were happy to see me, though, even if Gladys didn't appear overjoyed at my arrival. I don't think she really cared much, though, since I noticed she was again paired with Dr. Homer Fellowes at a bridge match being waged in the living room. Mrs. Winkworth was partnered with John Bohnert, poor fellow, who had probably been finagled into staying for dinner and bridge. The only problem with bridge, as I saw it, was that the proponents of the game always seemed compelled to rehash the last evening's game again the following day. Everyone I knew who played bridge did that. I wasn't enamored of card games or I might have learned bridge and done the same thing myself, thereby boring all my acquaintances who didn't play the game. Odd how life works sometimes, isn't it?

However, I was there to conduct a powwow with Monty and Harold, so I forgot all about bridge as soon as Monty opened the door to his suite of rooms. He seemed happy to see me, and even gave me a little hug. The sitting room was as pleasant as ever, and it held a scent of some masculine cologne and some probably very expensive pipe tobacco.

"So you found the culprit, and it's Granny!" He broke into laughter.

I think I was glad about that; I mean his sense of humor about what had been a harrowing ordeal seemed considerably better to me than him wanting to seek revenge on his nasty old grandmother. I told him so.

"Oh, Gran's all right, really. It's only that she disapproves so strenuously of the dissipated lives of so many picture people."

"Your life isn't dissipated," I pointed out with some bitterness. "And I think she was a beast to send you those letters."

"I think so, too," Harold piped in from the sidelines.

Monty gave a most elegant shrug. I swear, every single gesture the man made might have been choreographed. He dressed well, too. That evening he wore tan flannel trousers, a white shirt, and a rather raffish scarlet neckerchief. His smoking jacket was dark brown and had those leather patches on the elbows. I'm not altogether sure what use those patches served, but they looked good. Of course, just about anything would have looked good on Monty Mountjoy.

"Gran's only old and set in her ways," said Monty.

"I think you're being very generous," I said.

"But we still have to figure out how to get her to stop writing the letters," Harold said, bringing our attention back to the matter at hand. "Do you have any thoughts on the matter, Daisy?"

"Actually," said I, rather proud of myself, "I have, and I think I can do it."

"You do?" Monty's eyes opened wide, and he appeared both surprised and pleased.

"I figured you'd know what to do." Harold's voice held a

note of satisfaction that I appreciated.

"Let's all sit down and get comfortable, and you can explain your idea to us, Daisy," suggested Monty, gesturing to a sofa and two chairs neatly arranged before a fireplace, unlit this warm evening.

So we all sat, Monty offered us all drinks, I refused, Harold took a cream sherry, and our session began.

"What I recommend is that I perform another séance. During that séance, I can have Rolly make a general announcement to those present that the writer of the letters is known to the spirits on the Other Side, and they disapprove. Heartily disapprove, in fact. Then he can say something along the lines that if the writer doesn't stop sending the letters, something *truly* awful will happen. None of your grandmother's innocuous threats for Rolly, Monty. I fear Rolly might have to put the fear of God—"

"Or the devil," Harold slid in slyly.

I nodded. "Or the devil into her, but at least she'll stop sending the letters. I can almost guarantee it, your grandmother being more amenable to discipline than Lola. I truly tried to get Rolly to make Lola behave, but—"

This time it was Monty who interrupted me. "He did, though. I mean you did. She's at least a hundred percent better than she was before you got Rolly to talk to her." He shook his head. "Good God, what a strange conversation we're having."

I laughed. It was the first time I'd felt like laughing in days. But it really was an absurd conversation. It might make anyone laugh, talking about a patently spurious spirit giving advice to misbehaving adults and those adults actually taking the spurious spirit's advice.

"Say, Daisy, I'd like to take you and your family out to dinner at the end of this shoot," said Monty then, surprising me. "You deserve to be feted for your hard work on the set. You're the only one I've ever met who's been able to affect Lola's behavior in any way at all, and it would be my great pleasure. Besides, Harold's told me of your many sacrifices on his mother's behalf, and I know full well how you've sacrificed yourself for this picture."

I could feel myself blush. "Oh, but really, that would be too—"

"No, it wouldn't," said Harold, as if he'd proffered the invitation and not Monty. "If anyone deserves a night out, it's you. Besides, you know darned well your family would love to meet Monty. Well, maybe Billy wouldn't, but your mother and father and aunt would."

"Well . . . thank you, Monty. I'd love it. And I have a feeling Billy would enjoy it. That's very nice of you."

"I was thinking about the Hotel Castleton. They have a beautiful restaurant there, and . . . well, Harold's told me about your husband's afflictions, which he incurred in freeing Europe from the Kaiser's iron grip. If we dined at the Castleton, your husband wouldn't have very far to go to get there. It would be my true pleasure to host a party in your honor and his."

Darned if his words didn't bring tears to my eyes. What a swell person Monty Mountjoy was. "Thank you," I said, feeling humble. "That would be wonderful."

"Thank *you*. You not only assisted us with Lola, but you and Harold discovered who was writing those letters, which had been fretting me for weeks now."

"I still can hardly believe your own grandmother wrote the letters, Monty. I think . . . well, I think it stinks, and I think you're being overly nice in forgiving her."

Yet another elegant shrug. "I've known my grandmother all my life, Daisy, and I understand her perhaps a little better than you do."

"You must, if you can forgive her for writing those horrid letters. And to think of all you've done for her, too."

He gave a more-or-less whimsical smile. "My mother and I came to grips with the old lady's prejudices and idiosyncrasies a long time ago. Gran will never be brought to see that the glorious South lost the Civil War and that it's never going to 'rise again,' as they like to say. Besides, South Carolina was the very first state to secede from the Union. For Gran and folks like her, that's a point of pride."

"Oh, brother," I said before I could stop myself.

He chuckled. "I know. However, it's difficult for Yankees to understand how some Southerners feel about the conflict. And Gran's own grandfather was a high-ranking Confederate officer, don't forget. A colonel, in fact. He was even wounded in action."

I thought, but didn't say, proving yet again that occasionally I pause before I speak, that that was the way wars ought to work. Make the high ranking people or, even better, the guys who start the wars, fight them and leave the young men at home where they belong. What I said was, "I see. I suppose I can understand that."

"Not only that, but she believes all the publicity she reads in the papers," said Harold, "even though Monty's told her it's mostly bunkum. She honestly believes the bright lights of Hollywoodland are leading her grandson astray."

"That's only because she worries about the state of her grandson's moral health," said Monty, grinning. "She's had many burdens to bear as regards her family, don't forget. She was totally appalled when Mother began teaching dog-obedience classes, considering anything to do with dogs except hunting beneath the dignity of a fine old Southern family. Then, when I went into the pictures, she nearly died of horror."

"Even though you lifted her from poverty to all this." I waved my arms in an all-inclusive gesture.

"I probably should have bought her an old plantation in

South Carolina, but it seemed a stupid thing to do, since it would have cost more to fix up one of those dilapidated places than it cost to buy this entire complex. This way I got a home for Mother, too. And even one for me, should I ever need a retreat. I do like being around my family, even if it is . . . odd."

"Your family's no odder than any other family I've met," I told him. It was the truth, too. My work had taken me into all sorts of homes, mainly those of the rich and foolish, and there wasn't one of those homes that didn't keep, or at least try to keep, the secrets of its owners. No matter what the family, it could be guaranteed to contain people who were eccentric, if not downright evil. Heck, Harold Kincaid's own father was a rotter through and through. I could go on listing prominent families in Pasadena and tell you their oddities from now to kingdom come, and there'd still be some left over.

"I know you're right," he said. "Still, I understand Gran's reasons for being unhappy about living here and about Mother and me and how we earn our livings. If we lived life according to the tenets of her childhood, we'd be sitting on a dilapidated plantation, growing tobacco and owning slaves."

"Slaves," I said, and shuddered.

"You got that right," said Harold.

"I couldn't agree with you more," said Monty. "But she's old and set in her ways."

"So you've said." I didn't mean to sound as unkind as I did. But really. If ever there was an abomination perpetrated on earth, it was the practice people had of enslaving other people. I know slavery still goes on today; that doesn't make it right.

"Getting back to Granny, when would you like to conduct this séance?"

I blew out a considering breath. "The sooner the better, I guess. Lola will have fewer reasons to throw temperaments if the letters stop."

"Good point," said Harold. "What day is today, anyway?"

I had to think for a minute. "Wednesday."

"How about Friday night? The shooting is nearly done, and that will give Daisy an evening home with her family before she has to spend another evening out." He glanced at me with sympathy. "Her husband doesn't like having her working day and night."

"I don't blame him," said Monty, the gallant gentleman.

"That's for sure. I guess Friday will be all right," I said. "Billy's almost used to me conducting séances on Friday and Saturday nights, even though he doesn't approve of them."

"Rather like my granny doesn't approve of my acting?" Monty asked in a sugary voice.

"You have a point," I admitted. "A valid point." I thought about something else. "By the way, I think I'm going to have to tell Sam Rotondo it's your grandmother behind the letters."

"Why?" Harold demanded.

"I don't want the police involved." Monty sounded as adamant as Harold.

"I don't either," said I. "Which is the whole point. Don't you see? We don't want Sam snooping into the matter and discovering things we don't want him to discover. If I tell him who's behind the letters, he'll stop snooping. If I don't, he's sure to continue. He's like a bulldog that way." As I had reason to know from personal experience.

It took a mere second or two for the two men to understand my meaning.

"Oh," said Harold. "I guess that's true."

Monty said, "Oh. I suppose it is. But . . . what about Gran? Will they arrest her? I don't want that to happen."

Thinking bitterly of my questioning of Sam Rotondo before I left home that evening, I said with regret, "I don't know. I asked Sam if a person had to press charges against another person in order for an arrest to be made in a poison-pen case, but he didn't answer me." I sniffed. "He doesn't trust me."

"Hmm," said Harold in mock seriousness. "I wonder why that is."

"Darn it, Harold, there's no reason on the face of this green earth that Sam shouldn't trust me. I've helped the Pasadena Police Department more than once to catch criminals, don't forget."

"How could I ever forget?" asked Harold with a shudder. He'd been picked up with me at that accursed speakeasy.

"You know, Daisy," said Monty musingly, "I do believe I'd have to press charges in order for an arrest to be made, although I'm not entirely sure. See if you can find out from your detective friend. Or maybe I can have someone else ask him." He frowned. "No. I'd better not do that. I don't want anyone even thinking that I've been getting letters, too."

I sighed as I rose from my comfy chair. "I'll see if I can find out. Maybe I can make a general-interest telephone call to the police station and someone will answer the question. It's a simple question, after all." I said that mostly to make myself feel better.

Anyhow, we agreed that I'd visit the Winkworth mansion yet again, this time on Friday night, to conduct a séance and, with luck and strong words from Rolly, get Monty's grandmother to cease and desist writing her poison-pen letters.

Sometimes I hated my job.

CHAPTER TWENTY

"Again?" Billy sounded disgruntled, as well he might.

"I'm sorry, Billy. But this is the last time. I promise. Besides, the shooting will wrap up next week, and then there will only be publicity shots to do in order to advertise the picture, and then I can come home and stay home."

"It's about time," he grumbled.

I agreed with him. We were again seated at the breakfast table, Vi having set before us bacon, scrambled eggs and toast. You'd think scrambled eggs and bacon would be the same the world over, but I swear Vi's were better than any others I've ever eaten. Of course, she baked her own bread, too, and it was so good, it was probably sinful. Most delicious or fun things were sinful, after all.

"Besides," I said, remembering Monty's generous offer to treat my entire family to a wonderful meal at an elegant restaurant, "Monty Mountjoy wants to take us all out to dinner at the Hotel Castleton once shooting wraps up. He said he owes it to all of us."

Billy squinted at me. "How does he figure that?"

"Well, because I've had to spend so much time away from home, of course."

"He wants to take *all* of us?" Vi asked, her eyes wide and her coffee cup stalled halfway to her lips. It was nice to have Vi home with us during the morning hours, although her vacation would be over soon, because Mrs. Pinkerton would be coming home from her trip with her new husband soon. "Oh, my!"

"Say, that's swell of him," said Pa, who was surreptitiously feeding Spike bits of buttered toast under the table. Truth to tell, there was no need to be sneaky about feeding Spike tidbits. We all did the same thing. Spike was going to have to start watching his waistline pretty soon if we kept it up, too.

"I thought it was a nice offer. He said the Hotel Castleton has an elegant restaurant, and that it's close to home."

"I've heard that," said Vi, sipping coffee and looking as if someone had offered her the moon and the stars. "Wait until Peggy hears about this!"

Peggy was my mother's name. Well, her name was Margaret, but everyone called her Peggy. Except me, of course, and my siblings. We called her Ma.

"She'll be thrilled," agreed Pa. "I've seen pictures of that hotel. Even picked up and deposited rich folks there a time or two when I was a chauffeur. Won't that be something? Imagine dining with a famous picture star like Monty Mountjoy. Won't Jacob be jealous?" He grinned, pleased that his brother in Massachusetts would envy Pa's hobnobbing with what might be considered American royalty.

"Monty's a nice fellow," I said. "He's not at all spoiled like Lola de la Monica, who's a wretched person. Now *she's* truly been ruined by her fame, if she wasn't rotten to begin with."

I saw Billy eyeing me with misgiving and realized I shouldn't have voiced my appreciation of Monty's goodness. It galled me that Billy mistrusted the purity of my loyalty to him, although I did understand. Sort of. I'd probably be worried about him straying if I were confined to a wheelchair, too. On the other hand, it seemed to me that men were granted a great deal more latitude when it came to sins of the flesh than were women. Naturally, that was as unfair as everything else regarding the sexes, but there wasn't much I could do about it. I hadn't even been able to vote yet, since I'd turned twenty-one after the last election. But none of that mattered.

"I'm not sure when this gala evening will be planned, but I'll let everyone know as soon as I find out. I suspect it'll be next Saturday night."

"Isn't that the last day of Spike's training, too?" Billy asked.

I was glad he'd changed the subject. "It is indeed," I said. "And Mrs. Hanratty said she'll be giving out graduation certificates. This evening when I come home from work—if I survive another day with Lola on the set—we can practice with him. I want him to come in first."

I glanced at the floor. Spike, looking up at me with great hope in his big, brown eyes, wagged his tail as if he knew we were discussing him. He probably did, actually, since we'd mentioned his name. Knowing even as I did it that I was doing something wrong, since Spike was in danger of becoming plump, I said, "Spike, speak."

Spike spoke, and I tossed him another scrap of buttered toast. That dog would do virtually anything for food, which came in handy when it came to his obedience training. "Good dog."

Billy shook his head, but he smiled, so I guess he'd forgiven me for having a fictitious affair with Monty Mountjoy. I could have set Billy straight in seconds by revealing Monty's secret, but I couldn't in good conscience do so; therefore, I'd just try to be a good wife and show my husband by my good works that I was faithful to him.

After I washed and dried the breakfast dishes, I went to our bedroom to stare into the closet and decide what to wear that day. This was the first day of June and, as I said before, sometimes June and July are overcast and cool in southern California, but the *Pasadena Star News* had predicted warm weather for a while, so I chose a lightweight, light-blue French serge dress that hung straight from the rounded neckline to the

calf-length hemline. I'd sewn pretty embroidered ribbon—
purchased dirt-cheap at Maxime's Fabrics along with the bolt
end of French serge, also dirt-cheap—at the neckline, the three-
quarter-length sleeves, and down the middle of the dress. The
belt was made of the same blue serge as the dress, and it tied
loosely below the waist. The ensemble would be cool enough to
withstand the heat of the day, and easy enough to maneuver in
so that I could, if called upon to do so, wrestle Lola into submission. I prayed hard that I wouldn't have to do that, although
why God would listen to me after all the lies I'd told recently, I
couldn't say.

"You look bright and cheery today," Harold greeted me as I
walked toward the set. I hadn't been waylaid by Sam Rotondo,
for which I was grateful. Maybe God had listened to me after
all. Probably not. The fact that I'd arrived, parked, and made it
to the set unscathed was undoubtedly just an oversight on God's
part.

"Thanks, Harold. I do my best."

"You succeed admirably, my dear."

You can see why I adored Harold.

"What's going on?" I asked, interested that I hadn't heard
any screeching or hollering. I considered that a good sign,
although perhaps I was being overly optimistic.

"So far, Lola's behaving, if that's what you're asking me."

It was exactly what I'd asked him. "Glad to hear it." I
squinted at the set, which had been altered to reflect what
looked like dozens of wounded men laid out in various poses of
misery, some with dark substances strategically painted on them,
I presumed to appear like blood. Ick. "What are they doing
now?"

"Big hospital and reconciliation scene," said Harold. "Lola's
searching for Monty after the battle of something or other.
She's eventually going to find him among the wounded and

take him home and nurse him."

"Lola?" I asked, feigning astonishment. I knew it was a picture, honest.

"Lola's character," said Harold with a cynical twist of his mouth. "Tomorrow, we're going to be shooting indoors."

"Where indoors?" I asked curiously.

"The set decorators are creating a ruined plantation out of the dressing-room house even as we speak."

"I'll be darned."

"Probably," said a voice at my back. I jumped a couple of inches. I knew that voice.

Turning, I said savagely, "Darn you, Sam Rotondo, don't sneak up on me like that!"

"I'm too big to sneak," he said, smirking.

He was big, all right, although clearly not too big to sneak. But I didn't want to start an argument with Sam. I had to weasel information out of him. Besides, I didn't want to spoil what had started out being a beautiful day. Heck, if it weren't for all the wounded soldiers lying around, the day would be perfectly glorious in that almost-perfect setting. The trees were green, the flowers glorious, and birds chirped from their many nests on the property. Therefore, although it pained me, I smiled at Sam. "Good morning, Sam."

"Good morning, Daisy," he said with insincere solemnity. Turning to Harold, he said, less cordially, "Morning, Mr. Kincaid."

"Nice day, isn't it? Not one tantrum so far, and it's almost nine."

"Yeah," said Sam, offering a small chuckle in honor of Harold's attempt at humor. Then he turned to me. "To answer your question, Daisy, if you know who's writing the damned letters, Lola would have to press charges in order for the police department to arrest the sender. Now, tell me who's writing the letters."

Irked, I asked, "Why didn't you tell me this last night?"

"Because I don't like it when you keep information from me regarding a case."

Harold and I exchanged a significant look, and Harold shrugged. "Better tell him, Daisy. I'm sure the studio won't let Lola press charges. Hell, it's better for everyone involved if she never even learns who the writer is."

I considered Harold's words for a second or two. It annoyed me that Sam hadn't answered my question when I'd asked it and I'd like to make him suffer for his recalcitrance, but I knew Harold was right. Therefore, I said, "All right. But I don't want to go into this here and now. Let's go to one of the gardens away from everyone, and I'll reveal all." I said the last two words as if I aimed to impart unto him the secret of life.

Sam, naturally, rolled his eyes. "Fine," he said. "Let's go to a garden."

"I recommend the rose arbor over there," Harold said, pointing vaguely westward. "There's a gazebo there that's nice to sit in."

"Oh, yeah," I said, brightening. "When I first saw it, I thought I'd like to sit there for days on end and do nothing but read detective stories." I gave Sam a look. "Books about fictional detectives, needless to say."

"Totally needless," said Sam.

So we walked to the rose garden and settled in the gazebo, and I told Sam all about finding the newspapers, glue pot, scissors and pen in Granny Winkworth's desk drawer.

"The old lady's been writing the letters?" he asked incredulously.

"Yes. She disapproves of picture people and believes Lola has been leading her grandson astray. I guess that's why she wrote the letters. To scare off Lola."

"Damn," said Sam, who was as baffled by her attitude as I was. "That's flat stupid."

"Yes, it is. But according to Monty, she's old and set in her ways. He just doesn't want her to get in trouble with the police."

"You told him all about it, I suppose," said Sam resentfully.

"Of course I did. I figured I'd better. She's his grandmother, after all, and I was pretty sure he wouldn't want to see her hauled off to jail, or anything. That's why I asked if a person would have to file charges against the letter writer before being arrested. Shoot, Sam, I generally have reasons for the questions I ask, you know."

"I do know. That's why I didn't answer you last night. I don't trust you."

"You've made that abundantly clear, Sam," I said, feeling picked on. "But see, the thing is, Mrs. Winkworth is an old lady. She may be a misguided idiot, but Mr. Mountjoy doesn't want her hurt by all this. That's why I don't want Lola to know Mrs. Winkworth is the culprit."

"Well, crap, Daisy, that's not fair to Miss de la Monica, is it?"

My eyes paid a glance to the ceiling of the gazebo. Somebody kept the place swept clear of cobwebs and stuff. It was positively pristine. "Lola de la Monica is a cretinous egomaniac, Sam Rotondo. If we tell her the truth, she'll be screeching the news from now until doomsday and undoubtedly increase her quota of temper tantrums from zero to sixty within minutes of being told the truth."

Sam chuffed out a heavy breath. "Well, we've got to tell her something. If she thinks she's going to get more of those damned letters, she'll still screech from now until doomsday."

"Yes, but I've figured out a way to put a stop to the letters without her being the wiser."

"Yeah? How?"

He sounded as if he didn't believe me and wouldn't approve if he could ever be persuaded. His attitude annoyed me, but his attitude always annoyed me, so I didn't take him to task. "I'm going to conduct another séance and have Rolly, my spiritual guide, give a specific warning that the writer of the letters has disturbed the spirits with her antics, and she'd better stop it or something bad will happen to . . . well, I haven't figured that part out yet. Maybe I'll have Rolly talk to her ancestor, the general, and have him be stern with her. I'll have to talk to Mr. Mountjoy and find out what she'd hate most if it were taken from her. But Rolly will tell her that something dire will befall her or a loved one if she doesn't cease and desist."

Sam stared at me for what seemed like an hour and a half. I was utterly astounded when he finally said, "That sounds like a good plan."

I could feel my eyes go wide. "You mean it? You actually approve of something I'm planning to do?"

After another moment of hesitation, during which he pursed his lips and thought, I'm sure, about my many transgressions—or what he considered my transgressions—he said, "Yeah. It sounds as if that'd be best all around, and the police department won't have to get involved in a messy situation. We don't like messy situations," he said with a meaningful look at me.

"Well, then . . ." But I didn't know what to say next. I hadn't expected Sam to be so easy to persuade. I'd figured I'd have a fight on my hands. His capitulation almost felt like a letdown, which was downright silly.

"When do you aim to throw this séance of yours?"

"It's *conduct* a séance, Sam, not *throw* one."

He shrugged. "Whatever."

"Friday night. Tomorrow." I heaved a sigh. "It'll be good to have the matter settled. I'm so sick of Lola's tantrums, I don't think I can stand many more of them."

"You're not alone there," said Sam grimly. "This whole picture nonsense is a load of baloney."

Standing, I said, "I know you don't think you belong here."

He joined me, and we walked back toward the set together. I didn't want to leave the gazebo. "I *don't* belong here. Neither do the two uniforms. This has been a total waste of taxpayer money."

I thought about that for a moment. "Well, I suppose the picture is bringing business and revenues and stuff like that to the city. I mean, think of all the businesses that are getting trade from the folks working on the picture. Restaurants, and so forth. Department stores. Those sorts of businesses. That's important, I reckon."

"I reckon."

I could tell he didn't believe it.

The rest of that day on the set went well. Lola didn't throw a single temper tantrum. Not one. Mind you, I did have to encourage her a time or two, reminding her of Rolly's messages and so forth. Still it was, all in all, a red-letter day on the set of *The Fire at Sunset*. I could scarcely believe it when I drove home at an appropriately early hour and pulled into our driveway.

My family had a pleasant evening at home, too. After another one of Aunt Vi's excellent dinners—fricasseed chicken with dumplings, peas and carrots, and spice cake for dessert—I played the piano and we all sang, and then we all read for a while, and then we all went to bed. It would have been a normal evening for a normal family, except that our evenings since the beginning of the picture shoot hadn't been at all normal. I was grateful for that one evening, though; very grateful.

Friday rolled around, as it inevitably does after Thursday. Again, Lola caused no problems on the set, perhaps because she'd been told about the anticipated séance that evening and she didn't want to be scolded by Rolly again. Little did she know she wasn't going to be the center of attention at this particular séance, or she'd probably have made it a point to disrupt the filming.

Lucky for me, it was so crowded inside the dressing-room house that I didn't have to lie in wait to be of assistance to Lola. Rather, I hied myself to the gazebo, where I took out *The Case of the Deserted Wife*, a Sexton Black novel I'd thoughtfully stuck in my handbag in hopeful anticipation of a quiet day on the set. To tell the truth, I hadn't expected to be able to read the thing, but everything seemed to be working in my favor that day, much as it had the day before. I didn't quite trust my luck, although I told myself not to be absurd.

When I was about halfway through the second chapter of the book, enjoying the comfort of the padded gazebo bench and wishing I lived someplace on the Winkworth estate, Harold Kincaid joined me. I was glad to see him and laid my book aside for the nonce.

"Detective Rotondo told me where you were," he said by way of greeting.

"Yeah. I had to tell Sam and John Bohnert where to find me in case Lola starts cutting up."

Sitting next to me, Harold said, "So far, she's being quite amenable to direction. Not a single cross word has passed her lips, and she's actually doing what she's being told to do."

"How odd."

With a shrug, Harold said, "Not really. I think she's scared about the séance."

"That's exactly what I've been thinking," I told him with a grin. "Say, did you discuss with Monty what sort of threat would still his granny's venomous pen? I thought maybe I could dredge up her uncle—or was it her grandfather?—who was a general in the Civil War and have him tell her to stop writing the letters."

"Colonel," said Harold.

I blinked at him. "Beg pardon?"

"Her grandfather was a colonel, and that's exactly what Monty said. Get gramps to tell her he's ashamed of her actions. Monty thinks that will cure her pronto. She'd do anything to keep her family's name and the great Confederate cause unsullied."

"Oh, brother."

"My sentiments, too, but there's no accounting for taste."

"I guess not."

I spent the rest of the day plotting how to present the facts of life to Mrs. Lurlene Winkworth, doyenne of the Southern Cause in Pasadena, California—which to me seemed like a stupid thing to be, but I was a nobody. I thought I had a pretty good plan in hand by the time I went home that evening.

In order to keep Billy entertained while I was conducting the séance, Sam again came to dinner that night. He and Pa and Billy would spend the rest of Friday night playing gin rummy in the living room whilst I plied my trade. All in all, it felt good to be doing something of which Sam Rotondo, the bitterest of my enemies—he was my only enemy, come to think of it—approved.

CHAPTER TWENTY-ONE

In order to impress upon my audience the solemnity of the occasion, I wore my most spectacularly subdued spiritualist garb that evening. I'd worn the ensemble before, but only Harold had ever seen it, and he wouldn't mind. Heck, he knew that, while I did wonders with the White side-pedal sewing machine I'd bought for Ma—but mainly used myself—I wasn't rich. I did a whole lot of sewing with the money I made, but I was frugal when it came to fabric and accessories.

Anyhow, the dress was a long black silk number that tied at the side hip with glossy black-satin ribbons. It was supposed to be straight, but I've already mentioned my assorted curves that marred its sleek lines. The gown sported (if sported is the right word for such a somber occasion) a big, scalloped appliqué of shiny black beads and silk embroidery that glimmered in the lights of various lamps, and that would be truly stunning by the glow of the one cranberry lamp I permitted in the middle of the séance table.

Naturally, I wore black shoes, carried a small beaded handbag—I'd done the beading, of course—and was ready to set out. I was honestly optimistic about the outcome of this evening's work, and I smiled at those assembled in the living room of our comfy little bungalow on Marengo Avenue. Vi had already gone up to bed, but Sam, Pa and Billy were, as anticipated, gathered around the card table. Ma sat in her favorite chair, embroidering something for one of my brother's or sister's children.

Billy glanced up and saw me. "Gee, Daisy, you look great."

My heart plummeted. Not that I didn't appreciate his words, because I did, but Billy never used to hand out compliments, and I got the feeling he didn't like me looking good for other people. Nevertheless, I smiled some more and said, "Thanks, Billy. I want to impress Granny Winkworth."

"Granny Winkworth," Billy repeated as if he doubted my words.

Sam said, "It's the truth, Billy. Daisy's got to get the old lady to stop writing nasty anonymous letters to Lola de la Monica, and I think she'll be able to do it with this séance of hers." He pronounced the word *séance* as if it smelled like rotten eggs, but I was grateful to him for setting Billy's mind at rest.

Ma's head jerked up from her embroidery hoop. "Nasty anonymous letters?" she asked, astonished. "What nasty letters?"

The rest of the group appeared equally interested. Pa said, "Letters to Lola de la Monica? Oh yeah. I remember now."

"Sam can tell you all about them," I told them all. "I'd better get going. Wish me luck."

"Good luck. I guess," said Billy, clearly puzzled.

"It's like this . . ." were the last words I heard before I closed the door behind myself, and they were spoken by Sam.

Fortunately for my black silk stockings, Spike resided on Billy's lap, so I didn't have to fight him off at the door. I drove to the Winkworth mansion with a heart full of hope and a mind troubled with thoughts of Billy and his altered attitude toward my work and me. It seemed a little late in the game for him to have suddenly arrived at an appreciation of my spiritualistic efforts to keep the family's finances afloat, but I supposed stranger things had happened. Heck, people actually believing in the tripe I fed them was stranger than a change in Billy's attitude. Maybe.

I hadn't come to grips with anything by the time I gave the guard at the Winkworth estate my name, and the huge iron gate silently opened on its hinges through some magical automatic device unseen by yours truly. I parked the Chevrolet in front of the massive marble front steps, sucked in a deep breath of soft June air, scented that evening with gardenias and jasmine, and climbed the steps to the porch. There I rang the doorbell and waited for the butler to admit me. A butler. Paid for by Monty Mountjoy, whose grandmother appreciated absolutely none of the material comforts Monty had showered upon her. Ungrateful, demented woman.

When the butler led me into the front parlor, I was pleased to see Harold among the assembled guests. By the by, I allowed no more than eight attendees at a séance as a rule not because it made any difference to me personally, but because strict rules impressed my clients. You figure it out. It's beyond me. Along with Harold were Mrs. Winkworth and Lola de la Monica, both of whom appeared slightly apprehensive, Monty Mountjoy, who smiled at me happily; Mrs. Hanratty; Gladys Pennywhistle, who surprised me with a smile; and Dr. Homer Fellowes, who gladdened me by sticking close to Gladys. If you added me to the group, that made eight, which was fine, although I wasn't sure I trusted Dr. Fellowes not to make a hash of things once the séance got started. After all, he was even brainier than Gladys, and he might balk at the nonsense I intended to perpetrate.

To my surprise, Mrs. Winkworth came up to me with her hands outstretched. "Good evening, Mrs. Majesty. It's so good of you to come this evening."

"Thank you," I said in my deep, soothing, spiritualist voice.

"Er . . . Monty said it was most important that this séance be held," continued Mrs. Winkworth, who had a voice of her own to project: that of a dignified Southern lady whose ancestry was impeccable, although I aimed to peck at it some that night.

"Yes," I said softly. "The spirits are anxious that some extremely important matters be taken care of." I aimed to sound as mysterious as I could, and I guess I succeeded because I saw Mrs. Winkworth gulp and wondered if she knew she'd been a naughty girl. If she didn't know it yet, she sure would by the time the colonel got through with her; I could almost guarantee it.

"I . . . see."

She didn't seem awfully happy when we all traipsed down the hall to the dining room, which was once more being used for the séance that evening. I set out my cranberry lamp, lit the candle, sat at the head of the table, bowed my head and sat in silence for a moment as if bracing myself for torture to come. After a little bit of that, I told those assembled to take hands and signaled the butler, who evidently had gone to the same butlering school as Mrs. Pinkerton's Featherstone, to turn off the electric lights. He did so, and the room took on a wonderfully creepy aura. Exactly what I wanted. So I began to do my stuff.

Dr. Fellowes must have been warned by someone not to interrupt the séance, because I didn't hear a peep from him or from Gladys during my entire performance. In fact, the only noises audible as I perpetrated my fraud on Mrs. Winkworth and Lola de la Monica were a couple of gasps from one or the other of them when the colonel showed up and scolded Mrs. Winkworth—not by name, of course.

In a Southern drawl copied precisely from that of Mrs. Winkworth herself, and in a tone an octave or two lower than my normal speaking voice, I had the colonel say, "I know who has been writing the letters that are causing so much distress for someone present at this table. Such behavior is disgraceful and must cease at once." I swear, the colonel had more authority in his voice than even I knew I possessed. Probably Mrs. Hanratty's dog-obedience classes had helped me there. "Writing letters like that is beneath contempt and all human dignity and won't be tolerated by those of us who are on the Other Side. We spirits believe perpetrating such actions show an abysmal lack of gratitude and respect, are inappropriate, and are, to be blunt, shameful. If the letters don't stop, untoward misery will ensue for their writer and those close to the writer. I can guarantee it." I didn't want Lola to go guess who I was talking about, and I certainly didn't let on that the letter writer was present at the séance. All I wanted to do was to let Lola know that the letters would stop coming, and to scare Mrs. Winkworth so much that she'd stop sending them.

I went on in that vein for another few minutes until I heard soft, gulping sobs coming from the other end of the table—from Lurlene Winkworth, in actual fact—so I had Rolly return. He added his strong disapprobation of anonymous letter writers to that of the colonel. Then, in order to give Mrs. Winkworth time to get her emotions under control, I had him say a few words of endearment to me. What the heck, why not? When I deemed the old lady was in possession of her dignity, I slumped in my chair as a signal that my spirit control had left me and that I was limp from the exhaustion of having had my body possessed by various ghosts. It worked.

The lights went on a moment or two later, and I saw through my slitted eyes that Monty was supporting his grandmother as she rose from the table on what I presumed to be wobbly legs. As well they should wobble, darn it!

It was Harold who joined me at the head of the table, ostensibly to give me support as I rose to my own supposedly wobbly legs. He whispered in my ear as he did so, "Well done, Daisy! I swear you scared the pants off the old woman!"

271

"Lordy, I hope not," said I, also whispering.

Harold didn't dare laugh, but I heard a suppressed chuckle. "You scared her, anyway. I have a feeling Lola doesn't have to worry about getting any more letters, and neither does Monty. That bit you had the colonel spout about ingratitude and beneath-the-dignity-of and so forth was perfect."

"Thank you, Harold," I said modestly. "I did my best."

Monty came rushing up to us then. I presume he'd deposited his grandmother in the front parlor or somewhere else appropriate.

"Daisy!" he said.

Harold shushed him, so he repeated in a whisper, "Daisy! You were magnificent! Have you ever considered taking up acting as a profession?"

"Hell, Monty, she already acts as a profession. You saw and heard her yourself."

Trying to suppress his own laughter, Monty agreed with him. "But you succeeded. I know you did. You frightened the socks off Gran. I'm sure there will be no more letters."

"Better her socks than her pants," I muttered.

"Beg pardon?" queried Monty.

Harold said, "Never mind."

Supposedly supported by the two men—séances being theoretically very hard on the séance-giver—I, too, slowly made my way into the front parlor, only to see Mrs. Winkworth downing what looked to me like a glass of whiskey. My, my. And she was a genteel Southern lady. I didn't know genteel Southern ladies imbibed distilled spirits, especially in those days of what was supposed to be Prohibition, not that you'd know it to judge by the Hollywoodland folks and their bootleggers.

Harold and Monty sat me down gently into a chair across the room from Mrs. Winkworth. I was seemingly recovering my wits after having performed a difficult and valuable service but, naturally, Lola de la Monica never thought of anybody but herself. She came barreling over to me even before I'd made myself comfortable, much less had a chance to recover my purportedly scattered sensibilities. Because I resented her selfishness, I put the back of a white, beautifully manicured hand to my forehead and groaned softly.

Lola didn't care about anyone's sensibilities but her own, and she fell at my feet and grabbed my hand from my forehead. "Oh, Daisy! Oh, how can I ever thank you? You did it all for me, didn't you? I *know* you did it for me!" And she began to weep all over my beautiful black silk evening gown.

Monty, bless him, came over and carried her off. I noticed that Dr. Fellowes was looking upon Lola's performance with disdain, and I was glad he'd finally come to his senses. I just hoped Gladys wouldn't find Monty's gallantry enough to wrest her affections away from Dr. Fellowes and back to the actor. When I glanced in their direction, she appeared as disdainful as Dr. Fellowes, perhaps because she disapproved of séances or Lola or both, but at least it didn't look as though she aimed to leave Dr. Fellowes's side to assist Monty with Lola.

By the time I wended my way home from the Winkworth estate that night, I felt almost good for a change. I was almost positive Granny Winkworth would produce no more poison-pen letters, and I was guardedly optimistic that Lola would continue to behave herself for the duration of the shoot, which was scheduled to end early the next week. What's more, Billy and I could take Spike to dog-obedience training tomorrow! That was definitely something to look forward to.

Even better, the house was dark when I got home, so I didn't have to confront Sam Rotondo.

The Pasanita Dog Obedience Club proved to be as much fun on Saturday morning as it ever was. Hamlet, the Great Dane, had not merely the small Tommy to guide and hold him, but Tommy's father also participated in the Dane's training. Too bad Shakespeare's Hamlet didn't have Mrs. Hanratty to guide his actions, or the stage might have been littered with several fewer corpses at the end of the last act.

Fluffy the poodle continued to train her owner, Mrs. Hinkledorn, much to Mrs. Hanratty's displeasure, but it didn't look to me as if anything was going to change in that department any time soon.

Spike performed magnificently. Billy, Pa and I had spent a good deal of Friday evening before dinner practicing with him, and he would obey any one of us instantly. That morning at breakfast, I think Pa had even taught him to sneeze when he said, "geshundheit," although I still had to test that theory for accuracy. But it so happened that Spike had sneezed, and Pa had said, "geshundheit" and thrown him a piece of toast. Spike had sneezed again, again Pa had said "geshundheit" and again thrown him a piece of toast.

Which just goes to show that if one seizes an opportunity, great things can happen. It was pure chance that had caused Spike to have a sneezing fit that morning, and also pure chance that Pa had said "geshundheit" and given him toast. We didn't have long enough to find out if that particular bit of training would stick in Spike's head because we had to get to Brookside Park, but my money was on Spike. He'd do pretty much anything for food, even sneeze. I aimed to teach him to add, subtract, multiply and divide next.

Not that I was a whiz at mathematics, as you might have gathered by some of my earlier statements, but Mrs. Hanratty had demonstrated how her dog Theodore—a bulldog named after the late Theodore Roosevelt because they looked vaguely alike—could do simple math tricks. It isn't too difficult to train a dog to do anything once you get the hang of it.

Anyhow, class was a pleasure, as it always was. The June day was perfectly glorious, Brookside Park gorgeous, and I enjoyed being around Mrs. Hanratty and all those dogs. Dogs are ever so much easier to get along with than people as a rule. You can't fool a dog with such idiocies as séances and tarot cards or Ouija boards. Dogs know a good person when they meet one, and they can smell a rotter a mile away. That's my theory, anyway. It was nice to be around creatures who didn't believe in anything but what they could see, hear, taste and smell. You wouldn't find a dog trying to communicate with its dead relations; that was for sure.

The rest of that day went well. Billy actually condescended to go for a walk with Spike and me, although he refused to try to walk.

"There's no point to it, Daisy. My legs just don't support me any longer, and my lungs can't take it."

I wanted to argue, to tell him that if he put a little effort into walking, he might surprise himself, but I held my tongue. Life with Billy had become easier in the last few months, but that was only because he seemed to have given up on himself. I wasn't about to try bullying him. I'd already talked to everyone I could think of who might help with his problems, from Johnny Buckingham to Dr. Benjamin to Sam Rotondo, and there didn't seem to be much more I could do for Billy than be agreeable.

So we went for a nice walk, down Marengo, waving at the neighbors as we passed, Spike trotting obediently at heel as I pushed Billy's chair. Pa went with us as far as the corner, where he aimed to turn. There he planned to walk another block farther to the little grocery store on the next corner, then he aimed to detour into the store to see what goodies he might find. His mother, my grandma Gumm, had sent him a recipe for Boston brown bread, and I had a feeling we'd be having baked beans again sometime soon, this time with the official bread to go along with them. Pa said I'd love the stuff. I didn't argue. I liked most food.

"It's a nice day," said Billy at one point.

His words surprised me. Generally when we went out into the world, he griped and grumbled because he couldn't get up and enjoy it. I didn't trust this mood of his. Then again, what did I know? "It's about perfect. Hope it doesn't get too hot."

"I doubt that it will. September's when it gets really hot around here."

"Too true. I remember the first day of school was always the hottest day of the year, and we had to bring a hundred pounds of books home with us to show the folks."

Billy chuckled. I stared at the top of his head, which was covered with a soft cap, and prayed silently that this acquiescent mood of Billy's didn't mean anything awful. Then I took myself to task for being dramatic. What could it mean? My mind skipped back a few months to the stash of morphine syrup I'd discovered in our closet, but my heart gave a giant spasm, and I told myself I'd been hanging around Lola de la Monica too much. Billy was only becoming resigned to his fate. That was all.

I wished I believed it.

At any rate, we walked around the entire block and when we got back home, Aunt Vi had prepared lunch for us: chopped chicken sandwiches and a mixed fruit salad—rich folks called this type of thing a fruit compote—to go with it, and chocolate cookies for dessert. Yum.

The following day, the entire family walked to church on the corner of Marengo and Colorado. As I sang the alto part of our anthem for the day, "O For a Thousand Tongues to Sing"— which is the first hymn in all Methodist hymnals, by the way, although I don't know why except that it was written by Charles Wesley, but then again so many hymns were—I looked at my family. They always sat toward the front, so that Billy's wheelchair wouldn't get in the way of the departing throng when the service ended and everyone headed to Fellowship Hall for food. We Methodists like our food. I understand Baptists do, too.

Anyhow, I saw my family as I sang, and I noticed Billy watching me, a dreamy expression on his face. Again my heart lurched. What was going on here? Blast it, I wished I could stop worrying and take Billy's altered behavior as a good sign instead of a disquieting one.

Oh, well. There wasn't a blessed thing I could do about Billy's health, mental or physical, from the choir loft, so I decided to stop worrying, watch Mr. Floy Hostetter, the choir director, and sing. Maybe the words to the hymn would penetrate my heart and give me some peace.

CHAPTER TWENTY-TWO

The rest of that day passed peacefully enough. As usual, Vi presented us with a delicious dinner, which we took at noon on Sundays. I don't know why, either, except it was traditional to do so. That day she fixed pork chops and served scalloped potatoes, acorn squash and green beans with them. Butterscotch pudding for dessert. I swear, Aunt Vi was the best cook in the entire world.

Then it was Monday again. Darn.

"But this is the last week," I assured Billy and Vi at the breakfast table. "The shooting is scheduled to wrap up about mid-week, and then the only thing left to be done is the editing. So I'll probably not have to go back to the Winkworth estate until next week, when they aim to take publicity pictures."

"Why do you have to be there for the publicity pictures?" asked Billy, not accusingly, but as if he was honestly interested.

"Because Lola de la Monster will be there, and when she's there, I'm there," I said, feeling grumpy about it. "But then it's over."

"I think it's swell of Mr. Mountjoy to be taking us all out to dine on Saturday," said Pa, who loved his food as much as I loved mine.

"Me, too," I said, a trifle cheerier than before.

"It's very nice of him," said Billy.

I waited for a cutting comment about how Monty could afford to feed us all and a hundred like us, but it didn't come.

He saw me staring at him. "What?" he asked. "Did I drip on myself?" Vi had fixed waffles for breakfast, and we were eating them with genuine maple syrup sent to us by Ma's sister in Auburn, Massachusetts.

Oh, as an aside, Pa *had* taught Spike to sneeze on cue, if anyone's interested. The brilliant dog managed to sneeze his way through an entire waffle that morning.

"No. You haven't dripped," I said. "It's just that . . . never mind." It was just that I wasn't accustomed to him not showing his bitterness and envy of people like Monty Mountjoy, whose only claims to fame were that they looked good on a picture screen. I couldn't say that. Nor could I say that Billy would have looked good on a picture screen, too, if he hadn't been ruined by the cursed Kaiser and his cursed mustard gas. I dropped the subject, which was one that only frustrated me.

Billy smiled at me, and I tried not to think his smile a sinister portent.

Bother. I was truly good at making mountains of molehills, wasn't I?

However, my mood had improved a good deal from the prior week, now that I knew this would be the end of my durance vile and that Mrs. Winkworth had been dissuaded from writing any more horrible letters to her grandson and Lola de la Monica. I could almost understand somebody wanting to give Lola a good one—or even two or three, for that matter—but I still thought the old lady was a miserable specimen for trying to frighten the grandson who had done so much for her. Monty was much more forgiving than I when it came to his grandmother.

Sam awaited me with arms crossed over his chest when I parked the Chevrolet at the Winkworth place. I tried to maintain my almost-good mood from plummeting into my sensible shoes. Well, they were about as sensible as I could get away with and maintain my act as spiritualist extraordinaire. At least they had low heels, so I wouldn't be forever getting them stuck in the dirt.

I have a funny anecdote about high-heeled shoes, and it has nothing to do with my story. However, whenever we saw mushrooms growing in either the front lawn or the back lawn, Ma, Vi and I went out in our highest heels and walked around on the grass, stamping heavily. This was supposed to aerate the soil and prevent fungi from growing, according to an article Ma read somewhere. I doubt that the article had advocated puncturing the soil with high-heeled shoes, but what the heck. It worked, so we did it.

That day, however, my shoes were low and comfortable, and the rest of me aimed to be as relaxed as possible, too. I figured calm shouldn't be too difficult a thing to accomplish, what with Lola's worries put to rest and Sam unable to arrest Mrs. Winkworth.

Bracing myself, I left the Chevrolet, the door to which Sam had thoughtfully opened for me. Only I don't think he meant only to be polite. He wanted answers, and it was up to me to give them to him.

"Well?" he demanded before we'd even greeted each other. "Did it work?"

"Good morning to you, too, Sam," I said.

"Good morning. Did the séance work? Will the old lady write any more letters?"

Understanding that I'd get no politeness from this quarter, I answered his question. "Yes, the séance worked beautifully. And, no, she won't write any more letters. What's even better is that Lola was at the séance, and she's sure I conducted it for her own benefit. She wept all over my silk skirt in gratitude, in fact."

Sam shuddered. "Good God."

"All part of the job," I told him.

"I like my job better than yours."

"You'd be lousy at mine."

"Probably."

"I'd be lousy at yours."

"I know."

Gee, I'd aimed to rile him with my comment, but he must have been so relieved to have the problem of the poison-pen letters cleared up, he didn't take exception. Mildly astonished, I walked at his side as we headed for the dressing-room house. "Do you know when the filming on this picture is scheduled to end?" I asked, even though I knew the answer.

"Wednesday," Sam said.

"You must be glad it's almost over."

"I am." He shook his head and began muttering about wasting the taxpayers' money on frivolities like moving pictures and things like that.

I let him rant. His indignation was well-earned, as far as I could ascertain. It did seem rather excessive to have a detective and two uniformed policemen at a picture set for weeks on end. I'd begun to disbelieve, as much as Sam, the studio's claim about Germans wanting to steal Dr. Fellowes's invention.

Boy, did we get that one wrong! As we approached the dressing-room house—which was still pretending to be an old Southern plantation—we heard the uproar.

"What the devil is going on?" Sam asked.

It was a rhetorical question, of course, since I'd just arrived at the Winkworth estate and didn't know any more than he did. So I said, "Beats me," and we hurried our steps.

Poor John Bohnert was throwing a fit almost equal to those pitched by Lola de la Monica when we finally got the set.

"I can't *believe* the damned thing was stolen from a gated estate!" he bellowed in his best directorial voice. "It's insane!"

The two uniformed policemen appeared as puzzled as John.

One of them spotted Sam and me and ran over to us.

"What's going on?" Sam asked, his aura of authority having taken full command of him.

The uniform, the same Thomas Doan who'd approached my automobile on my very first day at the picture shoot, said, "Somebody stole Dr. Fellowes's invention."

"Somebody *what?*" Sam roared.

I decided this was a job for the police and not a spiritualist, so I sneaked away to where I saw Harold, Lillian and Gladys standing in a clump. I didn't see Dr. Fellowes anywhere. I expect he was tearing his hair out someplace else.

"Did someone really steal Dr. Fellowes's invention?" I asked the trio as I approached.

"Sure did," said Harold. "Unless the studio's done it as a publicity stunt."

"Would they do that?" I asked, appalled.

Harold tilted his head to one side. "I honestly don't know. I wouldn't put too much past the publicity folks."

"Well, if they did, they ought to be arrested," said Gladys. "Poor Homer is beside himself."

Boy, I'd like to see that. Imagine it: two Homer Felloweses. The mind boggled. "I'm really sorry. I guess they actually did need the police."

"Not that the police helped in this case," said Lillian.

I glanced over to see Sam, who looked as if he was really steaming. Officer Doan appeared cowed, and his fellow uniform was cringing. Sam in a rage was something to avoid if at all possible. "I'm sure that's exactly what Detective Rotondo is explaining to his men right this minute."

"Glad I'm not a policeman," said Lillian.

"Me, too."

We all heard John Bohnert holler, "But we *can't* shut down production! We're already behind! Damn it, at least let us shoot inside the house!"

"Oh, Lord," muttered Harold. "First Lola, and now this."

"Speaking of Lola . . ."

"She's not being any trouble," said Gladys. She added, "So far."

"It's true," said Harold. "The séance calmed her down a whole lot."

"Well, I'm glad for that, at least."

We watched Sam and the policemen argue with John Bohnert for another little while, and then John snatched his tweed cap from his head and flung it to the ground. He said, "Fine, then. Do your damned search." He raised his gaze to heaven, from whence, evidently, cameth no help. "This picture will *never* get finished!"

"You can start filming again after my men have searched this house. If we don't come up with anything here, we'll search the rest of the grounds and the other houses. I've got to make a telephone call right now." Sam clearly didn't care about the picture shoot. His detectival instincts were finally being called into play, and he was in his element. "I can't see how anyone could have got a piece of equipment that large out of this place without anyone noticing. It's probably just been stored in the wrong place or something."

"My men don't store equipment in the wrong places," said John angrily.

Sam said, "Huh," and turned to give directions to Officer Doan and his cohort.

I said stupidly, "I guess they're going to search the place."

"Hope they find the invention," said Harold. "I've got to plan costuming for another picture and can't be spending much more time here. Besides, Mother and Algie are returning next weekend, and I aim to host a welcome-home party for them. I have to plan that, too."

"It'll be nice to see your mother again," I said politely, not really meaning it. Mind you, Mrs. Pinkerton was by far my very best client but she tended to panic over trifles, and I was forever being called to drop everything and rush to her mansion to read tarot cards or manipulate the Ouija board or something. Although I needed the work, life had been quite peaceful during her absence—well, except for the last couple of weeks.

The missing-invention problem turned out to be a tempest in a teapot after all, and Sam turned out to be right. Dr. Fellowes's precious machine was found to have been packed in a case meant to house some other piece of equipment. Don't ask me what, because I don't know. Anyhow, John's precious schedule was only delayed another hour or so while the police conducted their ultimately successful search of the premises.

Lola didn't throw a tantrum all day long.

Nor did she throw one the next day or the next. Thus it was that I learned something, now that everyone seemed to be behaving themselves: motion-picture making was a big, fat bore, just as Harold had told me it was. In fact, Sam and I played gin rummy during that final Wednesday. I'd asked Billy if he wanted to come to the set to see how pictures were made but he declined, saying Sam had told him all about it and he could be bored at home quite nicely and didn't care to go out to accomplish the same state of ennui. I couldn't blame him.

On Thursday and Friday of that week, I was happy—no, elated—to stay home with my husband and father while Ma was at work and Aunt Vi returned to the Pinkerton place to prepare for the homecoming of the happy couple.

The entire family and Sam, too, went to the Pasanita Dog Obedience Club's last class on Saturday. That evening we were all going to dine with Monty Mountjoy—Monty had invited Sam as a thank-you for not arresting his grandmother—at the

Hotel Castleton, and I was excited about both the anticipated evening's entertainment and that day's obedience class.

Mrs. Hanratty had already explained to us that we were going to show off everything our dogs were supposed to have learned during the six weeks of class. I was almost certain that Spike would show up the competition, but you never knew how these things would turn out. Maybe he'd get nervous. Maybe *I'd* get nervous. Actually, the latter was more probable than the former, Spike being a most confident doggie, even if he was shorter than most of his fellow students.

There were about forty dogs all in all, and Mrs. Hanratty called out commands to us humans, which we then conveyed to our pets. We went one by one into the center ring, and darned if Spike didn't perform to absolute perfection. I don't think I've ever been as proud of anything as I was of Spike that day. After our last event—sit, stay, walk away, come, heel, sit; which sounds more complicated than it was—Spike's entire fan club and even some of the other watchers applauded, making both Spike and me very happy.

"That was perfect, Daisy," Billy told me, looking happier than I'd seen him in months, if not years.

"How'd you get him to do all that stuff?" asked Sam. When I squinted at him, he appeared honestly interested, so I acquitted him of being sarcastic.

"You just have to be firm," I told him.

"And have some food handy," added Pa.

"Yes," said I. "That part is very important." I glanced down at our happy dog. "I'm afraid we're being slightly too generous with the food, though." From my perspective, which was far above Spike where I had a perfect view of his long body, I could tell he was developing a distinct paunch. Mrs. Hanratty had told me explicitly that dachshunds were greedy little hounds and that it was very important to keep their weight within reasonable limits, because their backs couldn't support too much weight. The notion of losing Spike worried me so much, I decided then and there that he was going to go on a diet. How I'd convince the rest of the family to go along with my plans was a matter I'd have to tackle later.

None of the other dogs, in my admittedly biased opinion, performed anywhere near as well as Spike had done when their turns came. Little Tommy was patently anxious, and he made Hamlet nervous. Poor Tommy burst into tears when Hamlet loped for the comfort of his owner's Model-T Ford during the heeling-without-a-leash process. Tommy's father fetched Hamlet, and Mrs. Hanratty told Tommy that he'd done a wonderful job with such a huge dog as a Great Dane, and Tommy felt better after that.

Fluffy led Mrs. Hinkledorn on a merry chase that ended with them both winded and none the wiser for having spent six weeks and several dollars at dog-obedience school. Mrs. Hanratty only shook her head sadly as the pair, Mrs. Hinkledorn carrying Fluffy, left the ring in disgrace.

After the last dog and master were finished, Mrs. Hanratty prepared to hand us our certificates of completion.

"I'm going to give these out in the order in which the dogs and their owners placed in the class. In other words, the first certificate goes to the teacher's pet." She laughed one of her honking laughs, and everyone else laughed with her.

All of us Gumms and Majestys—and the one Rotondo— braced ourselves. Here it came. Glory or infamy. Which was it to be?

Oh, very well, that's a little dramatic. I'd been practically living with Lola de la Monica for weeks by that time. I think I deserved the benefit of the doubt under the circumstances.

"In first place," Mrs. Hanratty went on as my heart thundered in my chest, "I want to present this certificate to a person and a dog who have both worked very hard and who have profited greatly from their diligence. It is my pleasure to present the first certificate to Mrs. Majesty and Spike!"

I darned near screamed, "We won!" but I didn't. Not quite, anyway. I was grinning from ear to ear, though, when Spike and I walked up to Mrs. Hanratty to receive our certificate. We had worked darned hard for it, and it was nice to be appreciated.

The whole family, and Sam too, were applauding like crazy people when Spike and I rejoined them.

"That's my girl," said Pa with honest pride.

"All that time and effort were worth it in the end," said Ma.

"Well done," said Vi. "I don't know why a body can train a dog the way you've done and not be able to follow a recipe."

I didn't know, either.

"Good job," said Sam. I think he meant it.

"You're the best, Daisy," said Billy. He patted his knee, and Spike jumped into his lap. "And so are you, Spike."

Spike licked his chin.

On the way home, I became a little melancholy, knowing I'd never again be able to take Spike to classes at Brookside Park again. Silly of me, but there you go.

There was nothing, however, to prevent me from driving Billy and Spike to Brookside Park on a Saturday morning and taking a good long walk. That thought perked me up again.

CHAPTER TWENTY-THREE

It had been decided among us that we would need two automobiles to transport all of us to the Hotel Castleton that evening, so Sam came to our house early. He looked quite respectable in a dark suit and tie. I'd sewn evening duds for the entire family a couple of years earlier—I loved to sew not merely for myself, but for everyone—so we were all more than presentable.

Ma wore the ankle-length black gown I'd made for her out of the same black silk I'd used for the gown I'd worn to last week's séance. It was plain, that being one of Ma's specifications, had long sleeves, another of Ma's choices, and tied just below the waist with a black sash. Ma thought the sash too dashing, but I told her it wasn't. She didn't argue, since I was the acknowledged fashion leader in our household.

I'd made Aunt Vi's gown out of a pretty lavender satin I'd found on sale at Maxime's. Her dress was a trifle fuller than Ma's, Vi being a little plump. Plumpness was a hazard of cooking so well, I guess, and she definitely wasn't fat. Only a little plump. Anyhow, her gown was also straight, but I'd managed to disguise her slightly pudgy form by sewing it in layers. The result was beautiful, especially with the embroidery and the beading around the neck and three-quarter sleeves, if I do say so myself.

As for me, I wore a sleeveless blue satin dress with a scooped neckline. My gown ended at mid-calf, had a tiered skirt with a matching blue corsage pinned at one side of the low waist. I'd made the corsage myself, needless to say, with bits and pieces I kept from my endless sewing sessions. What's more, it was perfectly gorgeous. I had a light blue shawl to drape over my shoulders, although the June evening was warm.

Billy and Pa looked elegant in their black evening jackets, trousers and discreet ties I'd made for them.

"I feel like an undertaker," said Billy to Sam at one point.

"You look great," I said to him, feeling a trifle miffy, since I'd provided the garb for the entire family, and we *all* looked great.

Sam only laughed as he wheeled Billy's foldable chair out to the Chevrolet. Ma and Aunt Vi were going to ride with Billy and me, and Pa aimed to ride with Sam. Sam appeared neat and sober in his own black suit. My heart twanged a bit when it occurred to me he'd probably bought it to wear at his late wife's funeral.

The parking lot at the Hotel Castleton was crowded, but Monty had instructed Sam and me to drive right up to the entrance, under the canopy that had been draped from the marble columns of the vast hotel. I was a little nervous, but Monty had thought of everything. As soon as I'd brought the Chevrolet to a stop, a young man in the hotel's livery stepped up to the door and said, "Majesty?"

I blinked at him and said, "Um, yes."

"Very good," said he. "Mr. Mountjoy is awaiting you on the Palm Terrace."

Whatever the Palm Terrace was. Nevertheless, I exited the motor while other liveried young men opened doors and escorted Ma and Aunt Vi from the auto. It soon became clear to all of us that Monty had done his homework, because before I could think to ask for help with Billy's folding bath chair, yet another liveried gent rolled the chair right up to the passenger's door and helped Billy into it. It occurred to me that money might not be everything, but it could sure buy a lot of help, and Monty was a sweetheart to be spending so much of his on us.

Sam's Hudson had arrived right behind our Chevrolet, and the same gang of liveried . . . footmen, I guess I should call them, although I don't think we have footmen in the United States . . . assisted Sam and Pa from the Hudson. Pa, who used to be a chauffeur for rich folks, was accustomed to stuff like this, but it appeared to me as if Sam could have done without all the attention.

And then, darned if Monty Mountjoy himself didn't bound out of the hotel's front doorway and hurry up to our group. "Daisy! It's so good to see you again!"

"Thank you, Monty. This is very special for my family and me."

He kissed my hand, believe it or not. Better that than my cheek or anything, or Billy might have been unhappy. "Believe me, you deserve more than this for helping out so much in the past weeks." He glanced at Billy. "And this must be your husband."

Before I could answer him, Monty stepped up to Billy and held out his hand. "This is a singular pleasure for me, Mr. Majesty. I only regret that you had to suffer for the sins of those monsters who wanted to enslave the world. It's an honor to meet you."

Billy's mouth fell open. He hadn't expected this gracious reception from a man who made his living via his pretty face. So to speak. After hesitating for a second, with his hand being firmly shaken by Monty, he said, "Pleased to meet you, too."

I made the rest of the introductions, recalling my lessons in manners by introducing Ma and Aunt Vi before I introduced Pa. I thought it was swell of Monty to greet Billy the way he had, even though I suppose he should have waited for the ladies to be introduced first. But darn it, Billy deserved all the thanks and appreciation he could get. All of our soldiers did.

After introductions had concluded, Monty led us into the hotel. Boy, what a place! Talk about elegance, the entire hotel reeked of it. Monty had a way with people, and chatted with us all as he guided us to the Palm Terrace.

"I've decided to take it for the evening so that our party can be private," he said. "Things can get . . . ticklish sometimes when people recognize me." He grimaced. "I like the money that comes with my job, but I could do without the recognition. Can't go anywhere anymore without people recognizing me."

Billy and I exchanged a glance, and I'm pretty sure we were thinking along the same lines. I wouldn't mind a little recognition if it paid as well as Monty's. Mind you, I'm sure it got old to be swarmed by fans all the time, but it was clear to me by that time that Monty could well afford to pay for his privacy.

Anyhow, the evening was a grand success. No booze, since we were in a classy hotel, but that was all right with me. I knew, because I saw him, that Billy had secreted a flask on his person that I'm sure contained morphine syrup. He needed the stuff, and there wasn't a darned thing I could do about it. Twice during the evening, he took little sips out of that cursed flask.

I was pleased to see Mrs. Hanratty again, and reiterated how much I'd enjoyed her classes. I was less pleased to see Lola, but she'd evidently been instructed to behave herself, because she did. In fact, she went out of her way to be gracious to Billy, who was a little put off by her constant hovering. Harold was there, too, which was slightly off-putting for Billy, too. But I figured that was his problem. I thoroughly enjoyed myself, and so did the rest of my family.

We went home full and happy, and we would have something to talk about for months, if not years. My siblings were going to be green with envy, which was always a pleasant prospect.

"It's only for today, Billy," I said as I dressed to go to the Wink-worth mansion. "One last day, for the publicity shots, and then I'll never have to deal with these people again."

"Is that a good thing, or will you miss them?"

I gaped at Billy in the mirror, into which I'd been squinting in order to place my hat properly on my head. He was in his wheelchair petting Spike on his lap, and gazing at me with a gentle expression on his face. I frowned. Why did he have a gentle expression on his face? Generally when I went out to work, he picked on me for being sinful and wicked and fooling people for a living. Then there was the fact that for this job I was working with a bunch of picture folks, for whom Billy harbored no respect at all, although he'd gone a bit easier on Monty since Saturday night.

"Miss them?" I asked, astonished. "Are you kidding me?"

He shrugged. "Well, it must be sort of exciting to be working with the people who make the pictures we all flock to see in droves."

I shook my head. "Picture-making is boring as heck, Billy, and most of the people are idiots." I felt guilty after that barb, so I backtracked some. "Well, that's not really true. John Bohnert and Lillian Marshall are nice people, and so are Monty and Harold. I could happily do without ever seeing Lola de la Monica again."

He grinned, and I turned to gaze sharply at him. What was going on here?

"Are you all right?" I asked.

"I'm fine," he said. "Why?"

It was my turn to shrug. "Nothing, I guess. You just seem . . . I don't know. Different lately, or something."

"I don't know why you think that. I'm the same as always."

Turning back to the mirror, hat pin in hand, I said, "If you say so."

He only chuckled. "Have I told you lately that I love you very much, Daisy?"

This time I not only whirled around, but I dropped both the hat and the hat pin and dove for Billy. Spike yipped, startled, so I put my arms around the both of them. "Oh, Billy! I love you, too. I love you so much, I'll die if anything happens to you!"

Spike licked my cheek. Billy returned my hug. "The worst thing that could happen to me has already happened, Daisy. If anything else happens, you won't die. You'll probably be a little sad, but—"

"A *little!*" I shrieked. "Don't talk like that, Billy!"

I felt his lips on my hair, and I turned my face to his. We kissed for a long, long time that morning, but eventually I had to pull away and get ready for work. I didn't want to go, and I was very uneasy as I drove to the Winkworth estate. I told myself I was being ridiculous, but I couldn't be convinced.

Now that the filming was over and Dr. Fellowes's special invention wasn't needed, a uniformed policeman no longer guarded the gate. I might have been mistaken, but I got the impression Mrs. Winkworth's gatekeeper was glad for his absence. He let me in, and I drove to the regular parking spot on the so-called "north forty." Far fewer automobiles resided there, and I didn't meet anyone at all on my way to the set.

I was a little surprised to see that the dressing-room house had been given a change of clothes since I'd last seen it. Honest to Pete, the set directors had covered it with a fake Southern plantation front and it looked as if it had stepped straight out of South Carolina. Kind of like Mrs. Winkworth, only with more brains probably. Those set guys were awfully clever.

The mob was gone. No longer did a throng of people mill about, doing this and that. I only saw John Bohnert and Harold

Kincaid, Lola and Monty and a cameraman, who was having trouble getting Lola to hold a pose long enough for him to get a decent shot. I guess some things never changed.

As soon as he saw me, Harold came over to chat.

"Did Billy enjoy himself Saturday night?" was his first question.

"Actually, he did. At least I think he did. He liked Monty."

"Monty's a nice guy," said Harold. "Just don't tell Billy about his little aberration, and Billy will probably go on liking him."

"Probably." I sighed, thinking how unfair life was. The idea was far from revolutionary; I'd known about life's unfairness for years by that time.

Believe it or not, the publicity shooting was even more boring than the motion-picture shooting. Eventually, Harold and I got sick of watching Lola misbehave and Monty blot sweat from his brow—the day was hotter than heck by mid-morning—and we wandered off to sit in the pergola.

We were still there, Harold telling me about the party he was planning for his mother's return from her latest adventure, when Sam showed up.

"Sam!" I said, startled. When last I'd spoken to him on Saturday night, he'd said he was through with the Winkworth place and never wanted to see it again. Then I noticed the grim expression on his face, and I knew why he had come. With a hand at my throat, I rose unsteadily from the bench. "No."

"I'm afraid so," said Sam. He held out a hand, and I took it.

"What happened?"

Sam glanced at Harold, decided he posed no threat and that he'd learn soon enough anyway, and he said, "Morphine syrup."

My heart crashed to my feet. "Is he . . . ?" But I couldn't say the word.

"No. The doctor is with him now."

"Dr. Benjamin?"

"I guess. Your father said he's your regular doctor. They're at the Castleton Hospital. Your dad sent me to get you. Your mother and aunt are there, too, and I think your mother called the Buckinghams."

I stood there, confused, thinking all sorts of tangled thoughts, one of which ultimately got stuck on our Chevrolet. "Our motor . . ."

Harold materialized at my side. "Don't worry about your car, Daisy. Give me the keys, and I'll have someone drive it to your house." He looked at Sam, and I guess Sam read the question in his eyes.

"We don't know. The doctor is doing everything he can."

I said, my incoherent thoughts snagging on my job, "Lola . . ."

"To hell with Lola," said Sam.

"Right," said Harold. "Don't worry about Lola. Don't worry about anything except Billy now. I'll take care of everything here."

"Thanks, Harold."

And, with my insides leaden and my eyes burning, I went with Sam Rotondo to the Castleton Hospital, where Dr. Benjamin, our faithful family physician and friend, was gallantly trying to save the life of my husband, Billy Majesty, who didn't want to have his life saved.

It was the worst day of my life.

ABOUT THE AUTHOR

Award-winning author **Alice Duncan** lives with a herd of wild dachshunds (enriched from time to time with fosterees from New Mexico Dachshund Rescue) in Roswell, New Mexico. She's not a UFO enthusiast; she's in Roswell because her mother's family settled there fifty years before the aliens crashed. Since her two daughters live in California, where Alice was born, she'd like to return there, but can't afford to. Alice would love to hear from you at alice@aliceduncan.net. And be sure to visit her Web site: http://www.aliceduncan.net.